From the dark, murky streets of Gotham, Selina Kyle emerged, talons bared, transformed. . . .

THE WEAPONS . . .

With cat-o'-nine-tails and steel claws she prowls the city, wealth her prey. . . .

THE CAT . . .

Nine lives—and she would give them all to face her nemesis, Batman. . . .

CATWOMAN!

The Further Adventures of Batman 3

Featuring Catwoman

 ™

Edited by

Martin H. Greenberg

  ™

BANTAM BOOKS

NEW YORK · TORONTO · LONDON · SYDNEY · AUCKLAND

THE FURTHER ADVENTURES OF BATMAN VOLUME 3:
FEATURING CATWOMAN

A Bantam Spectra Book / March 1993

*SPECTRA and the portrayal of a boxed "s" are trademarks of
Bantam Books, a division of
Bantam Doubleday Dell Publishing Group, Inc.
BATMAN, CATWOMAN and all related characters, slogans,
and indicia are trademarks of DC Comics, Inc.*

ISBN 0-553-56069-7

Published simultaneously in the United States and Canada

*Bantam Books are published by Bantam Books, a division of Bantam
Doubleday Dell Publishing Group, Inc. Its trademark, consisting of the
words "Bantam Books" and the portrayal of a rooster, is Registered in
U.S. Patent and Trademark Office and in other countries. Marca Reg-
istrada. Bantam Books, 666 Fifth Avenue, New York, New York 10103.*

PRINTED IN THE UNITED STATES OF AMERICA

RAD   0 9 8 7 6 5 4 3 2

Contents

GOTHAM CITY SPRING: a suite
MORT CASTLE
PAGE 1

CREATURES OF HABIT
PAUL KUPPERBERG
PAGE 45

A KNIGHT AT THE OPERA
JEFF ROVIN
PAGE 89

CATWOMEN
GREG COX
PAGE 129

CATACOMBS
ROBERT WEINBERG
PAGE 159

THE CAT'S-EYE CROWN
KAY DEMIJOHN
PAGE 197

THE CITY THAT COULD NOT BREATHE
WILL MURRAY
PAGE 231

DEADLY PREY
GARY COHN
PAGE 279

ON THE WINGS OF ANGEL
KRISTINE KATHRYN RUSCH
PAGE 311

COPYCAT
JOHN GREGORY BETANCOURT
PAGE 347

AN UNAUTHORIZED BIOGRAPHY
BRIAN M. THOMSEN
PAGE 383

A HARLOT'S TEARS
ED GORMAN
PAGE 403

C&W
JON HAMMER and KAREN McBURNIE
PAGE 427

The Further Adventures of Batman 3

Featuring Catwoman

Gotham City Spring: a suite

MORT CASTLE

How to maintain the peace of society and the peace of the soul?

—An Unasked Question of
Shakyamuni the Buddha

There are no coincidences.
Everything happens as it must. This is karma.
Freedom? Of course you have perfect freedom!
—S. L. Yamashita Roshi

artist

Kyu Matsumoto is an artist: calligraphy, poetry, gardening, flower arranging, killing. Matsumoto himself, an enlightened man, one who has experienced satori, would never differentiate between these arts, set one apart from another. Each is "in the Tao," the Great Way, each is all, and all is all.

The morning light is good. Birds sing in his garden. Kyu Matsumoto sits in his robe at his kitchen table, the screen door leading onto the deck letting in a mild breeze that promises both warmth and humidity later.

He remembers an April day in 1949. Beautiful blond girl on the other side of the street. Peach-colored sleeveless dress. A fist-sized vaccination mark on her upper arm. How sure of her loveliness and place in the world!

Still he writes poems about her, even in his seventieth year.

But now he wishes to paint and so he prepares, and there, at the table, he begins.

A Zen painting is a wordless poem. It is an intuitive capturing of an instant.

This spontaneity is achieved only after years of practice with the traditional sharp-pointed brush set in a bamboo stem.

The touch of the brush is light, fluid; it dances. You might say that Mr. Matsumoto is a master, yet *he* would not say this. The flat-stone ink dish, the brush, the variations of the tones of the black ink, the absorbent paper, why should one seek to *master* these things? How *might* one do so? One might as well declare, "I have mastered the night."

Mr. Matsumoto begins with the moon.

After all, he can look outside and not see it.

Thus he affirms the invisible.

Kyu Matsumoto paints—

—NOW!

> *The moon*
> *eccentric*
> *and out of shape*
> *the brush line*
> *twists*
> *how comic*
> *the roundness*
> *the moon*
> *unborn*
> *undying*

Gotham City Spring: a suite

how alive
how perfect

sister, sister, tiger

Your world and the cat's world are not the same.
            —*Taisen Deshimaru*

The zoo opened at ten, and fifteen minutes after that they met (where else?) by the felines. Eyes nearly closed, the sole cat willing to show itself was a yawning tiger. Bored or quietly seething with rage or half dreaming of the good, hot throat blood of a kill, you could not say. Gotham City's zoo had not been modernized, so its animals lived on concrete and behind bars.

"Tiger, tiger, burning bright . . ."

"No poetry, please," Selina Kyle said, "assuming that is the start of a poem. I didn't ask you to meet me so I could hear your rendition of 'I'm a Little Teapot.' "

So early and a workday, there were not many zoo goers. Maggie the nun, Sister Magdalene, in her habit, all social conscience and Christian compassion, with a crucifix big enough to ward off King Kong Vampire.

Selina wore a white dress. Long sleeves. A white hat. Too heavy on a day headed for a record high. In an hour or so, she'd feel sweaty, and usually she *hated* that because it reminded her of some of the . . . *things* she'd been paid to do with men. And with women. There was a lot Selina Kyle hated. She'd placed herself pretty high up on the list.

"What did you want, Selina?"

"Talk, I guess."

The tiger yawned. It rose slowly, rippling movement, front to rear, retreating into shadow at the back of its cage. Its eyes glowed at Selina. *We know each other,* Selina thought. *We are each other.*

"Maggie, I . . . Look, this will sound stupid and it probably is stupid."

"So only you and I and a tiger and God will hear."

"Maggie, are you . . ."

Tiger eyes glow, burn bright. I ask Maggie a question and the tiger asks me . . .

"Are you *happy*?"

Maggie says, "Let's walk, can we?"

No lions to be seen. No panthers. *Cats hide in darkness.*

"You're asking because of my vocation, Selina," Maggie said.

"Nuns are *supposed* to be happy, right? Doesn't Mother Teresa think it's a grand day when she Scotchtapes a leper's nose back on."

Maggie laughed.

"You can't laugh at that. It's a sin!" Selina said.

"Don't worry, I'll make sure I bring it up in confession." A pause. "Selina, you're not happy."

"Wrong, Sister Sis. I do an aerobic workout twice a week, I've got cable television—"

"And you put on a cat suit and do whatever you can to get yourself killed."

I put on a cat suit—and become someone else . . . something else!

Ahead, under a flowering crab tree exploding with new purple was a bench in need of paint. They sat.

Selina turned to look at Maggie. A discomforting twinge as though she were looking at herself. No. Maggie was softer. There were no hard edges. And while her eyes were the exact same shade as Selina's,

Gotham City Spring: a suite

Maggie's held no bitterness in the infinite green depths. No rage.

"I am *not* 'always happy,'" Maggie said seriously. "I'm not the Flying Nun or the Singing Nun or the Lobotomized Nun. But I'll tell you, I have experienced happiness. Ecstatic happiness. Beyond that. Beyond words. I have known the profound and perfect peace of God that 'surpasseth all human understanding.' But it would mean nothing had I not also known the endless emptiness of despair."

Selina felt something hot and envious in her throat, a sudden flare on her face. She rose, glared at Maggie. "I don't need bumper-sticker religion, thanks."

"And I can't offer you any. I can only tell you what I have found."

"Let me guess. You've got—what's the name again?—*Jesus!* Do I win a Singer sewing machine?"

"There's a prayer, Selina. It's called the 'Jesus prayer.'"

"Catchy."

"'Jesus.' That's all you say. You don't say it aloud. You say His name in your heart and in your mind and in your soul. And you keep saying it and saying it. If you're washing the bathroom floor or cooking soup or arranging books on a shelf, you say His name, so that *everything* you do bears witness for Him, and then—"

"You wind up winning at bingo next Thursday."

Maggie looked at her sister. "Don't," she said. "Please."

Selina closed her mouth. Maggie said, "What happens is that Jesus is within you. The kingdom of heaven is within you, His kingdom. And yours. Selina, there doesn't have to be a gap between God and His children."

Selina abruptly turned her back. *She's stronger than I am,* she thought.

Maggie got up, stood alongside her, touched her elbow. "Sister Selina, always feeling neglected. Always so mad and so full of hate."

"No," Selina said. "Not always."

"Tell me."

She couldn't help herself.

"It was one time Pop took us fishing. Maybe I was six. We went out in a rowboat. You remember?"

"No. I don't know."

"We didn't catch any fish. Pop let me light his cigarettes all afternoon."

"Pall Mall."

"Uh-huh, Pall Mall. Even though you wanted to light 'em, Pop made it *my* job. Remember his beat-up lucky Zippo? He told us these silly jokes, and he drank beer and blew smoke rings. . . ."

I can smell the oily-sting of lighter fluid and the smoke and the wood of the boat and it's almost like I can smell Pop, and then, suddenly, I don't know how, the Zippo is tumbling from my hand, and disappearing into the water, and I don't even think about it, I just toss myself after it, so what if I can't swim, and I see it, and it's going down, and down, and I'm going down after it, and then Pop's in the water and he's got me and he's tossing me in the boat, and he's all red in the face, yelling at me, "You little idiot! I love you! Baby, baby girl, you could have drowned because of a goddamned stupid *lighter! You could have died."*

And then Pop plopped her bottom side up over his knee and paddled her hard, yelling, "Don't you ever, ever, EVER . . ."

She wonders if she's ever again felt so fully loved in her whole life. . . .

Gotham City Spring: a suite

"Selina?"

Clumsy in the dress, Selina ran—

—Away from memories. From family. From "could have beens" and lost possibilities.

—And from herself.

shadow in shadow

> *Even in warmest*
> *glow,*
> *how cold my shadow.*
> —Issa

It was 2:30 in the morning. It was warm, warmer and far more humid than you might expect or wish for spring. On the rooftop, in the unreal light of the half-moon, the Batman was a shadow within his own shadow.

In the alley below, the dumb drug deal he'd been tracking. Ultra-dumb, super-dumb, dumbhead in a drum dumb, the pilot for a TV series *Let's Make a Dumb Deal!* This transaction out of doors, perhaps so that if shooting were required, there would be no "surprises at the Holiday Inn."

Four on the seller team, four buyers. Clothing and mannerisms, unremarkable middle-class, living examples of the banality of evil. Among weapons visible, an economical and dependable Sten gun.

The Batman was about to explode. Just over seventy-six straight hours without sleep and he was hard *into* it, the zone beyond the zone. He watched, focused utterly, fully alive, almost amused that his gaze did not incinerate the lawbreakers.

The Batman was silent, but there was no quietness within him. There was a heart perfectly synced to the pounding rhythm of Justice's stern drummer. There was the rush-roar of his blood in vital response to the blood of all the innocents that had been shed by Crime. There were the billion points of hyper-awareness, the tinglings, the nerve twitchings, and barely controlled anticipations. Vengeance was a *living* need within him; it defined the Batman.

Gotham is *mine*, the Batman thought. Whatever is wrong, *all* that is wrong, I will set right. I am the Caped Crusader. I *am* the Dark Knight.

His thinking was flamboyant, melodramatic, and he knew it. A psychiatrist might have had other evaluations, might have used the term "paranoid," "manic-depressive," "obsessive-compulsive," and "delusions of grandeur," and he knew that, too.

And . . . the Batman attacks!

Even as he threw himself from the roof that was his thought. He distanced himself from himself, regarding his self-created and fate-willed persona in the third person. More, he could *observe* the Batman, put himself outside himself to see the night city's guardian in awesome, cape-flapping descent as—

—There! His left hand shot out, *precisely* grasped the fire escape he'd planned to grasp, and the ladder smoothly tipped and slipped (WD-40ed), clatter-rang as it shot out and he rode it down, *down at them*—

From below: "Huh!"

"Damn!"

Confusion and shock. And terror. *Panicked* terror. Exactly. Perfect.

"Get him!"

Get him? Not likely! Can't you understand? All the

Gotham City Spring: a suite

Dark Angels protect him and guide him! All the Dark Angels swoop down with him as—

"He's . . ."

—The Batman's right hand snapped a batarang.

"Shoot him! Get . . ."

The batarang shattered a wrist. He heard the particular sound of breaking bone. The Sten rattled to the pavement. Other weapons sought to lock in on him. Futility. Stupidity! He was invulnerable.

He was the Batman!

He hurled himself from a height of just better than nine feet above the drug dealers. He landed with his boots on a man's shoulders, like in a circus springboard act.

A scream of astonishment and hurt!

Beautiful, that's what he thought as the Batman felt-heard bones fracture and tissues rip. Using the crumpling man as his launchpad, he propelled himself into a forward midair roll, to land, precisely balanced. He—

—Snapped a *savate* kick to the point of a jaw and immediate unconsciousness to a brain.

—Cut off a curse with the edge of his hand across an Adam's apple.

—Struck with an inverted forefist directly into a solar plexus. Felt the leaping spasm swirl back up his arm from the man's traumatized body.

Ludicrous and surreal images. Bundles of silly-looking green coming undone in a whirlwind explosion! Eyes cross, like a cartoon, attempting to focus on the gauntleted fist that pulps a nose.

"Let's get serious, okay? We can deal, okay? Batman, let's deal, all right? Okay?" A quavering tone, but it was meant to be the Ultimate American Voice of Reason: *Talk* deal *when your butt is in the blender.* . . .

—Blink of an eye and high-impact dentistry, courtesy of the Batman. Teeth spewing, white and jagged.

"Don't hit me! Don't hit me!" The Batman did not hit him. The brick wall the Batman slammed him into did the hitting.

Then he stood, hands on hips, surrounded by eight men out. He was posing—for himself. He took a breath, and another, and another. He understood Tarzan's victory cry after a kill.

There was blood on the alley walls. Blood on the cracked pavement. Blood looked rich and thick at night. This was the way he *expected* blood to look, the Batman realized, and it was a most matter-of-fact realization.

A groan from . . . *one* of them. He could not distinguish which one, which of the *scum*, perhaps stirring toward consciousness, had made the sound. They were all alike.

They were criminals.

The enemy.

This was war.

What he should do was just *kill* them. At the very least, society would be spared expense and annoyance. A single, simple blow per man. Dole out death like a third-grade teacher passing out identical valentines to the class so as not to favor one student over another. "Here's one for you, and one for you, and one for you," and that would be that. *Finis.*

And then—

—*The mark of . . . the Bat!*

On their foreheads, *his* seal, the bat sign, a warning to all who would dare prowl the nightmare roads of the dark side. . . .

He felt himself smile, and a genuine smile was so rare for him that he took notice and savored it.

Gotham City Spring: a suite

No. Just . . . no.
Despite the temptation, he did not kill.
He was better than that.
He had been summoned to cowl and cape by destiny and the night and the ghosts of martyred mother and father, and whatever he was, whatever (and he was still determining that)—he was *not* a killer.
He was the Batman.
Police time now, the mop-up crew, and bring the big mop. Commissioner Jim Gordon, District Attorney Harvey Dent, he had allies in this war, men he could trust . . .
(*Allies? Trust?* Certainly, and Peter, make sure you deny Me *three* times, so they *really* get the message, and Judas, how's about you make arrangements for the Passover, okay? Put it on the Gold Card.)
Trust no one except yourself, said the Batman to the Batman. *Rely on no one.*
Carrying a briefcase in either hand, the Batman stepped from the alley.
He felt it. An instantaneous change in the air about him as he entered the sickish-yellow, humidity-steaming cone of light that radiated from the lamppost at the entrance of the alleyway.
(Perhaps he felt an indefinable shift in the very *aura* about him, that aura that distinguished him as *more* than a man. . . .)
The attack came.

green eyes in the night

Longing cat, sad
how you must cry with

*your love—
or worse still,
without!*

—Yaha

The Batman spun, dropped the briefcases. He ducked instinctively and moved in low, shifting from side to side, cautious, checking it all out, taking it all in. Focused.

Over him, the Catwoman's whip slashed the air. She made another try, whip cobra-striking out, but now he was in too close. He grabbed the lash. He rooted himself and yanked. No resistance. She let herself be reeled in—

—Then the Catwoman . . . *hissed*. He'd heard it before, and yet the sound disconcerted the Batman. It was not a woman imitating a cat. It was a cat's anger, and there was spit and fury in it. It was menacing, unnatural—and intriguing.

Slowly, slowly, the Catwoman, hips swinging, stepped toward him. There was something about her. There was something about her costume. Something that hid *and* revealed her.

The Catwoman purred. She licked her lips. Her eyes were a cat's green eyes and her eyes were a woman's eyes and there was no difference.

The Batman felt . . . confused. He thought of fingers stroking down a spine, grown-up sounds overheard (strange, so strange) when he was a child who should have been asleep, he thought of flesh on flesh, whispers in overheated rooms, he thought of earth smells and sweat, a half-heard laugh in the night that leads to murder or passion, a touch of roundness and softness unexpected, and then she came closer still, and there was that *tail* on her costume, moving as though

it were *her* tail, and he tried to tell himself it made
her ridiculous, but it did not.

The Batman felt an *unease* that was almost a fear,
a fear of all he felt and did not understand.

The Catwoman purred.

She talked in a purr.

"I can make you happy, you know."

He could honestly say he did not understand happiness, but he did not say it. He desired her, feared her,
but he could not say that.

What he said was, "What is it? What do you want?"

A shrug. A cat's loose and casual shrug. "Money,"
she said. "Money is good. Your playmates back in the
alley had money, and I'd been planning to relieve
them of it. Then you showed up."

"Yes," he said, surprised he didn't stammer. It was
like being in third grade, giving an oral report on your
dead bean-plant science-fair project.

As though it might lessen her . . . *power* over him,
he wanted to call her by her name, *Selina,* Selina
Kyle. Her "secret identity" wasn't much of an enigma
even if it hadn't yet been reported by CNN—but all he
could say was, "I picked up on them—"

"And then I picked up on you," she interrupted. She
purred.

She'd been following *him*, trailing him, he thought,
and he hadn't known, and he wondered how long. . . .

She came at him.

No warning, no subtle body language, no tensing of
shoulder, narrowing of eye. Nothing. She was all cat,
split-second metamorphosis, repose to assault.

The Batman jerked back, rattled, letting go the
whip, and her left cross missed his chin as she yanked
the whip from his hold, and he snapped back again as

the Catwoman's straight-arm returning backhand flew past—claws out!

And simultaneously the Catwoman kicked.

The Batman turned into it, moved closer, taking the blow with his thigh and not his crotch.

He threw a left uppercut. There was little behind it. But it was on the button, the chin, and she went back, and rolled, and then—

On all fours.

Coming at him.

Smiling.

Smiling a cat's inscrutable smile.

And he wanted to make her *yowl*. He wanted to claim her, to *tame* her, and make her *his*, and for an inarticulate instant he understood age-old combat between men and women, understood John Wayne, understood misogyny and a half-dozen other issues that are endlessly blathered about on talk programs hosted by the drippingly sensitive.

She was the Woman Animal and he WANTED her and she scared the HELL out of him!

This time her eyes *did* give her away. He moved with cautious sidesteps. Kung-fu attack/defense "basic horse" stance. Waited.

She leaped.

Rolled.

The other way.

Grabbed a briefcase.

And ran.

He took a step.

Another.

Tired. He was tired.

I am the Batman, he thought. I am Guardian, I am Justice, I am Victory, I am Righteousness . . .

I am . . . JERK!

Gotham City Spring: a suite

Sherlock Holmes, the world's greatest detective, had Irene Adler. For Holmes, as Watson put it, Irene Adler was *the* Woman.

And he had the Catwoman....

Or she had him.

the cat's meow

> *i am an orphan*
> *at this party*
> *envious even*
> *of scolded children*
> —Issa

Happy? Want happy?

Then go the hell elsewhere, because I was happy— not! The green reasons lay spread on my saggy bed in my East End *el floppo grande*, a "studio apartment" with hot-and-cold-running roaches.

Sweaty and feeling like I'm sweating dirt. The dirty city itself. Welcome sweet springtime. I'm wearing panties and a T-top, sitting on the couch, pouring drink number three, *sans* ice. Styrofoam cup. House of Stuart. It was cheap and it burned and it suited one Selina Kyle. I felt cheap, and sure as God made ingrown toenails (try rapping your Jesus prayer at the podiatrist, Maggie!), I felt BURNED!

Damn it.

Damn him!

Gotham City's daring cat burglar. The Catwoman, Ms. *Live it hard and on the edge*! Breathe in the danger, roll around in its prickly vibrations, get into it.

"Oh, hell," I said.

"Meow?" Otto said. He leaped up onto the middle sofa cushion. Otto was black, and as double ugly and raggedy as you'd expect pure alley cat to be. He was my only companion these days; he was also the only cat I ever encountered that actually went "meow," just as though he'd learned from a first-grade primer.

Otto put his head on my thigh. He snuffled. He sounded more like an adenoidal bulldog with a deviated septum than a cat.

"Otto," I said, "philosophy time. Why is it everything in my life is so incredibly *wrong*?"

Otto snorted.

"Stupid cat," I said.

I stood up. Otto meowed as I let him drop to the floor. I assumed it meant, "Stupid bitch."

And he wasn't wrong. I put the bottle of Scotch for the downwardly mobile and my Styrofoam crystalware on a tottering lamp table and went to examine . . . my loot. The take. The spoils . . .

Check the dictionary, chum, and you'll learn that what is spoiled usually *stinks*!

And the goddamned *counterfeit* money, the queer, the *snide*! STUNK, just as sure as God made stomach cramps. A scanner and a laser color printer, and voilà, hundred-dollar bills that looked slightly less genuine than what you get in your Monopoly set!

Oh, you can be sure Mr. Batman was laughing (oh, no, he's got heavier status than that—he is Mr. *THE* BATMAN!), laughing his bat-butt off right now. The joke's on guess who?

A flashback kicked in: Not so long ago (it seemed so long ago), when I was just discovering the—*power*— the Catwoman outfit bestowed on me—

—And the power it held over me—

Gotham City Spring: a suite

The Catwoman: The Batman. A rooftop encounter. Only fitting.

The Batman: So it's to be a war between us.

The Catwoman: It's always a war between the sexes.

The Batman: And who will draw first blood?

She *did! You* bet *she did! First round to the Catwoman. She cold-cocked him. Ka-Thwok! And she cut* him, *made him bleed. And she'd* touched *his blood. And smelled it.*

It's always a war....

Time to escalate the war, Mr. *the* Batman! Time to *win* the war.

How do you win a war?

You destroy your adversary.

You *kill* him.

Zap! I had it all put together in my mind.

Take the Batman out and I would conquer my own weakness. I'd know it and the world would know it. Take him out and turn my own life around. Nothing would stop me, not ever again—

(—hurt me . . .

—again . . .)

Take him OUT! The cop, the vigilante, the Hey-hey A-OK Gotham Good Guy, and it would set everything right! Take him.

Hell. I couldn't even take out the garbage without the bag ripping and dumping coffee grounds, eggshells, and an empty cat food can on my feet.

Selina Kyle—not even a wimp. Try wimpette.

I did not cry, even though my eyes sort of stung. You start crying when you're alone with just your damned cat, and maybe you'll never stop.

I am the Catwoman, I told myself, and I knew, I KNEW what I had to do.

an old man

My old thighs—
how thin
by firelight.
—Shiseki

Matter of public record: Mr. Abraham Itzak Cohen, aka Abie the Patch, owned and operated the Chez What? which he opened in 1933. He presented the top jazz acts to what he persisted in calling "café society," even after there were no real cafés and damned little left of what he could consider society.

It was the rock-and-roll thing. It was the Vietnam thing. It was urban blight and shifting economics and nobody knowing how to tie a damned tie anymore, and so, in the early 1970s, Abie the Patch, no schmuck he, closed the Chez What? and retired from the life of a cabaret entrepreneur.

Not a matter of public record but decidedly a matter of not infrequent public suspicion and speculation: *Most* of Mr. A. I. Cohen's "other enterprises," from which he did not retire.

What Abie the Patch would tell you, plain *mamaloschen* (if he liked you) was he was a gangster. He'd been termed "Patch" because of his talent for "fixing up." Etymology: In the days of touring carnivals, you had to have a "Patch." The Patch handled community relations and PR. He made sure the local officials got properly bribed and, upon request, properly boffed by the kooch-show entertainers, and that no carny popped a biscuit into the oven of the mayor's daughter, etc. "Everyone's all right now, right? Right!" was the Patch's responsibility.

Gotham City Spring: a suite

For a long time Abraham Itzak Cohen made sure everything was all right now in Gotham City.

So that was why, this afternoon when he should have been listening to Miles or Monk or Montgomery, he was at a meeting at which he did not wish to be, a meeting at which virtually every other person present wanted him dead.

He felt like hammered dreck. He was too damned *old* for springtime, the crap in the air always making him cough, an embarrassing *eck-ick* cough.

Of course, maybe he didn't feel any too chipper because of the cancer. Liver, lung, and pancreas . . . Thanks very much, we can stop the inventory right there. A secret. He knew he was soon going to be dead, and his doctor, who didn't want to soon be dead himself, was good at withholding information.

So Abie the Patch coughed, and behind him, Brian Roberts, his "bodyguard," patted him gently between his chicken-pointy shoulder blades. Brian the bodyguard was very big, very blond, and very bland, and had orders to kill Abie the Patch, Abie knew, "when the time was right."

The Right Time = When we figure out where the old bastard stashed the stuff he has on us. And Abie did have it—something *choice* on every one of them that would be an interesting piece of news for A) the cops; B) up-and-coming criminals; C) the *National Enquirer*; D) all of the preceding.

But for now the death under discussion and the reason for this conference was certainly *not* that of Mr. A. I. Cohen, Esq.

"The Batman has to be terminated. It's practical, eminently so," said Melville Chamberlain, who had become CEO of the Syndicate four years ago in one of the fairest elections ever held in the city.

Mort Castle

The Syndicate: At the top, gone the rough edges. Also gone the high drama and low comedy. An equal-opportunity organization, bachelors degree recommended, MBA preferred.

Melville Chamberlain (do you *believe* such a name? thought Abie the Patch) was sixty, but looked forty-five to fifty because of a tuck-around-eyes and unwattling-of-throat surgical combo. He sat at the far end of the high-gloss, utterly anonymous, boardroom table, and, let's tick them off (thought Abie the Patch): Mr. Y. P. Park, produce-shop protection, of Korean extraction, who can say an "l" or an "r" better than William F. Buckley; Ms. Rowena Bromley-Stigers, proprietor of a number of united "escort services" that could provide for any desire ranging from "the cringing ostrich trick" (only hinted at in the *Kama Sutra*) to . . . you fill in the blank; Mr. Jesus (Just call me "Hey!") Nuñez, volume refining and distribution of recreational chemicals, and Roland Kirby, Whiplash Lawyers "R" Us, and . . .

Gottenu, Abie the Patch thought. They all look alike! *These* are today's mobsters, wiseguys, heavy-hitting *goombahs* and *schtarker menschen*? No Blind Louie or Joey Splats or Thumbs Garrity or Tony Two-Stomp or Curly Moonglow . . . These jamokes got on an elevator to dig the music!

Include me out!

I am eighty years old and I weigh 101 pounds, and my insides are eating my insides, and I think maybe I have lived too long—

"Mr. Cohen?"

Melville Chamberlain. Obviously not the first time he'd asked . . . something.

"Yes, yes." Cohen nodded. He coughed. "I was thinking."

Gotham City Spring: a suite

"The Batman, Mr. Cohen," said Melville Chamber-lain. "We cannot come to any sort of reasonable ac-commodation with him."

The Batman? Abie the Patch *liked* the Batman. The Batman had style. If the Batman played jazz, he would be Archie Shepp, the angry saxophone, tearing into it, trying to break it all down.

"He's a madman, Mr. Cohen. He cannot be reasoned with. No one is safe from him."

Everyone is a madman and no one is safe from any-one, Cohen thought, but we try to pretend otherwise.

"Last month, the Batman put the arm on one of our numbers runners. A few hours later he took down one of our affiliates active in the sports world who was at-tempting to, let us say, prearrange the outcome of a college basketball game. Both of our people tried to 'set it right' in a sensible manner, Mr. Cohen. The Bat-man told them both it would all be set right when ev-ery criminal was either in jail or in hell."

Style, thought Cohen, definite style.

"Mr. Cohen?"

Abie the Patch spread his hands. Such thin hands. Spiders at the end of willow branches. He said, "You'll pardon me, I'm old and I don't think as quickly as I used to. Why do you need me, Mr. Chamberlain? The Batman, he's a man. If he needs to be dead, then make him dead. You can find, I am certain, personnel with the . . . *requisite* talents to deal with this situation."

Melville Chamberlain rose. "Mr. Cohen, there's some-thing about the Batman." You didn't hear it in the voice. That was as bland as yogurt. But it was there in Chamberlain's eyes. He was *scared* of the Batman.

They were *all* scared of the Batman!

Oy!

"Mr. Cohen, we think you can be of help with this.

You have a friend. He is known for his ability to . . . to *arrange* things."

"Yes."

"Double his usual fee."

"Triple," said Abie the Patch.

"Triple," Melville Chamberlain agreed. "With his standard guarantee."

"Of course," said Abie the Patch. He started to get up, but he didn't have quite enough strength to push back his chair, and he almost flopped back to the seat. But then Brian helped him ("Such a helper he is!"), and steady now, Abie the Patch gestured magnanimously, ostentatiously—just what he wanted it to be. "When have I *ever* refused to accommodate my friends and associates? Of course, I will talk to . . . my friend."

Abraham Itzak Cohen smiled.

The smile was for his own pleasure and not at all for them.

beneath the moon

> *what a moon*
> *if only she*
> *were here*
> *my bitter*
> *wife*
> *—Issa*

Kyu Matsumoto finishes his cigarette. He thinks. He has been thinking too much. He remembers a wife who used to love him and now hates him. Thinks of a son who lives in California and does something with computers and has had three wives and makes a great

Gotham City Spring: a suite

deal of money and is indifferent to his father—indeed, indifferent to the idea of having a father.

Enough. He will paint. This morning he will add to the painting begun yesterday.

Kyu Matsumoto's brush. It skims, glides, twirls over the paper. The paper and the brush. *No separation.* The brush and Matsumoto. No separation. No division.

Everything one. This is the natural way of things.

He is creating. He is arranging a painting. He is *growing* a painting. Memory? A glimpse of the future? The past is the past. The future is the future.

Matsumoto is alive NOW and keenly balanced on that hairline instant NOW between past and future and the ink and the paper and the vision are NOW!

The painting—

—A capturing of impermanence.

—Yet a master's art need never die.

No contradiction.

No contradictions.

There are no contradictions.

> *the cat*
> *all slinking curves*
> *beneath the moon*
> *beneath the emptiness*
> *beneath the moon*
> *how unhappy*
> *until*
> *the brush*
> *and the paper*
> *and Matsumoto*
> *and the moment*
> *give the cat*
> *a Buddha*
> *face*

Mort Castle

mirror, mirror

> geese fly over the pond
> they do not
> seek to
> cast their reflection
> —from The Zenzrin

He slept for twenty-four hours straight. He awoke, stretched when he got out of bed, feeling centered and rested, and went into the bathroom.

When he was ready to shave, he stood at the lavatory, the heavy, old-fashioned razor, double-edged blade, in his right hand, and for the first time this morning he looked into the mirror—*really* looked—and—

—Nothing.

—No reflection.

—*No one.*

He blinked. How about that. He smiled. He *thought* he smiled, anyway, because he felt the tugging at his mouth, but could see no smile in the mirror. No eyes. No one.

—No Bruce Wayne.

And he thought:

Once upon a time—

—There was a boy named Bruce Wayne and he was much like any other boy except that he was the only son of wealthy parents and then the mother and the father of that boy were killed they were mercilessly slaughtered they were shot to death *before the eyes of the boy who was Bruce Wayne and at that moment— NOW I understand—at that moment Bruce Wayne ceased to be there was an end to him and what came*

into being was an embryonic being the Batman the Batman THE BATMAN—

—And that—he is—*THE BATMAN!*—is who I am.

—NOW!

—Bruce Wayne does not exist. There is a lie called Bruce Wayne.

—Proof! He opens the razor, takes out the blade, runs it across the pad of his thumb of his left hand.

Nothing.

And then—

Flesh divided on an invisible line, angled through whorls and swirls (the marks of identity individuality), and then the blood line appeared and beaded up, and it hurt, a vicious, deep and *real* hurt, and he thanked God that it hurt, and he held his thumb over the basin, and watched Bruce Wayne's blood swirl onto porcelain and glanced up—fearfully—and saw a fearful and white and unshaven face in the mirror. He only glanced, afraid it would disappear, and then he cried out: "Alfred!"

Alfred was there, with raised eyebrows and "Sir?"

Then an arm around the shoulders of the sobbing Bruce Wayne. "All right, then. I have you. You're all right, Master Bruce. You are all right."

No, he wasn't all right, but better now ... better. For the moment. Screwed up? *Definitely*, but at least he knew it. The elevator did indeed go to the top—and kept on going.

Alfred put a Band-Aid on his thumb. He took him down to the Batcave. In uniform, locking himself into his true identity, his nature—he—*the Batman*—was in control. He could even push back the cowl to permit Alfred to shave him.

"Master Bruce," Alfred said, "do you want to tell me—"

"No," he—*the Batman*—said. "I don't want to. But I
have to. I think . . . I think I had a genuine psychotic
episode, Alfred. Call it an existential identity crisis,
like you're supposed to have when you're a
teenager—"

"Forgive the interruption, sir," Alfred said, "but I
don't think we can say you were *ever* a teenager."

The Batman shook his head. "I don't know. I . . .
Alfred, I need help."

"I'm here, sir. You know Leslie Thompkins would—"

The Batman interrupted with his palm out. Social
worker Leslie Thompkins had comforted him that
hellish night Martha and Thomas Wayne were
gunned down; she knew about the Batman, the
Batcave, everything, she . . .

She loved him.

And Alfred loved him.

He had to turn away. It hit extremely hard.

"No, there's someone else I have to see, Alfred," the
Batman said. "I suppose I should have a long time
back. But the truth is, I was scared."

Then the Batman felt cold and neither the face of
the faithful Alfred, nor the sign of the bat upon his
chest, nor the familiar walls of the Batcave made a
difference as he whispered, "He still scares me."

ducks on the water

> *There's a little white duck
> sittin' in the water,
> Little white duck
> doin' what he oughta!*
> —American Folk Song

Gotham City Spring: a suite

His friend Mr. Cohen has invited him for three o'clock,
but Matsumoto has not gone walking in the city for a
while, and so he leaves early—

—If one were speaking of philosophy, one might say
Kyu Matsumoto walks in the Tao. He walks the Middle Path, the Great Way, with angels on one side and
devils on the other, and he does not choose between
them.

But Kyu Matsumoto seldom speaks of philosophy.
Why talk of what cannot be understood with words?
Better to save your breath—for breathing!

So, if you asked him (politely), "Where are you going?" and he knew you to be a student of Zen, he
might (politely) say, "Quite!" But if you were not a
Zen student, then Kyu Matsumoto might (politely)
say, "Ducks."

With an easy stride that makes it seem as though
he is going nowhere and certainly is in no hurry to arrive, Kyu Matsumoto heads toward the lagoon in
Gotham Park. He smells water and the special sea-
sonal scent that one must think of as "green."

Kyu Matsumoto is reflecting on death and poetry;
one cannot think of poetry without thinking about
death.

> Let us go
> over the river,
> and sit
> in the shade
> of the trees.

That is Thomas Stonewall Jackson's death song. Simple and elegant, but surpassing it, believes Kyu
Matsumoto, is Goethe's exquisite:

Mort Castle

More light!

How *good* to think of these words on so splendid a
day! How good to be wearing his favorite clothes: An
unlined, beige, double-breasted suit, which was quite
the style twenty years ago when he purchased it. His
footwear: Nikes. They make you feel like gravity is
the illusion that it is! They are satori shoes, and he'd
gladly endorse them as such.

But it is his tie that is the *best*! It has a bold picture
of the square-headed dog and the little redheaded girl
from the comic strips. Because she has no eyes, you
sense she can see all that needs to be seen! Yes, the
orphan child is very Zen!

In the water, riding on their reflections, the ducks!
Mothers and their young! Matsumoto lights a cigarette. Ducks quack counterpoint. Ducks bob here and
there, a ballet. Tails up and wagging, they seek food
in the bed of the lagoon.

Kyu Matsumoto inhales, exhales.

The ducks look funny in their hunger.

He should have brought bread for the ducks. He finishes his cigarette. Grinds it out in the dirt, takes the
butt toward a wastebasket.

Perhaps he can find something.

Matsumoto has his head in the trash can by the
tree, has just spotted several potato chips, when they
come upon him. He will get the chips later.

There are six of them, high-tops, baggy pants, a tat-
too, some acne, some scars, and for all of them, hair-
cuts that make them look as though they've booked an
imminent trip to the electric chair.

Skinheads.

Emerging from the trash can, Matsumoto says,
"Hi." "Hi" is his favorite English word—because it

Gotham City Spring: a suite

sounds like *hai*, Japanese for "yes," and thus your greeting is also an affirmation.

"Hi, your ass . . ."

Matsumoto sighs.

He knows they want a tangible reason to hate Japanese. Or Koreans. Or Cambodians. Or African Americans. Or Hispanics, Pakistanis, Jews, Laplanders, or Micronesians . . .

Very well, then. Very well.

Karma.

So, then. So. Quite. It must be done with as little commotion as possible. The ducks must be considered.

Matsumoto strikes. Without thought. Without hesitation. Spontaneous. *Mo chih ch'u.* Effortless effort.

—Ruptures a spleen.

—Breaks an arm in two places. White of bone wetly piercing the different-colored layers of meat of a forearm.

—Fractures a kneecap. A hundred lines of fissure radiate under the sole of his Nike.

—Breaks a nose.

—Dislocates a hip, shearing off the socket with the most grating "rasp" noise one could imagine.

—Walks a screaming skinhead into a tree and unconsciousness.

—Sees—happily so—one young man running off, leaving his former comrades sprawled about.

But the ducks have been frightened. They are far out in the lagoon.

When he comes to the park next time, he will not forget bread for the ducks.

And popcorn.

Ducks like popcorn.

So does he.

Mort Castle

old friends

> *So often the world in haze*
> *thinking of past things*
> *how far-off they are*
> *—from* The Zenzrin

The man took up too much space with his gracelessness; he had no idea how to breathe, Kyu Matsumoto thought as Brian Roberts conducted him to the living room. White-carpeted, the size of a municipal parking lot in a major city that had a balanced budget.

Matsumoto smiled a greeting at Cohen. *How old he was! How old I am!* He took the matching cushioned chair on the other side of a small table on which stood a cut-glass decanter and two shot glasses. Ceremonies.

The chairs were angled so that people might look at each other or not. Cohen was a gracious man, Matsumoto thought.

"You pour, please," Abie the Patch said.

"Yes."

Matsumoto doled out shots. They sat and sipped. Matsumoto thought it good to be with his friend. There were no others. Not anymore.

And Chivas Regal. Excellent.

"Do you want to hear something funny?"

"Certainly," Abie the Patch said.

"Suntory," Kyu Matsumoto said.

"That is funny," Abie the Patch said. "Japanese Scotch." He ran his tongue over his upper lip. "Mr. Matsumoto, you're younger, more in touch than me. What the hell kind of world do we have when people don't drink real booze anymore? White wine. French

Gotham City Spring: a suite

water with bubbles in it. *Gottenu*, you know what you do with water with bubbles? You make an egg cream, that's what you do. You spritz it on your plants."

"Or you sit and watch the bubbles," Matsumoto said. The Chivas inside his mouth, a hot, wet line descending to his middle, and then the warmth. Fine. *Very* fine.

Cohen had a remote control in his lap. He held it up. "Do you want to guess?"

"No."

"How many years and you *never* guess."

"So everything is a surprise."

"Even inevitability?"

"Yes."

"And destiny? And chance?"

"Yes."

Abie the Patch touched a button. Across the room, the obsolete reel-to-reel tape recorder ticked into play.

Almost lighter than the air it set in motion, the music came from the Jensen speakers. A bass, not keeping any set time, and drums, a steady hiss of cymbal, and the piano, individual notes. There were vast distances between the instruments, spaces and freedom between the singular notes of the piano. These were musicians who knew how to play silences, *Zen!*—and Matsumoto entered the music, the Scotch warmth easing the dissipation of any barriers, as this moment of NOW became (of course of course) the only moment, here with his friend. . . .

Then the music was done. *Nothing* gold *can stay. Nor can anything else. Buddha!*

"Bill Evans," said Abie the Patch.

"Thank you," Matsumoto said, deeply touched.

"You are welcome. Another drink?"

"No, thank you."

"Mr. Matsumoto?"

Business, and Matsumoto did not look at Cohen; it would have been impolite.

"The Batman," Abie the Patch said. "My—*associates*—want him terminated. These jamokes, they don't even know how to talk gangster. *Terminated*, not whacked, not hit, not rubbed out. If you told one of 'em you were taking him for a ride, he'd figure a test drive in a new Acura."

"I understand."

"Triple the usual. And of course your guarantee."

Kyu Matsumoto nodded, knowing that Cohen would sense it if not see it. When he consented to arrange a killing, he pledged his own life as bond. *Nothing at all—yet they considered it everything!*

"Of course," Matsumoto said, "you may tell them that should I not bring about the death of the Batman, then I will most certainly kill myself."

"Why don't you pour again," Cohen said. "Some things I want to . . ."

Matsumoto poured. The two old men drank and talked quietly. Mr. Cohen, Abie the Patch, very quietly, asked his friend for help, a favor that would fix up—everything.

dokusan: a meeting of master and pupil

> —cat leaps from the shade
> into the moment, where we are
> —Lucien Stryk

"Please come in," he says. "You are Miss Kyle."

It is the next afternoon. "Yes," she says. She wears

Gotham City Spring: a suite

jeans, a T-shirt proclaiming, DON'T SAVE THE WHALES—
THEY'RE ANNOYING, carries a duffel bag with her *gi* and
her whip—and her Catwoman costume.

Matsumoto's home is airy. There is something ethereal in the way the light enters, this afternoon. On the
wall over the sofa is a picture, not Japanese or European in manner. It is called *Cat Dreaming of a Fish*,
Kyu Matsumoto says, when he remarks her noticing
it. The cat, curled tight on a background the precise
shade of blue that you see in dreams, has above it a
fish—rather the *skeleton* of a fish. "You wonder if a
dream fish before it became a meal in a dream had
a dream of a worm, don't you?"

"I don't know," Selina said. "What will learning
from you cost me? Fighting skills. I didn't come here
for an art lesson."

"No," Matsumoto says. "You need a lesson in manners." He grabs her nose. He twists. She drops the
duffel bag. Tries to strike back. Tries to yell.

Can't.

The pain corkscrews down inside her—filling her as
though she were hollow—and corkscrews up, all the
way up into her hair. Consuming and paralyzing. The
only movement she's capable of: lifting up on her toes.
The only sound she can make: a peeping "Ow-ow-
ow—led go ob my node."

"Certainly," says Matsumoto. He seizes the lobe of
her ear. He twists. She's on her knees. Previous pain
a mere prelude for . . . PAIN! She's on the verge of
passing out.

Matsumoto calmly says, "The *Kyosaku* school of
Zen, just in case you have suddenly developed an interest in metaphysical considerations, uses a good-
sized stick to awaken a student to the Buddha nature.
I don't believe in that myself.

Mort Castle

"Let us speak together, if you please."

At the kitchen table, they sit. Talk. He lights a cigarette. He seems utterly at ease and, at the same time, utterly aware. His smoking is not something to do. He *smokes*.

When she talks, he hears.

Her *sensei*, she tells him, her teacher, Ted Grant, taught her his own style a mixture of gung fu, tae kwan do, and "down 'n dirty." Now Ted says there is nothing more he can show her, and so she has come here.

She must learn more.

—*Must*.

She has to kill someone.

She tells him who it is.

Karma, thinks Matsumoto.

"Come with me," Matsumoto says.

By the door to the basement, he opens the closet where he stores the cleaning supplies. He hands her a feather duster. He takes out a vacuum cleaner.

"This is a Eureka," he says. "Anything else you need, I'm sure you will find."

"I don't understand," Selina says.

"Quite," Matsumoto says.

"But . . ."

"Ah, this is *mondo*. You ask questions, I give answers. Very good."

"You mean like a koan," Selina says. "Kind of a riddle, like what's the sound of one hand clapping?"

Matsumoto slaps her. A good shot that instantly reddens her cheek and makes her blink. "That is the sound of one hand clapping. No, we are not playing mind games. There are other ways to satori, to achieve liberation.

"A Eureka is extremely spiritual. It's spiritually

spiritual. Cleanliness is next to godliness. Buddha, you know, was an atheist. The moment he was dead, his disciples made him a god."

"I'd rather pay money for you—"

"Again, one hand clapping?"

"No!"

"The dreaded Oriental nose-kneading technique . . ."

"No!"

". . . bend your ear . . ."

"NO!"

"You will clean the house. You will live here six days a week. I have a small room with a futon and a nice chest of drawers from the Goodwill. There's a nine-inch color television, too. My son sends me televisions. Either Saturday or Sunday is totally yours.

"I will pay you ten dollars a day. I will teach you what you can learn.

"Your training begins with the Eureka. In Japanese we refer to it as *if yu nu sushi*. That means Eureka-Zen. Traditional *and* technological. Quite progressive."

"I can't, Mr. Matsumoto," Selina says. "I have a cat."

"Nobody has a cat, Miss Kyle. But the cat is welcome here."

"I . . ." Selina swallows hard, thinks hard. She ought to get the hell out of this loony's house right now. Benny Hill meets Bruce Lee!

But somehow she doesn't really want to.

She thinks, He smokes Pall Malls.

mondo: questions and answers

*a three year
old child*

Mort Castle

> *sees the world*
> *as haiku*
> *a one year*
> *old child*
> *points at the moon*
> *what is*
> *is what is*
> *who needs*
> *more*
> —*from* The Zenzrin

It's ... Cleaning Woman! Uh, didn't she used to be, was it, uh, THE CATWOMAN! Yowl! Spit! Hiss!??? Were you starting to forget? Was she? Ten days of "domestic service," and starting to take pride in your ability, girl, to eliminate even *numero uno dust speck* on a venetian-blind slat or a water splotch on the kitchen-sink faucet.

It was crazy. That's what she thought when she thought about it, so she made herself not think about it.

She carefully wet-mopped the tile floor in the downstairs "family room." It was quite American. A twenty-seven-inch television console, a gift from Mr. Matsumoto's son on the top of the set, one of those hideously memorable "black jaguar ashtrays" from forty years ago. A Ping-Pong table. Ping-Pong was "very Zen," Mr. Matsumoto had told her, beating her three straight games last week.

Also very Zen (said the *roshi*, meaning "teacher"): Frisbee, especially if you played with a dog. Dogs were always "in the Tao," never bound by bad karma. Dogs did not bother with choice: "To Catch or Not to Catch the Frisbee"; no Airedale terrier felt compelled to be a canine Hamlet.

Zen ... Okay, she had questions—after first asking

if it was all right to ask questions. (She had not
wanted to get her nose tied into a knot or her earlobe
snapped like a rubber band.)

Zen was one of the martial arts? Like judo or
hapkido or . . .

No. Certainly not. It was more like fresh-baked
goods, but not quite.

Was it a religion?

No, definitely not. Except for those who had made it
a religion.

What about an afterlife?

What about it?

But . . . But . . . But . . .

Try these home-grown koans, "teaching riddles,"
from right here in the old red, white, and blue USA,
land of Ohio-assembled-Hondas:

"Who's on first. What's on second."

"Who's on second?"

"Who's on first . . . ?"

*Zen is now. NOW. Zen is being alive in the NOW.
Unity with the NOW and the mind and body. No hesitation. NOW. Confidence. Attached to nothing.*

*We do not seize the day. The day does not seize itself.
Nor does it seize us.*

*We are all into it NOW and that is what is what
is. . . .*

*That is all there is and it is quite sufficient, purpose-
less and perfect. . . .*

She knew plenty of koans. Pop had taught her—

—Do you walk to school or take your lunch?

—Where is it colder: in the winter or in the country?

—My father and your father went to different
schools together.

—How high is "up"?

Oh, and by the way, Mr. Matsumoto, how do you kill

someone? How do you make him deader than hell for double-damned sure?

Simple. Hit him very hard where and when he is very weak.

Enough! Better to mop-mop-mop the floor. Funny, she felt almost as though the mop were mopping and the floor helped it along and she had her hands on the handle and there was no exertion, not the slightest, that was required. . . .

WHACK!

Her mouth flew open. She let go of the mop handle. She spun, left buttock burning. "Hey!"

"Tag," Mr. Matsumoto said. "You're it." He stood holding a Ping-Pong paddle.

"Where did you . . . what did I do?"

"You cleaned the floor. You mopped so well that you were lost in your mopping."

"Isn't that it? Isn't that *part* of it?"

"Part? All is all. Nothing is nothing. The air is all to a flying bird, the water is all to the swimming fish."

"And All is Nothing? Is that what comes next?"

Kyu Matsumoto smiled. "After his satori, Buddha was asked, 'Are you a god?' He said he was not. 'Then what are you?' he was asked. 'I am . . . awake,' he said.

"From now on, I will sneak up on you from time to time. Catch me if you can."

Several times she did.

words

i speak nonsense
and begin again
—Bill Wantling

Gotham City Spring: a suite

One night, I don't know why, I just start talking to him, you know? And what I tell him is just about everything. I mean, it's stuff I have never told anybody else. It's stuff I haven't even told myself.

And I guess I get pretty carried away, because, next thing I know, I'm blubbering, just going liquid. I think, if Mr. Matsumoto had touched me, tried to hug me, or even just patted me on the shoulder or like that, I never could have stood another minute with him.

But what he did was hand me his handkerchief. Then he recited a poem of Shinkicki Takahashi:

> I don't take your words
> Merely as words.
> Far from it.
> I listen
> To what makes you talk—
> Whatever that is—
> And me listen.

I loved that old guy then.
And I knew it.

satori

Only when you have no thing in your mind and no mind in things are you vacant and spiritual, empty and marvelous.

—Te-shan

This is what happened to me.
One night we ordered a pizza and Mr. Matsumoto

had had a few drinks (he drinks *good* Scotch—not the Liquid Plumber brands), and I did, too, and the Comedy Channel was showing Laurel and Hardy. We were both, I'd say, a little on the *faced* side. When Laurel is saying, "I can but he can," I'm laughing like hell, saying, "Ah, so! Very Zen!" And Mr. Matsumoto is laughing like hell at me and Stan and Ollie.

A commercial. I want popcorn, so I say, "I want popcorn."

"I want popcorn, too," Mr. Matsumoto says. "I have some in the cabinet. Orville's gourmet."

"Not microwave. That sucks."

"Certainly not. And don't say sucks. It's vulgar."

So I'm in the kitchen, shuffling the frying pan, sure that I did get the oil hot enough, and popcorn is starting to tick, just a tick here and then there, and the outside sounds of Mr. Matsumoto's garden, all the little living things I maybe have never even thought about, are making sounds like popcorn, and all the sounds are coming together, and everything that exists is the sound of popcorn EXPLODING, a perfect moment of CHANGE—

tick-tick-Pop-
ticktick-the-seeds-pop-
change-tick—
And outside, in the garden, I hear Otto's cry, just a statement and a longing, and it's a sound maybe that could have come from me, but it means he is looking for love but will happily settle for the chance to kill a bird or a field mouse and I understand and have no need to understand as all these possibilities rush at me rush at me rush at me

tick-tick-tick
tick tick
—which we are

Gotham City Spring: a suite

                              tick TICK TICK
Butterflies!
    Fallen leaves
        LEAP back to the branch!
    Impossibilities!
    jesusjesusjesus
    jesusjesusjesus
    jesusjesusjesus
    jesusjesusjesus
    jesusjesusjesus

Effortlessly, wondering, I shifted the lid of the pan. A single kernel shot up. It burst at the height of its leap.

And it was me.

I was free.

Burst open. White, so very white.

And new.

And ready to begin.

—And later, Mr. Matsumoto showed me how to kill the Batman.

—Or anyone.

peace

---

        the charm's
        wound up
                —William Shakespeare

It was a Friday evening. In another two days, it would be summer. A half hour before sunset, Kyu Matsumoto called upon Abraham Itzak Cohen. On the end table between the old friends, a bottle of Chivas

Regal. Two shot glasses. And two candles in simple glass candlesticks.

Brian Roberts asked, "Mr. Cohen, is there anything else you need?"

"No," Abie the Patch said. He slipped his thin hand down under the cushion of his chair. He pulled out the .22-caliber snub-nosed Colt revolver he'd secreted. He shot Brian Roberts smack dab in the middle of the forehead, a third eye above a surprised look.

"Like riding a bicycle," Cohen said. "You don't lose the touch."

The old men drank Scotch. Cohen tapped his temple. "All in here. All of it. You know, the putz was supposed to take me out once he found out where I had it. Couldn't think for a minute that people can actually learn and remember things. Back in vaudeville, I knew a guy who'd memorized the entire Oxford English Dictionary. Died broke, the schmuck."

"Not just in your mind now, I'm sure," Matsumoto said.

"No."

"A death poem, Mr. Cohen?" said Matsumoto. "It is customary."

"Light the candles. I'll think a moment."

"Do you need to think?"

"Please, I'm Jewish," said Cohen. He thought. Then he said:

> Mr. Monk
> Mr. Coltrane
> I join you
> we share
> our silences

"Good," said Kyu Matsumoto. He lit the candle for his friend, then one for himself.

Gotham City Spring: a suite

"Good *shabbos*," said Abraham Itzak Cohen. He smiled. "Peace be unto you."

"And unto you peace," Kyu Matsumoto said. Cohen put the barrel of the pistol to his own temple, elbow stuck out at an awkward angle, and pulled the trigger. The noise was not very loud, nor was there much blood.

Matsumoto blew out the candle closest to him. Satori, the blowing out, the extinguishing of all desire. His death poem came to him without thought:

> *laughter*
> *cats*
> *bats*
> *buddha*
> *no regret*

He reached for the pistol.

in a garden

> *Don't weep, insects—*
> *lovers, stars themselves,*
> *must part.*
> —Issa

Melville Chamberlain, Y. P. Park, Rowena Bromley-Stigers, Jesus Nuñez, etc., if you are looking for the Syndicate (Gotham City division), try jail. Slammersville.

For a while at least. Until the right lawyer and the right judge make the right arrangements so that this sector of the American economy can continue to function.

Who put them there?

Who listened to Cohen's tapes?

The Batman.

The Catwoman.

The students of Kyu Matsumoto—

—Who sit in shadows and remembrance and contemplation, in Matsumoto's garden.

"We are not so very different, are we?" she says.

Once he said, "We are on opposite sides," and she said, "Of the same coin?"

But coins have an edge. And coins can have no sides at all.

"I am not others and others are not me," he says.

"We are what we are," she says.

As is the moon.

As is . . . everything.

Thanks to—

Sheldon Castle, my father, for the home-grown koans.

John Kamplain, of the land of sturdy tents.

Lucien Stryk, for permission to use his poetry and the poetry of the Japanese masters that he and Takashi Ikemoto have translated.

Creatures of Habit

PAUL KUPPERBERG

The cat padded across the alleyway, shrouded in the protective darkness of night, picking her way over the city's debris. From beyond the alley came the sounds of the city, the drone of car engines and the swish of their tires on the damp pavement, the murmur of a million voices, the muffled rumble of the subways filtering up from the tunnels below. The alley stank of the rotting discard overflowing the trash cans and Dumpsters over which she stepped. Car exhaust, the mingled odor of exotic foods from street vendors, vapors from the sewers that flowed beneath the streets all assailed her sensitive nostrils.

Gotham City was all sounds and smells around her. She purred, content with the comfort derived from their presence.

Gotham was where she lived and where she

Paul Kupperberg

prowled, the place that provided her with everything she needed to sustain her.

She leaped up onto the top of an open Dumpster, balancing delicately on the edge. What she sought was nearby, would soon be hers. All she needed was a few moments alone to ferret it out. But she was accustomed to the solitude of her activities. She needed no one. She . . .

Froze.

A footstep scraped across the pavement behind her. Perched on the Dumpster's edge, fur bristling, ears straining, nose twitching to catch scent of the source of the intruder.

"No, no, no," came the soft-spoken response to her alarm. "You've no need to be afraid, little pretty."

The brown, matted cat turned her head to the sound of the voice and blinked large, glowing green eyes. There, at the mouth of the alley, stood a tall, slender figure. A human. The cat had been born of the streets, in a corner of an alley not unlike this one, and had never lived among these beings, had seldom experienced anything but torment and abuse from them. She had rightly learned to fear them.

"I'll be out of your way in just a moment," the human whispered in reassurance, advancing slowly into the alley. "You have your work to do and I have mine."

The cat sat, fur settling. She watched the human and purred. Humanity was the enemy, but this one . . . this one posed no threat. This one was a friend, indeed a kindred spirit. This one possessed the spirit and soul of the cat.

The woman paused before the watchful feline and extended a hand to be sniffed before gently scratching the creature's head with a claw-tipped leather glove. She was tall, lean, and graceful, her sensuous form

Creatures of Habit

encased in a matte-black leather bodysuit, its lines broken only by the small leather pouch hanging at the gentle swell of her hip, capped by a sleek mask that hid the upper half of her face, except for the startling, catlike green eyes that peered out the mask's eye slits below a pair of cat ears. A full, red-lipped mouth set in a strong jaw turned up in a secret smile she shared briefly with the cat.

"This has been lovely, my dear," Catwoman purred, withdrawing her hand. "But I really must be going." She pointed into the air and the cat followed her hand with its wide-eyed, glowing gaze. "Up there."

The cat blinked as if in understanding and stood, stretching its thin little body as Catwoman leaped nimbly to the edge of the Dumpster beside her. She settled on her haunches to watch her newfound friend.

Several feet over her head was the extension ladder of a fire escape. Catwoman's eyes narrowed as she briefly judged the distance, then crouched and sprang up, her gloved hands grasping the ladder's lowest rung. She effortlessly swung her lower body up like a practiced gymnast on the parallel bars, landing with only the slightest rasp of shoe leather on rusted metal slats on the fire escape's lower landing.

The cat peered up at her for a brief instant, and with a remorseful meow in farewell to the only human ever to treat her with kindness, she turned back to the contents of the Dumpster to continue her search for the evening's meal.

Above her, Catwoman was on a quest of her own. On the balls of her feet, she ascended the fire-escape steps, her matte-black leather outfit rendering her nearly invisible in the night against the brick of the building darkened by years of grimy Gotham air.

Paul Kupperberg

She stopped on the third landing, poised, listening to the sounds from the city below. Car horns blared. Voices rose and fell as citizens passed by the mouth of the alley. Somewhere in the distance, a police siren wailed mournfully on its mission of intervention in someone else's misery. She didn't care where it was headed as long as her work was uninterrupted.

Reaching into the pouch at her hip, Catwoman smiled her secret smile once again. How accommodating that the treasure she sought was held by one who made its acquisition by her so simple. Certainly the window opening onto the fire escape where she stood was protected by an alarm. This she knew merely by looking at the grimy glass on which she could see etched the fine line of wire that was there to prevent its being broken by the crude method of entry commonly referred to as the "smash-and-grab."

But Catwoman was far too subtle a professional to engage in so brutal and crass a practice. She pulled from her pouch a small plastic box with a single toggle switch on its face and, attached to its other side, a suction cup. The box was quickly affixed to the windowpane, directly over the wire strip glued to the inside of the glass. The toggle switch was flicked on by a clawed fingertip, and within seconds the box let out a single, gentle tone.

The alarm was deactivated. The wonders of modern electronics, she marveled, available to those who knew the correct *wrong* people. Catwoman knew them all.

Now her work was simple. From the pouch she produced a slender tool, the tip of which she applied to the glass. With a barely audible hiss, she traced a circle in the windowpane with the glass cutter. A tap of her knuckle at the center of the circle sent the etched out glass to the floor inside the room with a crystalline tinkle. She reached through the hole left there, flicking open the simple latch holding the window closed.

Catwoman purred with delight as she slid open the window and stepped delicately inside. She closed the window behind her, disappearing into the dark office beyond the night.

A visit to this place the previous day in civilian garb and the guise of an interested customer had given Catwoman the layout of the office, so she had no need of a betraying light to guide her steps. She went straight for the wall on the far side of the office, snaking sensuously through the maze of office furniture and display showcases. Her goal was the large built-in, walk-in safe that dominated that wall. A Wm. Finger Deluxe Model M, Series A-194–. Installed here in the offices of the C. Paris Rare Book & Manuscript Co., her research told her, forty years ago. Security technology had, of course, grown by leaps and bounds in the forty years since the safe's installation, but the Model M was still regarded as a fine example of post–World War II safe building. A solid box consisting of three layers of one-inch-thick tempered steel plating, fireproof, bombproof, with inlaid door hinges and dead-bolt locks and four separate tumbler mechanisms that made cracking the locks next to impossible for all but the most experienced safecracker or someone equipped with a good supply of explosives.

All in all, a most formidable and impressive box. Except for someone in possession of the combination.

Someone, like Catwoman.

Once again, her acquaintance with the correct wrong people simplified Catwoman's task. In this instance, it was Buddy Wexler, a small, round-shouldered old man

Paul Kupperberg

with a perpetual squint and a thorough knowledge of
safes built in America during the last century. There
was hardly a model he had not, at some point in his
long career, gotten into before his retirement. And being a professional of the highest caliber, Wexler always sought the simplest way through the steel and
locks confronting him. In the case of the product of the
Wm. Finger Co. constructed over twenty years ago,
that usually meant consulting the installation records
copied late that same year from the company's offices.
Most people, Wexler told her, amused, never bother
changing the combination set at the time of a safe's
installation, not even forty years later. It's too much
trouble to memorize new combinations, he assured
her as he handed her a slip of paper on which a series
of numbers had been written in exchange for a sum of
cash.

The dial spun beneath her fingers, first right, then
left, then right again. Then, a metallic click and the
safe's handle giving under a gentle push.

The safe door swung open and Catwoman laughed
in delight.

Within the safe were shelves and on the shelves
rested a wealth of paper rarities, the crème de la
crème of the C. Paris Rare Book & Manuscript catalog: a first edition of Miguel de Cervantes's *El
Ingenioso Hidalgo Don Quixote de la Mancha* from the
sixteen hundreds; the original manuscript of *Alice's
Adventures in Wonderland* in Lewis Carroll's own
hand; a set of nine Shakespeare plays bound together,
the first published collection of the Bard's work
printed four years before the almost-as-rare and more-
well-known First Folio; first editions of *Moby-Dick*,
Robinson Crusoe, *Pilgrim's Progress*, and other rare
volumes, many inscribed by the authors.

Creatures of Habit

And the object of Catwoman's excursion into the night: the original, handwritten manuscript of T. S. Eliot's *Old Possum's Book of Practical Cats*.

There were far more valuable items housed in the safe, items that Catwoman would take with her for sale and profit in the world's extensive black market in rarities and antiquities. But the Eliot manuscript, she reflected with emotion approaching ecstasy as she lifted the leather folder containing the sheaf of papers, was for her own private collection. If she left here tonight with only this in her possession, she would consider the night's efforts an unqualified success. Little more than a bit of doggerel, this lesser of the poet's works was most famous for inspiring a long-running Broadway musical, but it had as its theme that which was close to Catwoman's heart.

Cats. Her life. Her pleasure and passion.

Her obsession!

"You've always been predictable, Selina," a deep voice rumbled behind her.

Catwoman knew, even as she turned with the manuscript clutched to her breast, whose voice it was.

He stood, framed in the doorway to the office, a tall, broad figure sheathed in shadowy gray and midnight blue. His face was hidden by a mask, pointed ears reminiscent of a bat's head rising from its crown. Shining on his broad chest was a brilliant yellow oval in which was emblazoned a jet-black emblem in the shape of a bat and, to complete the image, a billowing cape with a serrated edge hung from his imposing shoulders like batwings at rest.

"Hello, Batman," she said, her voice as casual as someone meeting a friend on an afternoon stroll through the park. "Fancy meeting you here, of all places."

Paul Kupperberg

"Not so very fancy at all," he said, pointing a dark-gloved finger at the leather folder in her grasp. "The auction tomorrow of the Eliot manuscript has been in all the newspapers. I knew it was only a matter of time before you tried for it."

"But how could you have known I would try to-night?" she asked with a slow, sensuous shrug of her shoulders. Catwoman's tongue flicked out, briefly touching her suddenly dry lips. But there was no fear or apprehension attached to the gesture. This was something else, something that always seemed to grip her when she was in the presence of this man.

It was Batman's turn to shrug as he strode into the office, his hand held out as if to take the folder from her. "I've been keeping tabs on this place," he said. "It was still in the safe this evening at closing time. To-night was your last chance at it before it was shipped to the auction house tomorrow morning.

"Now, hand it over, Selina."

Catwoman sighed. "You have no idea how you vex me, dear Batman. Don't you find it astonishing how our paths are always crossing!"

Batman stopped within a yard of her. "No. As I said, you're predictable."

"Oh, no," she cried in mock horror. "I'd hate to think that were so. But I do know what I can do to drive that silly notion out of your mind." Now Catwoman laughed, and her hand, which had been creeping toward the pouch at her hip as they spoke, came into plain view holding a Zippo cigarette lighter. She flicked it to life and the flame leaped up a full six inches to fill the dark office with flickering shadows.

"This"—she giggled with undisguised pleasure—"is something you *never* predicted!"

Batman started in surprise as Catwoman spun and

tossed the flaming lighter into the open safe. Into the midst of millions of dollars' worth of old, dry, and brittle paper.

Still laughing, Catwoman moved toward the window even as Batman sprung into the safe with a single leap. The lighter had bounced once on the floor inside the safe, the flame of the Zippo reaching for contents of the lowest shelf. The manufacturer of the lighter guaranteed its performance in even the stiffest wind, so its brief flight from Catwoman's hand to the safe didn't dim the flame.

A leather-bound book began to smolder. Batman grabbed for it, hearing as he did so the pounding of Catwoman's heels on the floor and the crash of glass as she dived through the window. As he swept the burning book and flickering lighter up in his hands, the sound of the rasp of her soles on the metal rungs of the fire escape reached him. He rolled out of the safe, holding both sources of fire away from the rest of its precious contents, snapping shut the lighter and slapping the small fire licking at the pages of the burning book out against his chest.

He was back on his feet in seconds, heading for the shattered window and the pursuit of Catwoman. But she was gone, swallowed by the night. Along with the Eliot manuscript.

A cat with matted brown fur sat on the fire escape among the shards of broken window glass, looking up at Batman expectantly. His lips set in a hard, grim line, the Dark Knight peered into the alley below. Catwoman had escaped him again because he had again underestimated her cunning.

He routinely faced and overcame foes who were both stronger and smarter than she. He survived the treacherous nights of encounters with danger and

death with physical prowess and wits sharpened to
the pinnacle of human perfection, yet this one woman
all too frequently bested him with little more than a
look from those startling green eyes.

What was the answer?

The cat's plaintive meow broke his train of thought
and he sighed. Catwoman's time would come, he
knew. It always did and always would, as long as she
remained the creature of habit she had always been.
Batman turned from the window to place a call to
Commissioner Gordon to report Catwoman's success
and his own failure.

The cat cocked her head to one side, waiting on the
fire escape. She sensed this human might love cats almost as much as had the first one.

Selina Kyle was disturbed by the night's encounter.
Oh, not by her failure to steal the wealth of books and
manuscripts that had been within her grasp. She was
happy just to have the Eliot manuscript, which she
now set in a place of honor on a display stand in the
bookcase in the den of her Gotham City penthouse
apartment.

No, she thought as she walked over to curl into a
large, cushioned chair facing the bookcase to admire
her new prize. No, as far as she was concerned, she
had fulfilled her mission. What was disturbing was
Batman's observation about her behavior.

You've always been predictable, Selina.

As the Joker sought out novelties and chaos, as the
Riddler persisted in taunting Batman with clues to
his plans disguised as riddles, as Two-Face based his
crimes on his strange obsession with duality, so was

Catwoman overly fond of items with cat-related motifs.

The only difference between them and her, of course, was that they were all quite insane.

So, yes, she allowed, in that way perhaps she *was* predictable. In some small measure. Lost in thought, Selina absently stroked the silky fur of Cassie, the Persian that hopped up on her lap. Why did she confine her activities to such *objets d'cat*? Could it be that like that ridiculous little Riddler, she had some sort of warped, subconscious ulterior motive?

"Nonsense," she hissed. The Persian perked up its ears and blinked at her. A tortoiseshell tabby and an orange tom leaped up to join the cat on her lap.

Criminals like Riddler and Two-Face acted as they did because they *wanted* Batman to catch them. They were psychotics and sociopaths whose obsessive behaviors were literal cries for capture and help. They were the ones who kept the padded cells of the Arkham Asylum for the Criminally Insane full and its psychiatric staff working overtime.

But Selina Kyle? She didn't fit that description. She had been arrested any number of times in the course of her criminal career. On those few occasions the authorities had been able to hold her, she had undergone psychiatric evaluations, each one resulting in her being judged sane.

And yet . . .

There was no denying that Batman had known exactly where to find her tonight. Nor was there any denying the feelings that gripped her when he was near. She had always tried telling herself that her feeling for the Dark Knight was that of respect for a worthy adversary. But she was being honest with herself now, thoroughly analytical. And if the absolute truth were to be known, even to herself, she had to admit there was more to her emotions than respect.

Selina Kyle took pride in needing no man to make her life complete. In her former existence, before there was Catwoman to sustain her and make her whole, she had lived an empty life, being used by any man who could pay the price for her services. But that was long ago, and now she would as soon kill a man before she allowed him to touch her.

So it was certainly not a matter of need.

But *want*. Now that was an entirely different matter. Could Batman be the one to make her forget the dirty, unwholesome touches of the strange men of her past?

Selina became aware of the low, pleasured rumble of feline contentment. But the cats stretched out on and about her were all asleep, silent.

The purrs were her own.

For Batman?

Selina sprang to her feet, startling and scattering the cats, more deeply troubled now than when she began dissecting her emotional state. She couldn't believe what she was thinking. Since their very first encounter, Catwoman had always sought to triumph over Batman. To dominate him as she would dominate all men.

But now she was no longer sure. Now she didn't know if she wanted to win out over him ... or win him over.

This was going to require some very long, hard thought.

"Tell me, sir," Alfred Pennyworth said. "Might I spend another hour in the kitchen preparing some *other* dish

Creatures of Habit

you can allow to grow cold while you ponder the mysteries of the universe?"

Bruce Wayne sat staring out the dining-room window, chin resting on steepled fingertips, brow furrowed in deep ridges of thought. "No, Alfred," he replied absently, eyes fixed on something beyond the dark of night outside the glass. "No, thank you. This is just fine."

Alfred sighed softly to himself, his professional demeanor preventing him from too ostentatious a show of his displeasure. Mr. Wayne was, after all, the master of the house. And though Alfred had been hired long ago as the butler of the household by Wayne's parents, and in spite of the fact that he had literally raised young Bruce from the time of Dr. and Mrs. Wayne's deaths, the elderly British gentleman's gentleman always insisted on maintaining the proper level of decorum.

Which was not, he admitted with no small amount of pride (but only to himself), the easiest of tasks.

Because how many men in his position were servant, confidant, friend, and provider of first aid to the Batman?

Alfred stepped to the table and removed the plate of cold, untouched food. "Am I to assume, sir, that something is troubling you?"

Bruce Wayne made a sound deep in his throat, which Alfred interpreted as assent.

"Might I suggest speaking of it as a method of alleviating your concerns?"

Wayne looked at Alfred at last. "I'm sorry, Alfred. Did you say something?"

"Yes, sir," the manservant said patiently. "I was asking if you might like to talk out your problem vis-à-vis Catwoman."

"Catwoman," Wayne repeated. "Selina. I suppose I should be grateful no one was killed tonight. Considering the murderous crime spree she's been on lately, that's some consolation."

"She is proving most vexing, yes, sir. But then, Miss Kyle is always a problem when she embarks on a rampage."

"The woman's insane, Alfred."

"Yes, sir," the butler replied dryly. "I accept the diagnosis from a man who wears leotards and a mask whilst leaping about the rooftops of the city in the dead of night."

Wayne suppressed a smile at Alfred's response. Sometimes, he thought, his old butler must have invented the fine art of sarcasm. "Point taken, friend, but you'll have to admit that there's a considerable difference between my motives and Selina's."

"Quite, sir. Flip sides of the same coin, as it were."

Wayne had come to expect this reaction from Alfred. The older man was as close to family as he had known since the murder of his parents by a mugger when he was a youngster. He had always been there for Bruce Wayne when he needed him, to talk or be comforted, when he limped home in the dark of night and the aftermath of his self-appointed crusade against evil. But Alfred Pennyworth would never approve of the way he spent his nights. He would support Bruce as best he could, he would mend his wounds when the crusade turned bloody, but how was he to approve of any activity that saw Wayne putting his life on the line night after night?

What was he to do but hate any activity that threatened the young man he loved as dearly as his own flesh and blood? Even if that was an admission Alfred would never vocalize, not even under the threat of the

most heinous torture. Because that, of course, would
be a breech of the decorum he so valued.

"Whatever my reasons, Catwoman's a criminal and
a killer, and it's up to me to stop her."

"If you say so, sir. Although sometimes I must
wonder . . ." But Alfred's voice trailed off and he shook
his head as he started to turn with the dish in hand to
leave the room.

"Wonder what?" Wayne asked.

Alfred stood with his back to Bruce Wayne for a
long moment before turning back to his employer with
a look of concern spread across his normally closed expression. "About Miss Kyle, sir. It would seem to me
that she appears to prey on your mind far more than
do other foes whenever you and she encounter one another."

"Meaning?"

"Meaning, sir, that you might wish to consider investigating your emotional state where Catwoman is
concerned."

Wayne laughed, or at least made a sound as close to
a laugh as he could muster in light of Alfred's words.
"What are you saying, Alfred? That I've got feelings
for the woman that are interfering with my work?"

"I merely think you have a tendency to . . . shall we
say, obsess over Miss Kyle and her activities. Her
crimes are terrible, to be sure, but no more, and certainly often less, than the acts of others, such as the
Joker. Or Two-Face."

"Don't be ridiculous, Alfred. Naturally I'm going to
think about her when she's active. But I think about
every criminal I go up against."

Alfred nodded and his features settled back into
their usual neutral repose. "If you say so, sir," he said,

but he allowed a hint of skepticism to creep into his voice. He wasn't hiding anything from Bruce Wayne.

"I do," Wayne asserted. But he heard his old friend's doubt and it bothered him more than he was willing to admit. He was too tired to argue, though. And he had too much to think about.

Mostly about Catwoman.

"Will there be anything else, sir?" Alfred asked.

"No, thank you."

"Then I shall clean up in the kitchen and be retiring."

"Good night, Alfred," Bruce Wayne said softly, turning his gaze back to the black stare of the window. Alfred was almost out of the dining room when Wayne called out to him, "Before you turn in, Alfred, could you fix me something to eat?"

Alfred looked down at the plate of cold food in his hand and shook his head. "Certainly, sir," he replied. "How silly of me not to have thought of that myself."

The cat is largely nocturnal, a creature prowling the jungles and hunting in the night. Like her feline namesake, the Catwoman seldom hunted before the sun had set and darkness veiled her jungle, the Gotham streets. She was uncomfortable in the daylight, believing that sunshine revealed far too many flaws and imperfections in both body and soul.

But the night was part of her obsession. In the soft glow of the moon and the harsh glare of halogen street lamps lie her predictability.

This time she would walk abroad in the light of day!

Of course, the need to change required a number of concessions to form. The comforting bodysuit of black leather was unquestionably too conspicuous. So, too, was she forced to abandon her trademark burglar's entrance to her goal. But, in the daytime, most targets she might strike would be open and accessible. All she need do was walk through open doors, welcomed like any patron or sightseer, and take what she wanted. Less challenging, to be sure.

But a definite departure from her established patterns. And oh, so infinitely dull in comparison.

Today Batman would not know where the Catwoman was to strike until after the deed were done. He couldn't possibly be waiting for her this time.

Selina Kyle slid smoothly from the rear of the taxi that came to a stop in front of the Gotham Gem Mart Building on Forty-seventh Street between Kane and Robinson avenues. The entire length of this one block was devoted to the buying and selling of precious gems, in storefronts, in stall-lined arcades, and in the hundreds of offices in the towering buildings along the street. Here, a hundred-thousand-dollar deal could be struck and consummated on the sidewalk, between two dealers in diamonds who were comfortable doing so on nothing more than a handshake. Forty-seventh Street, known in the gem trade simply as the Street, was perhaps the single most valuable stretch of real estate in Gotham City, its status having less to do with the property itself than with the commodity traded here.

The commodity that brought Selina Kyle here bright and early this sunny Thursday morning.

She paid the driver, treating him with a dazzling smile as reward for his services and sending him happily on his way as she entered the lobby of the Gem Mart.

Stylishly dressed in a black leather miniskirt, dark green silk blouse, and green pumps that accentuated her height and glorious stature, she moved past the security guard at the lobby desk, toward the elevators. She leveled her most dazzling smile at the uniformed guard, lifting her sunglasses to rest atop her short-cropped black hair, revealing dazzling emerald eyes that caused his breath to catch in his throat. He watched her, coming and going, his head swiveling as though on a pivot to keep his eyes glued to the long, slim figure until she boarded the next elevator and the doors closed on this green-eyed vision.

It was only after she was gone that he remembered it was his job to have her sign in and list her destination in the building.

What the hell, he thought. Prob'ly just some rich babe pickin' up a major rock she conned her poor schmuckuva husband into givin' up for her.

And she was probably worth every carat.

He hadn't been able to sleep.

Usually as the sun was rising he would be settling down for his few hours of daily sleep. He didn't need much to revitalize himself thoroughly, not if he did it right. Actually he didn't so much sleep as meditate, placing himself in a deep trance state where his mind and body refreshed themselves in the shortest possible time. A little bit of business he'd picked up in his study of a myriad of meditative disciplines over the years, one that came in handy since he didn't have eight hours a night to waste in unconsciousness. His days were spent immersed in business. His nights were occupied by the affairs of the night itself.

His natural element as the Batman.

But last night he lay there in his bed, eyes closed, breathing deep and regular, and totally unable to

Creatures of Habit

achieve anything approaching a trance as he replayed
in his mind's eye, again and again, his encounter with
Catwoman.

Something about it bothered him, something beyond
her having escaped.

Something he had said.

You've always been predictable, Selina.

She hadn't liked that. She had tried to make light of
it, but he could see the surprise in her eyes after he
said it, he could tell that he had hit a nerve. Selina
had never thought of herself as anything but a strong,
capable foe whose actions were as clever as they were
vicious. But now, by pointing out her greatest flaw, he
made a big mistake. He had unwittingly challenged
her and she was sure as hell to pick up the gauntlet.

To do that, Catwoman would have to act out of character.

That's what had been gnawing at the back of his
mind as he tried to find a few hours of rest from his
labors.

To accept his challenge, *she would have to act out of
character*!

What would that mean? Fortunately her very predictability made her denial of it equally predictable.
She would have to forsake the night. Give up her costume. Maybe even her burglary modus operandi.
Guessing that much was easy.

Where it got difficult for Batman to call it was her
obsession with cats.

Her theft of the Eliot *Old Possum's Book of Practical Cats* manuscript was the perfect example of her
obsession. To throw him off truly, Catwoman would
have to give up her signature crimes on top of everything else. But he didn't think she could go that far;
she probably wouldn't think she needed to. Not Selina

Kyle, whose own identity was so closely tied up in her feline counterparts.

Then he remembered an article he had read in the latest issue of *Lapidary Weekly*.

Which was why the Batman was perched on the tenth-floor ledge of the building on Forty-seventh Street directly across from the Gem Mart.

Like a magpie, Catwoman had a fondness for bright, shiny objects, particularly those of great value. Especially if they had some sort of connection to cats. And while she would hate the analogy with the scavenger bird, she could no more help her attraction than could it.

Batman raised miniature binoculars to his eyes, looking down to the street far below and the taxicab disgorging a passenger before the Gem Mart.

He smiled grimly to himself, taking what satisfaction he could from being right about Catwoman's nature. A nature that drew her, like a bee to honey, to the tenth-floor office of Krinick Fine Gems, current owners of the Katz Canary Diamond.

"Yes, ma'am, twenty-five carats *is* most impressive," Lewis Krinick agreed with the tall woman in front of him at the display counter. She was absently sifting through a velvet-lined tray of diamond earrings, a customer eager to spend money, he was certain, but unsure as to what to spend it on. Most of his day was spent with women such as this one, women with far too much money and way too much time on their hands.

Though few, he had to admit, as breathtakingly gorgeous as she.

"I was quite intrigued when I read about it. In fact,

Creatures of Habit

I was wondering." She started, hesitating, to lift a diamond-drop earring to one delicate lobe and admire the effect in the mirror on the countertop.

"Yes, ma'am?" Mr. Krinick inquired. But of course he knew what was coming. It had been the most frequent request since the acquisition, two weeks ago.

She turned her eyes from her own reflection to look into the face of elderly Mr. Krinick. "Well," she breathed, moving closer to him. He caught a faint whiff of milk on her breath. "I know this is probably an imposition, but I would so love to actually see the Katz Canary Diamond. That is, if it's available." She looked at him expectantly.

"I'm sure you'll understand that the Katz is a most valuable gemstone," he said. "Twenty-five carats, one of the most perfect canary diamonds in existence, and therefore one of the most valuable. I'm afraid insurance regulations require we keep it locked in our vault except when showing it for sale, Ms.—I'm sorry. I don't believe I caught your name, ma'am."

The woman waved her hand vaguely between them, smiling. "Well, no, I didn't give it. I usually avoid doing so on the Street. I find I get much fairer treatment if my identity isn't known during the negotiation process."

Krinick cocked his head to one side, intrigued now by something other than her beauty. "And, um, why might that be, ma'am?"

"Because of my husband, of course," she said. "Roger McDouglas."

Krinick's breath caught in his throat. Roger McDouglas was one of the richest men in the country, owner of the nation's largest privately held media conglomerate, and famous for his aversion to any media exposure of himself or his family. So while his name was famous, his face and the faces of his immediate family were virtually unknown. Krinick knew McDouglas was married to a woman much younger than himself, and that she was said to be quite the beauty.

And that, as some people collected stamps, she amused herself by amassing many of the world's most fabulous gemstones.

"Ah, Mrs. McDouglas," he said, almost stuttering out her name in the sudden rush of excitement that gripped him. He felt downright light-headed. Giddy. "I . . . of course, I would be honored to show you the Katz Canary. Please, if you'll just follow me."

Krinick snapped his fingers, signaling to his wife, who, engaged with a customer of her own on the far side of the showroom, looked his way. "Deborah," he said. "I'm going into the vault to show *Mrs. McDouglas* some items."

Mrs. Krinick raised an eyebrow at her husband and the stunned, stupid grin plastered across his face as he led the woman to the room at the rear of the offices where the vault was located.

Batman unclipped the compressed-air gun from his utility belt. Catwoman would be upstairs by now, working her way into the vault and the Katz Canary Diamond. He would be there when she emerged with it in her possession, catching her red-handed, with no room for doubt or trampling upon of her constitutional rights that might lead to acquittal in court.

He would have her this time. The *last* time she would ply her criminal trade on Gotham City.

From a pouch in his belt, Batman withdrew a small cylinder that he fitted into the barrel of the

Creatures of Habit

compressed-air gun. To that was hooked the end of a slim, strong nylon rope. Then he took aim and squeezed the trigger. With a muffled cough, the cylinder exploded from the gun and flew across the width of Forty-seventh Street, striking the concrete over the window in the corridor outside the Krinick offices. The head of the cylinder shattered when it struck its target, driving the diamond-hard spike beneath it solidly into the wall itself.

Batman yanked sharply on the nylon rope and, satisfied that it was firmly embedded across the way, pulled it taut and secured his end to a flagpole support beside him. A small pair of handles with a grooved wheel between them produced from a clip at the rear of his belt under his cloak and fitted atop the rope completed his preparations.

Gripping the handles on either side of the rope in his gloved hands, the Dark Knight leaped from the ledge, launching himself into the air high above the street, gliding across the open space with his scalloped cape billowing out behind him like the wings of his namesake.

Selina gaped, eyes wide at the sparkling riches that lay before her on the crushed-black-velvet-lined tray in Krinick's hands.

They were just outside the closet-sized vault in the back room of the jeweler's office, an armed private security guard standing at attention not a dozen feet from where they stood. All around them were dozens of drawers containing thousands of precious gemstones, but there was nothing that could possibly equal the value or sheer overwhelming beauty of the Katz Canary.

Paul Kupperberg

"It is amazing, isn't it, Mrs. McDouglas?" Lewis Krinick said softly, in reverential awe of the diamond.

"Yes," she said, her whispered reply almost a hiss. She could not take her eyes off the large oval-cut yellow stone.

"Yellow, so-called canary diamonds are quite rare, you know. Particularly of this size and quality," he said. "This one came from the Kimberly Mines in South Africa, dug up in 189–. It was purchased the following year by Marcus Katz, a London merchant, for his wife's birthday. He had it cut from its original form down to its current twenty-five-carat oval shape and presented it to Mrs. Katz on March thirtieth, 189–.

"The gem remained in the family until sixty years ago, when the Katz's daughter sold it. It's since passed through several hands until, naturally, it landed in my own just this past month."

"It's spectacular," Selina Kyle breathed. "I believe I read it's valued at over one and a quarter million dollars?"

Mr. Krinick smiled modestly. "On their own, yellow diamonds of this quality have sold at roughly fifty thousand dollars a carat. With its history and provenance, the Katz Canary is worth considerably more."

The woman reached toward the diamond and paused, her hand hovering over the large rock as she looked questioningly at the jeweler. "May I?"

"Of course, ma'am," he said smoothly. Behind them, the security guard narrowed his eyes, watching the tall, elegant woman carefully. While he didn't find her threatening, he was paid decent money to watch over the Krinicks' property. Besides, in this day and age, you could never be too sure about anyone, or too careful.

Creatures of Habit

She picked up the diamond between two fingers, holding it as carefully as if it were an eggshell rather than a rock of the hardest substance in nature. She lifted it, slowly, to eye level, turning it so that its multifaceted surface caught the light of the overhead fixture. Sparkling like a chunk of solidified fire.

Beautiful!

"Yes," said Selina. "Yes. I'll take it, Mr. Krinick."

Krinick's heart began pounding like a trip-hammer in his chest. "Um, v-very good, Mrs. McDouglas. If you would care to step into my private office, we . . . we can discuss price and—"

Selina turned her eyes, alight with the reflective glitter of the diamond, on the old jeweler. "No, Mr. Krinick, I'm afraid you don't understand."

"I . . . don't?" he asked, confused.

"I said I'd *take* it and I meant *exactly* that!"

Her fist closed around the diamond and she laughed as her other hand snapped open the purse hanging from her shoulder. As she did so a thick cloud of gray gas exploded from inside, spreading rapidly through the small room. The guard gasped, reaching for his gun, but before he could do more than clear the holster, he tasted the gray gas in his mouth and felt it burning his nose, all putrid and greasy.

He heard a thud, the revolver falling from his numbed fingers.

Another noise, fuller and less solid than the hard steel of the gun. It was the sound of his own body hitting the floor. He was unconscious by the time Krinick's body hit and Selina's laughter filled the room.

"Thank you, Mr. Krinick," she said to the elderly man huddled in a lump at her feet. "I think that will be all for today."

Paul Kupperberg

Still laughing, small filters in her nostrils rendering her impervious to the noxious gas swirling about her, Selina Kyle stepped over Krinick's still form and sauntered from the room with the Katz Canary Diamond growing warm in her clenched fist.

In the main showroom, she pulled the door to the back room closed as she called in, "Thank you, Mr. Krinick. I'll be in touch this afternoon about that. Good-bye now."

Mrs. Krinick looked curiously at the woman, who smiled and wiggled her fingers in a wave of farewell as she strode through the showroom. Her husband had seemed so excited about this Mrs. McDouglas's prospects. It was so unlike him to let so potentially a valuable customer leave unescorted. But she had to trust her husband's judgment on this, so she returned the woman's wave and wished her a good morning as the woman opened the door and left the office.

Into the corridor, where the Caped Crusader stood waiting for her.

"Going somewhere, Selina?" Batman asked.

Selina's surprise was genuine and, for a split second, paralyzing. "Batman!" she hissed. "How ... ?"

"I think it would be obvious," he said. "I mean, really, Selina ... the *Katz* diamond. Even changing ninety percent of your MO, you couldn't have been more predictable if you tried." As he spoke, before she could fully recover her wits, Batman's hand shot forward and grabbed her wrist, squeezing hard. The sharp, sudden pain caused her fist to open and the lump of yellow crystal to drop from her hand.

Selina Kyle screamed out in anger and pain.

The Catwoman leaped at Batman, her free hand curled into a claw, crimson-painted nails reaching for Batman's exposed cheek. Batman twisted back and to the side, causing her clawed fingers to miss their target. He released her other hand suddenly, unexpectedly, causing her to stumble back as she tried to pull free of his grasp.

Catwoman's back hit the wall, but she used it as a springboard to hurtle herself, growling deep in her throat, back at Batman immediately. The Dark Knight was waiting for her, once more sidestepping her lunge and using her own momentum to send her continuing on her way, slamming into the opposite wall.

She was dazed, but she shook it off and spun, kicking off her high-heeled pumps as she moved. She was face-to-face with Batman as he came in at her, his blue-gauntleted hands reaching for her. She whipped up her arms, her forearms slapping into his wrists, one two, opening up his guard. She went in low, head down, like a battering ram into the muscular ridges of his stomach.

Catwoman felt his gut ripple as the impact doubled him over, heard his grunt of surprise and the rush of air escaping his lungs. She reached up, wrapping her hands around his forearm and elbow, and as she stepped out from under him, twisted and turned his arm, simultaneously sweeping her leg between his.

Batman grunted again, hearing the tearing of muscle even as he felt his left arm pop out of its socket, his leg buckling as Selina's leg smashed into the back of his knee.

He went down, landing heavily on his side on top of the diamond, unable to suppress a brief gasp of pain as the sharp facets dug into his ribs. He started to roll off it, to get back on his feet, but as he turned onto his back, the flat, hard surface of Catwoman's foot struck him on the chin, snapping his head back.

Paul Kupperberg

Batman's eyes glazed over and he was barely aware
of the sound of bare feet slapping against the linoleum
floor, receding into the distance. The sound overpow-
ered by the pounding pain of his dislocated shoulder
in his ears. He decided, a little later, that he must
have momentarily passed out from the pain, because
by the time he was again aware of his surroundings,
Catwoman was gone, except for the faint lingering flo-
ral scent of her perfume.

And the Katz Canary Diamond.

The damned diamond!

Selina paced her living room like a caged jungle
beast, voicing her displeasure with a low, throaty
growl. None of the cats who shared her apartment
were in sight, hiding from her anger, having scattered
when she first came home, hurtling her purse to the
floor with a banshee wail of rage. She deserved to lose
the diamond. That was the price she had to pay for
vanity.

She had started off on the right path, the one leading to change and preventing Batman from anticipating her activities. But she hadn't gone far enough. Her
ego had overwhelmed her good sense and she had
wound up with Batman breathing down her neck for
her misguided efforts.

Selina had abandoned virtually every aspect of her
Catwoman persona. Except for the single, most telling
detail.

Cats.

The *Katz* Canary Diamond, for God's sake. Cats . . .
the cat eating the canary.

You couldn't have been more predictable if you tried,
Batman had said, mocking her.

Creatures of Habit

But he was right, damn him. Of all the prizes to be had in a city as large and filled with wealth as Gotham, she had picked one of the very few that would serve as a beacon to draw Batman to her. And she had done it *consciously*. She had thought all the other measures sufficient to throw Batman off her scent.

But even more disturbing was how well Batman was attuned to the way she thought. Hadn't she always before struck at night? Didn't she always operate in costume? Wasn't her method always to burglarize the premises?

And yet the first time she decided to change those things, he was right there!

She could understand his pinpointing the Katz Canary Diamond as something that would attract her larcenous attentions. She could not, for the life of her, see how he would know she would try for it *when* she did.

Had she somehow given herself away?

The only thing she could think of was her reaction to Batman's slap at her predictability. Selina had thought that she'd covered herself well enough, but she had obviously let something slip.

And Batman, dear Batman, knew her well enough to pick up on her slip and turn it to his advantage.

Correction.

Almost to his advantage. Even though she had not thought there was a chance he would show up, she had reacted well to his appearance. She had overcome both her surprise and Batman, escaping him easily.

Of course, she couldn't completely discount the idea that she had been able to take him out because she *had* been expecting him after all. Selina had to consider that the same subconscious motivation that

Paul Kupperberg

made her so long adhere to her feline trademark also caused her to stay with it one more time. Because she wanted to attract Batman?

As much as she wanted to deny that, she wasn't able to dismiss it out of hand.

But there was a way she could *prove* she wasn't irreversibly and irrationally attracted to her greatest nemesis.

And that was to put behind her, once and for all, her cats.

"She's going to have to take it to the next step," Batman murmured, to apparently no one in particular in the dark cavern far below the cellar of Bruce Wayne's mansion on the outskirts of Gotham City.

Alfred, occupied with flicking a feather duster over a computer workstation several yards from where Batman sat, *sans* mask, revealing the brooding features of Bruce Wayne, turned in response to his mumbling. "Excuse me, sir? Is it your shoulder again?"

Wayne shook his head. "It's fine, Alfred. You did your usual excellent job setting it."

"Lord knows I've had enough experience." Alfred shrugged in resignation. "By my count, this is the twenty-third time I've been required to attend to that same shoulder. You might wish to seriously consider the surgical option to permanently remedying the problem that your doctor suggested, what was it, going on two years ago now?"

"One of these days, Alfred. When I can afford to take a month off for the surgery and recuperation."

"I see, sir," Alfred said with disapproval. "In other words, you'll have the surgery about the time pigs learn to fly."

Creatures of Habit

"Something like that."

"Then am I to assume your sotto voce complaints were in reference to Ms. Kyle?"

Wayne scratched thoughtfully at his chin. "It occurs to me," he said slowly, "that if she's trying to throw me off her trail, she's going to realize now that she'll need to completely abandon her MO."

"Rather beyond the psychological capacity of your average costumed foe, I should think," the butler observed.

"Too far out of it. Selina's lived with her obsession so long, I don't think she *can* give it up. Considering what I know of her past, it's something she needs to maintain what passes for her sanity. She has to identify with the independent nature of cats in order to convince herself that she doesn't need anyone. Especially the men who abused her when she was younger. If ever there was a creature of habit, it's Selina Kyle."

"Hmm, yes. If you say so, sir. So where does that leave matters?"

Wayne stood and strode across the Batcave to the computer console Alfred had been dusting. "Slightly more complicated to anticipate."

"Ah, yes, I see." Alfred nodded as Wayne hit the switch to power up the computer. "Ms. Kyle will endeavor to break her habit by choosing a crime she feels to be unrelated to felines. But you believe her incapable of making so atypical a choice, regardless of her motivation for doing so."

"Exactly." Wayne began to tap at the computer keyboard. "Like I said, she's a creature of habit and it's going to be her habit that nails her."

Alfred watched as he accessed the computer bulletin boards. Within moments, Alfred knew, Master Bruce would be deeply engrossed in the flow of electronic information, seeking out some obscure little fact, some previously overlooked news item that would point the way to his final confrontation with Catwoman.

"Very well, sir. And while you're making Gotham City safe for honest citizens to walk its streets, I'll be upstairs making the manor safe from dust."

Wayne nodded without hearing, his attention rooted to the computer screen.

"It's a dirty job." Alfred sighed as he walked, feather duster in hand, to the elevator. "But someone must do it." He threw a last glance back at Bruce Wayne, oblivious to the world beyond the computer screen, as the elevator doors slid shut.

"Not that anyone would notice if it were not done . . ."

She had spent five days planning this one.

Five days, scouring the newspapers and criminal sources in the underworld. Five days looking at this job from every angle, exploring it down to the smallest, seemingly most insignificant detail. Because she had to be sure, one hundred percent certain, that nowhere in anything connected to this crime, in any way, shape, or form, was there anything to do with cats.

This was going to be the work not of Catwoman but of Selina Kyle.

This was going to be the job that broke for good her obsession with cats. And with Batman!

Wrapped in a tight, slinky white evening gown, her long, graceful neck accentuated by a delicate golden chain, more gold and diamonds in her earlobes and

Creatures of Habit

about her wrist, Selina sat back comfortably in the rear of the limousine as it wound its way up the drive of the Whittington estate. This magnificent mansion on the outskirts of Gotham City, set on fifty wooded acres, was home to one of the city's oldest and wealthiest families. The Whittingtons had arrived in the New World from England late in the seventeenth century and, coming from old wealth, had amassed an additional fortune in manufacturing and, later, in the railroad industry.

Today, Ivo Whittington VII oversaw a vast financial empire and, with his wife Alyce, was known the world over for charitable works. And it was charity that brought Selina Kyle, along with three hundred invited guests, to the Whittington estate tonight. A fundraiser, to be exact, for the Gotham Museum of Modern Art. The invited guests, the cream of Gotham society, would be pledging money, upward of three million dollars it was estimated, for the construction of a new wing to the museum.

But it wasn't cash that interested Selina Kyle. It was the Whittingtons' own collection of modern art, often separated and out on loan to numerous museums around the country, now reunited for display at the fund-raiser before being transported to the Gotham for exhibition.

And not a single picture of a cat in the bunch, Selina thought, smiling in secret satisfaction.

Her target was a specific painting, recently acquired by the Whittingtons and being displayed for the first time tonight, a seventy-five-year-old piece by German expressionist Franz Von Wolf entitled *Lying in the Glade*, valued at $12.3 million. Von Wolf was considered one of the true geniuses of the German Expressionistic school, but his anti-Nazi stance had led to the destruction of the majority of his works by the authorities and his own death in a Nazi concentration camp. Only three Von Wolfs had been known to exist until *Glade* was uncovered two years ago in the storage room of an Austrian collector.

The limousine braked to a halt before the brightly lit front entrance of the Whittington house. A butler in livery stepped forward, held the limo door open, and extended a hand to help Selina slide from the car.

"Your invitation, ma'am?" the servant inquired.

Selina produced an engraved invitation from her evening bag, a proof copy stolen just last night from the office of the printers who had produced them. Satisfied, the butler bowed at the waist and Selina passed by him, stepping into the mansion's elegant foyer. Stationed at either side of the door and in the foyer itself were large, attentive men in tuxedos, beneath which she could detect the bulge of guns.

Security guards, of course. With the wealth of jewelry on the necks and wrists of the guests, and the scores of millions of dollars' worth of art on the premises, security would be tight.

Selina wasn't worried.

She walked through the milling guests in the foyer, into the main salon, accepting a glass of champagne from a passing waiter as she went. She was in no hurry. She would take her time, double-check the layout of the house, make sure her escape route was feasible. If all went according to plan, she and *Lying in the Glade* would be long gone before the theft was discovered.

Selina wandered into the ballroom, her eyes scanning the crowd, determining the location of the stationary guards, guessing which of the men and women circulating through the crowd were undercover operatives.

"May I freshen that for you?"

Selina heard the words spoken behind her, but she didn't bother turning to respond. Instead she drained the champagne from the glass and held it up for the waiter to take and replace with a full glass. "Thank you," she said.

"You're welcome," he said, and a hand holding another glass reached around her to clink glasses in a toast. "To your health."

Selina turned now. Either she was dealing with a most impudent servant, or . . . a tall, dark-haired, handsome-as-a-Greek-god, cleft-chinned stranger in a tailored tuxedo that cost more than most people spend for a car.

He smiled at her, dazzling white teeth flashing beneath a straight, chiseled nose. "I'm sorry," he said in a deep, rumbling baritone. "I startled you."

Selina blinked. "Uh, no," she said. "Don't be silly." She wasn't startled, that was true, but she did feel suddenly . . . strange. Uncomfortably warm. She couldn't remember the last time a man made her feel this way.

"Good," he said. "So, are you a friend of the Whittingtons or a patron of the arts?"

No, that wasn't exactly true. There was *one* man.

"Patron," she said, sipping at the champagne, regarding this man over the rim of her glass. "And yourself?"

"Oh," he said, flipping his hand vaguely between them. "A little of both." He held out his free hand to her. "I'm Bruce Wayne," he said.

Selina lifted an eyebrow at him as she took his hand

Paul Kupperberg

in hers. "*The* Bruce Wayne, of Wayne Industries and the Wayne Foundation?"

"Guilty. And you are . . . ?"

"Mitchell," she said. "Rena Mitchell."

"Pleased to meet you, Rena Mitchell," he said warmly, holding on to her hand.

"We . . ." Selina started, narrowing her gaze at him. "Have we met before, Mr. Wayne?"

Bruce Wayne sighed heavily. "Bruce, please. And if we had met, I'd have hoped you would remember. I know I would, which means this is a first encounter."

"Strange," Selina said. "You seem somehow . . . familiar."

"That's me," Bruce said with an elaborate shrug of mock resignation. "A dime a dozen."

Selina shook off the strange feeling that had gripped her and allowed herself a bright, genuine laugh. "Hardly a mere dime for a man of your status, Bruce."

"A dime, a dollar," he said, apparently growing bored with the topic. "It's all just money, Rena."

She looked into his eyes, searching. Something there, in the deep pools of black, something veiled, guarded. Something the tall, handsome millionaire kept hidden from the rest of the world. The something that reminded her of Batman.

"Oh, no, Mr. Bruce Wayne," she said playfully. "You aren't fooling me with that bored, playboy facade of yours."

"Facade?"

She nodded and sipped some more champagne. "A man as successful as you couldn't possibly be as shallow as you're trying to make me believe with your line of practiced cocktail-party chatter and that patina of ennui."

Creatures of Habit

Wayne pretended to think that over and said,
"Have you considered I might be some sort of idiot sa-
vant? A genius in business but useless in all other aspects of life?"

Selina laughed, almost charmed by his line, and
then drained her glass. "No, Mr. Wayne. I most assur-
edly do not." Then, handing the surprised millionaire
the empty glass, she turned and walked away from
him, into the crowd.

Bruce Wayne held his smile until she was gone. He
might not have fooled her.

But then, neither had Rena Mitchell, aka Selina
Kyle, aka Catwoman, fooled him.

The Von Wolf was being held upstairs in a locked,
windowless inner room. The only way into the room
was through the door, with two uniformed and armed
security guards in the corridor outside and a third inside the room with the painting itself. All three men,
along with the undercover security personnel downstairs, would be on alert once the painting was
brought downstairs for the unveiling in about one
hour's time.

Selina checked her wristwatch as she walked up the
winding staircase, yet another champagne glass in her
hand. Plenty of time. The "chauffeur" who had
dropped her off earlier would be waiting outside, hidden in the bushes below the window of one of the
guest bedrooms at the rear of the house.

She paused on the upper landing and took a deep
breath. Her plan was deceptively simple, the hardest
part being some acting on her part. But the Catwoman was—

No!

She wasn't the Catwoman. Not tonight, not for this job. She was Selina Kyle, plain and simple. She had to put Catwoman and all her trappings aside and think as Selina would think.

The plan, she reminded herself. Time to go into her act.

Selina splashed a bit of the champagne from her glass onto the front of her dress and quickly mussed her hair as she reached the top of the stairs. She let herself go loose, wobbling unsteadily on her high heels as she staggered down the carpeted second-floor hallway, thoroughly into her role as a drunken society woman by the time she rounded the corner of the hallway and the two guards at the door of the room containing the Von Wolf came into view. She was humming loudly, off-key, a stupid grin plastered across her face.

The guard closest to her, a tall, dull-faced blond man, stepped from his post beside the door as she came closer. "Excuse me, miss, but you're not supposed to be up here," he said.

"Tut, tut, tut," she said, a hint of a giggle in the slurred words. "I'm just a poor l'il lamb looking for th' poor l'il lambs' room."

"There're powder rooms for guests downstairs," the other guard said.

Selina stopped, swaying ever so slightly. "Occupadoed," she said solemnly. She giggled, pointing to the wet spot on her dress where she had spilled the champagne. "I gotta clean myself up." Then she turned serious, frowning. "D'ya know if cham . . . cham . . ." She stumbled over the word and laughed. "Champagne. D'ya know if champagne stains?"

"I wouldn't know, miss," said the blond.

Selina stopped in front of the door and the guards. She smiled at the two men. "Y'know," she said deliberately, patting the blond's arm. "You're kinda . . . kinda cute."

And she belched. Which caused her to break into hysterical laughter. The two security guards exchanged looks, amused but trying to maintain a professional attitude. "Oh, God, I stink uv rumaki," she said, snapping open her purse. "You gotta think I'm some kinda pig."

"No, ma'am." The second guard grinned. "You've just had a bit too much to drink."

Selina pulled a tube of breath spray from her bag. She shoved the glass into the blond's hand. "Hold this," she mumbled, uncapping the tube. She raised it to face level and pressed the plunger.

The spray hissed out the other end of the tube, straight into the faces of the two amused security guards. They never knew what hit them, their eyes immediately rolling back into their heads as they slumped to the floor.

Slipping small filters into her nostrils, Selina knelt in front of the locked door and shoved the end of the tube into the crack at the bottom of the door. She pressed the plunger once again, emptying the dispenser of its contents. The gas would spread and fill the room in under thirty seconds. The guard locked inside with the painting would be unconscious in less time than that.

The empty tube went back into her handbag and she next took out a long, tapered wire with a hooked end. A lock pick. The door would no doubt be locked from inside, but considering this was an inside door, the lock would be more for privacy than security. Someone of Selina's skill could pick the lock faster than it would take to search the unconscious guards for the key.

Paul Kupperberg

Fifteen seconds later there was a muffled click, which, a twist of the doorknob revealed, meant the lock was open. With a swift look around her as she pulled from her handbag a paper dust mask with an elastic band to hold it in place over her nose and mouth, Selina pushed open the door and slipped inside the room to claim her prize.

But found instead the Batman!

"Looking for something, Selina?" he asked, standing in the middle of the room, his voice muffled by the small oxygen mask over his mouth and nose.

Selina was speechless. She stood in the doorway, staring at him, her eyes wide with the questions racing through her mind.

"The painting's not here," Batman told her. "Once I figured out this was where you were going to strike, I had the police convince the Whittingtons to move all their art to a place of safekeeping."

"But ... how?" Selina said, her voice a dry, thin croak. "I tried so hard ... there was nothing ... *nothing* that could have tipped you off."

She could see his smile through the transparent plastic of his protective mask. "I guess I know you better than you know yourself, Selina. I couldn't have missed this one with my eyes closed."

"No," she snapped angrily. "I checked this one from every angle. The Whittingtons don't even own a cat. The name of the artist is Von Wolf ... *wolf*, a canine, not feline!"

"I knew you'd look for a target that had nothing to do with cats, but I also knew your subconscious would trip you up." Batman held up two fingers. "It did, in the name Whittington, right down to Mrs. Whittington's first name."

"Her first ... Alyce?"

Creatures of Habit

"Her *nickname*," Batman said. "It's well known in their social circle that her husband refers to her almost exclusively by her old sorority name . . . 'Kitten.' "

Selina blinked, surprised. "Kitten? I . . . I didn't know. . . ."

"And then there's the name Whittington itself. I'm sure you must have heard of the English legend of Dick Whittington's cat. Richard Whittington was—"

Selina finished his thought for him, her voice a dull monotone. "—a poor boy who came to London, where he made his fortune, supposedly when his cat was purchased for a vast sum by the King of Barbary to combat a plague of mice, and was three times made mayor of London in the early fourteen hundreds. Yes . . . yes, of course I know the story. I know everything . . . about cats . . . but I never connected the name—"

"You can run from your nature, Selina, but you can't hide from it," Batman said gently.

She looked at him with dead eyes. "I tried, though. I *really* thought I could. . . ."

Batman shrugged. "Even the name of the painting you were going to steal pointed in your direction."

"I don't . . . oh. Yes, I see. *Lying in the Glade.* 'Lying.' Say it fast, drop the 'g' . . . *lion* in the glade."

Selina Kyle, the Catwoman, began to laugh, hysterically, uproariously out of control, and jumped at Batman. She landed on top of him, swinging, nails raking across his cheek before he could throw her off. She was still laughing as she hit the floor, rolling, and regaining her footing in a single, lithe movement. Batman plunged after her as she ran out the door, back toward the stairs she had come up by.

Waiting at the bottom of the stairway, however,

Paul Kupperberg

were several uniformed Gotham City police officers.

She hissed defiantly and, without pause, vaulted the railing midway down the stairs, landing in a crouch in the foyer. The partygoers had been cleared out of the area, so there was no one between her and the door.

Except for more cops.

She laughed, barreling into them, savagely smashing aside anyone who got in her way with slashing claws and pounding fists and feet. She knew Batman would be right behind her, and while she feared no police officer, she could not trust herself to take on Batman right now.

She couldn't trust herself with anything that had to do with the Caped Crusader. The man who knew her better, she was sure at that moment, than she knew herself. The man who could overwhelm her, if not physically, then emotionally. She had believed herself capable of overcoming the very thing that had sustained her all these years.

Batman knew differently.

He knew how her mind worked, even how her own efforts would work against her.

Without realizing how she got there, Selina Kyle found herself running into the edge of the woods that surrounded the Whittington mansion. Batman was far behind her now. She knew with certainty that she could lose him easily in the dark of these woods.

But not from inside her head. That was another matter altogether.

Selina Kyle had slept for almost twenty-four hours after making her way home from the Whittington

Creatures of Habit

estate. She had been physically and mentally exhausted by her efforts, and her earliest dreams were racked by visions of Batman, chasing her, catching her no matter where she turned, how she tried to hide.

And, later, of him overwhelming her. And of her willing acceptance of his mastery.

She had awakened from that last dream, drenched in sweat, her heart pounding. But not in fear. No, nothing like that. Because the events of the past week, coupled with her dream, finally convinced Selina of something she was sure she had known all along but had not admitted, until now.

Batman was inside her, for better or for worse. In her head, second-guessing her. But also in her heart, the two of them locked in some bizarre, love/hate relationship that provided her, at least, with a perverse and delicious thrill, with the heat between them when they met, the dreams that both haunted and sweetened her sleep.

She couldn't speak for Batman, of course, yet there he was, right behind her wherever she struck. How could he not be sharing her feelings when he was otherwise so close to her, so attuned to her actions? Oh, yes, even if he wasn't ready to admit it to himself, it was there. Because if their minds were so in tune, how far apart could their hearts be?

Selina sighed, feeling warm and curiously satisfied as she stretched luxuriously, sensuously on her sofa.

Her gaze fell on a page from the daily newspaper scattered about her. The Life-style section of the *Gotham Gazette* and its headline about a display of rare Oriental jade feline statues going on display at the Schwartz Galleries in downtown Gotham City caught her eye.

Batman couldn't help but pick up on that, she mused.

"It's *perfect*," she said to the Manx nestled contentedly in her lap. And Selina Kyle began to purr.

A Knight at the Opera

JEFF ROVIN

I

It was an early-winter night, chilly and threatening snow, but she felt invigorated.

She dashed across the rooftops of downtown Gotham's brownstones and prewar apartments, excited to be going out tonight, to see the work that had comforted and inspired her when she needed it. She would change in the alley beside the opera house, put on a gown she carried in her shoulder bag—clothes to prove to the men inside that she *did* belong here, that clothes do not make the man . . . or woman.

Except for the clothes I'm wearing now, she thought, laughing to herself.

Yes, *they* were different. These clothes not only made her, they freed her, allowed her to release the kind of energy that made tigers so feared, the kind of speed that made cheetahs so fleet, the kind of stealth that allowed the panther and the alley cat and the wildcat to survive in the jungles of trees or steel.

The skintight gray costume of the Catwoman.

II

The precious relic was made of pine, dark around the base where it had been held over and over by its distinguished owners. There were minor nicks up and down its length where it had been tapped—or on occasion slammed—against the edge of one music stand or another.

Hundreds of guests looked on in silence as a guard removed the magnificent baton from the glass display case in the opera-house lobby and placed it in an ornate gold canister. The case glistened in the light of the great chandelier above, throwing golden drops on the patrons, on the marble floor, on the busts of composers that ringed the lobby.

John Taylor watched as the guard carried the baton toward the stairwell that led to Maestro LaDolce's dressing room. When the guard had disappeared, Taylor exhaled and turned to the couple standing beside him. They were a strikingly handsome pair, a slender young woman dressed in white with her arm hooked through that of a tall, powerfully built man.

"How happy I am to be finished with *that* good fellow," Taylor said. He ran a hand through his silver hair. "Can you believe it? One hundred and fifty dollars *an hour* for a guard. My musicians don't earn that much!"

Bruce Wayne's brow arched as he looked at the chairman of the opera's board of trustees. "Don't sell

the peacekeepers short. They haven't a printed score
to follow."

"You're right, of course, but it's frustrating."

"In what way?" Cindy Merritt asked, adding under
her breath, "Like any of us cares."

Wayne squeezed her hand as he smiled out at
Megan LaDolce, daughter of Maestro Clifford
LaDolce, who had come upstairs with her mother,
Wendy. They were brave, those two, for coming up
from the dressing rooms.

Taylor said, "The guard is just another example of
our uncivilized age. Savagery in life, savagery in entertainment. Across town, the Gotham Stadium sells
out sporting events, monster-truck rallies, heavy-steel
concerts—"

"Metal," Cindy corrected him. "Heavy metal."

"Whatever. Every kind of violent or cacophonous ob-
scenity. Yet the Gotham Opera is three hundred thousand dollars in the red. If the Wayne Foundation and
the Savran Gallery hadn't agreed to match every dollar we made at tonight's benefit—"

Cindy Merritt said, "Bruce had to do *something*
with the oodles of money he made investing in Rap-
Around Records, right?"

Wayne winked at her.

"Touché." Taylor frowned. "But that only under-
scores my point. Our culture has gone to seed. Do you
know, the manager of the stadium told me that a rock-
and-roll band kept an audience waiting for two
hours—imagine that! Maestro LaDolce has his idio-
syncrasies, but at least he always shows up on time."

While Wayne listened his eye was drawn to a dark
area between the main entrance and a large bust of
the Italian composer Alfredo Catalani, whose opera
La Wally had opened the hall in 1892. Shadows al-

ways caught Wayne's eye, and he thought he saw something moving in this one.

"It's criminal," Taylor went on. "Look at what we've had here—the baton that Beethoven used for the inaugural performance of *Fidelio*, which Tchaikovsky himself wielded when he opened this hall one hundred years ago. A magnificent piece of musical history has been on display here for a week, and do you know how many people came to see it?"

Wayne didn't answer. He was watching the shadow as it moved and became two, the new one taking shape and color.

"Fewer than two hundred in a city of over seven million," Taylor complained. "I could have saved a fortune by not even bothering to insure it; no one cared that it was here! It's a disgrace, I tell you, and I sincerely hope that people are watching tonight's performance on public television. Maybe they'll see that Mozart, Wagner, and Puccini can be more exciting than the Beatles or—who are those other beasts? The Dead Lepers."

Cindy pushed a strand of long, blond hair from her eyes. "Def Leppard."

"Whatever. I'm sure it should be Tone Deaf Leopard."

The lobby was beginning to fill with operagoers, and Wayne took a step back so he could still see the bust. He watched as a woman emerged from the shadow—a tall, slender woman dressed in a tight-fitting, floor-length lilac gown. Her black hair was cut short, her lips were painted a bright red, and her eyebrows were dramatically upswept. She moved with grace that was uncommon . . . yet strangely familiar.

Taylor lifted his sleeve with a pinky and glanced at his watch. "Well, enough bellyaching. It's half past

A Knight at the Opera

seven and there are still a few babies to kiss, a few pledges I want to wrest from Gotham's rich and famous." He extended a hand. "Bruce—I can't thank you enough for everything."

"I'm always glad to help," Wayne said, giving the chairman his hand and an encouraging pat on the arm.

Taylor bowed slightly to Cindy and, almost at once, turned and embraced *Gotham Gazette* music critic Craig Ogan.

"Work that crowd," Cindy said.

"Don't be too hard on him," Wayne said, leading her out of earshot. "What Taylor's doing *is* work. In John's six seasons here, Ogan's panned almost everything he's staged."

"Then John should've gone over and kicked him in the shins, not slapped him on the back."

"And what would that have done for the Gotham Opera?"

"Nothing, except to make its chairman feel very good."

"His work makes him feel good," Wayne said. "I haven't approved of all of John's artistic decisions, but he's given his life to this place."

Cindy winced. "*Très* work ethic. If you weren't so big and tall and young and stunning, you'd remind me of my dad."

Wayne's eye returned to the woman in lilac as she crossed the lobby and glided through the door that led to the parquet circle. She stopped for a moment beside one of Taylor's assistants; when the young man noticed her and smiled, she walked on. She'd baited him, making for a curious moment.

It bothered Wayne that he knew her but couldn't place her. His success in his work—all of it—depended upon remembering details other people would have forgotten long before.

"Speaking of Daddy," Cindy said, "it's time we paid him a visit. I want you to meet his date—"

The lilac is wrong, Wayne suddenly realized.

"—Karen Egenes, the woman he wants to hire to run his franchise operation. I want you to tell me what you think."

I saw her in a different shade . . . something paler.

Cindy was frowning. "Bruce? Hello, *Bruce?*"

Wayne glanced down at his date. "Sorry. I was just thinking."

"While I was talking? Whatever happened to 'just listening'?"

"I was."

"You weren't. What did I say?"

"That you wanted me to meet Karen Egenes, the marketing wunderkind."

Cindy touched a finger to her tongue and marked the air with a "1." "Okay—you *were* listening. Now I don't want to prejudice you, but Karen couldn't be more *wrong* for the job. She's too glib, too independent, too ambitious—"

"Sounds as if she's too much like someone else on the payroll."

Cindy pinched Wayne's arm. "I knew you were going to say that, but we're *not* alike. *I'm* devoted to my father and the company. All *she's* after is a seven-figure salary."

"If she can deliver the profits, she deserves it. I read about the job she did for the Dances With Videos stores. Sounds like she knows the retail business."

"But this is cookies, Bruce, not videocassettes and laser disks. If she's a stiff and Cookies of Merritt goes under, Dad'll lose a chocolate mint and I'll have to go

A Knight at the Opera

to work for a living—maybe even at the Wayne Foundation."

"You wouldn't want to. I hear the boss is tough."

"Really? *I* hear tell the guy's a pussycat."

They started toward the stairs, Wayne trying—and failing—to put the mysterious woman from his mind.

III

Before taking her seat in the last row of the orchestra, under the balcony, the woman in lilac walked down the aisle to look up at the frescoes on the domed ceiling, vividly painted scenes from the great operas: *Madama Butterfly*, *Die Fledermaus*, *Aïda*, and of course *The Magic Flute*. She smiled as she picked out Papageno among the characters, with his costume of feathers and flute shaped like a cat leaping at prey. The bird catcher's eyes and smile were full of love and optimism.

How beautiful *The Magic Flute* had sounded when she first heard it by accident years before, when she was working in the streets, entertaining others without ever being entertained herself. It was raining, and she had popped under the marquee to get dry; something in the overture had reached out to her. The melodies, the delicate violins and proud horns, the gaiety it created on a dreary night in an even drearier life. And then there were the stirring, beautiful voices, especially during the Queen of the Night's soaring aria.

Dressed as she was that night, with unpleasant stares drifting her way from managers and assistant managers and deputy assistant managers and other self-important little fools, she had left the street and gone to the alley beside the opera house. There, she sat on the concrete, and listened. During an intermission, a stagehand who came out for air kindly gave her a blanket to sit on.

Maestro LaDolce had been the conductor that night, and the very next day she'd written to him to tell him how much the performance had moved her. He took the time to write back and invited her to a series of lectures he was giving at the Conservatory of Classical Music. She went, and there she met his daughter, Megan; later the two young women enjoyed many hours talking about music and Mozart.

It was so long ago, yet so wonderfully vivid. She looked down at the ticket stub in her hand. She hoped tonight would be memorable as well, now that she was finally going to see, not just hear, the opera.

Selina Kyle adjusted her over-the-shoulder bag and walked toward her seat; a smile broke through the sweet reverie. As a bonus, she got to mingle with some of the richest people in Gotham City—the criminally rich who would help to make her a richer criminal. She'd been watching them before, from beside the bust in the lobby, listening for names, cataloging the necklaces and brooches, diamond cuff links, and gold tie tacks.

Art and commerce, happily coexisting. What more, she wondered, could anyone possibly ask for?

IV

"So what do you think of Karen?"

Bruce Wayne followed Cindy Merritt into his private box. He leaned forward on the brass rail and

A Knight at the Opera

peered into the half-filled orchestra, looking for the woman he'd seen in the lobby.

"Good Lord, Bruce, don't jump! Karen wasn't *that* bad!"

He was only able to see up to row S, the overhanging balcony blocking the seven rows beyond. The woman wasn't there, nor was she in any of the boxes.

"Bruce? Bruce, is this 'just thinking'—the sequel?"

"No. I was looking for someone."

"Anyone I know?"

"I'm not even sure I know her," he said, settling into his seat.

Cindy frowned. "Another episode in the further adventures of *Bruce Wayne, Master of Evasion.* What about Karen? Can you give me a straight answer about her?"

Wayne steepled his index fingers under his nose. "Frankly I found her to be delightful."

"No—"

"She's articulate and sharp, with a good sense of humor."

"You mean those cracks about raising more dough for the business and having a chocolate chip on her shoulder? Bruce, those puns were terrible!"

"They'll work in ads."

"Puh-*lease,*" Cindy groaned. "We're charging two dollars for a quarter pound of baked dough. We've got to be classier than that!"

"Elitist. You're starting to sound like John."

Cindy's mouth twisted, but before she could respond, the door opened in the box to the left and John Taylor entered, followed by Michael Savran. Cindy smiled pleasantly while glaring daggers at Wayne.

Michael Savran took the seat nearest Wayne. The young conductor's longish black hair was parted in the middle, spilling over both sides of his face; his aquiline nose was raised slightly, his thin lips pursed.

Taylor waved at Wayne, and Savran reached across the partition to shake his hand.

"Good evening, Mr. Savran."

"Mr. Wayne," the conductor said, then smiled broadly. "Of course, after tonight that will be Maestro Savran."

"*After* tonight," Wayne agreed. "The baton is still Maestro LaDolce's."

Savran shut his eyes and nodded his head in acquiescence.

Savran would be taking over the musical directorship when seventy-year-old Clifford LaDolce retired after this evening's performance. The naming of Savran had been something of a surprise, the arts community having expected the position to go to LaDolce's daughter, Megan, who had substituted for her father on numerous occasions, to great acclaim. But John had campaigned for Savran, whose family had recently become generous patrons of the opera, and the board had followed his recommendation.

After Wayne had introduced Cindy, the door to the box on the right opened. The statuesque Megan LaDolce entered with her mother, Wendy; Savran sat back quickly as the women took their seats.

Wayne rose, positioning himself between Megan and Wendy and the adjoining box so they could look over without making eye contact with Savran.

Megan chatted with Wayne for several minutes, thanking him for the letter of recommendation he'd written in support of her candidacy, and telling him about her plans to teach a master class at the university and help her father write his memoirs.

A Knight at the Opera

"Maybe I'll do some writing myself," she said. "A rock opera about monster-truck rallies."

"I'll produce it." Wayne laughed.

During their talk, Wendy kept looking at her watch, humming along with snippets of melodies as the musicians tuned up in the orchestra pit. "It's eight," the white-haired woman announced. "Why is the orchestra still warming up?"

Megan glanced back at her. "Papa will be along soon."

"He should have been there by now."

"Give him time, Mother. This isn't an easy night for him."

"For any of us," Wendy said in a loud voice. "I wouldn't be surprised if he's still in his dressing room, crying. Not surprised at all. His own daughter—"

"Mother . . ."

"What they did to you—"

Shaking her head, Wendy turned toward the door, stared at it for a moment, then looked at her watch once again.

"Now it's *after* eight," she said. "Something's not right."

"Mrs. LaDolce," Wayne said, "would you like me to go and check on him?"

"Thank you, no. He won't see anyone but his wife, his daughter, or his assistant before a performance." She leaned toward the stage, then sat back again. "Megan, would you go?"

"Mother, just fifteen minutes ago he said he wanted to be alone."

"I know, but I'm worried. He's been upset all day." She glared toward Taylor's box, "All *week*, in fact."

Megan looked up at Wayne and shrugged. "I'll go," she said, "but knowing father, he's probably taking his time going to the podium, will be there before I get back, and I'll miss the overture."

Wrinkling her nose, Wendy said, "It's no *Don Giovanni*."

As her daughter rose Wendy handed her her ticket stub. "Take this. Otherwise the *traditores* may not let you back in."

Wayne told Megan he'd look after her mother, and then she was gone.

"Not a very happy Mrs. Maestro," Cindy said as Wayne sat back down.

"I wasn't happy about the snub either, but it was a political call. But the opera needs a regular source of revenue, and the Savrans are wealthy."

"So are you, but I'd *hate* to hear you on oboe."

Wayne grinned as Cindy excused herself to use the rest room. While she was gone he occupied himself by studying the rapidly filling opera house. There were many women in white and in black, a few in daring reds and blues, but no one in lilac. He had already decided that he must have seen the woman in something other than an evening gown, but where? On the racquetball court? At the stables?

Wayne checked his watch; it was seven after and now *he* was concerned. This *was* most unlike the maestro.

The door to Taylor's box opened suddenly, and Wayne listened as the head usher leaned close to the occupants.

"Mr. Taylor, there's a problem downstairs. Would you come quickly?"

"What is it?"

"Please, sir," she said, "just come."

Taylor left, followed by Savran. A moment later

A Knight at the Opera

Bruce Wayne hurried from his box and followed them downstairs.

V

The dressing-room door was open and the maestro lay motionless on the couch, his lifelong assistant, Alfonse, kneeling beside him.

Taylor stopped in the doorway; the color drained from his ruddy cheeks when he saw the conductor.

"Alfonse—what in heaven's name happened?"

"I don't know," Alfonse said, tears running down his face. "Maestro asked to be left alone, as always, but when I came down to get him, I found him on the floor."

Taylor ran his tongue over his lips as he studied the room.

From behind, the head usher said, "Dr. Trias is in the audience. I sent someone to bring him down."

Taylor nodded, and then his gray eyes settled on Alfonse. "Where is the baton?"

"I don't know. When I arrived, I saw neither it nor the canister."

"Dear Lord," said Michael Savran, shutting his eyes and rubbing his forehead.

"Ring the police," Taylor told the usher, then turned to Savran. "Get ready. You are going to conduct *The Magic Flute* tonight."

Savran's brow shot up. "What? You intend to go on after this?"

"We can't afford to cancel the performance."

"John, people would understand."

"Our creditors will not."

"But my *parents*," he said through his teeth. "They wanted to be here for my Gotham debut."

"*They* will understand. Please go and prepare. I'll make the announcement."

Listening from down the hall, Bruce Wayne turned and walked quickly toward the lobby. He knew something that these people didn't know, something that concerned him deeply: the baton wasn't the only thing that was gone.

Megan LaDolce was also missing.

VI

One usher approached another in the doorway between the lobby and the theater, a few feet from where Selina was sitting.

"Did you hear why we're delayed?"

"Let me guess. Taylor Scrooge decided to pass the plate like he did last year."

"No, this is better. Remember how he decided to let the guard go and save a couple hundred bucks? Well, someone hit Maestro LaDolce on the head, left him stone cold on the floor, and stole the baton."

Selina felt as though she'd been struck in the stomach; it was several seconds before she could breathe. "Is the maestro all right?"

"Don't know. He's still out."

"Did Taylor freak?"

"No, but I hear he was more upset about the baton than about LaDolce."

Their voices faded as the blood drummed in Selina's ears. *It's happening again and I can't allow it—I won't allow it.*

A Knight at the Opera

There was a time in her life when, just like a black
cat, she seemed to bring bad luck to those who had
shown her kindness. Her sister, who would have been
killed if it hadn't been for Batman; her devoted friend
Holly; so many others. *Too* many others. She had
thought that those times were past.

Apparently not.

She rose as though she were in a trance and headed
for the door. Maestro LaDolce's music had given her
hope and joy when she was friendless, had helped her
find peace when her life was in turmoil. Whoever had
dared to do this would pay.

Selina crossed the lobby and entered the ladies'
room; it was empty. She opened the window, went into
a stall, locked the door, hung her bag on the hook, and
slipped off her gown.

The gray leotard was underneath. She pushed the
gown into her shoulder bag and pulled out a cowl. She
slipped it on, then donned a pair of gloves, each finger
of which was tipped with a short, pin-sharp claw. She
flexed her hands, then took a cat-o'-nine-tails from the
bag and slid it into a loop that was attached to her
waist.

As Selina Kyle, she was never free of guilt and re-
grets, of mortal failings and deep emotional needs.
She probably never would be. But as Catwoman, she
was someone else, someone undaunted by rules or
conventions, by man or woman, by shame of the past
or fear of the future. There was only the present, and
Catwoman commanded *that* with the grace and power
of the creatures from which she took her name.

After listening to make sure that no one was coming, she grabbed the bag and hurried to the window,
went up and out into the dark alley in a quick, fluid
movement. Shutting the window, she left her belong-

ings behind the Dumpster then headed toward the street.

VII

Catwoman moved quickly, hunched over and leading with her eyes, ears, and nose. Her arms were out-stretched and her hands were open, claws at the ready. Her eyes were constantly moving, studying the street ahead, the dark brick walls on either side of the alley, the concrete alley, which was still wet from a late-afternoon hosing.

The opera house was in the theater district, and she knew that the night watchmen here usually went to Loree's Kitchen when they got off. Her plan was to go to the backdoor to see if she could spot the guard who'd worked here tonight, lure him outside, find out whom he might have seen coming or going, or if the baton even made it to the maestro's dressing room. Maybe he'd been paid to hand it over to someone, or to let someone in—

She stopped suddenly by the stage door and dropped to a knee. Her right hand darted down and she pinched a small rectangle of cardboard between two claws.

A ticket stub for a first-tier box. Someone who had been inside tonight had come out—probably through the stage door.

There were only two ways out of the alley: up the fire escape or into the street. It wasn't likely that who-ever had been holding this ticket had come out here and then gone back into the opera house, so they probably went to the street. And if that were the case, there might be a record of their departure.

VIII

"Harleigh, I've got a teed-off exec producer on the hot line, chewing my ear off, telling me *she's* getting calls from impatient viewers. Is there *anyone* in there who knows what's going on?"

Director Eric Berkowitz was sitting beside the controls of the mobile transmitter parked in front of the opera house. He had a telephone pressed to one ear and an earphone against the other, its mouthpiece relaying his words to host Harleigh Kidd.

"Eric," she said, "we're not getting anything up here in the booth, other than that there's been a delay."

"Which we'd never have figured out for ourselves," Eric muttered. He turned to the tape operator sitting next to him. "Aaron, go inside and see what you can find out."

After Aaron had left, Berkowitz turned his attention back to the screen. Harleigh's interview with arriving local celebrities had a minute left to run; after that, he told the executive producer he'd cut to a promo for other PBS offerings.

The director didn't hear the newcomer enter through the cab and creep back. The first he knew of her presence was when she unhooked the earphone and dropped it into his lap.

"Did you tape Thomas Avenue tonight?" Catwoman demanded.

Berkowitz shot a look to his left. The intruder's gray

mask was inches from his face, and his gaze shifted quickly from the wearer's icy blue eyes to the pert ears atop the cowl.

He laughed. "What did you do, get that from wardrobe? Is that what's going on, some kind of wildcat strike?"

"The street. Did you shoot it?"

"We shot everything. Hey, why don't you get back inside. We've got viewers, you know."

Catwoman looked at the wall of equipment, saw a tape machine beneath one of the monitors. She extended a slender finger, touched rewind. The tape began to scan backward.

"Hey! You can't do that! That stuff is going out over the airwaves!"

Berkowitz reached for the machine but froze as a needlelike claw poked the soft underside of his chin.

"Don't!" Catwoman hissed.

There was a voice yelling on the phone, but she took it from the director and hung it up. She watched as the tape showed the marquee, the gawkers, the street—and a black van leaving the alley.

The phone rang. Berkowitz rolled his eyes toward it but said nothing. Blood dribbled from the small wound under his chin.

Catwoman hit pause and noted the digital numbers in the corner of the screen. The van had pulled out at 8:11 then headed north on Thomas. She watched as it turned east on Robinson Avenue and disappeared into the darkness.

The phone continued to ring. Berkowitz glanced at it again.

"What do I do?" he asked. "If I don't pick up—"

The pinprick pain in his throat vanished suddenly,

and the director looked back. The rear door of the truck was open and he was alone.

The cold air washed over him. He didn't feel it. Slowly he picked up the phone and the voice on the other end exploded.

"Berkowitz! What kind of games are you playing over there? Why didn't you *answer*?"

"Would you believe," he said numbly, "that a cat got my tongue?"

IX

After leaving the hallway, Bruce Wayne hurried to his Rolls, which was underground in the private opera-house parking lot. He unlocked the door and, behind the big automobile's darkened windows, removed a suitcase from a compartment beneath the seat. He pulled off his tuxedo jacket, undid his bow tie.

The crime and the identity of the woman gnawed at him as he opened the suitcase and removed the costume. Why couldn't he shake the idea that they were related? He thought about the theft . . . about Megan's disappearance . . . about the woman and her lilac gown.

Her posture! He suddenly realized *that* was what was familiar, not her face. She walked with her shoulders well back, her head slightly forward, her arms very loose, slinking in her skintight gown—

Slinking . . . like a cat.

Bruce Wayne donned his costume quickly. After making sure the parking area was empty, he slipped from the car and ran up the ramp that would bring him to the front of the opera house—and, he suspected, a familiar adversary.

X

A light snow began to fall as the Catwoman crossed the street, leaped to the fire escape of the Finger Musical Library, and raced to the roof. She moved quickly, feeling that the van would be traveling very slowly and carefully so as not to be stopped for traffic violations. If she hurried, she might catch a glimpse of it.

The museum district was one of the oldest of the city, dominated by three- and four-story brownstones where artists, musicians, and writers had lived before the area became gentrified over the past ten years. Once atop the library, she crossed the low, tarred rooftops heading north and stopped on one overlooking Robinson Avenue.

The snow on the street made it easier to pick out the cars. Crouching on the sandstone parapet at the edge of the roof, Catwoman squinted into the night, her eyes moving slowly from the sprawling West Park to the highway in the north to the wharf district in the east, with its freighters, cavernous warehouses, and heliport.

The wharf district.

She studied it carefully. Could the thief be planning to get the baton out of the city that night, by boat or helicopter? Things would get *awfully* hot in the city, especially when the police and Batman became involved. Only a fool would stick around for long.

A Knight at the Opera

The highway would already be a nest of state troopers. The wharf made sense.

She looked along Robinson, which ran straight to the river, a mile from where she was. There were trucks, cabs, private cars, and she followed them as they moved east. She happened to notice an impatient motorcyclist, then a cab, pull left, around a slow-moving vehicle.

A van.

She couldn't tell if it was black, but the distance and timing were right. She watched as it pulled onto a side street—then lost it behind the tall Harbor Authority Building.

Rising, the Catwoman thought back over all the years she'd prowled these streets. She pictured the buildings, their facades, the little-known passages between or over them, places she'd discovered when trying to elude the police . . . or Batman. After taking a quick look down, she flung herself over the edge, snapping her whip as she dropped.

Her timing was perfect. The long leather lash caught the arm of a streetlight and the metal bent without breaking; Catwoman knew not to hang on it for more than the instant it took to slow her fall. Kicking up and over, she relaxed her arms to let the whip unwrap, pulling it to her as she completed her somersault. Landing on the sidewalk on all fours, she darted past a young couple out enjoying the snowy night.

"Alice, that was a superhero!" the man shouted. "Three years in Gotham City and I *finally* saw one!"

Catwoman was gone before the woman could turn to look at her. She used her whip and a protruding gargoyle to swing up and over a wrought-iron fence beside the small Museum of Western Art; landing on

the other side, she cut through the block and emerged
in a cemetery filled with the graves of artists and
writers. She made her way through it by leapfrogging
over the tombstones.

When she emerged on the other side, Catwoman
ran around the Harbor Authority Building toward the
river just two blocks away.

XI

Under the otherwise deserted marquee, police officer
Jack Gish was interviewing a distraught man in front
of the public-TV mobile transmitter. The man occasionally dabbed a bloody handkerchief to the underside of his chin.

"I don't know *who* she was, officer," Eric Berkowitz
said around gum that he was chewing rapidly. "All I
know is she had on a gray-blue bodysuit of some kind,
claws, and a tail, and she took off after looking at a
tape."

"Was she a cast member?"

"I don't know."

"You say she took off? Was she in a car?"

"I don't think so."

"Where did she go?"

"I don't know."

"Mr. Berkowitz, exactly what *do* you know?"

"That she just—*vanished.* One second she was
there, pressing a claw to my throat, and the next
second she was gone."

A deep voice said from behind the men, "Did anything on the tape appear to interest her?"

Both men spun and glanced at the imposing gray-

and-blue-costumed figure. The scalloped fringe of his cape flapped gently behind his dark boots; the gold and black of the famed bat symbol peeked out over powerful arms, which were folded against his chest.

Berkowitz's eyes went wide.

"Good evening, Batman," Officer Gish said, tipping his hat. He seemed to stand a little taller.

"The tape," the Batman repeated. "Did anything interest her?"

Berkowitz swallowed his gum. "She—she seemed hot and bothered about a black van. I don't know why."

"You're certain you have no idea where she went? Did you see a shadow, hear brakes screech, did anyone shout from the street?"

Berkowitz shook his head.

"This van she saw. Where did it go?"

"It swung up on Robinson," Berkowitz said, turning and pointing, "heading east. I could show you the tape if—"

The director bit off his words as he turned back; the caped avenger was gone. The police officer was looking up, squinting into the snow.

"Like that, officer." Berkowitz said, following the policeman's gaze toward the skyline.

"What?"

"I was saying that the cat person vanished . . . like *that*!"

XII

The wharf followed the river for nearly a mile. Catwoman climbed atop a boxcar parked beside a warehouse; to her left, tugs and barges knocked quietly against the pilings. There was some activity at the freighters moored farther downriver, but not here—which was obviously why the van had come to this section of the river. *Here* was where someone could transfer stolen goods without being seen.

Unfortunately the van *was* nowhere to be seen, and she guessed that it had pulled into one of the three warehouses on this side of the wharf. Leaping off the railroad car, she ran from one warehouse to the other, listening.

There were sounds coming from the second; she went around to the garage-type door and saw fresh tire tracks in the snow. She paused by the door and bent close, listening to the muffled voices within.

". . . don't like the idea of sendin' her for a swim."

"Neither do I, Harvey, but what *choice* do we have? If we leave her behind, she'll pick us out of a mug book inside of ten minutes. And if we leave her here, old Whispery will turn tail and run."

"We can take her with us—"

"And do what? Keep her forever?"

"Let Whispery decide."

"Whispery will decide it's our problem. And *then* what? We can't even finger him . . . or her."

There was a short silence, after which the first speaker said, "Then I'm for bailin' out, Alex. I didn't sign on for murder."

"You're already in for kidnapping and stealing the baton. That's fifteen years. You might as well go all the way."

What scum, Catwoman thought. These were the thugs she was looking for, and hissing in anger, she took a step back and looked up. There was a spotlight ten feet overhead, and a window over twenty feet

A Knight at the Opera

above it—too high to get to. Opening the door could be disastrous: the men were probably carrying guns and had a hostage, which made things trickier still.

The only thing to do was to get them to come to her.

Catwoman leaned close to the door. "Pssst! You two!"

The men stopped moving.

"I know you're in there!" she said. "I'm a friend who's got some news for you."

After a long silence Alex asked, "What kind of news?"

"I happened to be driving by the opera and saw what you guys did in the alley. Don't worry—I'm cool. But remember that TV truck out front?"

"Yeah—"

"Well, they saw you too."

She heard Harvey swear; Alex told him to shut up.

"How do you know?" Alex asked.

"Because one of the men came running out with a video camera as you drove away. He caught you turning up Robinson."

"I don't believe you."

"Suit yourself—in stripes. I was only trying to help."

"And even if they did see us," Alex said, "what of it? None of them will have a clue about where we are—unless somebody tells them."

"It won't be me," Catwoman assured him. "I've been on the wrong side of the law myself. That's why I thought you might need help. A lift somewhere—use of the car phone. Anything."

Harvey shouted, "Anyway, how could they know what we were up to? We could've been loading a prop dummy."

"What about the baton?" Catwoman asked.

A short silence. Then Alex said, "How do you know about that? You couldn't have seen it. It was in a sack."

Catwoman heard footsteps, Alex's voice getting louder, coming nearer. She slipped her whip from its loop.

"I listen to the radio," she said. "It's all over the airwaves. The police'll put two and two together—or the Batman will."

Alex stopped moving a yard or two from the door. Catwoman edged back, out of the line of fire. Either he was coming out to negotiate or to shoot. In any case he'd have to open the door and she'd be ready.

"Hold on," Alex said. "I want to think about this for a second."

"No problem," Catwoman said, and snapped her whip straight up.

XIII

Pulleys groaned as the door rolled up. There were three flashes—left, center, right—and then the gun was silent.

No light spilled from within; Alex had killed it. But crouched on the spotlight just above the door, Catwoman had inferred his position from the direction of the gunfire. Her whip still coiled around the light, she gripped the handle tightly and swung down, legs stiff, toes arched toward her head so her heels were extended.

She caught Alex against the chest with her left foot; he fired as he stumbled backward, the bullet hitting the top of the door and ricocheting into the night.

A Knight at the Opera

Catwoman landed on her right foot and crouched in front of Alex, springing against him with her shoulder. He hit a stack of crates and she pinned him there, squeezing his throat with her right hand and grabbing his gun hand with her left. The weapon spat its remaining bullets off to the side, against the van.

"Alex!" Harvey yelled, and the second thug began edging forward in the dark.

Catwoman released Alex's throat and wrist, grabbed his jacket with both hands, and pulled him around, slamming him against the side of the van. Spinning once, her left leg extended, she brought the bottom of her foot against the side of his head. He slid to the floor without so much as a moan.

Crouching again, she listened and then threw herself toward the shuffling footsteps.

"Al—"

Harvey bit off the shout as Catwoman charged, both hands extended in the direction of his voice. The claws of her right hand caught his chest and tore through his coat and shirt to his flesh.

"Gawwwwd!"

Catwoman dropped to her back as he screamed, then watched him fire two bullets where she'd been standing. She grabbed his wrist with both hands and wrenched down; bone snapped, he dropped the gun, and his knees buckled. As he fell toward her she put her feet against his waist, bent her legs at the knees, and flung him forward.

She scrambled to her feet and looked back. In a dark corner she could barely make out the figure of someone—a woman, it looked like—sitting bound and gagged in a chair. The captive would have to wait a few minutes more.

Harvey was down and Catwoman was on him in an

instant, pressing a knee to his chest and hooking two clawed fingers under his chin. With her other hand she grabbed a fistful of hair and tugged. He shrieked in pain.

"Are you going to talk to me, Harvey?"

"Yes, yes!" he screamed. "I didn't want this, it all just got outta hand! It was Alex!"

"Slow down—"

"Look, I needed the cash, I admit it. The union, my ex-wife, Joe O and his boys. I don't know why I'm always in over my head—"

Catwoman rose, grabbed the front of Harvey's jacket, picked him up, and heaved him hard against a crate. His lungs emptied in a hot burst, and she did it again.

Now he was quiet.

She let him drop, then knelt on him again with one knee, her claws against his throat. "Would it be okay if we started at the top?"

He nodded weakly.

"Good. What's all this about?"

Before he could answer, Alex stirred to their left. Catwoman's free leg shot out and hammered him back to sleep, then her gaze returned to Harvey. Even in the pale glow of the spotlight, she could see the whites of his terrified eyes.

"I'm waiting," she said. "Start by telling me who you two are."

He swallowed hard. "I'm Harvey Helper. I work on the docks—me and my supervisor there, Alex Burgess."

"Who hired you? Who's Whispery?"

"I don't know—"

Catwoman pushed her claws harder against his throat. "Make a quick and educated guess."

A Knight at the Opera

"*I honest-to-Gawd don't know!* They had a whispery voice, coulda been a man or woman."

"Okay. Go on."

"This whispery person just called one day, outta the blue. Said they knew we do odd jobs after hours—"

"Odd jobs?"

"Like moving furniture or breaking kneecaps and collecting overdue bills. This voice told us to go to the stage door at the opera. When we got there, Whispery opened it a crack—told us how to get to the dressing room, then left. After we clocked the conductor, *she* walked in." He rolled his eyes toward the captive. "We didn't expect that—I swear it. I didn't want to hurt her."

"But she saw you, so you had to take her."

He nodded.

"Will Whispery be coming here?"

"I don't know. We were just supposed to park the van in here and put the key to the warehouse in the boxcar. We were gonna get our money in a couple of days."

"Where is the key?"

He pointed to his pocket. She nodded and he reached in, handed it over.

"No special signals?" Catwoman asked.

"Nothin'. When we finished here, we were just supposed to turn off the light and go."

Catwoman rose and drove the steel-reinforced toe of her boot into the man's right temple.

"You're gone," she said, and hurried over to the captive.

XIV

As she neared and got a closer look at the prisoner, the Catwoman stopped abruptly.

"Megan?" she gasped. "Megan LaDolce?"

The captive grunted and wrestled with her bonds as Catwoman hurried over. But before she could free her, a deep, familiar voice came from behind.

"Don't move."

The Catwoman straightened slowly, then faced the imposing figure standing in the doorway, silhouetted in the spotlight.

"Batman! How did you know I was here?"

"Not many people go crosstown on the rooftops. I followed your footprints in the snow." He strode forward, bending over each man in turn. "When did you take an interest in musical artifacts?"

"You've got it wrong," she said. "I didn't steal the baton."

Catwoman noticed the batarang he held at his side, ready to snare her if she tried to run. She'd tried that before: wrist, ankle, waist, his aim was uncanny.

"I know you didn't steal it. But were you helping these two find it? Is that why you were at the opera house tonight?"

That one caught Catwoman off guard: sometimes she wondered if Batman was psychic. But indignation quickly supplanted her surprise.

"I was there to hear the music, Batman, and you know what you can do with your presumptions."

"I'm sorry," he said. "But then, wouldn't a music lover find the baton that much more desirable?"

While he was speaking Catwoman had slipped a claw under the gag, where it crossed the prisoner's cheek. She slit it with a tug, and the words literally exploded from Megan's mouth.

"Batman, this woman *helped* me! If it weren't for her, I'd be dead!"

Batman stopped, intimidating and impenetrable in the dark. Catwoman slid behind Megan and began undoing the ropes.

"It's all so horrible," Megan said. "Were either of you just at the opera? Is Papa all right?"

"I don't know," Batman said. "Before I do anything else, I'll bring you to him." He fixed his gaze on Catwoman. "The baton?"

"In the van."

Batman went over and checked, then used the rope that had bound Megan to tie the hands of the thieves. After loading them into the van, he walked over to the women.

"Thank you," he said to the Catwoman, then indicated the men in the van. "Did they give you any information?"

"Nothing. Whoever hired them didn't tell them much."

Rubbing her rope-burned wrists, Megan walked up to Catwoman. "Your voice sounds familiar. Don't I know you from somewhere?"

Catwoman nodded.

"I won't ask where, but thanks for everything you did."

Batman said to his nemesis, "Can I give you a ride back?"

"I think I'll stick to the rooftops. But why don't you meet me on the roof of the opera house in an hour. I have some thoughts on who might be behind this."

He nodded, then walked to the warehouse door and

reached up. "Don't forget this," he said, flipping Catwoman her whip.

She saluted him with it, then watched as Batman helped Megan into the van and drove off. When they were gone, she dashed into the night to wait. . . .

XV

The powerboat came humming up the river in the dark. The driver throttled down, cut the engine several yards from the dock, and drifted in. When the rub rail butted against the wharf, the occupant hopped out with a guy rope, secured the boat, and waited.

Lying atop the boxcar, Catwoman smiled. She knew that someone would come as soon as the media reported that the theft had been successful. Something like the baton was just too valuable to leave lying around.

She studied the figure as he stood on the pier, staring first at the warehouse, then at the boxcar. He strolled a few paces left, then right, then stood still again—presumably to make sure his arrival hadn't attracted any attention.

Convinced that no one was there, the figure headed toward the boxcar—briskly, confidently, expectantly.

Catwoman waited, her hand draped slightly over the side; she watched as he reached the car, slid the door open a crack, reached in—

The costumed feline made her move, the man screaming as the door closed on his hand. He was unaware of the Catwoman as she somersaulted off the boxcar and landed behind him. Swearing, he pushed

A Knight at the Opera

the panel back, liberated his hand, turned, and walked into the cat burglar.

"The key man," she snarled with contempt, stiff-arming him with a palm to the chin. He staggered against the railroad car and she pinned him there with her whip, pushing the handle and pressing it up against his throat.

The man gagged under the pressure of the whip; blood trickled from the sides of his mouth.

"You ruined my night out," Catwoman said, "and if you don't tell me what you know, I'm going to take it out of your hide."

He reached up to push her back, but she pressed harder, causing him to choke.

"*Don't* tick me off, mister!"

"Can't ... *breathe*," he wheezed.

"You want to breathe?"

"Yesss—"

Catwoman stepped back and he staggered forward, dropping to his knees. She stepped behind him and slipped the whip handle under his chin.

"How's that? You like breathing?"

He nodded.

"Well, if you want to keep doing it, tell me who you are."

He did.

"I've heard of you. Where do I know the name from?"

He told her who he was. Things became clearer.

"Are you the one who hired those two bozos, Alex and Harvey?"

He said he wasn't—someone else did.

"Someone at the opera house?"

He hesitated. She pulled up on the whip handle and got his attention.

"Who hired them and why?"

He spilled his guts.

When he was finished, Catwoman stepped back and looked down at the pathetic figure.

"I'm going to let you go," she said. "Call it a hunch, but I think the fallout from all this is going to end your embarrassingly short criminal career and get you a nice vacation where all the crooked hoteliers and Wall Street shysters go."

With that, Catwoman ran west toward the Harbor Authority Building and the museum district beyond.

XVI

The wind blew in cold, gentle gusts as the Batman crouched in the open turret atop the opera house. A weather-worn gold statue of Gotham City's noted nineteenth-century conductor Roberto Kanini towered over him, baton raised, ready to lead the beat of the city.

Maestro LaDolce had come to before his daughter returned, and had refused to go to the hospital until she was found. Batman had brought her to the dressing room, given the maestro the baton, handed the two goons over to the police, then left to wait for Catwoman—assuming she planned to show.

He looked out at the city, thinking as he often did about the myriad secrets beneath the rooftops, the countless mysteries behind the lights. Secrets like the Catwoman and her love for opera. He regretted his assumption that because of who she was and what she was, she wouldn't appreciate Mozart. He felt ashamed but blameless.

A Knight at the Opera

As he peered through the snow, scanning the roof-tops, he felt vindicated in trusting Catwoman's word as a vague, sleek shape appeared on the horizon. Catwoman had said an hour, and true to her promise, she was coming. He was intrigued by what else she might possibly know about the case; that she would share it with him was more interesting still. So many of his enemies were unpredictable, but greed and megalomania were still the motivating factors. Catwoman was more complex than that. Like the animals from which she took her name, she had demons and a soul he could barely begin to fathom.

From across the alley, Catwoman's whip caught the fire escape at the second floor, and she swung over. When she reached the top, she lashed one of the iron bars that surrounded the turret and scurried up the dome. She was breathing heavily when she reached Batman's side, her breath forming little clouds. He gave her a moment to collect herself.

She gripped the pointed tops of two of the bars and twisted her fists around them.

Batman moved in closer. "I'm sorry if I insulted you back at the warehouse."

"You couldn't have known why I was there, or how much respect I have for Maestro LaDolce."

"No, but it's good to be reminded once in a while how unreliable stereotypes are."

Catwoman relaxed slightly. "You were in the theater tonight—as your other self, I mean?"

He nodded.

"And you recognized me. What did you think of me as *my* normal self?"

"I'd have watched you even if you weren't the only woman not wearing black or white."

Catwoman turned away, her hands twisting the metal again.

Batman took a step closer. "Things don't have to be the way they are. Would you like to talk?"

"Not about me," she said. "I *like* my life."

"Do you?"

"Considering what I started out as—yes." She looked back at Batman. "The truth is, it's the rest of society that frustrates me, especially the white-collar thugs who prey on the rest of us. People like Arthur Savran. Name mean anything?"

"Of course. Michael Savran's father—owner of art and autograph galleries worldwide."

"And would-be fence for the Russian baton."

Batman started visibly. "How do you know that?"

"Sorry, but I lied back there—I had a score to settle. Those two clowns told me someone was coming for the baton, so I waited around and had a little chat with him. He told me who his partner was and who let the men into the opera house. Maybe you'll recognize the name."

Catwoman told Batman, and gave him the details of the deal.

When she was finished, he said, "How can you be sure he was telling the truth?"

"The only man who doesn't lie is a dead one—but Arthur was pretty close to that when I asked him. He didn't have the guts to lie."

"Wait here for me," Batman shouted, then hopped the fence, jumped from the dome to the fire escape, and disappeared into the darkness.

A Knight at the Opera

XVII

Batman entered the opera house through the fire escape so as not to cause a commotion—yet. Standing inside, in the shadowy recess of one of the emergency exits, he listened as Pamina and Prince Tamino pledged their love at the end of Act I. Then he waited as the doors to the boxes began to open.

The glitterati of Gotham City stepped into the hallway, startled and falling silent when they became aware of the Batman, not sure whether to acknowledge him or turn away. Most gave him nervous smiles or small nods as they passed.

Then the occupants of boxes four and five stepped out.

"I could *murder* Bruce," Cindy Merritt huffed to John Taylor. "If I'd wanted to see this thing alone, I could've rented the Bergman videotape. From Dances With Videos, just to make the evening a total disas—"

She bit off the sentence and stared. "Is that Batman?"

John Taylor turned from Cindy to the niche where she was looking.

"Good evening, Mr. Taylor," Batman said, stepping into the light.

All sound and movement in the hallway stopped, every eye on the costumed figure.

Taylor coughed into his fist. "I hear you helped us find the baton. Congratulations and our deepest thanks."

"I'd like to have a word with you."

"Would you? Is there new information about the crime?"

Batman nodded once.

"I see. Uh—where would you like to talk?"

Batman pushed open the door and stepped back.

"Ah, the dark city—your office."

The chairman pulled on the hem of his tuxedo jacket and walked stiffly to the door. Once he was on the landing, he turned and faced the Caped Crusader.

"Now, what is this all about?"

"We have a confession from Arthur Savran."

"A confession? What did he do?"

"Struck an unfortunate deal with you, it seems. He agreed to serve as the middleman in the sale of the stolen baton to a foreign collector. The two-million-dollar insurance would have gone to the Russians, but the Savrans would have taken in two or three times that from the collector, endowing the opera with the bulk of it and keeping the rest."

Taylor chuckled. "A plot worthy of Puccini."

"In exchange for the money," Batman went on, "you agreed to name Michael Savran the new conductor over Megan LaDolce. He's a mediocre talent, but you were willing to make that compromise. Anything to survive."

"That's absurd. And so are you, for that matter—another pop hero with a bad tailor."

Batman said, "How are you spelling that, John?"

Taylor glared at him.

"The odd thing is, Mr. Taylor, I can't fault your goals, only your methods. Why did you resort to crime?"

"Crime? What crime? Assuming what you've said is true, who was hurt? The public didn't care about the baton, and all the Russians are concerned with these days are good, dependable wheat fields. The insurance money would have been welcomed there. I repeat, Batman: Where is the crime? What was destroyed?"

A Knight at the Opera

Batman took a step closer. He looked down into Taylor's angry eyes. "Several careers, Mr. Taylor, including your own and Michael Savran's. He'll have to resign—"

"No! I did nothing *morally* wrong."

"The courts may not agree."

"The *courts*?" Taylor dropped all pretense. "You expect me to be judged fairly by the same people who have shunned art in Gotham City for over a century?" He backed toward the fire escape and started down. "Give me a jury of my *peers*. They'll not only acquit me, they'll *thank* me."

"Come back up, Mr. Taylor."

"I can't do that, any more than I could allow the opera to wither during my stewardship."

"No one was blaming you before tonight."

"And after tonight? I won't go to prison! *I had to do it!*" He turned and started running. "It was all for art."

Batman reached for his batarang, but never got to throw it. He watched as Taylor was jerked up and back, exhaling loudly. He swung to and fro several feet above the ground, held by a purple lash around his waist. The top half of the makeshift lasso was looped around a gargoyle—the grinning face of a lion.

Catwoman looked down from her stone perch.

"You let Maestro LaDolce take a crack on the head, Mr. Taylor. For that alone, I ought to come down and use you as a punching bag." She snickered. "Now who looks absurd, you pompous little bug?"

Batman came down the fire escape, and with a tug on the whip, Catwoman released her captive into his arms.

"Make sure they put that rat where the sonatas don't shine," she said as she went back up the dome and around the turret, out of view.

XVIII

After handing Taylor over to the police, Batman returned to the top of the opera house, hoping to find Catwoman still there. But she was gone, disappointing if not surprising him.

From below, through the dome, he heard a thunderous welcome as Maestro LaDolce was brought to the stage. He felt a sense of satisfaction, as always, but as he looked across the city he also experienced an emptiness. He felt he'd come close to connecting with Catwoman, and then lost her.

Perhaps there'll be other times, he thought hopefully. She does have eight other lives I can try to reach.

As he turned to go his eye caught a message that had been scratched in the snow of the dome. Hooking his batarang to an iron bar, he lowered himself down and read it:

BATMAN—
I'VE GONE BACK TO HEAR THE REST OF THE OPERA. AND
WHILE BATONS ARE NOT MY SPEED, I DID SEE AN EMERALD
NECKLACE THAT CAUGHT MY FANCY. WILL I GET IT?

He shook his head. So they would meet again, and sooner than he'd expected. But he wouldn't go searching for the woman in lilac. He would let her have the opera for herself, and pursue the Catwoman later.

Lowering himself from the dome, he was quickly lost in the night and the music and his thoughts. . . .

Catwomen

GREG COX

Catwoman strolled through the front door of Wayne Manor at exactly 7:00 P.M. . . . and at 7:07, and 7:12, and 7:15, and 7:24. . . .

In all, Bruce Wayne noted, nine women wearing the same black, skintight, and very notorious cat costume, complete with pointed ears and sinuous black tail, had arrived at his mansion—along with numerous pirates, cavemen, witches, vampires, Roman emperors, gorillas, pharaohs, cowboys, gangsters, and even one or two superheroes.

His Valentine's Day Charity Ball and Banquet was off to a grand start; at two hundred dollars per ticket, the event would provide a much-needed windfall for the Gotham Orphanage. All that was very good and important, Wayne acknowledged to himself, but he had other plans in mind as well. Another part of his soul, deeper and darker but never far away, watched each Catwoman with the eyes of a hunter.

Nine possibilities so far, he thought. This is going to be trickier than I thought.

"Congratulations," Vicki Vale said from beside him. She took his arm and leaned her head against his shoulder. "It looks like you've got a hit on your hands."

"Not me," Bruce said. "The orphans." One of the Catwomen has to be the genuine article, he thought. But I'm ready. She's not going to escape this time.

They both stood in the grand entry hall of Wayne Manor, where Bruce, as host of the masquerade, had been dutifully greeting each new arrival. They'd already met over a hundred partygoers; another hundred were expected . . . fashionably late, of course.

Vicki was dressed in a flowery, almost Elizabethan-style gown, with lots of ruffles and beads and a billowing skirt that fell in wide drapes toward the white marble floor. Her reddish-blond hair, which usually fell about her shoulders, was perched high on her head and adorned with strings of pearls. The gown was cut low in the front, revealing the spectacular heart-shaped ruby pendant that hung neatly between her breasts.

Bruce's own costume complemented Vicki's: it consisted of a silvery tunic with lacy ruffled sleeves and collar as well as a pair of tight blue leggings. Romeo to her Juliet. An appropriate disguise for Bruce Wayne, he observed. What was Romeo but a wealthy playboy?

A man dressed as Cyrano de Bergerac—his disguise consisting of an oversized rubber nose, lavender doublet, feathered hat, black velvet cloak, and shiny aluminum épée—swaggered in through the open front door. Bruce gave Cyrano a polite nod and murmured greeting. Cyrano gave them both a flamboyant bow, kissed Vicki's hand, then proceeded into the main ballroom, where tables of hors d'oeuvres stood waiting.

Vicki laughed quietly. "That rubber nose tickled," she whispered. "I wonder if he realizes that."

Bruce managed a suitable chuckle, but inside he chafed at the restrictions of this costume. Cyrano and small talk didn't matter, not while Catwoman was loose among his guests.

The entire first floor of Wayne Manor had been decorated for the charity ball. Giant red-and-pink-paper cutouts of hearts—made by the orphans—decorated the walls. Overhead, garlands of heart-shaped paper lanterns crisscrossed from wall to wall. Each lantern hid a tiny electric candle, which flickered warmly and cast a pleasant pink glow across the normally gloomy entryway. The lanterns' radiance reflected off walls of dark, polished wood, but couldn't quite illuminate the vaulted ceiling or disperse the shadows lurking high above. Grim suits of armor, polished to a steely sheen, guarded the wide entryways to the main ballroom, the salon, the library with its huge open bar, and the other rooms open to partygoers.

The guests certainly seemed to be enjoying themselves. The party was scarcely half an hour old and already raucous laughter and the tinkle of ice in fine crystal glasses rose from the main ballroom. Wayne tensed at the sudden sound of gunfire . . . then, realizing it was just champagne corks popping, forced himself to relax.

A man dressed in the forest-green hose and tunic of one of Robin Hood's Merry Men ducked out of the library and hurried over to Bruce and Vicki. Beneath the man's brown mask, Bruce recognized Detective

Crouper, one of Commissioner Gordon's men. The walkie-talkie in Crouper's hand chattered constantly.

"The mayor's over the river now," Crouper said. "He'll be here in a minute."

"Shall we greet him at the door?" Bruce asked Vicki. He could hear the distant thrum of an approaching helicopter.

"Just a sec," she said. She hurried over to the coatrack and pulled her camera from the top shelf. "Don't forget, I'm here on business. Let me get a couple of shots with you and the mayor, okay?"

"Sure." *Catwoman is waiting, though.*

Vicki quickly checked the camera's film and switched on its flash attachment. The doorman stepped aside for them, but by then the helicopter had already set down on the helipad a hundred feet away from Wayne Manor. Ignoring the cold, Vicki stepped out and began snapping quick shots as the mayor (dressed as Santa Claus, including an overstuffed belly) jogged out from under the still-spinning rotors. He looked rather comical, Bruce thought. Two tall, burly men wearing dark suits and ties followed the mayor. Clearly they were bodyguards, dressed as, well, bodyguards.

Bruce hoped they wouldn't be necessary, but with a full litter of Catwomen at the party, anything was possible.

Out of the corner of his eye, through the open front door, he observed the latest Catwoman crossing from the main ballroom to the library. As with her sisters, her lustrous black disguise clung like spray paint to a trim, athletic body that was striking enough to turn the head of every man, and most of the women, in her vicinity. Feral blue eyes, outlined in black, gazed coolly from behind her cat's-head mask. She moved with a careful, sultry confidence that practically radiated allure—and danger.

If this particular Catwoman was a fake, Bruce thought, she was a good one . . . just as the other eight had been. So far, with nothing more to go on than a brief handshake with each Catwoman as she arrived, every one of them seemed as seductive and menacing as the real Selina Kyle.

"Something wrong?" Vicki asked him. "You look worried."

"Oh, nothing serious." *Could Catwoman be after the mayor?*

Mayor Santa Claus reached the front door and shook Bruce's hand warmly, smiling and posing as Vicki snapped half a dozen shots. Then, patting Bruce's shoulder, he said, "You're doing a fine job here, Wayne, a fine job. Nice to have people like you helping out, yes indeed, you're a credit to the community. Which way to the bar, Wayne?" Then, calling a welcome to an old crony he glimpsed in the library, he brushed past them and headed into the thick of the party. Bruce could hear the mayor's booming voice long after he vanished from sight.

More guests strolled up the walk; valets, Bruce knew, were parking the limousines on the lawn to the east of the house. He and Vicki retreated inside, to the warmth of the entry hall, and greeted the latecomers one by one as they entered: a pair of ghosts, two Charlie Chaplins, one Henry VIII, and an overweight man dressed as an astronaut, who turned out to be City Councilman Graves. *Another potential target?* Bruce wondered.

"Come on," Vicki whispered. "You're getting moody on me again. What's bothering you?"

"I was just wondering whether Alfred can handle a sit-down dinner for this many people."

"Alfred could organize D day, and probably did," Vicki replied.

Bruce's gaze returned to the ruby pendant around her neck. No, he decided. Catwoman would not bother with mere politicians when a prize like the pendant is available. He knew her that well.

Two clowns and a belly dancer paid their respects to Bruce and Vicki before joining the rest of the party.

"It's the pendant, isn't it?" Vicki said suddenly. "I see the way you keep glancing at it." She fingered the large ruby nervously. "Are you sure it's safe me wearing it tonight? I mean, it belonged to your mother, not to mention it's priceless as both a jewel and an antique!"

"Don't worry," he said. "Commissioner Gordon is here, and he's provided plenty of security."

She snorted. "Robin Hood and his Merry Men. They're so conspicuous, it's pathetic." The crowd in the ballroom parted for an instant, revealing one green-garbed flatfoot slouching against a granite column and trying, unsuccessfully, to look inconspicuous.

"There are other, less conspicuous guards," Bruce said. "Besides, I like seeing you in the pendant. No one's worn it since my parents died. This is the first time it's been seen in public in decades—it generated lots of good publicity for the ball."

"Perhaps too much publicity," she said. "You jumped a bit when the first couple of Catwomen stalked in here."

"You have to admit it's a pretty stupid choice for a costume." Catwoman was no laughing matter, as he knew only too well.

"I don't know . . . maybe I'd look good in ears and a

tail." She smoothed her gown and did a couple of slinky cat steps. "What do you think?"

"It's not you." The last thing he needed tonight was one more Catwoman. Where was the real Selina now? What was she up to at this very moment? His Romeo costume felt tighter and more confining with each passing second.

Vicki laughed and gave him a quick kiss on the cheek. "Don't be so stiff. Want me to get you a drink?"

"Maybe later."

Nine cats. Nine lives. That must be all of them.

He glanced over his shoulder at the massive grandfather clock at the end of the hall. Its pendulum had a little red heart taped to it. "Nearly eight o'clock," he commented. "I think most everyone that matters is here already. We might as well join the party."

"The flood does seem to have gone down to a trickle," she answered. "If you don't mind ..." She took his arm and they headed for the main ballroom.

She's in here somewhere, he thought. I know it.

A gust of cold wind from the wide-open front door blew against their backs. Vicki glanced behind her. "Oh, hell!" she muttered under her breath.

Just coming into the entryway was another woman wearing a simple gold domino mask—and exactly the same gown as Vicki. Instead of a ruby pendant, however, she wore only a silver heart-shaped locket between her lightly powdered breasts.

"I don't believe it!" Vicki said, exasperated. "The costume shop swore to me that I had the only Juliet gown in Gotham!"

"Well, at least your jewelry is one of a kind tonight."

Vicki shrugged in resignation. "Just as long as she finds her own Romeo," she said. "C'mon, let's party."

"My pleasure."

They followed the sounds of laughter and live music
into the ballroom. Bruce scanned the crowd, his brow
furrowing.

Your move, Selina, he thought. Ready when you are.

Keeping an eye on nine identical Catwomen while simultaneously playing host to Gotham's movers and
shakers proved extremely frustrating to Bruce. The
spacious ballroom was packed with men and women
in brightly colored costumes, talking and laughing
over the music. A five-man jazz band performed on a
raised platform, bedecked with scarlet streamers, at
the northern end of the dance floor. In the center of
the room, Indians and Martians and stranger combinations danced enthusiastically on a black-and-white-
checkerboard floor. The less active guests mingled at
the opposite side of the chamber from the band, in
front of a cold stone fireplace adorned with carved
Gothic demons. Undercover Merry Men moved among
the celebrants, as well as waiters and waitresses in
formal attire, carrying glittering silver trays of expensive appetizers.

All in all, Bruce thought, I'd rather be in my cave.
Or, better yet, prowling the darkest alleys of Gotham.

While the band played a slow, sad ballad he glided
across the dance floor with Vicki in his arms. The
dance provided him with mobility, the better to stalk
his prey. Looking over Vicki's shoulder, he caught a
glimpse of a sleek feline form in taut black leather: a
Catwoman dancing with a delighted-looking octoge-
narian oil tycoon dressed as Prince Charming. Her
bright red lips, about all that her mask did not conceal, were moving. Bruce strained to catch a word or
two, hoping he'd recognize Selina's voice if he heard it,

but the music and the din of too many conversations
drowned out everything.

The music changed to a more upbeat swing number,
and Prince Charming twirled his Catwoman into the
crowd and out of sight . . . just as another Catwoman
boogied into view a few feet away from Vicki. Then
Bruce spotted yet another one across the ballroom,
flirting with a young musketeer.

This isn't working out like I planned, he realized. I
have to make other arrangements.

"Excuse me," he told Vicki, "but it's about time for
the dinner to start. I really ought to check with
Alfred."

"Do you want me to come along?" she asked.

He shook his head. "You stay here and have a good
time. I'll be right back." Commissioner Gordon, wearing Robin Hood garb and sporting a quiver of arrows
across his shoulder, had been hovering at the edge of
the dance. As planned, he was keeping a close eye on
Vicki's pendant—and, Bruce assumed, on the nine
Catwomen. He hoped it would be enough.

As he zigzagged through throngs of dancing couples
his mind raced ahead. None of the Catwomen had arrived with escorts, he'd observed. Too bad; that might
have helped eliminate a few. Still, perhaps there was
a way he could turn that to his advantage. . . .

Reaching the border of the ballroom, he darted
down a long corridor marked as off limits to partygoers. It led to the kitchens. There, he found Alfred in
the midst of chaos. The aging butler was the
unflappable center of a scene of frenetic activity.

Dozens of hired chefs and caterers rushed past each
other, hauling trays of food into or out of ovens, arranging platters, putting final touches on cakes and
pastries, wheeling carts of dishes in all directions. The

smells of roast pork and rack of lamb mixed with bak-
ing potatoes, sautéing mushrooms, and steaming car-
rots, string beans, and corn. None of tonight's guests
would leave hungry, that much was assured.

Bruce caught Alfred's eye and beckoned his old servant over. Alfred ducked past a cook carrying an enor-
mous bowl of Caesar salad and met Bruce at the
threshold. "Yes, sir?" he asked quietly.

Bruce's voice dropped the casual tones of an amiable
playboy. "Have the seating arrangements been
made?" he asked grimly. His unblinking eyes fixed on
the butler's with an almost searing intensity.

"Indeed, Master Bruce," Alfred said. "Markers cor-
responding to each guest's costume and ticket number
have been placed at every seat at every table."

"Change them," Bruce said.

The banquet took up nearly all of the mansion's huge
domed solarium. Electric frost-free glass skylights
kept out the cold February night while revealing a sky
full of stars. As there were far too many guests to be
seated at even the manor's longest antique table,
nearly a dozen huge circular tables had been installed
for the occasion. Cupids sculpted from blocks of solid
ice served as centerpieces on spotless white table-
cloths. Four kinds of caviar, fresh fruits and vegeta-
bles flown in from South America and California
especially for the party, and numerous other delicacies
had been set out as appetizers. Everyone dug in.

Most of the guests removed their masks during dinner. All nine Catwomen kept their faces covered.
Bruce had expected as much.

Bruce and Vicki sat at the one rectangular table, at
the far end of the solarium, up on a dais. A speaker's

podium took up the center of the table. Bruce sat to
the podium's right, with Vicki sandwiched safely between him and Commissioner Gordon. The mayor was
on the podium's left, with City Councilman Graves
and several other dignitaries. While Vicki chatted
with the commissioner about the Penguin's most recent trial, for the kidnapping and attempted murder
of two rare Japanese owls, Bruce concentrated on
Catwoman. Surveying the room, he was pleased but
not surprised to see that Alfred had followed his instructions precisely: every one of the Catwomen was
seated next to someone in a green woodsy outfit
straight out of Sherwood Forest.

No doubt some of the guests were wondering what
the connection was between Catwoman and Robin
Hood. And, hopefully, the genuine Catwoman had
been thwarted for the duration of the meal. Bruce allowed himself a private smile. He shared his table
with Juliet, Robin Hood, a robot, a flapper, Santa, and
an astronaut. The mayor's bodyguards lingered in the
background. Not a single Catwoman sat anywhere
nearby.

Maybe, he thought, if I go from table to table, saying hello to all present, and especially to the
Catwomen, I can locate Selina before she strikes.

Bruce started to rise, but Vicki stood up first. "No
need to get up," she said. "You guard my dessert while
I make a quick trip to the ladies' room. I'll be back in
a sec."

Before Bruce could protest, Vicki guided the volumi-
nous folds of her costume along the solarium's perim-
eter. As she passed a neighboring table a lithe woman
in a form-fitting cat suit got up and followed close behind her. Bruce's eyes widened. Beneath Romeo's tunic, his muscles tensed for action. Then Vicki glided

by the next table, and yet another Catwoman rose to her feet and padded gracefully after the first. Bruce's teeth ground together. Moment by moment, table by table, a train of dark, pantherish women formed behind Vicki, like bridesmaids at some sinister feline wedding. Within minutes, all nine Catwomen disappeared with Vicki into the privacy of the ladies' rest room.

Caught off guard, Merry Men half rose, exchanging nervous looks with Commissioner Gordon and each other. Damn, Bruce thought. Too many Robin Hoods and not a single Maid Marian. For a single angry moment he wished he had installed security cameras in the mansion's rest rooms. But no; Alfred would never have allowed it. Still, he should have planned for a moment like this. He should have been prepared. . . .

Without warning, the lights went out. Cries of surprise and fright surrounded Bruce. He thought he heard Vicki scream, but he couldn't be sure.

Somewhere behind him, a man tripped and fell, cursing loudly as he crashed to the floor. One of the mayor's bodyguards, Bruce guessed. With only the starlight to see by, the crowd was reduced to a mass of shadows.

He sprang silently to his feet. *Time to act.* "I'll check the auxiliary generator," he shouted to Gordon. "Make sure no one gets hurt."

Eyes long accustomed to the night rapidly adjusted to the solarium's dimness. Bruce dashed between the tables, past blinded partygoers just now stumbling out of their chairs. A closet-sized alcove was located in a hall right outside the solarium. In the dark, it looked like an entrance to a black and endless cave.

Just what I need, Bruce thought. In the impenetrable murkiness of the alcove, his fingers grasped Ro-

meo's tunic and tore it open. Silk and lace separated
as snaps and Velcro tabs came undone. Bruce's Romeo
costume parted to reveal the outspread wings of a bat
silhouetted against a golden emblem. Next he pulled
open a hidden compartment at the back of the alcove
and withdrew a feared and famous black cowl. . . .

When the lights came back on, Batman was already
helping a shaky Vicki Vale to her feet. Under the fluorescent lights of the rest room, amid the elegant
gold-and-marble fixtures, he looked like an avenging
demon loose in paradise. Though his ebony cloak and
cowl concealed mortal flesh and blood, they conveyed
an aura of almost supernatural power.

Thank Heaven for Alfred, he thought briefly. I knew
he'd get the power going again.

Vicki's gown was ripped, leaving her shoulders bare.
Her red hair fell in disarray about her shoulders,
while the bands of pearls that had held her hair in
place now rolled like dozens of tiny white marbles
across the tiled floor.

She was holding her gown in place, looking about in
dazed confusion. "Batman—" she said. "What're you
doing here—where's my camera—"

"Easy," he said in a low, gravelly voice. "Did you see
them?"

"Oh, my God," she gasped. "Bruce's ruby! It's gone!"

Batman turned and ran. He burst through the rest-
room door and found himself facing two Merry Men
with drawn pistols. One of them fired a panicked shot.
The bullet passed harmlessly through the swirling
black fabric of Batman's cape and ricocheted through
one of the solarium's glass walls. Plate glass tinkled

like sleigh bells as it fell into the room. A woman screamed.

"S-sorry—" the man stuttered sheepishly.

Batman shoved him out of the way and sprinted for the far wall. He saw two Merry Men struggling with one of the Catwomen there. He knew it was the wrong one—the *real* Selina Kyle would never be taken that easily.

"Amateurs!" he snarled under his breath.

He found the solarium's side door standing open. Outside, he deftly plucked a pair of infrared goggles from a compartment in his yellow utility belt, then secured them to his face mask and watched the neatly landscaped lawn leap out in sharp relief, displayed in shades of red and black.

To the east, two Catwomen on foot were being chased by three Merry Men. He dismissed them out of hand; his quarry never ran in packs. To the west, he saw a Merry Man tackle a Catwoman, rapidly cuff her, and begin reading her rights to her. Her mask had come loose, revealing long blond hair very unlike Selina's. As far as he knew, Catwoman still wore her hair short and dark.

That left the south—

To the south was the mayor's helicopter. He heard its motors revving up. The rotors had already begun to turn. Without a second's hesitation, Batman sprinted after it.

Funny, he thought, I didn't know Selina could pilot a copter.

He reached the landing pad and leaped. The wind from the copter's spinning blades caught his cape, so that it swelled about him like the dark and scalloped wings of a monstrous vampire bat. Still, he was seconds too late. His fingers grazed the landing strut,

then he tumbled back toward earth. Landing firmly
on his feet, he fired a grappling line from a device he
plucked from his gleaming gold-colored utility belt,
but the hook slid along the same landing strut without catching hold and plummeted down to land only a
few inches away from his boots.

Again he didn't hesitate. Turning, he sprinted toward the wooded area to the west of Wayne Manor.
There, hidden by scrub brush and guarded by electronic monitors, he kept a small secret helipad . . . and
the Batcopter.

Black and streamlined, the aircraft looked more like
an alien spaceship than a conventional helicopter.
Twin sets of compact, high-powered rotors sprouted
from batlike, horizontal wings that spread out on both
sides of the rocket-shaped, one-man fuselage. Jet
boosters in the tail allowed the Batcopter to zoom as
well as hover. Bruce Wayne had spent a fortune on
this unique vehicle; not even the Pentagon had anything faster or more versatile.

It didn't take long for him to strap himself into the
pilot's seat, manipulate the throttle, and bring the rotors to life. He lifted at once and soared toward
Gotham City. He knew Catwoman would be heading
for a secret lair in the city, some swanky cat pad hidden deep in the ever-changing maze of Gotham's underworld.

Switching on the radar, he sorted out the various
pings: two small planes headed for a private airstrip a
couple of miles south, what looked like a weather bal-
loon, and—yes—*there*—that had to be the mayor's
helicopter.

He opened the throttle as far as it would go and
soared through the night. Below, his infrared vision
made the passing trees, suburban streets, and little

matchbox houses into a surrealist's monochromatic nightmare.

He was closing quickly with the Catwoman. He saw her helicopter's running lights now, and a faint blur of motion where the rotor's blades chopped through the night.

He activated the Batcopter's weapons systems. The onboard computer ran a quick systems check, and one by one lights came to life in the panel before him:

> GRAPPLING LINE: READY
> SMOKESCREEN: READY
> LASERS: READY
> MACHINE GUN: READY
> AIR-TO-AIR MISSILES: READY

He punched the missiles' tracking system to life. The tiny viewscreen lit up, showing the area ahead in a series of radar pulses. The target finder instantly zeroed in on the mayor's helicopter and locked it in. He poised his finger over the firing button . . . and hesitated.

Could he shoot her down so callously? She was a different breed of criminal from the Joker and the Penguin: dangerous, yes, but in a different sort of way. A thief and an outlaw, but not a mass murderer, not so psychopathically violent, not without a human side. She belonged in prison, not Arkham Asylum. And she was a woman. Maybe *the* woman . . .

He deactivated the missiles. He'd bring her down, but not in flaming wreckage. There would be old-fashioned justice this time: the legal way.

He switched on the radio. "Catwoman," he said. "This is Batman. I have you locked onto my tracking screen. Land and surrender peacefully. You won't be hurt. I can promise you a fair trial."

Somehow he didn't expect an answer. But it came after only a second—scratchy with static, but close enough to Selina Kyle's smooth, silky tones.

"Batman ... how *pleasant* to hear your voice once more. You always give me pause ... or should I say, paws?" She chuckled.

"Selina—" he began, but she went on.

"Listen up for once, my dark knight. I have the mayor on board with me, plus a hungry kitty that would *kill* for a little delectable morsel of fresh meat. Say, a human liver. Back off, or he's cat food. Catwoman out!"

Furious, Batman increased speed. He didn't give the mayor *any* chance of survival if she landed with him. He knew how Selina Kyle hated men, *all* men, and that included government officials, no matter how important or powerful.

... if she even had the mayor. It could be a trick of some kind. Hadn't he heard the mayor being shielded by his bodyguards on his way through the solarium? Yes. He knew he had. It was a bluff on Selina's part, nothing more.

He drew up behind and just to the right of the mayor's helicopter. He could see Gotham City's official seal painted on the copter's door, and Catwoman, black and beautiful as obsidian, manipulating the controls. He aimed the machine guns, punched the trigger, and watched as lines of lead bullets, laced with tracer fire, arced through the air and neatly sheered the blades off the small stabilizing rotor at the back of the helicopter.

It veered wildly to the right and began to spin in helpless circles, angling toward the ground too fast for

Greg Cox

Batman's comfort. His shot had been *too* effective—
unless it was another of Selina's tricks. Well, he had a
trick of his own in store for her after their battle was
over.

Catwoman regained control of her helicopter only a
few feet above a set of power lines. She veered to the
left at the last moment and half crashed, half landed
in someone's wide backyard.

The house's back-porch light flickered to life.

Meanwhile Batman worked feverishly as he hovered overhead. Removing his infrared goggles, he activated the spotlights on the bottom of the Batcopter
and trained their powerful twin beams on the stolen
helicopter. Then he turned on the Batcopter's microphone and loudspeakers.

"The game's over! Don't even try to get away," he
said. His voice echoed like thunder across the neighborhood. "This is your only chance. Surrender peacefully and you won't get hurt."

People crept from the house, their arms held over
their heads—a balding, middle-aged man in a bathrobe, a woman with her hair in curlers and cold cream
on her cheeks and forehead, and a couple of boys
around twelve and thirteen years old dressed in pajamas. The younger boy seemed to recognize the
Batcopter. He looked more excited than afraid.

"Get back in the house!" Batman ordered them as
he hovered above the frozen lawn. They ran, the parents dragging the youngster behind with them as he
stared back over his shoulder.

The stolen helicopter's rotor blades were slowing; as
Batman watched they stopped. He saw a trickle of
something wet on the ground as its pilot climbed out.
She shook one fist at Batman, tried to run, and col-

lapsed. There was something dark and wet on her leg. Batman guessed it was blood.

Keeping the floodlights trained on her, he landed a short distance away. Then he climbed down and advanced inexorably upon her, a nightmarish specter of vengeance come to render justice.

She tried to drag herself away from him; couldn't. He read the pain and fear in her eyes. Her skin was white as a sheet, and she was shaking all over, violently, entering shock. He cuffed her wrists first, just in case she was faking, then hastily checked her leg with his gloved hands. A compound fracture, he guessed; nasty, but not fatal. Far off he heard an approaching siren. The police would be here soon. They would get her an ambulance. But first—

"You can keep the jewel, Selina," he said. A note of sadness crept into his stern voice. *Why did she always have to take things so far?* He hadn't wanted to hurt her.

"Wha—" she began.

"It was fake," he said. "Bait to catch you with, to stop you once and for all."

She barked a harsh laugh. "Then—the joke's—on *you*—" She shook her head violently and the cat mask, already ragged and loose from the crash, slipped away from her face.

Curly red hair tumbled out from beneath the black leather hood. Her exposed face, pale from loss of blood, bore a faint resemblance to Selina Kyle's, but Batman knew Catwoman's true features better than he knew his own, and this woman, however attractive she might be under better circumstances, was not even in the same league.

Blast it. I knew Selina couldn't pilot a helicopter.

She began to laugh, and couldn't stop—not even

when Batman bent and pried her fingers from the ruby pendant she still clutched. In the white glow of the searchlight, the gem shone like a frozen red flame against the blackness of his gloved palm. He ground it to paste in his fist and let the breeze blow the powder away.

She knew it was fake all the time. If she knew, then Selina must have known, and that means—

He swallowed. *What about the original?*

Turning, he ran for the Batcopter. He had to get home.

From above, Wayne Manor resembled a grim medieval stronghold. High, lightless towers speared the sky above gray stone walls. Carved gargoyles struck bestial poses, frozen in place as they clambered above and around the empty gutters and deserted balconies. A rooftop of black slate tiles trapped the weak starlight and consumed it, so that only bleak shadows could be seen where the roof covered the manor. The limousines had disappeared from the grounds, Batman noted, although a few police cars remained parked in front of the mansion. Obviously the party had broken up early . . . or, more likely, been shut down by Gordon in the wake of the robbery. The flashing red lights atop the waiting police cars reminded Batman uncomfortably of the ruby that had started this all, the precious heirloom he prayed was still safe.

Nine Catwomen, he recalled, but only one had snatched the fake gem from Vicki. What had the real Selina been up to during the confusion?

Flying without any lights, relying only on radar and Batman's own infrared lenses, the Batcopter executed a flawless vertical landing in a secluded clearing in the woods west of the mansion. Batman leaped from his seat and ran, his huge cape flying behind him, toward a large granite boulder nestled amid tall, brooding pines. A signal from his belt activated a hidden mechanism, and with only a quiet hum to betray the well-oiled apparatus concealed within, the giant rock slid smoothly back, revealing one of many secret entrances to the Batcave.

Batman raced down the open tunnel. He had neither the time nor the patience to deal with Gordon or his officers now. Maybe there was a chance he could still stop Catwoman, even though he feared he was already too late.

Behind him, the rigged boulder silently eased itself back into place, sealing off the tunnel. The underground pathway, marked by green fluorescent strips, slanted sharply downward for several yards, then leveled off. Batman's boots pounded savagely upon the rough stone floor of the tunnel. He felt his heart pounding beneath the dark gray tunic and emblazoned bat symbol. His breath fogged the cold cavern air as he ran, ignoring fatigue and despair, concerned only with finding out the truth as soon as possible.

Could she have known all along where the safe was? Of course she did. She was Catwoman. She has her sources, just like me.

Finally, after a few endless minutes, the tunnel opened up and merged with a wide-open space filled with darkness. Batman pressed another button on his belt and a battery of overhead lights came on. The dim illumination fought with but did not dispel the lingering shadows that haunted this level of the Batcave. Far above, hanging upside down from their rocky roosts, bats squeaked at the disturbance. A few flapped away toward gloomier, less crowded resting places.

Greg Cox

Batman gave his headquarters only a quick inspec-
tion, sweeping his gaze rapidly over the familiar
scene. Everything seemed in place, the computers and
state-of-the-art laboratory equipment juxtaposed
against weathered natural stalactites and stalag-
mites. In the distance, across a deep black chasm that
seemed to drop toward the center of the earth, he
glimpsed his trophy room, full of bizarre relics from
his previous cases: a stuffed tyrannosaurus, a Lincoln
penny the size of a monument, one of Catwoman's
long black whips . . .

Selina, he thought. When is this long war going to
end?

A monitor informed him that, far above, Bruce
Wayne's library was currently unoccupied. Good. Stepping into the closest elevator, he keyed in the coordi-
nates for the library. The elevator door slid shut and,
after a smooth ascent, opened again to reveal the back
of a one-way mirror. Batman looked through the glass,
spotted neither Catwoman nor anyone else, and gave
the mirror a firm push. The door swung outward, and
he stepped decisively into the empty library. Shelves
of thick hardcover books, mostly medical texts left behind by his father, occupied heavy wooden book-
shelves. Nothing appeared to be disturbed, but that
didn't surprise him. Cats are neat and tidy creatures.

He went straight to a slim collection of novels on
the opposite wall. A rust-colored, leather-bound edition of *Treasure Island* caught his eye. He pulled that
volume halfway out until he heard a metallic click
from somewhere within the bookcase, then one entire
shelf of realistic-looking books collapsed together like
an accordian being squeezed, compressing themselves
into a thin mass packed tightly against the right side
of the bookshelf. Behind the now absent display of lit-

erary classics, Batman found the front of an old-fashioned combination safe, recessed into the back of the bookcase and the wall beyond. The gray steel door looked deceptively secure.

Not even Vicki knew about this safe, he remembered. Only Alfred and Commissioner Gordon and few of Gordon's men.

Batman tugged experimentally at its handle. The front of the safe came open easily . . . too easily. He hadn't even touched the lock yet. He felt a sinking in the pit of his stomach, and knew the truth: he was too late.

Inside, nestled on the blue velvet pad where he had left the real ruby pendant, was a sealed red envelope—and a silver, heart-shaped locket. He recognized it instantly. The other Juliet. Suddenly all the pieces of the puzzle came together.

Nine Catwomen. Nine decoys. And the real Catwoman was right under my nose the whole time.

There was a tiny latch on the side of the locket. Flicking it open with a brush of his finger, he found inside a tiny portrait of himself, as Batman, trimmed to fit the shape of the locket: grim, unsmiling lips and a clenched jaw scowled up at him underneath the spiked bat ears of his cowl. Next he examined the envelope. A handwritten message on its exterior addressed the letter to, simply, "Batman."

For a second fear brushed his heart. Why had Catwoman left a note for Batman in Bruce Wayne's safe? Then he realized that from Catwoman's point of view, it was only logical to assume that Batman would eventually show up at the scene of one of her crimes. He let out a small breath of relief. His dual identity was still safe.

I should be thankful, he thought, *that she headed*

directly for the safe when the lights went out and
didn't stumble onto the Batcave instead.

He opened the envelope slowly. No need to rush; she
was obviously long gone by now. He found a paper valentine within, illustrated with a drawing of a sleek
black cat posed in front of a cheerful-looking red
heart. Opening the card, he recognized the stylish
loops and curls of Catwoman's handwriting:

> Dear Batman,
> Happy Valentine's Day!
> Thanks for the *purr*fect gift!
>> Love, Selina

Standing like an ebony statue, Batman read the message several times. Soon, before the night was over, he
would have to find Gordon and update him on the situation. There were nine phony Catwomen to interrogate, other clues to examine, possibly a leak in the
police department to track down. The Batcopter
needed rearming and refueling as well as other main-
tenance. Vicki Vale must be reassured that Bruce
Wayne was still alive and well. He had much to do before Wayne could sleep.

For now, though, he just stood alone in his father's
library and contemplated the fragile black-and-red
valentine in his hand.

Another trophy for the Batcave . . . or his first emblem of defeat? He felt a slow, simmering anger welling
up inside and knew he wouldn't rest until, one way or
another, he had his mother's ruby pendant back again.

For Gotham City, March swept in like a savage arctic
bear. The skies were gray and sullen, the winds fierce,

the snow frequent and unpredictable. The weather seemed more appropriate for Chicago.

Late one night, in an out-of-the-way alley, a lone figure sat and watched like a lonely, forgotten sentry. Icy winds whipped past soggy cardboard boxes and fragments of broken whiskey bottles. A graffiti-covered subway car rushed by, shaking a dilapidated stretch of elevated track and dusting the street below with clots of yesterday's snow. Dirty brown slush, melted during the day, had frozen to rock hardness with nightfall. The runoff had overwhelmed the drains and flooded the alley, so that the pavement resembled a skating rink designed by a madman, studded with hideous, jagged obstacles. It was a terrible night to be out and a worse place to be. To visit Palinko Street tonight you had to be desperate, greedy—or obsessed.

Batman crouched between the cracked and crumbling supports of the subway trestle, staring down at the alley several yards below. With his dark cloak wrapped about him, shielding him from both the elements and the view of others, he sat and waited, hunched over, his gloved hands gripping his knees. The wind blew harder, but failed to dislodge him from his perch. Intent upon the night's mission, Batman barely felt the cold.

Soon, as expected, a lone figure appeared at the far end of the alley. The new arrival wore a slick yellow raincoat with the hood drawn up over his or her head. Trembling visibly, head down against the oncoming wind, the figure trod gingerly across the ice and snow.

Batman's eyes narrowed, his muscles braced for combat, but he remained as still and soundless as one of the gargoyles back at Wayne Manor. Another train came over the tracks just a few feet above his head, vibrating the steel and wooden beams that supported

Greg Cox

him. Batman didn't look up. His gaze never left the
stranger below.

The figure in the raincoat approached the backdoor
of what looked like an abandoned building. It looked
furtively up and down the alley, then knocked three
times on the door. A few heartbeats later, the door
swung inward just a crack, casting a thin wedge of
light upon the alley floor. A copper-tinted chain kept
the door from opening any further. Through the narrow opening, Batman spotted a sallow-faced man
wearing a paper air filter over his mouth, an orange
wool scarf around his neck, and a small gray cap. A
bulky and extremely unconcealed bulletproof vest covered his entire torso.

Just as I thought. Batman nodded to himself. Percy
"Paranoid" Plummer . . . one of Gotham's most incor-
rigible fences . . . up to his old tricks.

Batarang in hand, Batman watched and waited for
the right moment. The figure in the alley and the man
behind the door held a hasty, whispered discussion.
Not yet, Batman thought, but soon. He calculated the
distance between him and his two targets, factored in
the strength and direction of the wind.

A handful of green bills appeared in Percy's grip.
The yellow plastic hood nodded, and a mittened hand
disappeared into the coat. A moment later the mitten
reemerged holding a bright red object that dangled
from a golden chain. The light from the inside of the
building made the ruby pendant gleam like a drop of
fresh blood. The money and the gem exchanged
hands.

Now, Batman thought.

Two black metal bats swooped, one after another,
from under the subway tracks. The first batarang flew
with surgical precision, the sharpened steel blades at

the edge of its wings hitting both the door and its
frame, wedging tight. Percy swore and tried to slam
the door shut, but the batarang jammed it open. The
second batarang, arriving only seconds after the first,
smashed into the hood of the yellow raincoat; the wet
plastic muffled the sound of metal colliding with bone.
The figure staggered, knocking the lid off a rusty
trash can, and dropped to its knees.

Batman hadn't waited to see his batarangs strike.
While his weapons were still in midair he had
launched himself from his elevated hiding place. The
bitter March wind caught his cape as he leaped, so
that it fanned out above his shoulders like the terrifying wings of an enraged fallen angel. His fists were
clenched in fury, but his every movement was precise,
controlled, and effective. From the moment he sprang
into action, he made every second count.

First: He landed solidly on the icy pavement, the
small spikes in his soles of his boots finding secure
purchase in the ice. As his black cloak billowed out behind him, shrouding him in spooky majesty, his grim
eyes searched the area. He listened for the click of a
gun or the hiss of a knife, but heard nothing.

Second: His right leg kicked out, connecting with
the target outside. The yellow figure flew face-first
into the garbage, twitched once, then lay still. *Fine.
That's one taken care of for the moment.*

Third: He slammed his shoulder into the partly
opened door. The chain snapped and the batarang
came loose. He heard footsteps echoing ahead of him
as Percy fled frantically toward the front of the building. *He's got the pendant,* Batman reminded himself.
I can't let him get away.

The building held the remains of a bankrupt department store. Batman rushed past empty display cases

and deserted dressing rooms. The walls were white and bare. Bits of fallen plaster crunched under his boots.

He gained rapidly on Percy. The fat fence was breathing hard through his surgical mask; the orange scarf streamed out behind him as he ran. Batman focused on the pendant Percy still clutched in his mittened hand: the ruby that had once belonged to his murdered mother.

A flying tackle brought Percy down. They crashed to the floor, arms and legs flailing, and rolled into the ruins of an old checkout counter. Batman was back on his feet before Percy had time to do more than groan and clutch his head. With one hand, Batman snatched the pendant from the fence's grasp; with the other, he gave Percy a swift chop against the back of the neck. The battered crook collapsed unconscious onto the dusty, plaster-ridden floor.

Batman allowed himself a grunt of satisfaction as he deftly wrapped the golden chain around the ruby and locked it into a compartment of his utility belt. The entire chase had taken less than four minutes.

The other target, the one in the raincoat, was still dragging itself back onto its feet when Batman returned to the alley. A gust of wind blew the hood back, exposing the face of Detective Crouper of the Gotham Police Department. The batarang had left a swelling purple bruise across Crouper's left jaw; he didn't look like such a Merry Man now.

A powerful hand, covered by a cold black glove, seized Crouper by the collar and slammed the back of his head into a brick wall. Batman tore open the raincoat and confiscated Crouper's gun. He removed the clip and threw it into a deep pile of garbage.

Only then, with his batlike visage only inches away

from the crooked cop's face, did he ask the one question he wanted answered: *"Where is she?"*

"Who?"

Batman snarled and squeezed the crooked cop's throat. "Catwoman. Where?"

"I don't know!" Crouper broke down. Tears streamed from his eyes, freezing quickly on his face. "It was all by phone, by messenger . . . I didn't even know where she was at Wayne's party! She made me tell her about the sting . . . and the safe. She blackmailed me."

The worst part was, Batman believed him. Catwoman always covered her trail well.

Disgusted, he dragged his captive inside the old store, where he handcuffed both Percy and Crouper to a heavy iron pipe. They'd be safe there until Gordon came for them. He'd have to tell Gordon where to find the gun as well.

Outside, in the desolate alley, the wind had finally blown the clouds from the sky. A pale, cold moon shone down on Batman as he recovered his batarangs, then paused amid the scattered trash and debris.

He had his mother's ruby back, but it wasn't enough. Gotham at night belonged to him, but not to him alone. Somewhere in the shadows a stray cat screeched in fury or in heat.

He opened another compartment on his golden belt and took out a shiny silver locket in the shape of a valentine. He stared at it for a long time, then pressed it to his cheek. Somehow he thought he caught a faint whiff of perfume.

Next time, Selina, he vowed. Wait until next time.

Catacombs

ROBERT WEINBERG

The mind of a madman is like the Catacombs—a twisted maze of dark corridors leading ever downward.

—Justin Geoffrey

Police Commissioner James Gordon shook his head in disgust. In all of his years on the police force, he had seen more than his share of bizarre crimes, but tonight's matched any he could remember. It wasn't just the brutality of the murders. Death was never pretty. It was the sheer *ferocity* of the crimes that bothered him.

Riordan, one of the investigating crew, wandered over. He was a burly, redheaded Irishman, his eyes normally twinkled with good humor. Not tonight.

"Six dogs, Commissioner," he said, drawing in a deep breath as if trying to banish the stench of blood from his nostrils. "As best we can tell, there were six of them. We won't know for sure until we wake somebody at the kennel."

Gordon shivered. Six of them—Dobermans, the

fiercest, deadliest attack dogs known—dead. He shivered, mentally correcting himself. *Not merely dead.* They had been ripped to pieces, torn to bits, as if by some monstrous jungle beast. *Slaughtered.*

"The jewels?" he asked.

"Gone," answered Riordan. "Just like at the other stores. Case smashed, all the gems taken."

"No clues," said Gordon, stating the obvious. "The thief, whoever . . . or whatever, was too clever for that."

"Nothing so far. Fingerprint boys are dusting the counters. But we ain't had much luck up to now."

"Nor will we tonight," said Gordon. "This maniac doesn't make mistakes. At least not foolish ones."

Pulling a package of gum from his coat pocket, Gordon stuffed several pieces into his mouth. Chewing gum was a terrible habit. It looked foolish and was bad for his teeth. He planned to quit. Someday. But not tonight. Not as long as a homicidal jewel thief stalked Gotham City.

The crimes had begun two weeks ago. The first attracted little attention. In crime-plagued Gotham City, a midnight robbery at a downtown jewelry shop was nothing out of the ordinary. That the criminal had managed to circumvent the elaborate store alarm system raised a few eyebrows. Just a few. To the police, it merely suggested an inside job.

Not so the second theft. Like all of the thefts, it also took place in the downtown, high-rent district. Flashman's Jewelry showcased some of the finest diamonds in the metropolis. Along with a state-of-the-art technology, the owners employed two full-time night watchmen. Ex-cops, they were tough, reliable, totally dependable pros, able to handle any emergency. At least they managed fine until that night.

The thief struck sometime between midnight and

Catacombs

dawn. Ghostlike, the burglar evaded all of the outer alarms and scanners with ease. The police found no sign of a forced entry or exit. The only evidence of the criminal's passing were the looted display cases. And the corpses of the two men set to guard them.

Gordon sucked in a deep breath, remembering those bodies. Both men had been horribly mutilated by their unknown assailant.

One guard had been savagely disemboweled, his ripped-out guts littering the floor of the showroom. The police discovered him facedown in the ruins of his own intestines. The dead man's horrified expression had shocked even the most hardened investigators.

The fate of the second watchman made it quite clear to the commissioner that they were dealing with a homicidal maniac. The coroner's report told a grisly tale.

Knocked unconscious by his attacker, the stunned guard presented no threat to the robber. The thief could have made off with the jewels without any further violence.

Instead the crook had ruthlessly slashed the man's neck and face to ribbons. There was hardly enough left of his features to make a positive identification. Worst of all, several huge gouges in the guard's body indicated that after killing him, his slayer had *devoured* parts of him.

More crimes followed. All involved jewels or rare gems. Another night watchman died, in as gruesome a manner as his predecessors. Tonight it had been six guard dogs, torn to pieces, their limbs scattered haphazardly throughout Beaumont's Department Store.

"You checked on the Joker?" asked Gordon, shaking his head to clear the cobwebs of memory.

"He's locked in tighter than a drum at Arkham Asylum," Riordan replied. "I made double sure of that as soon as the call came in. Just as you instructed me to, sir. No way that madman committed these crimes."

"I know, I know," said the commissioner, frowning in annoyance. "Besides, the Joker always kills for a reason, however twisted it might be. These murders are so . . . senseless."

"You pegged it, Commissioner," said Riordan, shuddering. "None of this stuff makes sense. You know what they're saying on the street?"

"That werewolf nonsense," said Gordon, snorting in annoyance. "Forget it, Riordan. No member of the animal kingdom other than man ever develops a taste for diamonds and rubies. A human mind is behind these crimes."

"Commissioner! Over here!"

It was Jacob, another member of the lab team. He was standing about twenty feet from the gem counter, excitedly pointing at something on the floor.

Gordon hurried over. Mutely he stared at what the officer had discovered. A pool of blood covered the floor. Outlined in the center of it was a paw print. A huge paw print—the paw print of a gigantic cat.

2.

THE KILLER IS A CAT! proclaimed the huge headline of the *Gotham Daily News*. Sipping a cup of black coffee, Bruce Wayne studied the story over breakfast. Features grim, he ate slowly, chewing his food mechanically. The gruesome details of the latest slayings were not designed for a hearty appetite.

When he finished, Wayne folded the newspaper

neatly and placed it beside his plate. A cold, righteous
anger burned in his heart, but as always he kept his
feeling under tight control. Temper tantrums too often
led to mistakes in judgment. And in his continual war
against crime, the slightest mistake might be fatal.

Closing his eyes, the millionaire contemplated the
facts as presented by the newspaper. Little had
changed since the first robbery. The police were still
baffled. They had no idea how the thief broke into the
jewelry stores, or how he evaded the security systems.
It was as if the killer walked through walls. Even Gordon, the best of the bunch, expressed bewilderment
over the bloody paw print. It was definitely a case for
Batman.

Wayne sighed, feeling incredibly weary though the
day had barely begun. Sometimes, late at night, unable to sleep, he wondered at the unceasing parade of
madmen who plagued Gotham City. Many times it
seemed that his entire life was spent dealing with one
lunatic after another. Was the gigantic metropolis a
breeding ground for insanity? Or, more to the point,
was it his presence, the opportunity to challenge Batman, that attracted the fiends? The question gnawed
at his conscience, but he had no answer. Perhaps
there was none. All he knew was that without him
more innocents would die. And that he would not allow.

Banishing all thoughts of doom and gloom from his
head, Wayne pushed away from the table and rose to
his feet. A big, powerfully built man, muscles like
steel bands rippled in his arms and chest. Because he
was so perfectly proportioned, the millionaire's size often surprised people when they encountered him for
the first time.

That no one had ever linked him with the mysterious Dark Knight was mute tribute to his consummate skill as an actor. "Sloth personified" was how one newspaper columnist described him. Wayne had laughed for days after reading it.

Ten minutes after breakfast, he entered the hidden underground sanctum beneath Wayne Manor he called the Batcave. A vast complex of workshops and laboratories, it was here that he transformed himself from man into superhero—Bruce Wayne into Batman. And, he hoped, it was here that he would find the answer to the phantom thief.

Using a computer grid of downtown Gotham, Batman pinpointed the location of each robbery. He noted that all of the buildings were located in the older section of the city, an area that had remained the same for nearly a century. Following a hunch, he called up the plans for all of the structures. Studying them, he was disappointed to note that several different architects had designed the stores. It seemed highly unlikely that four different firms would have constructed similar buildings.

Then, struck by another thought, Batman ran a secondary scan on the locations. Exactly what did the buildings have in common, if anything? A minute later he knew he had found the right answer.

The police continued to draw a blank because they were asking the wrong questions. They kept trying to discover how the phantom thief broke into the buildings. They were stumped trying to solve a series of impossible crimes. Only Batman realized the truth. The burglar was not breaking in. He was already inside the stores when the alarms were set.

The facts flashed up on Batman's computer screen as he accessed the proper reference file. A hundred years earlier, a huge network of underground tunnels

Catacombs

had been excavated nearly a hundred feet below the surface of downtown Gotham. These passages, nine feet high by six feet wide, had relieved street congestion during a time when wagon traffic was threatening to overwhelm the city's hub.

Connected directly to the railroad yards on the south side, the tunnel system offered direct access to numerous department and retail stores in the downtown area without contributing to urban gridlock. Small railroad handcars were used for deliveries. Over eighty buildings were linked to the network by offices in their subbasements. In the winter, even coal was transported through the passages.

The decline of railroad transportation and the rise of the trucking industry rendered the underground network obsolete. Trucks brought products directly from the manufacturer to the retailer, avoiding middlemen and costly handling charges. Fifty years ago, the tunnel system was officially closed, all of its stations sealed.

Now, Batman suspected, someone had reopened them for business. However, instead of using the tunnels for deliveries, the criminal mastermind was making withdrawals. The Dark Knight's eyes narrowed as he noted that the vast tunnel network had been dubbed the "Catacombs."

A movement in the corner of his eye caught Batman's attention. It was Alfred, his butler and confidant. His presence here in the Batcave meant he had something important to say. Alfred knew better than to disturb him while he was working.

"What?" asked Batman.

"The local cable-TV talk show just featured an interview with Inspector Lincoln," Alfred declared in precise, clipped tones. "I thought you might be interested in what he had to say about this case."

That Alfred knew he was working on the jewelry murders did not surprise Batman in the least. His butler had a sixth sense about such things. That Lincoln, one of the thickest, most incompetent police officials in the city, had any thoughts about any crime was much more astonishing.

"And what pearls of wisdom did the good inspector offer the good citizens of Gotham?" asked Batman with a faint smile.

"He intimated that Catwoman was behind these crimes," Alfred said solemnly. "As to evidence, he offered none. Evidently he saw no reason to confuse the issue with facts."

The grin disappeared from Batman's face. Catwoman was one of his most mysterious and deadly foes. A cunning and resourceful jewel thief, she had battled him to a draw a number of times in the past year. Trained in the martial arts, she was as dangerous as she was beautiful. Catwoman was as ruthless an opponent as any Batman had ever fought. But she was no killer.

That Lincoln thought otherwise was no surprise. The inspector's head was so wooden it attracted termites. Still, his opinion was bound to cause trouble. Catwoman would regard Lincoln's remarks as a personal insult. And she was not one to take an offense lightly.

"Let's hope Catwoman missed that broadcast," said Batman, turning back to the computer monitor. "This case is trouble enough without her getting involved as well."

3.

Unfortunately Catwoman did see the interview. It was hard to miss it. Lincoln's remarks were prominently featured on the local news reports of all the major TV channels at both noon and 6:00 P.M. And repeated endlessly as sound bites on twenty different radio stations throughout the day.

That Catwoman found the inspector's accusations offensive was borne out by the gaping hole that currently appeared in her television screen. She had angrily tossed a handy vase at the set only seconds after the police officer finished speaking. Unlike her nemesis, Batman, Selina Kyle, aka Catwoman, did not believe in keeping her temper under control. Especially when she was accused of crimes not of her doing.

Though over an hour had passed, she was still furious. Her long slender fingers, capped by sharp, pointed nails, clenched and unclenched uncontrollably as she paced the floor of her apartment. The claws of the cat, Inspector, she thought darkly, are unforgiving. And I do not forget an insult.

However, most of her rage was not directed at the blowhard official. Selina Kyle was nobody's fool. That cat's footprint had been no accident. The real mastermind behind the jewel robberies had hung a perfect frame on her.

By now everyone in Gotham City believed that Catwoman was responsible for the thefts and killings. Unless she proved herself innocent, she would be haunted by the murder rap for the rest of her days.

Grand larceny was one thing. If the authorities managed to nab her for robbery, it would be a long sentence in the state pen. Selina felt quite confident

Robert Weinberg

that no jail could hold her. Three premeditated murders, however, were a sure guarantee of the electric chair. And Catwoman had no illusions of returning from that.

Equally important, the fortune in rare gems called her. As the master cat burglar of Gotham City, she considered the jewelry trade her private territory. Selina hated interlopers. According to her twisted brand of logic, those diamonds and rubies actually belonged to her. Silently she vowed to even the score with the phantom thief. And make the stolen booty her own.

Eyes narrowing with concentration, Selina reached for the telephone. Time to call in some favors, she decided, dialing a well-remembered number. Her lips curled into a cruel smile. Nobody squawks better than a frightened politician.

Before embarking on her career as Catwoman, Selina had earned her keep in an equally illegal fashion. For years she had sold her body to the highest bidder. Specializing in domination and perverse pleasures, she serviced a wide range of both male and female clients. Many of them numbered among the glitterati of Gotham City. Though they had tried to keep their identities secret, no one ever managed to deceive Selina Kyle.

Always an opportunist, and gifted with an exceptional memory, she had filed away detailed notes on their secret vices, along with an extensive photo scrapbook, for darker days. If nothing else, Catwoman believed in preparing for the worst. That was why she was the best at everything she tried.

Three phone calls and an hour later Selina leaned back on the sofa, a sly smile caressing her lips. Sleep might come hard to several politicians tonight. A little

Catacombs

fear was good for everyone, including the stuffed shirts in city hall. After today, they might even consider celibacy. Though she strongly doubted that. Nor did she care.

What mattered was that she was sure she knew the phantom crook's secret. According to a very highly placed source in the mayor's office, Commissioner Gordon was convinced that the thief lurked in the old freight tunnels beneath downtown Gotham.

Another unimpeachable source, this one in the police department, confirmed that story and added that a full-scale manhunt in the notorious Catacombs was scheduled for the day after tomorrow. The wheels of justice spun slowly in the vast metropolis. Which suited Catwoman fine. Tonight she planned to invade the underground maze. And deal out her own brand of justice.

4.

Far beneath the city streets, a solitary figure stirred on a makeshift bed of huge pillows and expensive throw rugs. Scattered about the huge chamber, a thirty-foot square with the dark mouth of an old freight tunnel embedded in each wall, sat stacks of treasure from more than a dozen merchants of downtown Gotham. Not all the prizes were of equal value. Rare gems filled antique goblets while only a foot away rested half-finished boxes of potato chips. And cans of Coca-Cola stood side by side with rare vintages of fine wine.

Yawning, the reclining man sat up, rubbing the last remnants of sleep from his eyes. His skin, the color of

old ivory, gleamed in the light of two ornate candles
that cast strange shadows on the far wall. Tall and
lean, he wore a long flowing white robe that left only
his head and hands uncovered.

His face resembled an ancient Egyptian death
mask. Thin bloodless lips framed a gash of a mouth.
Narrow ears pressed flat against his skull. Short
black hair matted his head, emphasizing the deep yellow of his complexion. Gaunt cheeks and long, needlelike eyebrows that met over his beaklike nose
combined to draw attention to eyes of unusual power.

Dark green, hypnotic in intensity, they glowed with
a seemingly supernatural brilliance. Strange, catlike
eyes, they perfectly matched in color the one piece of
jewelry that he wore—a huge multifaceted emerald
dangling on his chest, held in place by a thin chain of
purest gold. With each breath the man took, the massive gem pulsed with unnatural life.

In one swift, fluid motion, the yellow man rose to
his feet. All around him, as if in response, the floor
rippled with life. Cats—cats everywhere—rose to
greet their master. Black cats, gray cats, gold cats,
striped cats, alley cats and Siamese cats, hundreds of
cats stretched and arched their backs as the robed figure raised his arms above his head as if in prayer.

He smiled, a death's-head grin that held no humor.
His gaze swept across the room, and he laughed cruelly at a joke only he understood. In seconds, reacting
to the slightest change in their master's mood, the feline horde howled in delight. The dimly lit chamber
exploded with sound.

Grimacing with annoyance, the yellow man flicked
one hand in a sharp gesture. On his chest, the emerald flared green, reflecting his displeasure. As if cut
by a knife, the noise ceased instantly. Here, truly, was

the master of this immense pack. He was the Lord of Cats.

"Silence, my pets," he whispered, in a harsh voice that echoed from the concrete walls. "Your wailing disturbs my concentration."

For an instant he stood frozen in place, a faraway expression in his deep green eyes. A brief look of satisfaction crossed his face. "The Midnight Slayer returns," he declared, sounding pleased. "As I command."

From out of the nearest tunnel emerged a patch of darkness darker than the dark, blacker than the night. A killer beast, with glowing yellow eyes and a mouth full of flashing teeth. Nine feet long from head to tail, and weighing more than two hundred pounds, it killed with a casual grace and ferocity unmatched by any other member of the animal kingdom. A monster rarely captured and never tamed, the Midnight Slayer was a giant black panther.

Growling deep in its throat, the big cat padded its way across the concrete floor to the Lord of Cats. On the man's chest, the great green emerald pulsated with raw energy. Gradually the menacing rumbling in the beast's chest quieted, then stopped. Almost docile, it came to a stop less than a foot away from the robed figure.

Clenching the blazing jewel with one hand, the yellow man bent down and gently scratched the panther behind the ears. Incredibly the monster purred with satisfaction like a giant kitten. Slowly, ever so slowly, it sank peacefully to the ground.

With a sigh of relief, the Lord of Cats straightened. Even when he used the full power of the emerald, it was enormously difficult controlling the mind of the huge leopard. Most big-game hunters considered black panthers the most dangerous of all predators. Savage beyond belief, they lived only to kill. Still, as long as the Lord of Cats held the Heart of Sekhmet, *he* was beast's master.

Originally captured in Central Africa, the Midnight Slayer had spent most of its life in a major California zoo. The Lord of Cats had "liberated" the monster soon after embarking on his unique quest. It had served him well with fang and claw ever since.

"Tonight I sense she will come," he whispered, kneeling beside the unmoving panther, as if telling the beast his deepest secrets. "The one I desire as my bride. Who more fitting a mate for the Lord of Cats than the Catwoman?"

Lazily the panther lifted its immense head and snarled, baring immense fangs. "No reason to be concerned," said the man, chuckling. "There will be others to slay—many others. Our work here is almost finished. I baited a trap for Catwoman with your paw print. She had no choice other than to investigate.

"Once Catwoman joins us, we shall abandon these tunnels. I grow tired of the darkness. There are other cities to plunder, other treasures to take, other deaths to savor."

The Lord of Cats raised the emerald to his forehead, placing the throbbing jewel on the bridge of his nose, directly between his eyes. An eerie green light filled the chamber. Instantly all of the cats were on their feet, their eyes fixed unwaveringly on the man holding the gem.

"Go now," he commanded. "Spread throughout the Catacombs. Serve as my eyes and ears. Let no human walk through these tunnels undetected. Obey me, for I am your lord." His hands pressed the emerald even tighter. "I am the Lord of Cats."

And, like the wind, they were gone, scattered throughout the maze of Catacombs, leaving the Lord of Cats alone with the Midnight Slayer. Patiently they awaited the arrival of Catwoman.

5.

Entering the Catacombs proved quite easy for Batman. He only hoped that leaving would pose no greater difficulties.

At six that evening, millionaire playboy Bruce Wayne arrived as scheduled at Lewiston's Gem Emporium, located in the heart of Gotham's exclusive jewelry district. Accompanying him was a small army of caterers, decorators, and unidentified craftsmen. While the tradesmen hurried about, transforming the store's main showroom into a lavish reception hall, Wayne cheerfully discussed his plans with William Lewiston, the tuxedo-clad, white-haired manager of the place.

"I'm having a small, intimate party for a few friends tonight," he confided, sipping a glass of white wine handed to him by his ever-present manservant. "Things get so boring at the mansion sometimes. I thought a little night on the town would be much more entertaining."

The wrinkled look of disapproval on Lewiston's face made it quite clear what he thought of Wayne's plans. However, the older man wisely kept his opinions to himself.

Unknown to the general public, Lewiston's had suffered a major cash-flow crisis a few months ago. Sluggish sales forced major cutbacks at all levels of the operation. Bankruptcy seemed only a matter of time.

Then, unexpectedly, a sudden influx of hard currency changed everything. The emporium carried on with no interruptions in sales or services. As the economy recovered, so did the jewelry business. The momentary crisis past, the store flourished.

Only a few members of the Lewiston family were aware of the source of those necessary funds. Control of the century-old family business had quietly shifted to Bruce Wayne Enterprises. Day-to-day operations of the firm were still handled by the regular employees. But financial operations were tightly controlled by a board of overseers responsible only to the flamboyant millionaire.

Tonight was the first time Wayne had indicated anything more than a passing interest in the jewelry store. Face white, his lips tightly pressed together as if to keep from screaming in outrage, William Lewiston escorted his new boss on a tour of the premises.

"Where does that lead to?" asked Wayne, waving his wineglass at a padlocked door at the far end of a dusty storeroom.

"Down to the subbasement," Lewiston replied. "Dreadful place actually and no longer used for anything. Long ago the furnace was located there. This building is one of the oldest in the city. Our establishment has been situated here for over a hundred years."

"How fascinating," said Wayne, his bored tone indicating his true feelings. Then, casually, he asked, "In the winter, coal was delivered . . . ?"

"Through the Catacombs," answered Lewiston. "You are aware of the tunnel system?"

Catacombs

"I own a number of properties in downtown Gotham," said Wayne. "Though none quite so close to the old central routing office of the passageways."

"We boarded up the entrance to the maze years ago," said Lewiston. "The city stopped using the tunnels back in the early forties." The older man chuckled. "Though there was some talk in the sixties, during the Cuban missile crisis, of using them for fallout shelters."

"Wasn't the Cold War wonderful," said Wayne. Grasping the store manager by the elbow, the millionaire steered him back into the main showroom.

"No reason to worry about your fancy displays," Wayne said soothingly, patting Lewiston on the shoulder. "I would never do anything to jeopardize an important investment. Trust me on this. When you arrive tomorrow, you'll swear that no one was ever here."

It took five minutes and several dozen more assurances before Lewiston could be convinced to depart. Another half hour passed before everyone else had cleared the showroom. Finally only Bruce Wayne and Alfred remained.

"Nine o'clock," said the millionaire, glancing down at his watch. "The phantom thief never strikes before midnight. That gives me three hours or more to locate his lair."

"You refuse to let the police handle this matter?" said Alfred, disapproval sharp upon his face. "There is still time to make an anonymous phone call to Commissioner Gordon."

"I suspect Gordon knows all about these tunnels," said Wayne, opening a large box brought in by the workmen but left untouched during the preparations. "But department procedures limit his capacity for fast

Robert Weinberg

action. By the time he sends men into the Catacombs, our murderer will be long gone. Besides," he concluded as he carefully checked the contents of the container, "a single man stands a much better chance of finding the killer than a squad of policemen."

"Especially if that man is Batman," said Alfred, with a heavy sigh.

"Correct," said Wayne, emptying the special apparatus onto the floor. "Give me a hand with this stuff, Alfred. It's time for me to visit the Catacombs."

Five minutes later Batman stood ready to enter the underground maze. Few people would have noted that somehow the Dark Knight appeared different than usual—bulkier, bigger, his muscles not as well defined beneath his costume. Only his long cape, dark and mysterious, seemed unchanged.

In one hand he held a small but powerful flashlight. Built to exacting specifications, it cast a pale white light that was visible for only a few feet. A second similar device was hooked to his belt. In dangerous situations where a normal light would betray his presence, Batman relied on such lanterns until he was extremely close to his quarry. Of extremely rugged construction, the lights were built to take a beating. In the absolute blackness of the underground maze, they were a necessity.

Gripped in his other hand the crime fighter held a small lightweight dart gun. It was loaded with the most powerful tranquilizer pellets available. Batman wasn't sure what beast lurked in the Catacombs, but he was taking every precaution. Three dead guards and a half-dozen dogs ripped to pieces demanded it. One scratch from these darts would knock an elephant off its feet.

"Don't forget to move the food around on the plates

a bit," he instructed Alfred as he pulled free the last of
the boards blocking the entrance to the abandoned
tunnel system. Like the gaping mouth of some ancient, gigantic dinosaur, it waited silently for him to
enter. "After all, Bruce Wayne entertained his friends
here for hours. Or so we told Mr. Lewiston. And our
employees."

"I will make sure the evidence is properly faked before the workmen arrive tomorrow to carry it all
away," said Alfred, gazing nervously into the darkness. "Shouldn't you be carrying some sort of map,
sir?"

"Memorized," said Batman, tapping the side of his
head. "Not that it matters much," he continued, taking his first step into the maze. "The Catacombs all
head in one direction. Downward. *Ever downward.*"

6.

Batman was not exaggerating when he claimed to
have memorized the map of the entire freight transportation system. Gifted with an exceptional memory,
he had spent years perfecting it through rigorous
mental training. One glance at most simple diagrams
was all he needed to master them. A more complicated drawing, like the maze, required greater concentration but not much more time.

Nor had he misled Alfred when he stated that all of
the tunnels led downward. The Catacombs converged
in one huge shipping depot well over a hundred feet
beneath the city streets.

The entire freight system had been designed to
serve an area stretching from the railroad yards on

the south side to downtown Gotham. Hundreds of
shipments passed through the corridors every day. In
order to keep operations simple, from the very beginning of the endeavor two sorting areas had been main-
tained.

One was centered at the train station, where goods
from all over the country arrived and were separated
for transportation downtown. The second, even larger
distribution area, was located scores of feet beneath
the buildings it serviced. From here, freight and coal
were sent to smaller sorting centers where they were
prepared for delivery. They were then shipped by
handcar through tunnels to their proper destinations.
Ruling out the main depot as too dark and dismal,
Batman was convinced that the phantom thief was
headquartered in one of the substations. The problem
was finding the proper room without alerting the
phantom killer to his presence.

Cautiously, he started down the tunnel leading from
Lewiston's Jewelry Emporium. The passage was a
concrete oval nine feet high by six feet wide, with a
flattened floor and roof. Wide metal tracks were the
only evidence that railway handcars once traveled in
this same direction. The corridor walls were flat and
unbroken, showing no signs of age. Every ten feet
there was a small niche for a gas lamp, but none was
in evidence. To Batman, it seemed as if he were walking through a gigantic tube thrust into the earth.

At first, the intensity of the darkness was not overwhelming. Especially since a sliver of light filtered
down the tunnel from the open landing. However,
forty yards into the passage, the tunnel angled thirty
degrees to the right. Now Batman's flash provided the
only illumination in what was otherwise a pool of ab-

solute blackness. The effect was startling, almost frightening.

Batman paused, abruptly conscious of an unnatural tightness in his chest. His breathing came in short shallow gasps. And he could hear the blood pounding in his head. The Dark Knight was afraid.

Normally the darkness held no fear for him. For years he worked with it, capitalizing on superstitious criminals' fear of the night and its supposed terrors. However, this darkness was different.

It was not merely the inability to see outside the small circle of light the flashlight provided. More than once he had been blinded in battle or caught in lightless traps. Always he managed to fight on without the least problem. In a moment of epiphany, Batman realized it was his present location that frightened him.

A thousand tons of rock rested over his head. Only a thin wall of concrete, more than a century old, stood between him and being buried alive. This darkness was so complete, so absolute, because light could not reach a hundred feet beneath the street. Walking through these tunnels was like traveling in the domain of the dead. The passageways were aptly named the Catacombs.

The air was heavy and stagnant, breathable, but stale and lifeless, like the air in a tomb. And silence hung over the tunnel like a shroud. The comparisons, apt as they were, did nothing to relieve Batman's apprehensions.

Shaking his head in annoyance, the Dark Knight forced himself forward. The more time he wasted worrying here, the better chance he gave the phantom to escape.

Another fifty yards and the corridor branched left and right. After a second's thought Batman took the right-hand passage. Downward, ever downward, the tunnel continued.

He walked in silence, the only noise the soft scrape of his boots on the old concrete. And the sound of his breathing.

Nothing stirred, nothing moved. The passage walls were remarkable in their sameness. Not a crack showed in the concrete, even after ten decades.

A thin layer of dust coated the floor. It was unmarked by footprints of any type. If a phantom haunted these corridors, he had never used this particular tunnel. Which suggested to Batman that there was little chance of him being discovered. His hopes of surprising the mysterious killer rose as he continued descending.

Again the tunnel split, and this time Batman took the left passage. Though supremely confident of his memory, the Dark Knight was still pleased to note that the tunnel sloped downward. And the dust covering the floor was still unmarked by human passage.

Ten feet ahead, at the fringe of the light, something moved in the semidarkness. Instantly Batman froze, instinctively raising the dart gun. Senses alert, he waited for something to happen. Nothing did. After a few seconds he took a tentative step forward, then another.

Two points of light glared at him from the blackness. Batman blinked in astonishment. A large tomcat silently entered the sphere of light cast by his flashlight. Without a sound, the yellow-and-black-striped cat circled him, as if checking out what he was doing here. Finally, as if signaling its approval of his presence, the cat meowed once. Then, without another sound, it bounded down the corridor and disappeared in the darkness.

Batman shook his head in bewilderment. He was positive that Catwoman was not involved in these crimes. Yet the presence of a cat in the tunnels seemed to indicate otherwise. Suddenly he realized that letting the animal escape might have been a major mistake. Hurriedly he set off after the beast.

7.

About the same time as Bruce Wayne first made his presence known at Lewiston's Jewelry Emporium, Catwoman entered the Catacombs. Selina found no special significance in the name given the tunnels. Nor was she the least bit afraid of what horrors might lurk underground. Though gifted with an exceptional mind, Selina Kyle possessed little imagination. She considered the darkness her friend and ally. The absolute blackness of the Catacombs held no fear for Catwoman.

An abandoned building on the far side of downtown Gotham offered her access to the tunnels. An old book she found in the library detailed the history of downtown and provided a map. Only whispered memories greeted her as she pulled back the few old rotten planks guarding the tunnels from the outside world.

As always when pursuing her lawless ways, she wore her cat costume. Originally designed for a rich man's party girl, the black cat suit had undergone a number of startling changes since falling into Selina's clutches. An underlayer of thin nylon mesh strengthened the garment so that it could not be easily ripped. Padding at her knees and elbows lessened her vulnerability, as did a layer of high-density foam packed in her face mask. While keeping the outfit's tail, she had reinforced it with a steel chain. In tight situations, it served as a dangerous surprise.

Her fingers ended in sharp, curved metal hooks almost an inch long. She thought of them as her cat's claws, and more than one man had felt their sting. Tucked through her belt, Selina carried a twelve-foot-long leather whip. She handled the deadly weapon with a skill born of many months of constant practice.

Her feet clad in soft, form-fitting boots, Selina jogged down the long concrete corridor. In one hand she held a tiny flashlight that emitted a pencil-thin beam of light. It was all the illumination Catwoman needed. She knew exactly where she was going. Like Batman, she was headed down.

Each time the tunnel branched into two, Selina pulled out her map. Always, she picked the passage leading deeper into the earth. She was convinced that the criminal mastermind behind the thefts and murders lurked in the lowest level of the Catacombs. Because that was the location she would have chosen if planning the crimes.

Twenty minutes and nearly a mile into the maze, Selina encountered her first cat. It sat peacefully licking its paws in the direct center of the tunnel, almost as if expecting a visitor. Catwoman rubbed her eyes in astonishment. The last thing she had expected to find in these tunnels was a stray animal.

She blinked, then rubbed her eyes again in annoyance. The cat was nowhere to be seen. It had calmly waited for her to appear, and then vanished. With a snarl of suspicion, Catwoman pulled the whip from her belt. Cats as sentries seemed unlikely, but so did killers who operated from Catacombs beneath

Catacombs

Gotham City. She continued onward, her every sense alert.

Five hundred feet farther, the corridor branched again. This time a big black-and-white-striped cat sat in the right-hand branch. It meowed loudly when Selina approached, then bounded down the corridor out of sight.

"Damn it," swore Catwoman, a touch of awe in her voice. "If this isn't a scene right out of *Lassie*. With me playing little Timmy."

Shrugging her shoulders, Selina followed her feline guide. Another two hundred feet farther, the tunnel split a third time. Waiting there in the mouth of the left branch was the cat she was following. Sitting next to it was a pale gray Siamese that stared at her with unblinking eyes. As Selina drew close the two animals, as if possessing one mind, turned into the passage and scampered away.

Each time their party crossed another tunnel, it picked up another cat. Soon Selina trailed nearly a dozen animals, all descending farther and farther into the Catacombs.

In a rare moment of self-doubt she wondered if entering the tunnels had been a terrible mistake. Her reception indicated she was expected. Though her ability to control cats was remarkable, it seemed to be nothing compared with that demonstrated by her unseen quarry. There was something uncanny in the coordinated responses of the animals. Something terrifying.

A sliver of yellow light far ahead was Selina's first indication that she was about to meet the master of the maze. By then she estimated she had been traveling through the passages for over an hour and gone several miles into the system. The patch of illumination grew larger and larger, showcasing the diverse pack of cats now only a few yards ahead of her.

Emerging from the tunnel into a large concrete vault, square-shaped, ten yards on a side, Selina immediately noted that each wall of the room opened into a tunnel exactly matching the one she had followed. Though she remembered her exact route here, leaving by the wrong exit might cause her serious problems. But before she could safely anchor the proper location in her mind, her gaze fastened on the center of the chamber—and her eyes widened in astonishment.

A man lounged on a throne of pillows, surrounded by more cats than Selina had ever seen in one place. There were hundreds of them—big and small, young and old, male and female—all watching her with an unwavering stare that was almost hypnotic in intensity. Still, it was their master who commanded her attention.

Long and lean, he was dressed in a long white robe that revealed only his head and hands. His skin was the color of old ivory, contrasting sharply with hair as black as night. Thin bloodless lips twisted in a smile of recognition as dark green eyes stared deep into hers. On his chest an emerald of incredible size and beauty throbbed with unnatural life.

"Welcome to my lair," said her host, waving one hand about the chamber in a sweeping gesture. His voice, deep and powerful, filled the room. "Welcome to the kingdom of the cats."

"The kingdom of the cats," Catwoman repeated, carefully noting the piles of expensive jewelry haphazardly scattered on the floor. "How nice. Then who the hell does that make you?"

"Can't you guess?" asked the yellow man. Reaching

to one side, he gently ran his fingers across the top of
a huge black pillow. Selina gulped in sudden shock as,
without warning, a massive head rose off the ground
and she found herself staring into the savage eyes of
a gigantic black panther.

Her host chuckled. *"I am the Lord of Cats."*

8.

She was all he had imagined and much more. A quiet
feeling of satisfaction engulfed the Lord of Cats. The
Catwoman would make a perfect mate. Once he sub-
dued her will to his.

"Sit," he commanded, gesturing to the cushions that
littered the ground. "Please make yourself comfortable. Would you care for a glass of wine? I've been anticipating your arrival all evening."

"You have?" said Catwoman, lowering herself to the
floor. He noticed with grim satisfaction that she carefully sat with her back to the exit, facing both him and
the Midnight Slayer. She did not trust him at all.
Which was exactly what he expected. Those who
trusted too easily made easy prey.

"Wine?" he asked again, raising a bottle and two
glasses. "A fine selection from the best Gotham City
has to offer." He laughed. "With disappearing gems
dominating the news, no one notices missing furnish-
ings or a few bottles of excellent vintages."

"Sure, sure," said Catwoman, her eyes never leaving his as she took a filled goblet. "But let's get back
to that remark about expecting me."

The Lord of Cats sipped his drink, as if assuring his
guest that the wine was not drugged. He was much

Robert Weinberg

too wise to attempt anything so childish with a huntress like Catwoman. For her he needed a much more
subtle trap.

"Come now," he said slyly. "After leaving not a clue
at any of my earlier crimes, did you really think I was
so inept as to miss a bloody footprint at my latest triumph? I instructed the Midnight Slayer"—the beast
growled at the mention of its name—"to step in that
pool of blood. It was my way of sending a message to
you. Call it an invitation, if you like. An invitation to
my lair."

He smiled again, very pleased with himself. "An invitation that obviously worked."

"I'm here," said Catwoman. "But on my terms, for
my reasons. Understand?"

"Of course. You are my guest. I assure you no harm
will come to you here."

"I appreciate your concern," she replied, a faint
touch of mockery in her voice. "Considering the blood
already on your hands."

"Bah." He snorted in annoyance. "Mere mortals.
Their deaths mean nothing to ones like us."

"Like *us*?" she repeated.

"Exactly," said the Lord of Cats, sliding his right
hand up across the Heart of Sekhmet. Like a jolt of
electricity, the power of the sacred stone flowed
through him, increasing the force of his mind tenfold.
Catwoman's eyes flickered with emotion as his words
battered her will with incredible mental force. "We
are the Chosen of Sekhmet."

"Sekhmet?" she asked, puzzled. And eager to know
more.

"The Mighty One," said the Lord of Cats. "The lion-
headed goddess of Egypt known as the Eye of Ra. You

Catacombs

and I, and those few others like us, are her disciples, her children. We are the people of the cat."

"I don't understand," said Catwoman, her eyes never wavering from his.

"Listen, then, and I will tell you the story of my life," he answered. "The story of my destiny. And yours."

Settling back on the cushions, he focused all of his attention on Catwoman. By the time he finished his tale, her mind would be under his control. Her will, what little remained, would exist only to serve him.

"My name is Landros Bey. I was born in Egypt, the most ancient of all lands, forty years ago, on a night sacred to the lion goddess, Sekhmet. My mother, a woman of unlimited wealth, owned a huge villa on the outskirts of Cairo and I was raised there. No mention was ever made of my father, and I learned through painful lessons never to raise that question. However, from time to time over the years my mother hinted of dark secrets best not revealed. It was soon quite clear to me that my birth was not the unexpected result of some casual liaison. My education reinforced that conclusion."

Bey paused, taking another sip of his wine. Catwoman remained motionless, mesmerized by his history and the power of the Heart of Sekhmet. "During the daylight hours, I was taught the arts and sciences by the most brilliant minds in Cairo. At night, my mother and I traveled to secret rendezvous in the oldest sections of the city, where I gained knowledge of a different sort."

His voice lowered, and the shadows in the room seemed to lengthen. "Ancient, wizened men instructed me in the ways of black magic. It was in Egypt that civilization first started. Modern history began less than two millennia ago. At the time of the birth of Christ, our culture dated back thirty centuries. The greatest sorcerers of the world practiced in the shadow of the Sphinx. Their wisdom became my heritage."

"Why you?" asked Catwoman, surprising him with the question. She was not yet completely under his psychic domination.

"I was the Chosen of Sekhmet," replied Landros Bey. "As are you. And probably others who never realize their full powers. We are people of the cat.

"There is no logical explanation for this gift. Nor were my teachers, wise in the ways of magic, able to offer me any answers. Certain individuals are born with a special *affinity* to cats. We are bound and bonded to the cat kingdom. We are drawn to felines, and they are drawn to us. We think like them, understand them. Our souls are in harmony. Perhaps, if those who believe in reincarnation are to be believed, we were cats in a previous existence."

The Egyptian raised the hand that held the giant green emerald. "My mentors and my mother instructed me in the old ways, the dark ways, because they feared me—they feared the power I possessed. This one treasure my unknown sire left with my mother, commanding her to present it to me on my thirteenth birthday. She dared not disobey."

Bey caressed the jewel. It pulsed with an inner light, the green glow reflecting off his green eyes. "In the ancient scrolls it is known as the Heart of Sekhmet. A living gem, it gives the owner the power to communicate with beasts. To become Lord of Cats."

He saw no reason to mention that the jewel's aura enabled the user to impose his will on lesser minds, including those of his feline followers. And on any human unsuspecting enough to let him weave his spell. A few more minutes of conversation and Catwoman would be his, body and soul, forever.

"My mother and her friends planned a great future for me. Unfortunately I had no desire to be a pawn in their schemes. My mind was my own. As soon as I was able, I took my leave of them and their petty dreams. Master of my destiny, I came to America, eager to sample the pleasures of the flesh."

Bey smirked. "For two decades I reigned supreme as the greatest animal trainer in the world. Never before had anyone handled lions and tigers with such ease. My skills were constantly in demand by movie and television studios. I earned astronomical sums each time I toured with the circus. No one ever questioned the source of my expertise, and I knew better than to tell them.

"Women, power, and fame were all mine. For years I wallowed in the excesses such power brings in its wake." He paused. "Then, when normal pleasures no longer excited me, I turned once again to the darkness of my youth. More than one innocent perished in my quest for greater thrills, new sensations."

Face flushed red with blood, the Egyptian knew he was revealing too much. But he could not stop. "Yet it was not enough. I wanted more. I hungered for companionship—a mate. *You.*"

Catwoman's eyes bulged in surprise. Immediately Landros Bey realized he had made a mistake, but already it was too late. Even the Heart of Sekhmet could not overcome Catwoman's innate distrust of men.

Sluggishly she struggled to her feet. Her eyes never left his, but now suspicion filled her gaze. No longer passive, she raised her whip and pointed it at him.

"You're not playing with a full deck, Bey. If you think a few tricks with kitties and a roomful of diamonds are gonna persuade me to call you sweetie, then you're really crazy."

They were both on their feet now. But before the Egyptian could answer, a yellow-and-black-striped tomcat raced out of the right-hand tunnel. Meowing loudly, it skidded to a stop only a few feet from its lord. Frowning, Bey pressed the Heart to his forehead. In seconds his grimace turned into a cruel, cold smile.

"What a pleasant surprise. The famed Batman approaches."

The Egyptian waved a hand and the monstrous beast at his side rose off the floor. Bey nodded once and the huge gem between his eyes blazed. With a savage growl that shook the chamber, the black panther hurtled forward into the right-hand tunnel.

"No man," said Landros Bey, laughing harshly, "not even Batman, can survive the fury of the Midnight Slayer. Tonight the Dark Knight dies."

9.

Batman fired only one shot. And it missed. Out of the darkness charged the black panther, moving with the speed of an express locomotive. The merest whisper of its paws striking the concrete floor provided the Dark Knight with his only warning. There was no time to think, no time to aim. Reacting by instinct alone, Batman raised and fired the dart gun just as the huge jungle cat burst into the white light of his flash.

Sheer chance triumphed over human competence. The exact instant Batman pulled the trigger, the pan-

Catacombs

ther launched itself into the air at the crime fighter. The tranquilizer dart passed harmlessly between the monster's widespread paws and clattered harmlessly to the concrete thirty feet away.

Batman got no second chance. The giant leopard slammed into him like a cannonball, the force of its impact knocking him to the floor. Huge jaws snapped at his face while the killer's massive front paws ripped and tore at his torso. An ordinary man would have died then. But Batman was no ordinary man.

Acting with astonishing speed, the Dark Knight shoved his left arm into the panther's gaping mouth. Desperately he pushed his elbow deep into the monster's throat, forcing its jaws open wider and wider. Angrily the beast responded, trying to rip the offending limb to shreds. But its gigantic fangs drew no blood. Nor did its claws, tearing with mindless rage at Batman's chest.

The night watchmen's deaths had made a strong impression on the Dark Knight. He had recognized the mark of a killer beast and acted accordingly before entering the Catacombs. Beneath his uniform he wore lightweight, fiberglass body armor, similar to a bulletproof vest. The panther's claws and teeth battered him terribly but could not cut through the protective gear or rip his mask.

Using his free hand, Batman grabbed the giant cat by the throat. Squeezing with all his strength, he pushed the leopard back. The monster's rear paws desperately clawed the floor, but the concrete offered it no purchase. Inch by inch, the black panther slid off Batman's chest and onto the ground.

Adrenaline pumping, the Dark Knight forced himself up to his knees. His main concern was not to let the panther bring up its rear legs so that it could rip

Robert Weinberg

at him with all four claws. Armor or not, his body could only withstand so much punishment. After an eternity he made it to his feet.

His breath coming in short, sharp gasps, Batman clenched his strong fingers even tighter on the beast's throat. Mewling in pain, the panther relaxed its jaws for an instant. Immediately Batman wiggled his trapped arm a few inches forward.

Seconds ticked by as man and beast remained locked in deadly struggle. Each time Batman felt the panther loosen its grip, he pulled his limb forward another few inches. Finally only his hard fist remained in its mouth. Pulling it free, he knew, would offer the leopard a new opportunity to bite his unprotected face. Instead he jerked to the side, lunging with his whole body. Together, he and the cat crashed to the cement.

This time, however, Batman was on top. Powerful knees dug into the panther's rib cage. The crime fighter's elbows pressed into the leopard's upper front paws, holding its slashing front claws apart. And his mighty fingers continued to tighten on the beast's windpipe. And tighten.

Five minutes later Batman wearily rose to his feet. The gigantic beast on the floor remained inert. It was dead, strangled by the Dark Knight. Later, when the body was discovered and examined, the police found that along with a crushed windpipe most of its ribs were cracked. Man and beast had fought to the death. And man had triumphed.

Shakily Batman grabbed his dart gun and flashlight, dropped in the first instants of battle. The killer beast no longer threatened anyone. But the Dark Knight's mission still remained. It was time to confront the monster's master.

10.

"Enough idle chitchat," said Landros Bey, turning to Catwoman. His voice rang with simmering passion. "You have heard my story. And my offer. Reign with me as Mistress of Cats. *Or die.*"

Selina forced herself to remain calm. The Egyptian's hypnotic spell broken, she now recognized Bey as a homicidal maniac. All of his promises meant nothing. Sooner or later he would grow tired of her or find himself attracted to another woman. His proposal amounted to nothing more than a death sentence.

"I've always been a loner," she said quietly, revealing none of her inner thoughts. "Adjusting to a mate, even one as desirable as you, might be difficult."

The Egyptian smiled, visibly relaxing. Which was exactly the response Selina expected. Megalomaniacs, especially male ones, were so easily fooled. Their monstrous egos made them willing victims. For all of his mystic powers, Bey was still governed by his lust. Catwoman intended to take full advantage of it.

"You mentioned astronomical sums?" said Selina, letting a trace of greed creep into her voice. The thought did excite her. But she was playing for much higher stakes—her life and liberty.

Bey nodded. "Wealth beyond your wildest dreams," he declared. "These jewels amount to nothing more than tawdry trinkets when compared to the treasures in my possession. As my queen, you will share in the finest collection of gems ever assembled."

"You make it sound quite inviting," said Selina. She was playing for time, waiting for the right moment to strike.

Unexpectedly the huge emerald on Bey's chest

flared brilliant green. The Egyptian staggered, almost
losing his footing, as if punched in the head.

"Impossible!" he screamed, his face turning bloodred with rage. "It cannot be!"

"Bad news?" Selina asked, inching her way forward.
She suspected that her necessary diversion was about
to arrive. Landros Bey was guilty of a sin made by
many, many others. He had underestimated Batman.

"*He* killed the Midnight Slayer," said Landros Bey,
anguish rippling through his voice. The Egyptian's
hands curled into fists. "But he shall not escape my
wrath. I swear it!"

Selina's face betrayed no sign of emotion, but inwardly she exulted. Though she hated to admit it,
Catwoman was relieved to hear that the Dark Knight
had survived the panther's attack. Few men attracted
her, least of all cops. But deep within her soul, Selina
Kyle knew there was something special about Batman.

Cautiously she slid another step closer. This time
Bey noticed the movement. His green eyes narrowed
in anger. "Do you think to play me for the fool?" he
said venomously. "Beware. I am Lord of Cats."

"And I," answered a deep, resonant voice from the
mouth of the right-hand tunnel, "am Batman."

Landros Bey gasped in fear. Standing in the mouth
of the black passageway, the Dark Knight presented a
frightful, menacing figure. Tall and powerfully built,
huge cape draped around his broad shoulders, he
looked almost superhuman.

Ever alert, Catwoman noticed the numerous rips
and tears in Batman's uniform. Though he appeared
unharmed, the barest hint of a tremor indicated to
Selina that the battle with the Midnight Slayer had
seriously weakened the crime fighter. He was in no

condition to fight Landros Bey. And the hundreds of cats the madman still controlled.

Evidently the Egyptian realized that, too. "This will be a great pleasure," he said, the Heart of Sekhmet throbbing with energy. His voice turned shrill with passion. "Kill—"

Catwoman acted. Like the tongue of a snake, her whip flicked out at Landros Bey's chest. The Egyptian, caught completely by surprise, shrieked in horror as the dark leather snapped against his skin—and cut through the gold chain holding the telepathic jewel.

The Egyptian grabbed for the emerald, but he was an instant too late. Like a streak of green fire, the Heart of Sekhmet plunged to the concrete floor. With a blinding flash, the gem exploded on contact, shattering into a thousand fragments of brilliant dust.

Kill, Landros Bey commanded before the destruction of the Heart of Sekhmet. But he never completed his order, never named his victim.

Kill, demanded the Lord of Cats. And his word, unchecked by any further wish, was law.

With one voice, five hundred cats howled madly. Landros Bey, his expression puzzled, waved his hands futilely in the air. "Stop, stop," he shouted. "I demand you to stop!"

Catwoman, immediately sensing the horror to follow, sprinted for the right-hand tunnel and Batman. Grabbing the Dark Knight by the arm, she pulled him into the black corridor. As she suspected, he had no strength to resist.

"Let me go," he protested feebly. "I can't let the Lord of Cats escape."

"Nothing to worry about," said Catwoman, dragging Batman farther into the passage. Behind them, a man's high-pitched voice bellowed in incredible pain.

The scream followed them for a long, long way up the tunnel. "Nothing at all."

11.

The next night the police staged a major search expedition through the Catacombs. Nearly a hundred men participated in the raid, hoping to discover the lair of the phantom thief. In the third vault they searched, they made a grisly discovery.

Dead cats filled the chamber. There were hundreds of them, terribly mauled and mangled; bitten, scratched, clawed to death. For some unknown reason, they had turned on each other in an insane orgy of destruction. Not one animal remained alive.

Buried beneath them was the horribly mutilated body of a man. No one had any idea of who he was, nor did positive identification seem possible considering the condition of the corpse. The body of a huge black panther, discovered in a tunnel leading off the chamber, only added to the mystery.

Even Bruce Wayne wasn't sure of the whole story. Once she was convinced he was not too seriously injured to ascend the Catacombs on his own, Catwoman had vanished into the darkness. Bruce was not terribly surprised that none of the reports about the police dragnet mentioned recovering the stolen jewels. Catwoman believed in taking advantage of every opportunity.

Somehow Batman knew he would encounter her again.

The Cat's-Eye Crown

KAY DEMIJOHN

Do you think Catwoman will show up?" Vicki Vale asked.

"I wouldn't be surprised." Bruce Wayne's expression remained neutral, but his sharp blue eyes missed nothing as he scanned the crowds around them. "Everyone else in Gotham seems to be here tonight."

It was eight o'clock sharp, and the opening reception at the new *Treasures of the World* exhibit at the Gotham Museum was already in full swing. Movie stars, local celebrities, politicians, museum trustees, reporters, and wealthy patrons of the arts had been invited to the black-tie affair.

Like most of the men already present, Bruce was nattily dressed in a tuxedo. With a red cummerbund and matching silk bow tie, he cut quite a handsome figure. Vicki Vale, at his side, wore a shimmering red evening gown and a beautiful ruby pendant that nestled gently between her breasts. The pendant was a flawless replica of a family heirloom; the original was safely stored in a bank safety-deposit box. Only the small flash camera Vicki carried gave away her true purpose in attending: she was here on a special assignment for the *Gotham Globe*, photographing the event and its famous guests.

"Hey, there's Chiller T-Bone," Vicki said. "Hey, Chiller!" she called, snapping up her camera for a quick shot. The rap star, dressed in his trademark black raincoat, did a slow spin, flashing Vicki a dazzling smile. The dozens of diamond rings on his fingers and in his left ear sparkled. Vicki said to Bruce, "I did a story on him last month. Nice guy."

"Ah." Bruce nodded absently. He had more on his mind than hot new rap singers . . . he was worried about Catwoman. Where is she tonight? he wondered. On a nearby rooftop? Mingling with the crowd in some ingenious disguise?

"Where do you think that crown thing is?" Vicki asked. They passed Commissioner Gordon, who was busy talking with the mayor and several other politicians, and Vicki snapped his picture.

"That must be it over there." Bruce pointed to the far wall, where dozens of people were pressed up against velvet ropes, leaning over them to peer into thick glass display cases.

"Let's take a look," Vicki said. "That's what we're here for!"

The centerpiece of the *Treasures of the World* exhibit was the Cat's-Eye Crown, a gold-and-jewel-encrusted crown from the fabulous Carciofi Hoard uncovered the year before in a remote part of Greece. An archaeologist named Luigi Carciofi had excavated the unplun-

The Cat's-Eye Crown

dered tomb of an ancient king, and it had yielded up
scores of priceless artifacts. The best pieces were touring the United States, the exhibit currently on loan to
the Gotham Museum.

Vicki headed for the display cases, snapping a few
shots along the way. The crowd around the Cat's-Eye
Crown was thick, but finally an opening appeared and
she and Bruce slipped to the front.

There, in the center case, on a simple black velvet
pedestal, sat the Cat's-Eye Crown. Bruce had seen pictures of it before, but he had yet to see it in person.
The crown was magnificent in every way, from the
deep red of its egg-sized rubies—found only in gems
from the Alepha kingdom, they were rarer than flawless diamonds, and far more valuable—to the soft gold
of the ancient settings that had been wrought by master goldsmiths long dead. The jewels around which
the metal had been intricately woven captured the
color of the sky just after sunset, and the pearls shone
with fresh-buffed luminosity.

But the true marvel of the crown, the one thing that
set it apart, was the extraordinary cat's-eye orb that
surmounted its tip like a little glowing sun. It was
pierced on its horizontal axis by a golden spike set
with pearls and rubies at either pole. The cat's-eye orb
was half the size of a man's fist and its stripes shim-
mered in browns, golds, and bronze colors of un-
earthly beauty.

"Wow," Vicki breathed. She forgot to take a picture.

Even Bruce, accustomed as he was to beautiful jeweled treasures—his family mansion had more than its
share of priceless antiques, after all—could scarcely
believe his eyes. The pictures hadn't begun to do the
crown justice. It truly *was* a masterpiece in every
sense of the word.

He also knew, deep inside, that Catwoman would go after it. She'd *have* to have it. This was the sort of prize that came along once in a lifetime.

Others were waiting to view the Cat's-Eye Crown, and Bruce and Vicki soon found themselves forced to move along to the other display cases, which held rings and bracelets and other jewelry from the same dead king's tomb.

Clearly bored—and Bruce had to admit everything else *was* a letdown after the crown—Vicki soon slipped a telephoto lens onto her camera and went back to snapping pictures for her feature story.

"I see it coming," she commented to Bruce as she caught Gotham's mayor gesturing broadly as he spoke to Artemis MacIntyre, the museum's curator. "Catwoman's going to snatch that crown."

"Oh, I'm sure the police have taken precautions," Bruce said.

"Come on!" She snapped a shot of three famous musicians munching caviar. "Commissioner Gordon's pretty good, but he's no match for a master burglar like Selina Kyle."

Bruce grinned. "Have some faith in the system, Vicki. I'm an honorary trustee of the museum, remember—"

"It's amazing what huge donations will buy these days," Vicki cut in with a laugh.

"—and I know they've taken all sorts of extra precautions. There are laser beams crisscrossing the floor, hidden surveillance cameras, and lots of extra guards for this exhibit."

Vicki still shook her head. "It won't be enough."

"And if I were Batman, I would've had the curator bug the crown for me. You could slip a miniature transmitter in among all those jewels and Catwoman would never notice. That way I could track her if she steals it."

Vicki snorted. "We'll see. When I was at the *Globe* this afternoon, they were already digging through their morgue for old Catwoman stories. They're working on a history of Selina Kyle's criminal career. It will run as a companion piece to the story of her knocking off the crown."

"*If* she knocks it off."

"*When* she does."

"You newspaper types are such pessimists."

She gave him a kiss on the cheek. "And you're such an optimist. That's why I like you so much, Bruce. Now give me a hand and see if you can spot the vice-president. Rumor has it that he'd be here tonight."

Arm in arm they headed for the tables on the far side of the cavernous special exhibit hall.

The reception officially ended at midnight. It took the museum staff a good half hour to shoo the last few lingering guests out the door.

At 1:15 A.M. the caterers finished cleaning up; they folded up their equipment and carried their tables and trays and bags of garbage out the side door, under the watchful eyes of Commissioner Gordon and a dozen security guards. They drove away in their company's vans without so much as a suspicious glance at the crown.

At 1:20 A.M. the cavernous hall was completely empty. Commissioner Gordon himself threw the switch that activated the alarm system. Invisible laser beams crisscrossed the floor in random patterns; anyone who broke a beam would trigger a silent alarm, and dozens of policemen would converge on the museum within minutes.

At 1:45 A.M., a large ceramic urn standing next to the door to the special exhibit hall where the *Treasures of the World* was on display began to rock gently back and forth. The urn, decorated with a mixture of Egyptian figures—mostly involving Bast, the Egyptian god of cats—developed a jagged crack along its side, then slowly split open an inch.

A fine mist jetted out. It hung in the air like a haze of smog, and slowly began to spread throughout the exhibit hall.

Twenty minutes later, when the mist had dispersed throughout the room, the urn opened another few inches. Hands clad in black leather gloves, complete with razor-sharp claws, appeared at the edges of the crack. They pushed the sides of the urn all the way apart.

Catwoman emerged, stretching luxuriously, like a cat waking from a nap: tall, sinuous, and thin, dressed in her black leather cat suit. A small transparent mask covered her mouth and nose; she breathed easily through it. The mist contained a mild narcotic gas: it would put anyone who inhaled it into a deep, deep sleep. It would also reveal any laser beams without breaking them. She was, after all, a master burglar, and took no chances.

Gently she patted the black pouch at her waist. It held every tool she could possibly need in her work tonight.

As the mist settled Catwoman studied the web of interlaced beams of light passing along the floor at ankle level. So simple; did they take her for a fool? She padded forward silently, stepped over every beam as

she came to it, heading swiftly and surely toward the
now dark display cases against the far wall.

When at last she stood before the Cat's-Eye Crown,
she drew out a palm-sized flashlight and flicked it on.
The jewels and gold and cat's-eye leaped to vibrant
life, radiating warm colors. Breathing oh so softly, she
stared in at it, entranced. *Marvelous. Absolutely marvelous.* Her taloned fingers curled and uncurled; her
thin lips twisted up ever so slightly. All mine, she
thought.

After a long moment of contemplation she stepped
back and allowed herself to breathe again. Business
first, she decided. She would have the rest of her life
to appreciate the crown's beauty.

The glass in the display cases was wired for vibrations, she knew; it had been a simple matter for her to
break into the security company that had designed
them, copy the plans, and slip out. After all, who
would break into a security company?

She drew a small power drill from her pouch,
crouched at the foot of the display cabinet, and mea-
sured exactly two inches out and six inches over. Then
she drilled a quarter-inch hole in the floorboards, fast
and neat. Drawing a dentist's cleaning hook from her
pouch, she reached into the hole, fished around until
she looped something, and pulled out a small black
wire. She stripped off the plastic coating, exposing
copper, and left it that way. Then she drilled another
hole two inches away, pulled out a red wire, stripped
it, and connected the two with little jumper cables.

So much for security, she thought, standing. An
earthquake could shift the museum off its foundations
now and the alarm system in the display cases
wouldn't register a thing.

She drew a glass cutter from her pouch, cut her way

into the case, and scooped out the crown. It was heavier than she'd expected. She tried it on experimentally. It was several sizes too big for her, and she had to hold the rim to keep it from slipping down over her forehead. Perhaps I can have it altered, she thought. She took it off, popped it into a sack, and slung it over one shoulder.

From there it was a simple matter to cross the room—avoiding the laser beams—and follow little glowing red arrows to an emergency exit. A sign said an alarm would ring when it was opened. She snipped the wires (this sort of door wasn't even a *challenge*) and went out. She found herself standing between two immense concrete columns, far to the right of the museum's front entrance. She moved forward cautiously, looking, listening.

The September night was cool but not cold. Trucks rumbled distantly on the west-side highway four avenues over. Catwoman scanned the tall, ornate old buildings around the museum: offices mostly, all dark now; even the cleaning crews had gone home. The wide street, with its rows of parking meters, was completely deserted. Halfway up the block, an all-night diner's sign flashed in neon pink and blue.

For a second she thought she saw a dark figure on a nearby rooftop, but when she blinked, it was gone. She gave a soundless mew of disgust. I must be getting paranoid in my old age, she thought. There hadn't been anybody there. She'd been careful; not even Batman could've stopped her tonight.

Like a phantom, she drifted from pool of shadow to pool of shadow, heading for the public parking garage located two blocks away. Reaching the broad, garbage-strewn steps leading underground, she started down.

She rounded a corner, arriving at the first level. The

garage was silent save for the faint sound of dripping
water. She continued her descent. On the second level
she turned and headed for section B-44 and her car.
Smells of gas fumes and oil permeated the air. Then,
from somewhere ahead, she heard the unmistakable
sharp *snick* of a switchblade opening. Her heart began
to beat faster. She could sense danger. It exhilarated
her.

Without breaking stride, she thrust her hand into
her pouch. Her fingers curled around a smooth, polished wooden handle. She began to smile.

Twenty feet from her car two figures leaped out
from behind concrete pillars. They both held knives
pointed straight at her.

"Money!" one of them snarled. Then his eyes went
wide as he realized his mistake.

"Whip!" Catwoman snarled back, and in one movement she pulled a small whip from her pouch. The
cat-o'-nine-tails lashed through the air with lightning
speed, striking her would-be assailant across the
hand. He screamed in pain. Knocked from his grasp,
the knife skittered off and vanished under a nearby
Jeep.

Catwoman hissed at the other thug. Dropping his
knife, he turned and ran, the first thug following close
on his heels. They vanished into the dark, distant re-
cesses of the garage.

Nodding in satisfaction, Catwoman coiled her whip
and returned it to her pouch. Then she continued to
B-44, where a boxy little red car was parked. It was
an Electric Leopard, a battery-powered car: nondescript, economical, and environmentally sound.

Opening the trunk, Catwoman stashed the crown,
her gloves, and her cowl. She donned a mousy-brown
wig, glasses with heavy horn-rim frames, and a pale

green sweater, which she buttoned to her chin. Disguised, she climbed in and brought the car to silent life.

Safe.

Now, at last, behind her own locked doors, with her disguise off and her cat suit put away, she could allow herself the luxury of exulting over her successful heist.

With the eyes of a dozen lounging cats fixed upon her, she pulled out the crown. In the bright light, it seemed more magnificent than ever. She turned it this way and that, and light sparkled off the bloodred rubies and across the walls. Intrigued by the show, an old Siamese stood, stretched, and padded over to investigate.

"What do you think, Arthur?" She lowered the crown for him to examine.

Arthur leaned forward, sniffed once, then again, as if disbelieving what he'd smelled the first time. Suddenly he began to back up, hissing and spitting. Fur bristling, he turned and fled.

"What got into *you*?" Selina asked, shaking her head.

She crossed to a mirror, where she put the Cat's-Eye Crown on again, this time padding it until it fit comfortably. The weight was oppressive, though; it made her neck ache. But the crown itself . . . magnificent. A fantastic, glorious, gem-bedecked extravagance.

"You're mine," she crooned, setting it carefully onto her dining-room table. She stepped back and continued to stare in fascination.

She knew she'd never part with it; the crown would be a prize she'd treasure forever. How many heads

had it adorned? How many kings had fought to the
death over it? How many fair maidens wept, how
many ancient warriors fought to the death?

She would gladly have sat up all night admiring it.
But her shoulders ached, and truth be told, she was
growing sleepy. She headed for her bedroom. In the
doorway she turned for a last look at the crown, and
purred in quiet satisfaction. A good night's work, she
told herself. A very good night's work indeed.

She switched off the lights and went to bed.

Selina awoke to the smell of coffee percolating in the
kitchen: the automatic timer had started it right on
schedule. The television's remote control sat on the
bedside table. She flicked it on, and an eight-foot-
square section of wall became a picture, projected
from a state-of-the-art home theater system she'd had
installed over the bed.

"—robbery at the Gotham Museum," a gray-haired
anchorman was saying with practiced solemnity. "Details just ahead, but first this message."

During the commercials, Selina wandered into the
bathroom to start drawing her bath. As water flowed
into the tub she heard a tiny meow. It was Charlotte,
a long-haired calico kitten, hiding under the sink.

"What's wrong, baby?" Selina asked softly. She
knelt and picked up the kitten, cuddling it. "What
frightened you?" Usually the only thing that spooked
her cats were strangers in the house. They always retreated to the bedroom when she had visitors . . . unless she had need of their special talents.

Then she remembered the crown. Hurrying out into
the living room, she knew at once that something was

wrong. There wasn't a cat in sight. Depositing Charlotte on the sofa, she ran into the dining room.

The crown was still on the dining table, exactly where she'd left it. She sighed in relief. It hadn't been touched. But something was *very* wrong: normally cats sat or sprawled on every flat surface in every room.

Perhaps the crown spooked them, she thought. Arthur certainly hadn't liked its smell the night before.

Puzzled, she went back to catch the rest of the news story while her bath filled. It had just come on. "The crown, with an estimated value of twenty-five million dollars in jewels alone," the anchor said, "is one of the earliest pieces of goldsmith's work to come from that region of Asia Minor. Its discovery as part of the Carciofi Hoard last year was one of the archaeological events of the century. Let's go live to reporter Alan Hart at Gotham Museum."

The picture cut to the museum's exterior. A reporter in a brown trench coat stood on the museum's wide steps, framed by two massive columns. Selina watched long enough to hear Alan Hart say, "Not yet, but rumors say Catwoman is responsible. She certainly seems the most likely suspect. Especially since she is renowned for cat-related crimes."

She flicked off the program and headed for the kitchen and coffee. She certainly needed a cup, and after that, a long hot bath.

As she walked through the living room she called her cats' names one by one. And one by one her cats crept out into the open. They'd been hiding under chairs and behind curtains. What didn't they like about the crown?

Selina poured herself a cup of coffee. Well, perhaps her little friends were just a bit overexcited. Luckily

The Cat's-Eye Crown

she'd be home for the next few days, lying low, and that would calm them down; they'd get used to the crown. In a month they'd treat it as if it had always been there.

She took a sip of her coffee, grimaced, and nearly spat it out. It was far too weak, almost like dishwater, and tasted awful. She didn't understand it; the machine was only a few weeks old, and it had been functioning perfectly until now.

Angrily she dumped the whole pot of coffee into the sink. She attempted to reprogram the coffee machine, but all the lights on its control panel began to blink. When she pushed the reset button, a thin curl of acrid smoke rose from its center panel. Quickly she unplugged it.

Maybe that's what was wrong with the kitties, she thought. They must have smelled smoke from the coffee machine and run away to hide.

Thoroughly disgusted, Selina made a cup of instant, then wandered in for her bath. The hot water felt wonderful when she climbed into the tub, and it managed to soothe her frazzled nerves.

Afterward, wearing a leopard-patterned terrycloth robe, with a towel wrapped around her head, she came to the next part of her morning ritual: reading the newspapers. She had all three city papers delivered each morning, and today she read the banner headlines with special care.

From the *Gotham Globe*: CAT'S-EYE CROWN NABBED! *Police Puzzled; No Clues Apparent.*

From the *Gotham Daily News*: GOTHAM MUSEUM ROBBER FOILS POLICE SECURITY. *$25M Crown Stolen; Museum in Uproar.*

From the *Gazette*: CAT'S-EYE TREASURE GONE! CROWN THEFT ROCKS ART WORLD!

The preliminary stories, written sloppily in the middle of the night by bleary-eyed rewrite men, didn't have many details. Basically the police had no clues and no leads to follow up, other than their suspicions of her guilt.

Selina gave a little laugh. They hadn't found her yet, and they wouldn't find her this time either. Indeed, the crown theft had been a perfect crime.

The newspapers would need another day to get the full spread out, the photos of the crown, the background of its discovery, the list of earlier great museum thefts around the world. But this was a good first item for her scrapbook.

She cut out the articles and pasted them into the leather-bound volume. Someday, far in the future, when she was old and withered and living in some tropical paradise on a fine income from the stocks and bonds she'd purchased with her ill-gotten gains, she would enjoy leafing through the records of her exploits as Catwoman.

It was time to get ready for the day. She returned to the bathroom. First, a touch of scent—Chat Noir, her favorite perfume, just a dab behind each ear, at the hollow of her throat, and between her breasts.

When she picked up the fan-shaped bottle, though, it slipped from her hand. She tried to catch it, bobbled it like a crazed juggler, then helplessly watched it fall to the green-and-white floor tiles. It smashed to pieces.

Selina cursed her own clumsiness. Thoroughly disgusted, she stared at the glittering ruin of nearly three hundred dollars' worth of imported scent. The bathroom began to smell like a French cathouse. First the coffeemaker, then her perfume. This was not starting out to be the kind of day she had envisioned.

The Cat's-Eye Crown

She bent to gather up the shattered glass. Fumes rose from the floor, and the strength of the liberated perfume's scent made her eyes water.

"Ow!"

An iridescent glass sliver was stuck in the palm of her hand. She pulled it out and blood began to flow. Slapping a wad of tissue over the wound, she scrabbled in her medicine cabinet for adhesive bandages and disinfectant cream. Once she had doctored herself adequately, she fetched a whisk broom and dustpan from the kitchen and returned to the disaster on the bathroom floor.

Nursing her bandaged hand, she swept, then wiped the last of the perfume up with a sponge. She tossed the debris into a plastic bag, which she sealed firmly.

With a sigh, she stood in front of the bathroom mirror. Never mind the perfume, she'd do her hair. At least the towel couldn't hurt her if she dropped it.

As she unwound the towel from around her head, though, several long black locks fell into the sink. She studied her reflection carefully. Was that a tiny bald spot just above her left temple?

Panicking, she grabbed a brush and ran it through her hair. A huge clump came loose, leaving a bald spot the size of a quarter. She let out a yowl of fear, tried to push the hair back in, realized it wouldn't work, and frantically searched the rest of her head. She found two more bald spots exactly like the first, one on the left side and one on top.

This can't be happening, she thought. My hair can't be falling out! She paced angrily. Police search or no police search, she had to see a doctor—a specialist. What study did hair fall under, dermatology? She'd try the Yellow Pages after she was dressed.

Deciding that it wasn't worth tempting fate, she put

on a faded old Gotham Griffins sweatshirt, blue jeans, and tennis shoes. She tied her hair in a kerchief to protect it. After changing her eye color to a brilliant green with contact lenses, she dug out her phone book.

Sure enough, she found a whole section devoted to dermatology. Then one name leaped out at her:

KATZEN EMILY MD
Certified Amer. Board of Dermatology
Adult & Pediatric Dermatology
Diseases of Skin, Hair, & Nails
Hair-loss treatment
M-F Appts. 10:00 A.M.–4:00 P.M.

Her hands trembling, Selina dialed the number. Three rings later a receptionist answered.

"Hello," Selina said. "My name is Sally Lynx. I'd like an appointment to see Dr. Katzen, please . . . no, I've never seen Dr. Katzen before. . . . I'm having a hair-loss problem. . . . Can you fit me in this morning? . . . How about this afternoon? . . . Fine. I'll see you then. Thanks."

It was barely nine o'clock, which meant she had over six hours to kill. She knew she couldn't just sit there waiting for more hair to fall out. She had to do something—*anything*—to keep busy.

She'd admire her crown, she decided. She went into the dining room, sat down, stared at it. It was still breathtakingly beautiful. She reached out to fondle it. She loved how cool it was to the touch, and how heavy. Picking it up, she turned it this way and that, admiring the gems.

Her hands were drawn to the cat's-eye knob on top—she couldn't resist it. She rubbed the shining

The Cat's-Eye Crown

surface. As she did so she felt it turn in her hands. There was a click and a small latch opened inside the crown. Two thin amber pieces of what looked like horn slid out.

A secret compartment! Selina felt goose bumps prickle the back of her neck. She'd discovered it herself. She was the first person in thousands of years to see these little hidden artifacts.

The two golden slices of horn were as thin as a fingernail, buffed and polished. When she held them up to the light, she could make out some oddly shaped scratches . . . writing of some kind? It looked almost like hieroglyphics.

Intrigued, she found a magnifying glass and examined the markings more closely. They were a real mystery, all right . . . just the thing to kill time while waiting for her appointment with Dr. Katzen.

An expert was what she needed.

Gotham University, just outside the city, had a department of ancient languages. Perhaps she could consult one of its professors. But that could prove dangerous: he or she might recognize the inscriptions, whatever they were, and call the police.

Nevertheless Selina's curiosity was too great. She had to know what it said.

She reached for the phone and had an operator connect her with the proper department at Gotham U.

"Linguistics," a perky woman's voice answered. "Sarah speaking. May I help you?"

"My name is Diana Cheshire," Selina said glibly. "I'm working on an article for *Gotham* magazine, and I need to speak with someone who's an expert on early-Greek writing."

"Dr. Janitz, he's our best."

"Yes. Of course. Dr. Janitz. Certainly Dr. Janitz

would know. Can you arrange an appointment with him for me?"

"He's not in yet. If you'll give me your number—"

"I'm not at my office now. If I were to call back in— say, an hour?"

"I'm sure Dr. Janitz will be in by then."

"Thank you." She hung up. Then she began to pace.

The two horn wafers were distracting, all right. She chewed a fingernail, deep in thought. What could they say that was so important someone would hide them? Made in Japan, probably, she thought sarcastically.

When she called back an hour later, Sarah told her Dr. Janitz would be glad to see her. He had an opening at 11:30 that morning, if she could make it. Selina agreed: the sooner the better, after all.

The speed with which Janitz had set up the appointment made her a bit suspicious. Still, Selina was sure she'd be able to handle his type without any trouble.

She rose. It would take at least an hour to drive out to the university campus, and probably another fifteen minutes to find the right building. If she was going to make their appointment, she'd have to hurry.

An hour and a half later Dr. Janitz met her in his dark, book-lined office in the basement of the Gotham School of Linguistics. The room smelled of camphor and dampness.

Selina wore a short curly red wig, sunglasses, a purple miniskirt, purple fishnet stockings, and high heels. She felt like a beacon, the only spot of color in the place.

The professor, a tall, thin man with a prominent

The Cat's-Eye Crown

Adam's apple and receding hairline, was mushroom pale. He looked as though he lived underground. His watery blue eyes, magnified by thick glasses, kept straying down to her legs as they spoke. His decade-out-of-style suit, with the leather elbow patches, didn't help her confidence in his abilities, either.

Selina slowly crossed her legs. "Oh, Dr. Janitz," she said breathlessly, "I'm so grateful you could see me on such short notice."

Dr. Janitz's eyes seemed glued to Selina's panty hose. "Uh, what was this about, again?"

"I'm doing an article on the wonders of ancient languages," Selina said. "We're going to feature some artifacts from different cultures as illustration, and just for a kick I thought I would try and get one of them translated." She swung her right leg gently at the word "kick."

"Well, I don't know. I'm very busy . . . and of course there's the matter of a fee for any sort of outside consulting service I might do."

"I'm sure our publisher will be happy to compensate you at your usual hourly rate. Just send us a bill. And, of course, we'll give you full credit for the translation."

"Hmm. In that case—"

She placed the two amber slices with their peculiar inscriptions on his stained gray desk blotter. "What do you make of these?" she said.

Dr. Janitz forgot all about her legs and stared in fascination at the faint inscriptions. "Horn, I'd say. Very old. I don't recognize the script right off, but let me see—" He pulled a magnifying glass out of his desk and peered through it carefully. "I'll take a wild guess and peg it as Thraco-Illyrian, some hybrid of Thracian and, perhaps, Phrygian." He looked up for a

Kay Demijohn

moment and curiosity sparkled in his pale eyes. "Where did you get these?"

Selina shrugged and wrinkled her nose. "They belong to a friend of the publisher. I don't really know him."

"I see." Dr. Janitz nodded, muttered to himself, and made some notes on his desk blotter. "Curious. I'll have to cross-check these marks before I can tell you anything."

"Of course."

She watched him pull down two huge, dusty books from the top of a corner bookshelf. He opened one, paged through it for a moment, then shook his head and closed it. A cloud of dust particles shot from between the pages.

Grumbling, he opened the other book. There was no sound in the room except for the dull buzzing of the fluorescent light overhead and the pages turning under Dr. Janitz's hands.

"Aha," he said.

"What?"

"Very interesting. Very interesting indeed." He was chuckling in a peculiar way.

"Can you read it? What does it say? Tell me quickly!"

"My dear, whoever owns these pieces had better be careful." He shook his head. "This is an ancient Illyrian curse."

"Really?"

"Well, unless it's a clever forgery—and I'd have to run some chemical tests to tell you about that."

"I'm afraid we wouldn't have time for that. I'm on deadline. And if I go back and tell the publisher that his friend's artifacts are fake—well, I'd just as soon not get involved with that."

"A shame." Dr. Janitz shrugged. "Well, then, let's

assume the pieces are legitimate, just for the sake of making the translation. It's all here, clear enough." He cleared his voice and said in stentorian tones, "Ill fortune and ill health plague all but the rightful owner of this crown."

Selina tensed when he mentioned the crown, but the reference didn't seem to mean anything to Janitz. Probably doesn't watch the news or read the papers, she thought.

She forced a bubbly giggle. "Oh, come on now. That's not much of a curse! What does it really say?"

"But that's the gist of it, as close as I can tell. Some of the inscription has worn away."

"You're holding out on me. It must say more than that."

"Well, as a matter of fact, it does go on in that vein for some time, enumerating a variety of unpleasant things. Boils, blindness, and broken bones, just to begin with."

"And baldness?"

"Yes, it mentions something about that, too." He leaned forward, studying the bits of horn. "There it is: mange. And then—oh, my. My dear. Yes, it's a very disagreeable curse." His face reddened. Plainly some clauses were involved that he didn't feel like uttering out loud to an attractive young woman.

Despite herself, Selina shivered. "But you said it might be a forgery."

"More than likely. One never knows." Dr. Janitz closed the book. "In any case, I hope the owner has a legitimate bill of sale, or a close relationship with a dermatologist, ophthalmologist, and orthopedist." He smiled weakly. "And perhaps—pardon me—a proctologist also."

Kay Demijohn

"Yes," Selina said, managing a chuckle. "I'll be sure to warn him."

"Will I get a copy of the article, Miss Cheshire? For my files, you know."

"Of course."

"And where may I reach you? After business hours." He was staring at her legs again.

Smiling sweetly, Selina gave him one of her business cards, the one with the name of a long-dead veterinarian and the phone number of the Tokyo stock exchange—minus the country code. "There you go."

"A pleasure to meet you, Ms. Cheshire."

"Oh, no, professor. The pleasure was all mine." With a wink she sashayed triumphantly out the door and up the stairs of the Gotham School of Linguistics.

A curse, huh? That would certainly explain what was happening to her: first the coffee machine, then the bottle of perfume and the sliver of glass in her hand, then her hair falling out. It was a good thing she didn't believe in curses, though, otherwise she might be tempted to sell the crown and be done with it.

She retrieved her steel-gray Cougar from the campus lot, paid the attendant, and was halfway home when the car began lurching strangely. Alarmed, she pulled over to the shoulder, shut off the engine, and climbed out.

You didn't have to be a mechanic to spot the problem: a flat tire. And not another car in sight.

Selina contemplated walking to the service station she'd passed, but it was several miles back. She didn't belong to an auto club, so she couldn't call anyone for help—not that there was a phone around, anyway. She looked up and down the road and didn't see anything, not a building, not a driveway, *nothing*. She really was stuck.

Best to do it herself, she decided, opening the trunk. Huffing and puffing, she wrestled the spare tire out and cranked up the jack under the car. The jack handle caught in her skirt and tore a ragged hole in her stockings. Her wounded hand throbbed. But she managed the job: she was nothing, if not a survivor.

By the time she finished, she had grease all over her hands and a long smear next to her nose. She rolled the flat into the bushes beside the road, got into the Cougar, and brought the motor to roaring life. Then she peeled out with the accelerator floored, little bits of gravel pinging up against the underside of the car.

Her mood was dark. Her triumph at the university had been marred.

Two minutes later the car started lurching again, exactly as before. She pulled over, climbed out, and saw to her disgust and fury that the new tire she'd just put on had gone flat, too.

She kicked it, stubbed her toe, and did a very undignified one-legged dance next to the car. There weren't any other vehicles in sight . . . and she still couldn't see any houses or driveways. Just the forest of pine trees lining the road.

That does it, she thought. Curse or no curse, I'm going home.

She climbed back in, turned on the emergency blinkers, and drove slowly on the shoulder for the next three miles. There, at a service station, she had the mechanic on duty replace all four tires plus the spare.

While he was working, she went to the ladies' room to freshen up. She looked atrocious, she decided, studying herself in the mirror. Her wig was slightly askew; she straightened it. Then she washed her face, getting off most of the grease, and dug out her compact to fix her makeup.

Kay Demijohn

With dismay she noticed what appeared to be a rash developing below the left corner of her mouth, marring her otherwise flawless skin. Perfect, just perfect, she thought. She'd always had flawless skin; now she was breaking out.

What had Dr. Janitz said? *Ill fortune and ill health plague all but the rightful owner of this crown.* There had been something else. *Boils, blindness, and broken bones just to begin with.* She thought of her face. Then she thought of the strange bald spots on her head. Mange? she wondered.

It's a good thing I'm not superstitious, she told herself again. But this time she didn't sound so sure.

When she finally made it back to her penthouse, she replaced the two pieces of horn in their little secret compartment in the crown. She changed clothes quickly, checked her head to make sure no more hair had fallen out—none had—then headed downstairs. She was through with cars for the day. She planned on taking the subway to Dr. Katzen's office.

The trip was uneventful, which was a pleasant enough surprise after what was turning into a day of disasters. Dr. Katzen was even running near to her schedule. At 3:20 P.M., Selina found herself ushered into an antiseptic, gleamingly white medical room. She seated herself on the stainless-steel edge of the bed and waited.

Dr. Katzen—a short, middle-aged woman in a white lab coat, her hair in a bun—came bustling in, clipboard in hand. "What seems to be the trouble?"

"I've developed some bald spots," Selina said, removing the kerchief from around her hair.

Dr. Katzen pulled a lamp closer, tilted Selina's head,

and examined the three hairless areas. "Um-hmm," she muttered several times.

"Do you know what's causing it?" Selina asked.

"No, but we can certainly try to find out. It could be any number of things—as simple as an allergy, as complex as subdermal mites."

"Mites?" Selina asked, a sinking feeling inside.

"Yes. It's more common than most people realize. In dogs and cats it's called—"

"Mange," Selina finished. She swallowed; there was a huge lump in her throat.

"Yes, that's right," Dr. Katzen said, a puzzled look on her face. "But don't worry, it's treatable. Most people who are diagnosed with subdermal mites recover one hundred percent; the hair loss is only temporary."

"I also seem to be developing a rash," Selina said. She indicated the redness around her lip.

"Yes, not too uncommon. Might be poison oak or poison sumac, though you don't see that much this time of year. I'll give you some ointment. You did the right thing in coming to me. We have to catch this sort of thing before it gets serious. You can get some nasty facial boils if you're not careful."

Dr. Katzen took a blood sample, then sent Selina to the front desk to schedule a follow-up appointment.

Selina took a taxi home, brooding on her problems. She really *didn't* believe in curses, she kept telling herself. But why take chances? She'd get rid of the crown. The gold and gems were valued at twenty-five million. She ought to be able to get a million or two for it, cash.

She knew a lot of fences. In her profession, you had to: each had a different specialty. Some dealt with

Kay Demijohn

artwork, some sculpture, others dealt in bonds and negotiable securities, and still others specialized in jewelry.

She sprawled on her sofa with Charlotte, her long-haired calico kitten curled up on her tummy, as she went through her Rolodex. Of course, her apartment's telephone was neither registered under her name nor billed to her address. Records were such bothersome things. She preferred to keep her calls private, and saw to it that no one could find, much less figure out, her phone statements. A smart cat leaves no obvious paper trails.

"Ah," she said. "No-Look Louie." Louie specialized in moving high-priced works of art to private collectors overseas. The crown was valuable for its gold and gems, but it was more valuable as an artifact . . . priceless, even. If anyone could get top dollar on the overseas market, Louie could.

She didn't like dealing with Louie because of his one big eccentricity: he had a small head—a very, *very* small head—and had an inferiority complex about it. He couldn't believe anyone would just look at him out of politeness. The slightest glance could set him off on a tirade about how you were making fun of him. When you met Louie, you literally had to keep your eyes averted at all times. Despite that, he was a good fence, with a steady European customer base.

She punched his number. The phone rang twice, then Louie's gruff voice answered: "Yeah?"

"Louie, darling, it's me." She let a sexy, slinky purr into her voice. "Have I got a package for *you*."

"Listen, sweetheart, whoever you are, the cops were in here today hassling me about some stolen crown I don't know nothin' about and *don't want* to know nothin' about. Get it?"

The Cat's-Eye Crown

"Got it." Selina hung up, frowning. "Dancing Donna," she muttered. "She can handle it."

Dancing Donna was one of her favorite fences. Tall, black, slinky Donna Washington had once been a top fashion model, until age had caught up with her. Now she moonlighted as a topless dancer at night while running a second-rate fencing outfit during the day. You didn't get top dollar from Donna, but you got respect. And Selina actually *liked* her: they had a lot in common.

Donna's phone rang once, twice, then her answering machine came on. "I'm out," it said. "Leave a message or call back later." *Beep!*

"It's me, Donna," Selina said. "I've got a little bit of business for you."

"Darling!" Donna cried. "Don't hang up. I'm screening my calls."

"As usual."

"But of course I'd pick up for you. What's this little bit of business? Tell me all about it."

"It's big. *Very* big. Golden. Jeweled. Ancient."

There was a meaningful silence.

"It was you, then," Donna said at last, in awe.

"As a matter of fact, yes."

"Honey, I'm proud of you. And I'd love to hear the whole story. We ought to do lunch and you can tell me about it then. In two or three months, maybe?"

"What are you saying, Donna?"

"You know how much I wish I could handle this deal for you, honey."

"But?"

"I can't. Simply can't touch it. I don't dare."

"Come on. What are you trying to tell me?"

Donna sighed deeply. "I wish I could help you, dearest. I really do. But I'm being watched, I'm absolutely sure of it. Twenty-four-hour surveillance. I can't even

flush the toilet without some cop making a notation
about it in his little black book. We shouldn't even be
staying on the phone this long. They've got eyes on all
of the best fences in Gotham. No one will touch that
crown, nobody, N-O-B-O-D-Y. Don't waste your breath
calling X or Y or Z, and you know who I mean. You'll
have to fence it yourself, and abroad. Try Japan."

"You're kidding."

"Wish I were. If this line weren't scrambled, they'd
be after you even as we speak. But I shouldn't stay on.
I'm going to flush the toilet some more. It drives them
crazy. Good luck, Selina. Stay in touch."

Donna hung up.

"Just great," Selina muttered. "How do I get this
thing to Japan? Mail it?"

Feeling frustrated, she flipped through her Rolodex,
looking for some fence—any fence—who might be able
to unload the wretched crown. She dialed one, then
another, then another. All gave her the same sad
story: sorry, not this one, no way. Still she dialed,
gradually growing more and more frantic. Surely
someone somewhere would want the blasted thing.

Boils—broken bones—blindness.

She was wrong.

When she'd exhausted her list of fences, she just sat
there in numb shock. Nobody wanted it.

It had been a long day already; she felt tense and
near the point of nervous collapse. Better catch a
quick nap, she thought. Let my subconscious work on
the problem.

She stretched out—Charlotte still curled up on her
stomach—and closed her eyes. Sleep came quickly, but
it was uneasy, full of troubled fragments and images.

Finally she began to dream. In her dream she was
being surrounded by every person who had ever worn

The Cat's-Eye Crown

the crown. Beggars and thieves, noblemen and noble-women, they formed a jostling, angry mob in her living room, tearing the upholstery with their swords, getting fingerprints on the silver, and leaving muddy footprints on the rugs. They called for the crown—or her blood.

She kept trying to explain it to them, to make them understand that she really wasn't to blame. She was a victim of society. Then she tried to give them the crown, but she just couldn't find it. If they would just be patient, give her some time, she was certain that she would locate it and give it to them. She promised she'd do it just as soon as she possibly could.

"Please," she said. "Please, just wait a little longer."

"Your time has run out," said a beggar with Dr. Janitz's watery blue eyes and weak smile. "You know the rules. Boils, broken bones, and blindness."

"Please," Selina said. "No, not yet."

"Boils, broken bones, and blindness . . . boils, broken bones, and blindness . . . boils, broken bones, and blindness . . ."

Selina woke with a gasp, sitting up. The kitten gave a startled meow and hopped to the floor. Selina was soaked with sweat and her arms and legs felt shaky.

"Some dream," she said to the kitten. She shook her head, then stood. It was just as well she'd awakened; it was time to start dinner.

At 6:00 P.M. the microwave blew out while Selina was thawing a steak for her supper. It took half the apartment's circuit breakers with it. Muttering under her breath, Selina unplugged the microwave and switched the power back on.

At 6:40, as she was boiling potatoes, a sudden burst of gas from the stove created a fireball. It seared her

Kay Demijohn

eyebrows and sent her diving for cover—but it only lasted a second. Shaking, she switched off the gas, stuck the pot (water, potatoes, and all) into the refrigerator, and phoned out for pizza.

At 7:15, the television in her living room went out.

At 7:18, the television in her bedroom went out.

At 7:24, the pizza arrived. It was cold, smelled funny, and had little green specks on it that seemed to be moving. Selina threw it out. She didn't even bother calling the pizza place to complain.

At 7:50, the refrigerator died. She noticed it when she got out a diet soda: the light inside didn't come on. She spent ten minutes checking fuses and power cords before giving up. It just *quit* as far as she could tell.

At 8:05, her telephone rang. She scooped it up, puzzled. Nobody had this number. It was *completely* unlisted.

Instead of a voice on the line, though, there was a weird electronic warbling. She slammed the receiver down. Instantly it began to ring again.

Boils—broken bones—blindness. Her hand throbbed where she'd caught it on the sliver of glass that morning.

"All right!" she screamed at the crown. "Enough! I can't stand it! Stop it, stop it, *stop it!*"

The phone stopped ringing. In the kitchen, she heard the refrigerator whir to life. It only lasted a second, then died away—like a ray of hope being offered to her, if only she cooperated.

I've got to get rid of you, she thought as she looked at the crown. Right now. Right away, before everything I own goes to pieces. Including me.

But how? She couldn't simply call up the police or Batman and just give the crown back. No, that would be far too embarrassing, and far too complicated to

The Cat's-Eye Crown

manage safely. Somehow she would have to get back into that museum and leave it there. That would amount to restoring it to its rightful owner—which ought to serve to lift the curse. She hoped.

The decision made, she felt as though a weight had been lifted from her shoulders. She would take it back, return it to its rightful owners, and never so much as *look* at ancient artifacts again.

Flushed with energy, Selina packed up the crown and put it into a small padded box. The sun was already down; since the museum closed at 6:00 P.M., she hoped to find it deserted.

She put on her cat suit except for the cowl, a black biker's jacket, and shiny spiked heels. Then she hurried down to the garage.

Rather than the Cougar on her Electric Leopard, Selina went straight to a tarp at the back of her storage area. Underneath sat a classic bike—the Triumph Tiger, glossy blue gray, graceful, powerful, and best of all, customized for speed, maneuverability, and silence.

She put on her cowl, becoming Catwoman, then pulled a custom-built black safety helmet over her head. Her cowl's cat ears fit neatly inside. When she strapped the helmet on and lowered the transparent visor, her head was completely covered.

She wheeled the vehicle out of the garage and down the street, hopping on the seat to coast a good two blocks downhill before starting the motor. It purred to life. She switched on the headlight, turned, and headed downtown.

Even this late, traffic was heavy. She bypassed all of the major arteries, taking a series of alleys and side streets across town to Gotham Park. The lights of the towering apartment houses blazed above her, but there were few people out. Now and then she saw an occasional pedestrian walking a dog from lamppost to lamppost, but that was it.

Gotham Park at this hour was quiet and deserted, the trees a looming presence against the night sky. Gotham Museum was only two blocks away; it would be easy to get there unseen.

Catwoman stopped the Tiger, killed its motor, and dismounted. The museum, long after closing hours now, would be protected only by its ancient security system and a few sleepy guards. In minutes she'd be inside.

She carefully concealed the bike in some bushes. With an almost gay abandon in her walk, anticipating her liberation from the weight at her waist, she headed for the museum.

A block away, she rounded a corner and came to a halt, frozen in her tracks. If she had had a tail, she would have twitched it in a frenzy of alarm.

Everything was very different now. The place was floodlit and almost as bright as noon. Two armed guards stood outside each exit. There was no way she could get close to the building without being noticed. Not tonight. She would have to take the crown back home again.

A small voice inside her head told her just to leave the crown in the employees' parking lot. Somebody would find it sooner or later. For a moment she weakened: it was so tempting to be done with the problem.

But no. What if somebody else took it? Or it was never found? Would she ever be free of the curse? Somehow she didn't think so. Not unless she returned it in person.

She backed up, hissing under her breath, and crouched in the shadows to think things through. A dozen plans ran through her mind, but she quickly rejected them all as impossible. Perhaps she could get to the museum's roof from an adjacent building—

The Cat's-Eye Crown

She turned to try for the roof and collided with a tall, dark shape. Her eyes traveled up past the golden emblem of a bat to the familiar black cowl with its tall, pointy ears.

"Batman—" she gasped, taking a step back.

"How do you feel, Selina?" he said. "You don't look well."

"I—I—" She swallowed, forced her voice to silky smoothness, and started over. "You know things are rough all over, Batman dear."

He took a half step forward; she took a full step back. "Why have you staked out the museum tonight, Selina?" he demanded. "Wasn't the crown enough?"

"You're toying with me, lover," she said. "Not nice."

"I want the crown back," he said. "Where is it, Selina?"

"I have it with me," she cried, thrusting the sack into his hands. "Take it! It's all yours!"

And, as he opened the sack and reached in, she turned and fled. Batman didn't follow.

Batman drew out the magnificent Cat's-Eye Crown. Even in the dim light, its gems sparkled with inner fire. Nodding, he put it back into the sack, turned, and strolled at a leisurely pace to where the Batmobile waited. He'd return it to Commissioner Gordon the next day; now he had some sleep to catch up on . . . but first he had a phone call to make.

When he reached the Batcave, he dialed a number he'd memorized when he broke into Selina Kyle's apartment the night before. It had been an easy thing to find it, with the secret transmitter Artemis MacIntyre had hidden in the crown for him.

Kay Demijohn

A sleepy Selina Kyle answered on the second ring: "Hello?"

"Hello, Selina. This is Batman," he said.

"Batman?" Her voice went up an octave. "How did you get this number?"

"It's written on your phone."

There was perfect silence for a long moment. When Selina spoke again, it was with a sexy, husky voice. "What can I do for you, lover?"

"I just wanted to let you know that your appliances will work right if you remove the miniature radio-activated super magnets I stuck next to their motors."

"What?"

"And you don't have to visit Dr. Katzen again. It's not subdermal head mites; the crown was coated with a thin layer of an invisible hair-removal powder. Your bald spots will grow in."

She made a hissing sound through her teeth. "And I suppose you shot my tires from the woods."

"With an air rifle."

"And called my phone with some weird electronic device."

"Yes."

"And broke my bottle of perfume by remote control."

"No, that was your own clumsiness." He chuckled apologetically. "You were very quick to blame it on the curse, though."

"How do you know about it, then?"

"From the microphones I planted all over your apartment. The crown had a tracking device, so I found your current lair with no trouble."

"That was *so* unfair of you."

"Crime doesn't pay, Selina. I hope you've learned your lesson."

He hung up on her sputtering protests.

The City That Could Not Breathe

WILL MURRAY

The first night the air turned blue over Lower Gotham, no one died.

It happened at a quarter to midnight. There was a full moon. A blue moon, oddly enough. The second day of the coldest December in a decade. The rare moon rose in the east, a chimera of crystal. Seen from Gotham Village, it appeared to climb the Art Deco spire of Gotham Tower, once the tallest man-made structure in the world, and now merely the oldest Depression-era skyscraper still standing in Gotham.

At a quarter to midnight the cold blue moon stood poised atop the Gotham Tower Spindle in a rare juxtaposition of the celestial and the earthly. A malicious-looking cloud scudded along, dragging a tattered gray domino mask across the lunar face. A moment later the swelling cloud swallowed the moon, and there was darkness.

The blue shine came then. It was brief. Beyond the six-square-block blight called the Rust Scab, home only to the homeless, it was visible as a lambent glow—sourceless and ethereal. Like foxfire.

Lower Gotham slumbered. Few beheld the sight. Even cabdrivers avoided the Rust Scab.

The few who saw the dome of sapphire radiance swell over the Rust Scab were drawn to apartment windows by the roaring.

If the blue radiance was soft, the accompanying sounds were harsh, discordant. The roaring was the least of it. There were cries—throaty shrieks and growlings, commingled into one angry knot of sound as if the beasts of Gotham Zoo had all gone mad at once.

Except the cages of Gotham Zoo were empty—and had been for months.

Abruptly the blue light collapsed, and the low subterranean rumble of the G train rattling northward drowned out the feral symphony.

After the subway had passed, the sounds were gone as well.

Then the blue moon returned and Gotham City slept on, undreaming, unsuspecting, unprepared.

The next morning, the *Gotham Gazette* carried a brief item on page 28 about the feral din heard in the vicinity of the Rust Scab. It mentioned no blue glow, only the fact that police had been dispatched to the area and, hearing no sounds, dismissed the reports. The cops didn't venture far into the Rust Scab. People who did—even those wearing badges—were sometimes found with their throats slashed by tools not quite sharp enough for the job.

The item neglected to mention that unpleasant fact of city life. But it did wonder in print if the ghosts of the now closed Gotham Zoo hadn't come back to haunt the city that had allowed it to wither away like some exotic garden.

The morning talk-show jockeys picked up the item and soon the airwaves were buzzing about "phantom lions." But it was no joke. Gotham Zoo was sorely missed, and the man believed responsible for its demise, millionaire developer Kendall Sharp, was pilloried for buying the landmark on the cheap and allowing it to slip into bankruptcy and decay.

Sharp, on the verge of going belly-up himself, at first declined all offers to enter the public discussion. But as the day wore on and he increasingly found himself the target of scorn, he flung his two cents' worth into the argument.

"Listen," Sharp said peevishly. "That zoo was on the ropes when I took it over. And the people wouldn't support it. If you want my opinion, this city isn't classy enough to support a world-class zoo."

An opinion that only enraged proud Gothamites.

That evening local newcasts reported homeless people taking up residence in areas where they normally weren't seen. Reporters were sent out to interview this latest wave of the disenfranchised. Those few willing to talk on camera explained that they wanted to get away from "the jungle." Reporters assumed they meant the various hobo jungles that dotted the city's outskirts.

They assumed wrong.

Later that evening the blue radiance completely enveloped the Rust Scab for five minutes to the exact second, and seventeen people died.

There was no moon, no roaring sounds, and the seventeen who died were too busy trying to suck air into their starving lungs to cry out. No one knew they had died until the morning, when their purple-faced bodies began turning up in Dumpsters all over the city and floating in the noisome river.

That day, the talk-show hosts were calling it the work of the worst strangler to stalk Gotham City in a generation.

By the time the six o'clock news was aired, Police Commissioner James W. Gordon was doing a live remote in front of police headquarters.

"There is no reason to panic," he insisted in his gruff voice. "Repeat, citizens should take only the usual precautions they normally take against random crime. While we are ruling nothing out at this time, there is no evidence that these deaths are homicides."

The statement was as clear as it could possibly be. Nevertheless reporters began badgering him.

"Commissioner Gordon, do you have any suspects at this time?"

"Commissioner Gordon, why is this monster striking the homeless?"

"Commissioner Gordon, have you any witnesses?"

Commissioner Gordon's face slowly turned a beet red. He took a deep breath and said in a voice as calm as he could make it, "Pay attention. There may not *be* a strangler!"

"Commissioner Gordon," a print reporter asked as he absently recorded the previous statement, "how does this crime compare with the Boston Strangler case?"

"Listen to me!" the commissioner shouted. "These are not strangulations! There are no ligature marks,

The City That Could Not Breathe

no neck bruises, no signs of foul play. In every case, the deceased died from simple asphyxiation."

A short silence descended on the gathered press. Camcorders whirred monotonously. Occasionally a pencil scraped shorthand marks on a notepad.

Then the questions flew again.

"Commissioner Gordon, are these deaths smog-related?"

"Commissioner Gordon, what is the city planning to do about these toxic fumes?"

This time Commissioner Gordon turned thermometer red and swallowed his peppery opinion of the media.

In his palatial estate, Bruce Wayne fingered his square jaw as he watched the comic inquisition, his midnight-blue eyes thoughtful. Gordon, in his attempt to avoid panicking the populace, had instead been trapped into inciting a health crisis.

Wayne rang for his butler, and when he appeared, lean and very correct, Wayne said, "Coffee, Alfred. Lots of it."

"Very good, Master Bruce."

Alfred withdrew.

Then Wayne went to the great casement windows and ran the curtains apart. The skies were overcast, like low-hanging slate. Perfect bat-signal weather.

He smiled tightly. If he knew his old friend Gordon, it would be just a matter of time. . . .

The Gotham County Morgue was booked solid. On a normal night there were at least five homicides, and an accidental death or two.

Tonight every refrigerated drawer was occupied, and the three stained porcelain autopsy tables overflowed with the dangling limbs of purple-faced corpses.

The Batman moved among the dead, his gloved hands touching dead throats, his glittering eyes alert behind die-cut eyeholes.

"Not a mark on any of them," Commissioner Gordon said tightly. "If there were, we could make sense of this travesty."

Choosing one at random, Batman pulled on a drawer handle. A slab squeaked out on steel rollers badly in need of oil. He plucked the sheet off the body. This wretch was more lavender than purple in the face. The eyes were closed, the mouth contorted. And like the others, his weather-beaten face bore deep care lines made harsher by the agony of his death.

"Not drowned?" Batman asked in a faraway voice.

"No water in the lungs."

Batman lifted the corpse's stiff-fingered hands. The nails were longish and blackened by grime.

"They were not locked in an airtight chamber," he said. "No broken nails. A man fighting for his life would claw and scratch at the walls around him."

Gordon nodded soberly. "In extreme cases, at one another. But none of the bodies bear scratch marks. They were murdered separately, although the times of death coincide exactly—if the coroner can be believed."

The Dark Knight returned the protesting slab to its niche.

"Killed at the same time, in the same weird manner, but not in a confined space," he said slowly.

"I know it makes no sense."

"Read the *Gazette* yesterday?"

The City That Could Not Breathe

Gordon spat. "That rag!"

"Skip the editorials," Batman said dryly. "Yesterday's edition made mention of roaring sounds heard in the vicinity of the Rust Scab."

Gordon cocked a grizzled eyebrow. "Roaring?"

"Described as the greatest cat fight heard outside of the Serengetti Plain."

"How does this—"

"Remember the homeless who began turning up in unlikely parts of town yesterday? Some of them claimed that they just wanted to get away from what they called 'the jungle.' "

Commissioner Gordon narrowed wise old eyes. "The Rust Scab! It's been practically taken over by homeless people since it was condemned. Is it possible? These poor wretches—killed in the same place, their bodies dispersed?"

"Very possible."

"But why?"

"I think I'll take a spin through the Rust Scab," murmured Batman, turning in a swirl of scalloped-edged wings.

Gordon called after him, "Good luck." It sounded like a prayer.

The passing of twenty-four hours had shaven dull the eastern edge of the now waning moon as the Batmobile, running without lights, skimmed into the Rust Scab.

Batman had prowled the blighted spot before. It had not changed. Plywood still sealed off building entrances and windows. Windblown trash surged along cracked gutters, as always. Only one thing was different.

Will Murray

The rusty fire-blackened ash cans stood cold and empty, like depth charges dropped from some higher realm. No tattered-gloved fingers hovered over smoky embers for warmth. No furtive figures withdrew into alley mouths as the Batmobile's headlights raked the still emptiness. Rats lay dead everywhere.

And more surprisingly, no brickbats sailed from shattered upper-story windows to bounce off the Batmobile's titanium-and-ceramic hull.

The Rust Scab, once the last refuge for the city's worst elements, the rudderless and the depraved alike, was a ghost town of crumbling skyscrapers and abandoned office buildings.

The Batmobile coasted to a stop. The Dark Knight popped the cockpit hatch and climbed out, a black-and-gray specter.

Under his cowl, his ears strained to pick out sounds. There were no indications of life. Nothing but the unforgiving night wind whistling through concrete canyons and shattered windows.

Batman stalked the Rust Scab, his exposed mouth thinning in distaste.

Once, in the days of his father, this had been the heart of metropolitan Gotham. Here were erected the first true skyscrapers in the city—indeed, in the world. Now it might have been a small city depopulated by a neutron bomb and left to corrode and decay.

All things age and fall into disuse, but the builders of multiple-story skyscrapers like the Gotham Tower never envisioned the day when they would have to come down. To date, the City Commission on Urban Renovation had not figured out a way to raze the Rust Scab without the thousands of linear rods of concrete and steel-girder debris spilling out into the still-viable sectors of the city surrounding the blighted zone.

The City That Could Not Breathe

From his utility belt, Batman plucked a handheld
shotgun mike. He thumbed it on and aimed the para-
bolic dish around.

The wind, amplified, shrieked metallically at him.
He eased down the volume.

On the backsweep, the device picked out a soft mew.

At the sound, he stiffened his gloved hand and
waited. Another mew came. And following it, a
breathy voice saying, "Go, Spooky!"

The sound seemed to be coming from the Gotham
Tower. Once a magnificent landmark. Now every
window—all sixty-five hundred—boarded up with
weather-beaten plywood.

Following the mike, the Batman floated toward the
entrance door. The old revolving doors lay broken and
twisted, glittering with glass-shard teeth.

The Dark Knight gathered up his cloak and wormed
through the bent brass frame into the marble lobby.
Despite his best stealthy technique, glass gritted
under his blue-black boots.

Cages long removed from their banks, the elevator
shafts stood exposed, stained with long streaks of oil
and rust. Batman moved to a fire door and passed into
the stairwell beyond. The door valved imperfectly
shut, cutting off all but a thin triangle of light.

His mike picked up no sounds from below. From
above, Batman detected soft—very soft—footfalls. He
went up, his heavy batwing cloak quaking with every
step.

There was no light now. Debris lay scattered on the
well-worn steps. Each step was a moment of nervous
anticipation. Once, his right foot came into contact
with a hard round shape. Batman moved his foot
slightly and felt the unsettling sensation of a loose

glass bottle. Steadying it, the Dark Knight stepped over carefully.

He continued mounting the steps, placing his feet with care. The bottle might only have been a discard. More likely it was a crude burglar alarm set to trip the unwary.

On a landing, the Dark Knight paused and powered up his mike. The sounds coming out of the tiny loudspeaker were faint, scuttling. A mouse or rat might have made them.

Batman dismissed that theory a few steps along, when his descending boot produced a squishy noise mixed in with the brittle breaking of thin bones. He nudged the thing into a corner and, using his spread cloak to muffle the backglow, thumbed on a penlight.

It disclosed a rat, jaws frozen in a death gasp.

Grimly he continued on.

The Dark Knight did not detect the trip wire below the sixth-floor landing until his shin made contact and a sharp click made him aware of the presence of a booby trap.

In the flash of a second a thousand thoughts can go through a man's mind. Batman had visions of an antipersonnel mine taking off his legs, poison gas squirting out of hidden nozzles, and—not as wild as it might sound because it had actually happened to him once before—a cocked crossbow sending a hardwood shaft toward one of his major organs.

None of these dire things happened. Instead the impenetrably dark stairwell became alive with din—a roaring, snapping, snarling cacophony as if a dozen jungle cats had unexpectedly happened upon one another and had the feline equivalent of a freeway pileup.

The sounds were overwhelming. Batman was forced

to clap his hands over his ears. Amplified. Loudspeakers. He whipped out his penlight and thumbed it on, splashing light around the stairs, seeking the ear-punishing source.

The trip wire at his feet, the light disclosed, remained taut. The line went to an eyelet screwed into the wall and continued up to the wall-mounted loudspeaker at the next landing.

Quickly Batman stepped over the wire and went to it.

The loudspeaker had a microcassette recorder attached to it. The capstans were turning slowly. Batman hit the off switch, and the feral cacophony stopped in midhowl.

He popped the tape and stowed it in his utility belt.

The Dark Knight was about to resume his climb when a cool, ultrafemale voice purred, "Don't look so smug. Some of us had sense enough to step *over* the wire."

Batman whirled, eyes straining upward. His flash found a form.

Midway up the next flight of steps, a supple black-clad figure stood, hands resting on svelte hips, a cupid-bow mouth forming a self-satisfied smile.

"Selina!" Batman hissed.

The slinky figure gave a low hiss and said, "Please! Tonight I'm Catwoman."

Hands coming off hips, she came down the steps to stand before him. Selina Kyle—aka the Catwoman—smiled through her furry cat mask. In the dim light it was hard to tell where human flesh left off and the pert-eared cat cowl began. Her entire body was sheathed in gray fur. Perfect winter attire—for Gotham's most notorious cat burglar.

"What are you doing here?" Batman demanded.

"Breaking no laws for one thing. So lose the attitude."

"I asked a question," Batman said coolly.

She ran steely glove claws down his chest bat insignia, producing a metal-on-metal scritching. "You heard the cats," she purred. "Need you ask?"

"Taped sounds."

"Maybe. Maybe not."

Batman grabbed the slim wrist and squeezed. "What do you know?"

"Ease off!"

"People are dead, Selina. I want answers."

"Remember when Gotham Zoo was more than a collection of empty cages?" Catwoman asked in a low throaty voice.

"Yes."

"Me too. One of my favorite places, in fact. I had a favorite inmate, too. Bast. Name ring a bell in your belfry?"

Batman nodded grimly. "Black panther. Sumatran."

Catwoman smiled in return. "Describes Bast to a whisker. She was supposed to have been shipped to the San Diego Zoo when Gotham Zoo was liquidated."

"Supposed?"

Catwoman disengaged her hand and shrugged. "I got sentimental and I flew out there. No Bast. The curator never heard of her. I checked. None of the other cats from the zoo have been seen either."

"The papers get their facts mixed up sometimes," Batman pointed out, searching her half-masked face for any signs of truth or deceit. He found neither. Selina Kyle was made that way. Perhaps she had never learned the difference.

"That's what I thought. But I heard all that roaring the other night. Mixed in was Bast's growl."

"Growl?"

Catlike eyes flared. "Don't look at me like that! I'd know that delicious growl anywhere." Her voice dropped seductively. "Wish I had one just like it—to keep the boys in line."

Batman demanded, "Curiosity brought you here? Is that what you're saying?"

"I think Bast is around here somewhere."

"Ridicu—"

Down the stairs came a furry flash of black and white.

Catwoman looked up. "Spooky!"

Bristling like a porcupine, a small black cat with tuxedo markings raced between Catwoman's legs and on down the stairs. Batman followed it with his penlight. On white paws, it bounded over the trip wire and continued on.

Catwoman jumped after it, calling, "Wait up, you cub!"

The gloom swallowed them both.

The Dark Knight caught up with them in the lobby.

Catwoman had cornered the cat, back arched and tail erect as it hissed, teeth bared, greenish eyes wild with fear. She dropped to her haunches before it, dropping her voice, too.

"Here, Spooky. Good Spookins. Come here, girl."

Reluctantly the tuxedo cat allowed herself to be gathered up. She was mostly black, with a white chin that swelled into a powdered-sugar breast.

Catwoman stroked her fear-ruffled fur and purred into one folded-back ear. The cat's needle claws clung to her furry arms like a kitten clings to its mother.

"Friend of yours?" Batman asked quietly.

"Spooky's a huntress. I sent her ahead to see what she could see."

"And report back?" Batman asked ironically.

"Unlike me, she can see in the dark. And she knows when to retreat. My early-warning system. Aren't you, Spookins?"

Batman ran a gloved finger between the cat's ears. Its pupils were very large and very black.

"Obviously she *did* come upon something that scared her," he admitted.

"Obviously," Catwoman said dryly.

The air turned blue then. All around them. It smelled of unleashed electricity.

Batman still held his penlight. It fell from his fingers, clattering to the floor. His hands went to his throat. His eyes locked with Catwoman's. A sharp uncomprehending glance passed between them.

The black cat leaped to the marble floor. Selina Kyle, self-styled Catwoman, strained to inhale oxygen.

Oxygen that was no longer present!

Quickly Batman dug a gas mask out of his utility belt, took a quick hit of oxygen, and then grabbed the back of Catwoman's neck with one hand. As he pressed the mask to her face she took in three quick breaths. Batman, feeling his lungs ignite with a low burning, brought the Plexiglas mask back to his own grim mouth.

Catwoman held her breath, eyes frightened. The Dark Knight held up five fingers to her face, flashed them twice.

Catwoman nodded. She understood. They had a ten-minute supply of oxygen. No more.

Batman then took her by the arm and urged her toward the twisted revolving door.

Selina broke free and knelt to gather up Spooky, gasping and contorting on the floor. Together, they hurried along, walking as if on eggshells.

When the mask was again passed to her, Catwoman put it to the cat's tiny lioness face. She revived. Then Selina took two long breaths and returned the mask to Batman.

They passed out into the ruin of Renwick Street, stumbling only a little. Out here, the night air was lambent with a soft azure glow that looked peaceful but was as breathable as methane.

Batman propelled Catwoman north, the two sharing the gas mask like scuba divers in distress shared an oxygen tank. It was taking too long. They dared not run because that would consume too much oxygen too fast. Around the corner, the Batmobile stood crouching. Not one hundred feet away. A short sprint normally. Under the circumstances, it might as well have been a mile.

Batman brought Catwoman to a halt, pulled her in front of him. She had the mask to her face now. In her free hand Spooky squirmed and clawed, gasping audibly, as if dying.

Eyes hard, Batman pointed a black remorseless finger at the struggling feline.

Catwoman understood instantly. She shook her head no. Batman repeated the gesture. Catwoman repeated hers. And Batman then drew a harsh finger across his own throat and hers.

Angrily she pushed the gas mask into his face with enough force to sting his upper lip.

Furiously he moved her along. They stumbled another few yards.

And then the voice came.

It was like the aural equivalent of the blue shining,

all around them. In stentorian tones, it thundered: *"Citizens of Gotham City! If a ransom of fifty million dollars is not paid by tomorrow midnight, all of you will writhe under my thrall! You have less than a day to decide your fates! I am the Unseen Strangler!"*

The voice was deafening. It forced them to their knees. Spooky leaped to freedom, and collapsed, contorting like a worm on a fishhook.

On her belly, teeth bared, Catwoman crawled toward her.

The Dark Knight felt a brief surge of admiration for the young adventuress's courage. But his gas-mask indicator told him less than two minutes of air remained.

He tried to shout sense at the valiant woman. No air remained in his lungs. So no words came out. Cursing inwardly, he went to her side, knelt, and fed her oxygen.

Catwoman angrily yanked the mask from her face. Batman forced it back. They struggled. Finally the Dark Knight relented and allowed the mask to be pressed to the thrashing cat's tiny nose. The hissing of the precious air, most of it escaping, made Batman's blood run cold.

He left them there.

It was a desperate move. It was a desperate situation. The Dark Knight ran, flat-footed, pacing himself. The oxygen in his lungs was too soon used up and they began crying for a fresh supply. The pumping of his heart was in his ears. His brain seemed to squeeze in his head like a sponge under cruel fingers. His vision went gray at the edges.

Once, he fell. Forcing himself to go on, Batman regained his feet. He ran on, no longer sure he was moving in the right direction. He saw only a gray field

The City That Could Not Breathe

now. There were crisscrossed black lines in the gray, like a test pattern. He was, cruelty of ironic cruelties, as blind as a bat.

A blood roaring filled his ears when he slammed into a hard obstacle. Swallowing a bark of pain, he reached out—and felt the sleek cold comfort lines of the waiting Batmobile.

Gasping, Batman groped for the cockpit hatch. It hummed back when he touched a hidden catch and he flung himself in, like a wounded winged thing retreating into its nest.

He fumbled for the overhead switch. Through the growing blood roar in his ears, he heard the cockpit hatch hum, catch, and lock securely.

Batman knew he was not safe yet. The dash was a baroque mélange of electronics. He reached out with all ten fingers for the oxygen release button. It was one of a nondescript array. Gloved fingers inadvertently triggered the windshield wipers, air conditioner, and rear-deck smoke dispenser before the unmistakable hiss of the chassis oxygen tanks releasing breathable air sounded faintly in what seemed to be the far, far distance.

The Dark Knight was breathing normally when he woke up. Adrenaline cleared his brain instantly. Straightening in the seat, he hit the main engine starter button and sent the sleek road machine squealing toward two prostrate figures just ahead. The Batmobile's gas turbine engine sputtered oddly, but he ignored the warning sound.

Braking before the two still feline forms, Batman cut the cockpit oxygen supply and cracked the hatch in one motion.

Out and to Catwoman's side in three long strides. He gathered up Selina Kyle, dropped her in the Batmobile passenger seat, and although it was a foolish thing to do, went back for the cat, Spooky.

When they were all sealed inside and oxygen was filling the confined space, Batman gunned the Batmobile as far away from the Rust Scab as possible.

Even beyond the outer edge of the zone, the blue lambency suffused the air. Here, cars had run into hydrants, one another, or just stopped, spilling gasping occupants from askew doors.

At an intersection, a multiple car crash blocked all traffic. Before he could hit the brakes, the Batmobile coasted to a dead stop, engine muttering like an angry predator.

Then it died completely!

Catwoman had her lungs working by that point. She blinked, looked about with dazed eyes, then remembered Spooky. The cat lay limp on her lap.

She gave it a nudge, muttering, "Wake up, sleepyhead."

The feline rolled over, unresponsive.

"Damn you!" Catwoman said, giving Spooky's chest a double-handed squeeze. Nothing happened. She pried tiny jaws apart with gloved thumbs and blew air into the slack mouth. Once. Twice. Thrice.

Batman was about to say something comforting when, with a rattly intake of air, the black cat began to gasp, choke, and then breathe in greedy gulps.

"Good Spookins," Catwoman purred, hugging the frightened feline to her gray breast.

Then her eyes fell upon the awful sight beyond the cockpit windows. People—ordinary people—lay like beached fish in the street, heaving, twitching, mouths working spasmodically, frightened eyes strained toward the beckoning eternity of the cold stars above.

"How far does this blue hell extend?" Selina asked thinly.

Batman said nothing. His hands on the steering wheel clutched and unclutched with suppressed fury. There was no room in the Batmobile for another soul. Not enough oxygen for the three of them if this awful phenomenon went on much longer. There was nothing he could do. He had never felt so helpless.

The Dark Knight was trying to get the dead engine restarted when abruptly the night went black again.

Catwoman gasped.

And on the ground, people started to breathe again. They stumbled to their feet, laughing, relief on their faces. Some whooped with joy. They had come to within minutes of excruciating death. And to breathe was intoxicating.

Batman sent the cockpit hatch sliding back.

The air outside had cleared. Tinged with an ozone tang of some sort, but tolerable.

And ringing through the night came a thunderous repetition of the demand of moments before: *"Citizens of Gotham City! If a ransom of fifty million dollars is not paid by tomorrow midnight, all of you will writhe under my thrall! You have less than a day to decide your fates! I am the Unseen Strangler!"*

"Somebody," Catwoman hissed, "is going to pay for this!"

"Somebody will," said Batman, hitting the main engine starter. The Batmobile's gas turbine engine coughed, rumbled, and as if unleashed, roared to life. He sent the machine surging up an unblocked side street.

"Where are we going?" Catwoman asked, puzzled.

Batman's voice was flint. "You owe me."

"Okay," Catwoman admitted, shifting the panting cat to her other arm. "Spooky and I owe you. But I'd still like an answer to my question."

"I want you to stay out of this."

"Not likely."

"This is serious." The Batmobile turned sharply, slithering into an alley. The hatch rolled back. Batman turned his masked face to stare coldly into Catwoman's. "This is as far as you go."

"What about the missing cats?" she said stubbornly. "What if this madman has them somewhere in the Rust Scab?"

"I promise to free them in that unlikely event."

Reluctantly Catwoman climbed out.

"Going back in?" she asked.

Batman stared through his windshield, avoiding her eyes.

"Be suicide. Whoever's behind this is prepared. The Batmobile needs air. And so do I. I'm going to look into this from another angle."

Hidden eyebrows lifted, making Catwoman's tufted ears seem to perk up. "Any suspects?" she asked.

"No."

"Liar!" And Catwoman faded back into the shadows, soon becoming only a pale blot framing a Cheshire-cat grin under which the green disks of her feline companion's eyes winked sadly.

The Batmobile roared into reverse and was soon lost in the cold night.

The next morning Commissioner Gordon was roused from sleep by the ringing of his bedroom telephone.

His "Hello?" was more mumbled than annoyed.

The City That Could Not Breathe

"I'm surprised to find you asleep," Batman's flinty voice said.

James Gordon looked at his clock radio, sighed, and said, "I turned in twenty minutes ago."

"Sorry."

"We lost four people last night. None of them homeless."

"I came close to being number five. And Catwoman six."

"What? How is that minx involved in this?"

Quickly Batman related the events of the previous night. He concluded by saying, "The Rust Scab is the epicenter of this disturbance. There's no doubt of that."

"From what you say, the blue light was strongest there. The dead were found immediately outside the zone. But people were affected as far south as Gotham Village. There, it manifested itself as a nagging shortness of breath. I felt it, too."

The line hummed. Then Batman said, "I have a theory."

"Go ahead."

"Some thing or force or machine in the Gotham Tower is doing this. The roaring sounds were meant to frighten the homeless out of the Rust Scab. Those who refused to evacuate after the first night were asphyxiated on the second and their bodies dispersed to send the police chasing in all directions."

"That much he succeeded in doing," Gordon growled.

Batman continued: "Now that he's taken over the Rust Scab, this Unseen Strangler is gearing up to extort Gotham City."

"But who?"

"Think about it. Who owns the Rust Scab?"

Will Murray

"Kendall Sharp? Preposterous!"

"Who purchased Gotham Zoo and sold off the animals?"

"Sharp," Gordon admitted.

"Who faces bankruptcy by January first, according to the *Gazette*'s gossip columnists?"

"Sharp!" Gordon roared. "I'll have him hauled in!"

"On what charge? You'll need proof. Why don't you leave that to me?"

"What do you propose?" Gordon asked dubiously.

"Think about how much better you'll sleep if I don't answer that question," Batman said just before the line went dead.

Kendall Sharp roamed the AM radio dial in the privacy of his cathedrallike office on the twenty-fourth floor of an uptown office building he built in the early 1980s now on the verge of foreclosure.

The radio callers were not talking about Kendall Sharp today. The topic of the hour was the Unseen Strangler.

Sharp never thought he'd see the day when he preferred to keep his name out of the public dialogue, but that was the sad state to which his fortunes had fallen.

Representatives of the city government, the mayor, and of course Commissioner Gordon, gave frequent statements calling for calm during the newsbreaks. But when programming returned to call-in shows, public opinion was sharply divided between those who called for the ransom to be paid and those who believed the city should never knuckle under to terrorist demands.

More than two thirds of the callers added that they

were planning to leave the city well before the midnight deadline, just in case. This brought a thin smile to Kendall Sharp's rather soft face.

For their part, the city fathers were firm: no ransom would be paid.

Sharp laughed aloud at that.

His secretary buzzed him and Sharp shut off the radio.

"Yes, Norma?"

"Mr. Bruce Wayne of Wayne Industries is here."

"Wayne? Does he have an appointment?"

"He's not on the calendar, Mr. Sharp."

Kendall Sharp narrowed his colorless eyes. Bruce Wayne was a major mover and shaker in Gotham City. Many times Sharp had tried to draw him into business alliances, but the mysterious millionaire had always begged off. What could he want now?

"Send him in," Sharp said, intrigued.

When Bruce Wayne stepped through the door, Sharp came out from behind his vast cherrywood desk with his right hand outstretched and his most ingratiating smile on his face.

"Wayne! Great seeing you again! Great! Have a seat. Drink?"

Wayne stood. "Thanks, no."

"So what brings you to my domain?" Sharp asked, going to a bar setup.

"Business."

Sharp let his poker face settle before answering. "You? Gotham's most famous scion of the wealthy? I thought you just attended board meetings and collected dividends and interest, without any need to get down on the playing field with the rest of us hardscrabblers. What a life. I built my empire, Wayne. To the manner born I am not. You and I don't play in the same sandbox. Never will. But you know that, don't you?"

"I was riding by the Rust Scab today," Wayne said in a neutral voice. He was looking at the walls. Most were adorned with photographs of Kendall Sharp hobnobbing with various celebrities in his days as a high-flying developer.

"Mess, isn't it? I got that area—six entire blocks of once-prime real estate—for a song five years back. I had plans, Wayne. Big plans. Tear it all down and put up Sharp City. A city within a city. Television studios, office towers, malls, the works. Then the market went soft and I was left holding the bag."

"The city was not happy with your attempt to ... persuade them to raze the area at their expense and waive all property taxes until the year 2040," Wayne said in the same inflectionless voice.

Sharp puckered his meaty mouth unpleasantly. "A bargaining ploy."

"Which you played too long. When the market dropped, it was no longer feasible to go ahead with Sharp City."

Sharp shrugged, pouring himself a brandy. "The market will bounce back. And so will I. You watch. I earned every thin dime I lost. I'll earn it all back. And more."

"In the meantime," Wayne continued, "the Rust Scab is turning into a breeding ground for antisocial elements."

"My private security people had it under control until the city complained about a little necessary rough-house," Sharp said defensively. "But we're getting away from the subject at hand." The developer turned, saluting with his filled glass. "Or are we?"

"No, we're not. I'd like to take the Rust Scab off your hands."

Kendall Sharp was so taken aback at the unexpected offer he blurted out his reply. "You're crazy!"

"Am I?"

"Don't hype a hypster. You know the real-estate market. You must have an inkling of what it would cost to raze Sharp—I mean the Rust Scab. Even if I sold you the whole thing for a dollar, you couldn't make the bottom line work." He snorted derisively. "A silver-spoon blueblood like you? Not in a million years."

"Why not let me worry about that?" Wayne countered.

Sharp's eyes narrowed. "What's your offer?" he asked flatly, taking a sip of his drink.

"Five hundred."

"Million!"

Wayne nodded.

Sharp got his coughing spasm under control. He took another swallow, hacked once, and said, "No sale."

"Why not? It's a generous offer."

Sharp wiped his moist mouth on the back of his hand. "Exactly. *Too* generous. You got something up your fancy sleeve, Wayne. You're too savvy to pay through the nose for that herd of petrified white elephants. What's your game?"

Wayne rose to go. He looked into Kendall Sharp's suspicious eyes. "No game. I'm just a concerned citizen who thinks he can help beautify Gotham City."

"Crap! I don't buy it. You didn't get where you are by being a crusader for the public welfare."

Wayne paused at the door. "Neither have you." The door closed.

Will Murray

"What does he know that I don't?" Kendall Sharp muttered as he stared at the closed panel.

He was still mulling over that question later that evening at his co-op overlooking Gotham Park when the lights went out.

"Not another blackout!" he complained, tripping over an ottoman on his way to the telephone. He crawled the last few feet and brought it to his face.

The instrument was dead in his hand. No dial tone. He rattled the switch hook and got no response.

Going to the door, he poked his head out. Other residents were doing the same.

"No lights?" he asked.

"No nothing," Sharp was told.

The elevators were dead. No one on his floor seemed to relish the thought of descending nearly thirty flights to find out what was wrong, no matter how Sharp tried to fast-talk them into the chore.

Finally Sharp said, fuming, "Never mind. *I'll* do it. I can't be without a phone tonight!"

He had to pause every few flights to catch his breath. At the tenth-floor landing, winded, he changed his mind. "The devil with it!" he said, and retraced his steps.

There was enough moonlight on his floor to see that the door to his apartment was ajar. He had shut it. And locked it.

His heart beating high in his throat, Sharp hesitated.

Walking softly, he approached the door and put one ear to the panel, listening.

The only sound was his own pounding heartbeat. Emboldened, Sharp carefully eased the door open.

The City That Could Not Breathe

Someone was at his wall safe, he saw. The fake
Monet, gilt frame and all, had been taken down, exposing the round steel door. The burglar was indis-
tinct in the darkness. A blot of shadow in the gloom.
Dark hands—obviously gloved—were working the
dial.

Peering intently, Kendall Sharp caught a vague
glimpse of a shadow on the wall. The shadow of a
smooth head with pointed animal ears.

He withdrew, heart high in his throat. "Batman!"
he gasped.

He stood there a moment, eyes darting wildly, trying to calm himself. Then he heard the faint metallic
squeak of his safe hinges turning.

There was no choice now. He removed his Hermes
power-red tie and looped it around both strong hands.

Holding it before him, he padded into his living
room.

The tall pointy-eared apparition was still at his
safe, riffling through papers. It found one of interest
and unfolded it to reveal a section of blueprint plans.

Then the expensive garrote swooshed over and
down, and Kendall Sharp was exerting all his
strength into squeezing the interloper's throat.

He got a fight. He expected one. Gloved hands
reached around to grab at his face. He buried his shut
eyes in the burglar's left shoulder, protecting them.
Needlelike talons raked his thick hair, opening his
scalp here and there.

Grunting, he gave the garrote a hard twist and
dragged his opponent down. Together, they collapsed
on the rug, Sharp on top. His hands, bone white at the
knuckles, increased their terrible pressure.

Slowly the fight drained out of his opponent. When

Will Murray

the struggling form went limp, Sharp only squeezed harder.

Finally the developer released the tie and stood up, feeling his shirt sticking to his skin by cold sweat. He was breathing hard.

Then the lights returned.

Sharp blinked wildly, scrutinizing his victim.

He saw a slim feline form, attired in a gray cat suit, complete with long tail. The molded ears set high on the mask's head were, he saw, catlike. Not batlike.

"Who the hell are you?" he muttered.

Then he locked the door as other tenants came out into the corridor, expressing their relief at the return of electricity.

Snatching up the crumpled set of blueprints that had fallen to the floor, Kendall Sharp rushed to the telephone. It was working again. Quickly he stabbed out a number.

"Yeah?" a suspicious voice said.

"Chief, here."

"Yeah, Chief?"

"Someone is onto us. Bring the car. We have a disposal problem."

"What about tonight?"

"If you hurry, we can hold to the schedule. Snap on it."

Sharp hung up and dropped into his sofa. He let out a long, ragged breath, wiped sweat off his high forehead.

A knock at his door was followed by a woman saying, "The super found the problem. Someone tampered with a junction box. Isn't that awful?"

"Imagine that?" Sharp said bitterly.

When he had his nerve back, the sweaty developer got up and checked the body of the cat burglar. Her

mouth was open. He understood the process of stran-
gulation enough to know that the tongue should be
protruding. It was not. He knelt and put an ear to his
victim's mouth. It was instantly warmed. She was
breathing.

Kendall Sharp fumbled around the floor, looking for
his tie. But when he got it wrapped around his hands
again, he realized he was completely drained. He had
no strength to finish the job.

He decided it didn't matter. Nasty jobs like these
were what he paid other people to do. . . .

As darkness fell over Gotham City the Batmobile ca-
reened up and down the little-traveled streets. It was
a tortuous route the Dark Knight was following, but
he had no choice. The main arteries were choked with
people and vehicles—all leaving the city. The deadline
set by the Unseen Strangler was just hours away. No
one wanted to be caught, exposed, when the air
stopped supporting life.

Overhead, police helicopters clattered and sent spotlights creeping among the spires of the Rust Scab.
Batman frowned. Gordon had promised him a free
hand on the ground. The choppers were not exactly a
vote of confidence.

Eventually the Batmobile reached the outer periph-
ery of the Rust Scab. He throttled the low-slung machine down as his hard eyes drank in the sorry sight.
It was in every respect a blighted zone. Bruce Wayne
had been correct. It had to be brought down. Even
empty lots would be better than these crumbling sym-
bols of the great city's inability to renew itself.

The winter air was clear. No blueness. And no men
in blue. Gordon had at least kept his promise to keep

the police off the streets of the fatal zone. If Batman failed, many would die tonight. But Batman did not intend to fail.

Engine throttled down, he eased into the Rust Scab, the Batmobile's on-board life-support system hissing.

The car penetrated a block. Abruptly the blue light sprang into being. Without braking, Batman kicked the mighty machine into reverse.

It screeched backward, slewed to a stop just beyond the blue glow. The light stopped just at the edge of the Rust Scab. It was like a radiant curtain, cold as the winter air itself.

He had been seen. Batman waited for the Unseen Strangler's next move. In the sky, the police helicopters, engines sputtering in the rarefied air, seemed to limp off.

The light went out, as if inviting any and all to try their luck again.

In the dark confines of the Batmobile cockpit, Batman stared up at the spindle of the Gotham Tower, focusing exclusively on it. He glanced at his dash chronometer: 11:31. Three minutes went by.

Eventually he gunned the engine and raced toward his goal. At the last minute he cut across a side street and, skirting the Rust Scab, retreated into the night.

The night wore on. Gotham City held its breath, waiting for midnight. Zero hour.

Selina Kyle knew she was not dead because her throat hurt. Swallowing saliva was like swallowing a dry peach pit coated with sand.

The pain was reassuring, considering the dead numbness of her arms and legs and the frightening fact that she couldn't seem to open her eyes.

The City That Could Not Breathe

She groaned, just to see what happened.

A voice said gruffly, "Chief, the furball just came around."

"How bizarre," said another voice, one that sounded hollow and unfamiliar. "I thought if we had any trouble, it would be from Batman. Instead I get this interloper—whoever she is."

"I've heard of her, Chief."

"You have?"

"Catwoman. Calls herself Catwoman. She's a cat burglar. Likes jewels, cat statues, high-class stuff like that."

Footsteps came close and stopped very near. "Catwoman, huh?" grunted the hollow voice. "All right, Catwoman, why stick your paws in my mouse hole?"

The gag in her mouth was yanked down roughly.

"I'm waiting," the hollow voice prompted.

"Who . . . ?" Catwoman asked in a raspy tone that sounded to her own ears like a crone's last croak.

"Some nerve, huh, Chief?" the gruff voice grunted. "Her trying to pump you."

Catwoman swallowed again, wincing.

"Since you're not going to live out the night," said the hollow voice, "no harm in telling you. The name is Wayne. Bruce Wayne. Maybe you've heard of me."

And the voice of the Unseen Strangler laughed as if at a private joke.

"You're Kendall Sharp," Catwoman spat.

"And you haven't answered my question," the Unseen Strangler retorted, sounding not at all concerned.

"The big cats at the Gotham Zoo. Where did you *really* send them?"

The hollow voice sounded taken aback. "Cats? You burgled my safe over *cats*?"

"Where are they?"

"Bring her, Weederman," the Unseen Strangler ordered thinly.

Rough hands took Selina Kyle by the elbows and dragged her unceremoniously across a gritty floor and up a short flight of steps. A door opened, and immediately her nostrils were assaulted by a stench any zoo patron would recognize—that of caged animals.

The hollow voice at her ear said, "Back when this Art Deco monstrosity was first built, some over-imaginative architect thought the tallest skyscraper in the world would make a perfect dirigible launch-pad. So they built one up here in the Spindle. The one time they tried to use it, the updrafts practically tore the ship apart. To cover their embarrassment they erected a radio antenna in its place. There is where the passengers were to disembark."

A hand yanked off her blindfold and Catwoman found herself blinking at a row of dim caged shapes—the stripes, spots, and silky flanks of assorted jungle cats. She saw a lion, a clouded leopard, a jaguar, and what seemed to be an emaciated Bengal tiger.

"My Atmospheric Converter is too valuable to be left unguarded," the Unseen Strangler said hollowly. "Meet my last line of defense."

Catwoman turned around. Too late. The door shut. She was alone.

And then she noticed the machine. It sat high in a supporting girder over her head. Even seen from below, it resembled the blueprints she had found in Kendall Sharp's safe—the one labeled "Atmospheric Converter." It was studded with compressors and

The City That Could Not Breathe

great lengths of heavy-duty ducting. It hummed
faintly, as if waiting.

Time passed. Catwoman tried to wrest her bonds
free. They wouldn't budge. Her claw-tipped gloves had
been taken. She felt as weak as . . . well, as a kitten.

Her luminous eyes went to the cages and rested on
a sleek black coat. "Hello, Bast," she purred. "Long
time no see."

Bast, the Sumatran black panther, growled. When
she closed her yellow eyes in the gloom, her ebony
face vanished.

Without warning, the machine suspended above
kicked in with a high howl like some kind of enraged
air conditioner. In the confined space, the air turned
blue and thin and as cold as the breath of death.

And in their cages, the big cats howled their fear.

It was midnight. Straight up.

All over Lower Gotham, people awakened from sleep,
straining for breath and twisting in their bedclothes.
They crawled to windows and threw them open, hanging out gasping faces.

But there was no fresh air. No air of any kind.

Car engines sputtered and died. Behind the wheels,
drivers died, too.

And over the city that could not breathe, a silent,
batlike shape glided closer, closer to the Gotham
Tower, midnight-blue eyes hard and without mercy.

There was no oxygen. But that did not mean there
was no air. The black Mylar wings of the collapsible
batglider rode the cool air currents toward the Spindle, glowing evilly blue now.

From loudspeakers mounted high in its summit, the
snarl of jungle cats came, as if to warn him away.

"Chief!" cried an anxious voice.

Bathed in blue, the Unseen Strangler looked up from his control board. He wore a rubberized coverall garment. His head, like that of his subordinate, was covered by a fishbowllike Plexiglas helmet. Only his had a blue mirrored surface that prevented anyone from seeing in, while Weederman's was as clear as Lucite.

"What is it?" he snapped.

"Either the biggest moth I ever saw, or Batman's trying to make a run at us."

The Unseen Strangler clopped over to the ornately framed window. He walked heavily, encumbered by two oxygen tanks that fed into his helmet.

Bringing his burnished blue head to the glass, he made fists with his gloved hands. "Clever. Very clever. He must have launched himself from the Industry Complex roof. No doubt he has a gas mask, too."

"That's some kinda hang glider he's riding," Weederman pointed out. "No motor to conk out because of the ozone."

"Pick him off! I've no time for this. After tonight, they'll pay through the nose just to breathe this stinking town's dirty air!"

Weederman grabbed up a Dragunov sniper's rifle and took it to the eastern window. He locked and loaded, and got the rifle up on his rubberized shoulder. It was awkward. His oxygen tanks weighed down his arm and his helmet was in the way. He had to hold the sniper's scope nearly a foot in front of his aiming eye.

He squeezed off an experimental shot.

"Missed!"

The City That Could Not Breathe

"Try again."

Weederman brought the scope closer. Another report came. The recoil knocked the scope against the helmet, jarring him back.

"This ain't working out, Chief," he complained.

"Make it work, or suck ozone like the rest of them!"

Batman, balancing on a aluminum framework, gloved hands clutching the control bar, angled away from the Spindle. The sound of his own breathing, muffled by the gas mask, fought with the whistle of the wind in his wings.

The spiteful snap of the second bullet sounded off to his right. The first bullet had zipped by his left foot. It would not be long before the sniper found his aim.

Catwoman, gasping, struggled on her knees to the single portholelike window high in the Spindle. It faced east. She saw the black batlike shape fluttering in the blue radiance.

Over the machinery howl, she heard the crack of the rifle.

Wriggling back, she went to the nearest cage and stuck both bound hands through the filthy bars.

"Come, Bast! Play!"

Bast, the black panther, took a swipe at the offered hands that was anything but playful.

"I can't get a bead on this guy!" Weederman complained. He sounded like he was talking from some glass well. "My helmet is too big, or something."

The Unseen Strangler stomped to his side.

Will Murray

"Why do I pay you?" he complained, taking up the rifle.

He looked through the scope, found the black shape in the blue haze, and tracked it. When a black bat symbol in a golden oval was smack in the cross hairs, he squeezed the trigger once, deliberately.

"Blam!"

"Ooof!"

The air was driven out of Batman's lungs with such force it blew his gas mask loose.

He was slammed backward, his fragile wings buckling. A tangle of Mylar and aluminum, flesh, bone, and blood, he fluttered downward.

"Got him!" crowed the Unseen Strangler. He tossed the rifle contemptuously aside and returned to the control board, where a microphone was mounted on a flexible stalk. He leaned into it and spoke.

And over Lower Gotham, a voice like exultant thunder proclaimed: *"Citizens of Gotham! Your leaders have defied my demandments! Tonight, those within the sound of my voice will die! Tomorrow night, the zone of dead air will widen, and widen again on each successive night until my demandments are met! The new price is seventy million dollars! Heed my words— for I am the Unseen Strangler!"*

Bast took another swipe. Under the panther's angry lash, Catwoman flinched. Teeth gritting, she let the claws do their worst. They hooked the strands—tore flesh, too.

She bit her lips in pain. The next swipe forced her to pull away.

The City That Could Not Breathe

But the bonds felt loose, now! Catwoman twisted her wrists and wriggled them sinuously out of the ragged knot.

For some reason the air within the immediate sphere of the howling machine was breathable. It stank of ozone, but there were oxygen molecules still present. Selina Kyle felt as if she had just run the Gotham Marathon, but she could breathe.

Still on her knees, she got the window open. Crawling out onto the ledge, she saw a spiraling form with thin batlike wings. Spiraling downward.

"Oh, no!"

Sobbing, Selina Kyle hung her feline head. . . .

Batman plummeted. The center of his chest felt like a sledgehammer had hit it squarely. The sniper had aimed for his bat emblem, the only bright spot in his midnight regalia. Deliberately bright, since it masked a shield of bulletproof Kevlar.

The bullet, however, had not penetrated. He struggled to unfold his glider wings—first one, then the other. Mercifully he got them in position to catch the air.

Then he was sliding down, not falling. The straining wings filled. The Batman, once more an airborne shape of retribution, described a single vulturelike circle low over the Rust Scab. Then he found an updraft and began to ascend.

Nearby, a wayward sea gull strayed into the blue zone, folded up its wings, and crashed to the hard pavement below.

The Dark Knight remembered his gas mask then. He had been holding his breath in suspense. The pure oxygen had a reviving effect.

"Unbelievable!"

"What?"

"He's back, Chief! I don't know how, but he's back."

"You get out on that ledge and put him down for good! You hear me?"

"You got it, Chief!"

Fuming, the Unseen Strangler reached for the big dial that expanded the operating range of his Atmospheric Converter. He hoped the mayor hadn't joined the evacuation. It would teach him not to ignore the demands of the Unseen Strangler.

The Dark Knight saw the globe-headed figure ease out onto the ledge of the Gotham Tower and felt a cold sickness come over him. He was still too far from his goal. And the air in his mask was running low.

He would not make it. There was no way. He had lost too much time, and only a true course would get him to the Spindle. If he had to dodge another bullet, it would be more merciful to take it.

Below, a string of police cars, lightbars pulsating, converged on the Rust Scab. They got only so far before oxygen-starved engines died and thrashing blue figures spilled from open doors to stumble about in blind agony.

The sight brought new resolve to the Dark Knight's cowled features.

Selina Kyle heard the third rifle shot. Her head jerked up. She saw the approaching black wings and crawled out. Below her, a rifle barrel jutted. It spat another lance of reddish fire.

The City That Could Not Breathe

Batman held his course. He kept coming.

"Crazy!" she gasped. "He's crazy! He's not even trying to dodge!"

Scrambling back, Selina went to the cages and began opening them as the pent-up felines vented their rage at the awful noise and the stinking air that seared their sensitive nostrils.

Batman dug into his utility belt. The last bullet had gone wide. The sniper was lining up another shot. He was taking his time, picking his target.

Too much distance separated them for the Dark Knight to do more than guess. When the moment felt right, he closed his eyes and triggered the magnesium flare.

The evil blue night lit up, silvery white.

Weederman was looking through the cross hairs when the hot silver light stabbed his single open eye.

He screamed as he stumbled back to the safety of the window, off balance.

At the control board, the Unseen Strangler was oblivious to everything except a moving indicator that read "Oxygen–Ozone Balance." It was creeping toward the ozone end of the scale.

Then the door to the Spindle came open and Weederman screamed again, more loudly this time, as sinuous shapes began filing down the steps, making angry question marks with their colorful tails.

The sputtering flare fell from his hand and Batman opened his eyes. They went to the ledge. Empty!

He blinked. Was it some trick of the weird blue light?

A second later the sniper was back out. This time he was not alone.

A sleek black panther was stalking him, snarling its fury. And as the sniper backed away along the crumbling ledge, a jaguar and a wild-maned lion padded out from another window.

The sniper found himself surrounded. He did a crazy thing. Sensible by his lights, perhaps. He dropped his rifle overboard and threw up his hands in surrender.

The crouching panther uncoiled and slammed its big padded paws into his rubberized chest.

The sniper went out and down. The panther recovered and found its footing.

Batman followed the windmilling body with wide eyes.

The falling man struck a ledge that shattered his helmet, bounced off another, and fell another hundred yards or so, ending up on a setback, motionless.

The Unseen Strangler was focused on his control board when he felt something heavy brush his legs.

He ignored the sensation.

He couldn't ignore the squeaking of his oxygen-tank valves. Someone was turning them off. He realized that when he began gasping inside his protective helmet.

"Who!"

He turned to see a slim catlike female form standing behind him. Her smile was mocking. So he punched her in the stomach, forcing her to expel the air she had been holding in her lungs.

The City That Could Not Breathe

Catwoman had no choice but to inhale. Her face twisted as the stinking ozone entered her lungs. She folded onto the floor, gasping, gasping like the others.

"Fool!" the Unseen Strangler spat, restoring his oxygen supply.

Then he noticed the big cats out on the surrounding ledges. "Oh, no," he muttered.

A sudden cross breeze sent Batman shooting past the Spindle. He dipped his left wing and came around like a fragile black moth circling a beckoning blue light bulb.

Unfortunately all approaches were thick with pacing, snarling jungle cats. They were panting now. Some lowered themselves to their lean stomachs as their vibrant energy flagged.

The tip of Gotham Tower was a blunt dome, studded with anchor staples left over from its days as a dirigible launchpad.

A corded batarang looped out, snagged one of these, and the Dark Knight was soon tethered to the structure. Using a mechanical device, he reeled himself toward his objective.

The Spindle loomed closer. The topmost porthole was open. When it was within reach, he hit a disengage latch and his Mylar wings separated and fell away.

The Dark Knight was left clinging to a ledge. He worked toward the window, got his feet through, and reeled the rest of his body to safety.

He was prepared for anything—except the absence of a foe. He saw the empty cages, the faint blue tinge to the close air. And could not help but be aware of the howling machine over his head.

Will Murray

It was too complicated for easy analysis. Not so the portable gasoline generator off in one corner. Its dynamo spun and spun, throwing occasional blue sparks.

He removed his gas mask. The unpleasant air filled his lungs. He understood then. There was a breathable field surrounding the device—otherwise the generator powering it could not operate.

Batman took out a small packet he had brought along because he knew there was no electrical service to the Rust Scab. Ripping open the foil packet, he flung a powdery substance—emery dust—into the whirling blades.

Then he raced for the steps because he knew dynamos could do strange things when they went haywire.

Batman found Catwoman unconscious. He knelt and gave her his remaining oxygen. In one corner of the room, the Unseen Strangler attended to his controls. Red lights were blinking. Circuit breakers were popping. Frantically he reset them. They popped again.

Calmly the Dark Knight strode up to the iridescent-helmeted figure and, with a set of brass knuckles fitted over his right gauntlet, shattered the Unseen Strangler's protective helmet with a sharp, short blow.

The man froze as the shards rained at his feet. He gave a short, frightened gasp. Then he began gasping for air.

Like one of his own victims, he began to bend and unbend his tortured body.

Batman spun him around hard. "I've been waiting for this moment," he said tightly.

The Unseen Strangler lifted his head—and a finned black fist connected with the soft features of Kendall Sharp, changing them forever.

The City That Could Not Breathe

And Batman hadn't even used the hand weighted by the brass knuckles.

He turned, face slowly reddening. Above, the machine of death was whining and complaining. It wouldn't be long now.

He stalked over to the spot where Catwoman lay insensate, gulping down the last precious seconds of remaining oxygen. It was going to be tight.

He took the mask from her face and brought it to his own. Catwoman began to hack and squirm. Her eyes fluttered.

In the act of restoring the mask to the reviving adventuress's mouth, Batman became aware of slinking shapes padding into the close confines. He turned.

The dull, demented look of the approaching feline eyes told him all he needed to know. They were in pain suffocating, but they had enough energy left to vent their rage on anyone.

Coming to his feet, he unhooked his broad batwing cloak and began snapping it in their faces, fending the big cats off. They swiped back listlessly. Batman narrowly avoided losing his cloak to still-lethal claws.

One, a Bengal tiger, crouched, preparing to pounce. Its striped tail switched angrily.

The slinky panther coming through another window made for Catwoman. Soon they would be surrounded.

Batman yanked back his cloak. From his utility belt, he removed an atomizer filled with a pale greenish liquid. He pointed the brass nozzle at his cloak and squeezed the rubber bulb. A fine mist coated the cloak, and after waving it over his long-eared head, he let fly.

It plopped onto the tiger, now an ominous hump of stripes.

Abruptly the big cat rolled over onto its back and

began pawing at the heavy, enveloping shroud. Other cats, too, joined in. They began fighting for the prize. The lack of air made their movements slow, languorous. They panted slowly.

Then the generator blew. The door to the tower jumped off its frame and banged down the steps. The ceiling overhead cracked. Plaster cakes and white dust showered down.

Dynamo blades flew through the room with sizzling snarls, impaling the walls and floor with short *chuck*ing sounds.

One caught the fallen figure of Kendall Sharp in the throat, bisecting the larynx. Red fluid bubbled up in a dying fountain.

The blue tinge that made the air look so unreal abruptly faded.

Just in time! Batman took in a gulping breath and found it breathable.

The cats, momentarily shocked by the explosion, came to their feet, the fragrant bat cloak forgotten. Sniffing blood, they approached the ruin that was Kendall Sharp's throat, sniffing with curiosity. A broad pink tongue flicked out. Tasting sounds came.

And deliberately fangs sank into unresisting wrists and legs and other parts as the big cats tugged and pulled, each claiming the prize for his own.

By that time the Dark Knight was bearing the limp form of Catwoman down the first of a long, long series of steps.

Fortunately she came around after only sixteen flights. Batman set her down.

"What—what happened?" she asked, dazed.

"You evened the score," he told her. "Thanks."

The City That Could Not Breathe

Selina Kyle smiled wanly. "I'd say the bottom line hasn't been written yet."

"You were right about the cats."

Catwoman's eyes widened. "Where are they?"

"Upstairs. Snacking. It will take professionals with tranquilizer darts to get them off what remains of the Unseen Strangler."

"Spooky must have smelled their spoor," Catwoman mused. "That's why she turned tail." She frowned. "It was Kendall Sharp, wasn't it? I found blueprints for that weird machine in his apartment safe. He caught me in the act." She grimaced, feeling her bruised throat. "Lucky me."

Batman nodded. "It was Sharp. I conducted my own investigation and he gave himself away by refusing an offer for the Rust Scab no one in his right mind would have declined."

"Funny," Selina murmured. "He tried to convince me he was Bruce Wayne. Why would he do that?"

"We may never know," Batman said quickly, taking her elbow.

They started down the stairs.

"By the way, what *is* that scrumptuous minty cologne you're wearing?" Catwoman asked after a thoughtful silence. "It's driving me . . . crazy."

"Nepeta Cataria."

Catwoman purred.

Commissioner Gordon couldn't keep up with the incoming reports.

"The blue haze is gone, Commissioner."

"Casualty reports coming in from all sectors south of Gotham Park, sir."

"Sir, Unit fifty-five still not answering from the Rust Scab."

"Get men into the Rust Scab," Gordon instructed. "I want that place combed down to the last dead rat."

When the police aides had left, the office window slid up soundlessly, and a tall athletic shape in gray and black stepped into the room.

Commissioner Gordon became aware of the silent presence only when a shadow fell across his desk. He jumped in his chair.

"How do you *do* that?" Gordon blurted.

"I oil your window regularly," said Batman in a dry voice.

"Bah!"

"Kendall Sharp, the Unseen Strangler, is dead," Batman intoned.

"Good riddance. But what was his game?"

"What it appeared to be. Extortion, plain and simple. It was a way to get out of bankruptcy court and refinance his crumbling real-estate empire. If the city had paid tonight's ransom, Sharp would not have been satisfied. Eventually he might have been able to trick the city into razing the Rust Scab."

Understanding came into Gordon's narrowing eyes. He pounded his desk. "And, with the ransom money, build Sharp City, after all!"

Batman nodded grimly.

"The fiend! But there is one thing I don't understand. How did he do it?"

"A machine. Ruined now. Somehow it broke down the oxygen molecules in the air, converting them into chemically similar but unbreathable ozone, so the atmosphere no longer supported life. Ozone has a distinctive smell, you know."

"But why did the air turn blue?"

The City That Could Not Breathe

"Ozone tends to absorb light rays," Batman explained. "For some reason the blue band of the spectrum was all that showed through the electrical field."

"Where did he get such a device?" Gordon exploded.

Batman shrugged gray shoulders. He looked oddly naked without his enveloping cloak, like a masked circus acrobat.

"That is another mystery," he said. "Remember the Midnight Creeper and his light-bending exoskeleton?"

Gordon harrumphed again. "If he ever gets out of Arkham Asylum, I shall personally shoot him!"

"Someone built that devilish device, too."

Gordon looked perplexed. "Are you suggesting there's some free-lance—what?—renegade scientist building infernal machines for any madman with the wherewithal to purchase them?"

Batman went to the window. One foot on the sill, he paused.

"It's a working theory. Perhaps someone should interrogate the Midnight Creeper along those lines. After the tigers are cleared out of the Rust Scab, that is. I'd have your Special Operations Unit do it before anyone ventures into Gotham Tower." He tossed an atomizer. Gordon caught it. "That might help."

Gordon noticed a faint minty odor. "Perfume?" he muttered, reaching for the phone.

"Catnip," said Batman, and was gone.

Deadly Prey

GARY COHN

I liked this guy, I really did. He was the first one that I'd let myself like in so long. The first one to get me to let my guard down in so long. Of course he was rich. A Texas billionaire. A nice one ... as Texas billionaires go. Not oil, computer software. His daddy's money had come from oil, but there had only been a few million left when Arley and his sister Lynette inherited everything a dozen years ago. Seed money, Arley called it, laughing. Some of these guys, they start talking about their money, and all I can think of is how they look like big fat roast turkeys, waiting for me to carve them up. But not Arley Kincaid.

When he talked about his money, how he and little sister Lynette had earned a fortune, he made it sound like the greatest adventure in the world, a game of brinksmanship played against the coldest corporate

killers. He was gorgeous, too. That helped. He was tall
and tan and he walked like a cowboy. His shoulders
were broad, his hips were narrow, his eyes were a
smoky blue gray, with little laugh lines that crinkled
at the corners. His thick wavy hair was the color of
old gold. And that smile and honeyed drawl. The first
time I saw him I almost laughed, he seemed so perfect
he had to be some kind of joke. My kind.

Of course he was funny; that helped. A man who
can make me laugh, *with* him, not at him, that's rare.
When Arley talked about how his daddy had lost his
first fortune on a bet, or how he and Lynette had almost lost theirs the same way, those gray eyes twinkled, that big white grin flashed, his mockery of his
own comeuppance was disarming. Oh, yeah, Arley
Kincaid got me to let my guard down, all right.

I met him at the opera. A charity function spon-
sored by the Wayne Foundation. I wore low-cut black
silk, hoping Bruce Wayne would be there . . . and hoping he wouldn't be. He wasn't. I love those affairs.
Hate the music, love the company. Every fortune
within a hundred miles of Gotham shows up to do its
part for the unfortunate. In this case I think it was
the Victims of the Joker Survivors' Fund. All those
widows and orphans. Who knows? Who cares? I go to
meet and greet . . . and hunt. Mrs. Underhill Cox
might be wearing the Rani emeralds. Maybe I over-
hear her mention that she and Roddy are staying in
the Presidential Suite at the DuPree Palace Hotel.
Buffy and Hewitt promise to visit before she returns
to Philadelphia. I decide to visit that night. Late. In
costume. Hard to resist the Rani emeralds. So during
the intermission I was sipping champagne with some
fat, rich geezer in a tux. Of course, they're all in tuxes
at these things. A banker, I think. He wanted to get

inside my silk. I wanted to get inside his vault. We were negotiating. And then I noticed Arley Kincaid.

He was leaning against a marble column, drinking bourbon straight up. He was in a tux, too. One that fit damn well, I noticed. He wasn't talking to anyone. He was just watching me work the banker, and he had this arrogant, amused little smirk on his face. Challenging. Damned sexy. I never could resist a challenge. I met his stare. Our eyes locked, and the fat banker eventually noticed that he no longer had my undivided attention.

"I'm sorry, Errol—I just noticed my cousin over there. I haven't seen him in years," I told him. "Thanks for understanding." I gave his cheek an affectionate pat, just to keep him interested, and walked across the room to the guy with the smirk.

"Something amusing you?" I asked.

"Just you, darlin'. I would've expected Selina Kyle to hunt tougher prey."

"Meaning you?"

"Maybe."

"What makes you think you know anything about Selina Kyle?"

"I did some homework."

I gave him a once-over. "How do I know you'd be worth the effort?"

"Only one way to find out. Why don't we start with dinner?"

What the hell. He was handsome, he smelled rich, he had an attitude, and he was right—fat old bankers were beneath me. We skipped the rest of the opera and went to dinner.

His car was waiting out in front of the opera house. A red XJ12 Jaguar convertible. As I got in he said, "I

told you I did my homework." It was a warm June
night. He put the top down.

"I prefer older Jags—XK120s, XKEs," I said. "But
at least you got the make right."

He had a table waiting for us at the best nouvelle
restaurant down in Soho, Le Chat Noir. "Okay, pal,
I'm hip to the cat motif. Now why don't I think we just
met by chance tonight?" I asked.

He grinned. "I confess—I've been planning this for
a while. Ever since I first saw your picture in a magazine, I've always wanted to have dinner with the
Catwoman."

"You're out of luck. She's retired—you'll have to settle for plain old Selina."

"That's not what I saw back at that little soirée,
darlin'. You were *workin'* that room. I could tell. I
know you."

"What makes you think so?"

He leaned forward, took my hand. His voice was
soft but compelling. "I know you 'cause we're just
alike. We're predators, darlin'. We go after what we
want. Especially if someone else has it!"

"And what about this?" I asked. "Are you hunting
me?"

"Well . . . I'd kinda like to think it's mutual. Gives it
a nice little edge, don't you think?"

And then we were deep in conversation. That's when
I let my guard down. He was charming, he was clever,
he was handsome and funny. He ordered his steak au
poivre rare, like I ordered mine. He told me about
Texas, I told him about Gotham. He told me about his
family. I didn't tell him about mine. We drank a bottle
of wine. Then we drank another. We talked about
hunting.

"See, Lynette and I—she's my sister an' my business partner—have been hunting together since we were kids. Everything from squirrels and bunny rabbits to wolves an' cougars and bears. Fact is, my daddy's old desert ranch out in west Texas is kind of a private hunting preserve for us and our buddies. So anyway, when we went into business, we found it wasn't any different." He wasn't drunk, not at all. But there was more Texas in his voice the more he drank. "We picked off the competition like *they* were bunny rabbits! When we got to the wolves an' bears, well, some of 'em almost got us, but in the end, Kincaid Software Systems always comes out on top!"

"I know," I told him. "I own two thousand shares."

"Do you, now? It's up to a hundred and twelve a share."

"I know."

We grinned at each other. By now we were holding hands across the table. "You still just Selina, or is Catwoman here, too?"

I brought his hand up to my lips and gave his thumb a little bite. "I think she's on her way. . . ."

He owned a loft in Gotham, not far from where we were. I wasn't drunk, not at all, but when he asked if I wanted to see his place, I said yes. Oh, definitely.

The loft was big, open, and luxurious. Some of Arley's trophies were on display. The wolves and bears didn't bother me, but I disapproved of the big cats.

Then we were on his couch, tearing at each other's clothes. It was sheer animal passion, fierce kisses, bodies pressed hard, half-dressed, half-naked. And then it was over.

I lay in his arms, gently scratching my fingers through his chest hair. I really liked this guy. I purred in his ear.

Gary Cohn

"I think Catwoman *is* here," he said with a little chuckle.

"You may be right," I conceded.

"I surely would like to see you in that costume sometime," he whispered. "Fact is, I'd like to peel you out of it."

"Think you can handle her?" I teased. "The Catwoman has very sharp claws."

"I'd take my chances."

I decided I'd take mine. "I have it with me," I confessed. "In my purse."

"I thought you said you're retired."

"I lied." I slipped out of his arms. "Why don't you wait in bed," I told him. "I won't be a minute."

In the bathroom I shed my silk dress and pulled on the skintight costume. It made me feel strong, sexy, reckless—it always did.

I pulled the mask over my face, flexed the claws. This was something new, going to a lover's bed as Catwoman.

I left the bathroom light on, knowing it would back-light me. I stepped out.

Arley lay on the bed, waiting. He was beautiful. He saw me and said, "My, oh my."

I arched, I stretched, I flexed my claws. Why not give him a show? I thought. Build a little tension. I felt sinuous, slinky, sensual. "Are you sure you're ready for me?" I asked, letting a seductive growl into my voice.

"Oh, yeah, darlin'—right from the start," he said.

Then he pulled a gun out from under the pillow and shot me.

2.

I woke up in a cage. Dawn was breaking, and the sun
in my face woke me. Then I remembered Kincaid
shooting me. "Stupid, stupid, stupid," I yelled, bang-
ing my fists against the bars. Finally I stopped,
caught my breath, looked around. I was naked, lying
on a bed of straw. Over in the corner was a dish of water and some raw ground meat. In another corner was
a sandbox. Cute. What the hell was going on?

It was hot in that cage. It was eight by ten by seven
feet high, and it stood out in the hot sun. There was
nothing else around, just some low hills and scrub
brush, with mountains in the distance. The morning
dragged on, and soon it was sweltering out there, and
I felt lousy. Bleary. Locked in a cage in the middle of
the desert somewhere.

I checked under my ribs where Arley had shot me.
There was a little hole, nothing much. Tranquilizer
dart. There were a couple of holes in my right arm. I'd
been drugged for a while. I was starving and thirsty.
I ate the meat and drank the water. And waited.

After a while I heard an engine, and a Jeep came
rolling in across the hills. It stopped by my cage.
There were four people in it, three men and a lean,
hard, good-looking blond woman about my age and
height. The driver was Arley Kincaid.

The other two men were about Kincaid's age. One
was a little weasel with a great big single-action Colt
strapped low on his hip, gunfighter style. He dressed
like Glenn Ford in a cowboy movie, in a faded Levi's
jacket and a white Stetson cowboy hat. The other man
was big and slow looking. He wore a T-shirt, jeans,
and a cap that said "Winchester." The four of them

climbed out of the Jeep and stood in front of the cage, appraising me.

"Well," Arley said to the others, "is she fine, or what?"

"Damn, Arley, she's juicy—the Catwoman herself!" the big one said.

"She doesn't look so tough," the woman said. "You should have gotten Batman."

He patted her arm. "One thing at a time, Lynette. Let's see how this one works out, then we'll go after bigger game."

I hissed at the woman. That got her attention. "I'm tough enough to tear your eyes out, bitch!" I turned to Arley. "Kincaid, what the hell is this all about?" I demanded.

"Whoo! She's got spirit!" the big one said. "Settin' naked an' helpless in a cage, and she's makin' threats!"

"I told you we should cut out her tongue, Arley," the little guy said. "I don't like it when they talk back."

"Now Billy-Ray, we're not savages." Arley turned to me. "Selina, darlin', this here's Billy-Ray Jenkins, Bubba Buell, and my sister Lynette. Remember I told you about our little hunting club? Welcome to it.

"Now, here's what we're gonna do. I'm going to unlock your cage, and we're gonna head on out of here. We'll give you two hours to make yourself scarce, and then we're comin' after you."

"What do you mean, coming after me?"

"What's it sound like? Look, we've all been hunting together since we were kids. Local game started gettin' boring, so we started importing things—lions, tigers, elephants, rhinos. But you know, even that got boring after a while.

"One day Bubba brings out this wetback kid he

Deadly Prey

picked up hitchhiking. Kid was pretty resourceful—took us the better part of a day to get him."

"Now, *that* was fun," Bubba said.

"That's the sickest thing I ever heard of," I told them.

"Nah, it gets a lot sicker," Arley said. "That was about a year ago. We've done half a dozen hunts like that since. We keep trying to find tougher prey—last one was a Special Forces sargeant Lynette picked up in a bar out near Fort Bliss. She took him down her own self!"

"And now it's my turn?" I asked.

"That's right. Like I told you, I saw your picture in a magazine an' decided you'd be perfect. An' here we are."

"Damn it, I *liked* you, Kincaid," I whispered.

"I know, darlin'—that's what I was countin' on." He pulled out a key and unlocked the cage door. They all climbed back into the Jeep. Arley pointed off to the east. "I'd head that way, Selina. Plenty of cover just over them hills." Then they were gone.

I pushed the door open and dropped to the ground. I was starting to feel a bit better as the drugs wore off completely. But I wished I had some more water. As the sun continued to climb it got hotter and hotter. I was getting thirsty already.

Well, Selina, so much for romance, I told myself. Can this relationship be saved? It's the same old story. Boy meets girl, they fall in love, boy drugs girl and takes her out to his ranch so he and his friends can hunt her down and kill her. I wondered if he planned to stuff me and display me in his trophy room. Well, they'd have to catch me first.

I set off to the north, maintaining a light, steady lope. If Kincaid suggested I go east, then any other direction must be a better choice. As I ran I felt my head grow increasingly clear.

The scrub was tearing up the soles of my feet, but I willed the pain away, and I tried to avoid the worst of it, the mesquite and the brambles. I had a feeling I was going to hurt a lot more before this was over. I saw a fox, a couple of rabbits, spotted a pair of buzzards circling.

As I ran I evaluated my chances. Could I find a highway and get out of here? Not likely. I remembered Arley telling me this ranch covered thousands of acres, all owned by him and Lynette. No doubt the hunters knew this terrain far better than I could learn it. Would they come at me all together?

I thought about the gunfighter rig the little guy was wearing. They'd each have a specialty, each have his or her own game. They'd probably set a wager about who would bring me in. So they'd come after me one at a time. It would be about noon when they started out.

Could I find something to wear? Not unless my fashion sense ran to briars and brambles and cactus needles. What about a weapon? That was a better possibility. Then I thought about the Green Beret Lynette had killed. Those guys are expert survivalists, and the bitch took him down. That didn't bode well for me.

As I ran I counted seconds. I wanted to keep track of the time. After about a half hour I stopped to get my bearings. I figured I'd put somewhere between three and four miles between me and the cage. I'd run enough marathons to know that I could keep to that pace almost indefinitely as long as I didn't injure my feet too badly, as long as I found some water, as long as the heat didn't keep climbing.

I'd picked a little cluster of hills as my goal, and I

was among them now. There were mountains looming off to the northwest. I was sure I'd be better off up there than out here in the open. At least I might find some cover in the mountains.

Where the hell was I? Lynette had picked up the soldier at Fort Bliss. I'd met a few soldiers, in a past life. Some had been stationed at Fort Bliss, near ... where? El Paso. Near El Paso. Western tip of Texas. New Mexico to the north. I didn't know much about this area, but I did know that people were few and far between.

It was barren country, desert. A lot of it was salt flats. But up in the mountains I might find some water, something to eat. There were a few scrub pines, I could see them a mile or two off. Along my run I'd noticed cactuses in assorted shapes and sizes. Didn't I read somewhere that you could break a cactus open to get water? Which cactus?

Hell, I'm a city kitty. What did I know about Texas? I'd better learn fast. I started running again.

3.

The terrain opened back up into desert again between the hills and the mountains. The desert was a rolling, dipping place, with stretches of dry, scruffy, hard ground where nothing grew, and broad expanses of sand. The sand rolled into dunes, some a good twelve feet tall. Long gullies, some of them running for miles, split the desert floor. They must get a lot of flash floods around here during rainy season, I thought.

I'd guessed that the mountains were another five miles off. But distances are deceptive in the desert, and that guess was way short. Now I was figuring that they were more than twice that far away. I'd been loping along for well over an hour. The sun was intense, and the heat was really starting to get to me. Sweat pouring down my face stung my eyes, and it was getting a lot harder to ignore how much my feet hurt. A glance told me that they were torn and bloody, so I stopped glancing at them. A stiff wind had started to whip up, blowing stinging grit against my nakedness. It mixed with my sweat, making grimy rivulets that ran down my skin.

That's when the first of them spotted me. From way back behind me the wind carried a faint, high cry. It was a genuine cowboy "yee-hah!" I looked over my shoulder. Atop the dunes, about three quarters of a mile behind me, was a man on a black horse. It was the big guy Arley'd called Bubba. He came riding down the dune full tilt, his horse kicking up a cloud of sand. I broke into a sprint. There was no cover for at least a mile in any direction. If he wanted to take a shot at me, then I was already dead.

Shooting me wasn't on Bubba's mind at all. As his horse closed the distance between us he started twirling a lariat over his head. He was playing cowboy, and I was the steer. I twisted and turned, running in a broken pattern to make it harder for him to lasso me. When he was only a few yards away, he tossed the rope. It was a good throw, and the loop dropped over me, but I leaped out of it before he could yank it tight. I kept running.

"Damn, girl, you're quick!" he shouted. "You're makin' this big fun!" His massive stallion bore down on me. That horse was good. No matter how I twisted and dodged, it stayed with me, constantly gaining.

Deadly Prey

Bubba began to toy with me, using the horse to herd me this way, then that way. I was starting to get tired.

Then he tossed the lasso at me again. As it dropped over me I tried to jump free once more, but I didn't quite make it. The loop pulled tight, snagging my left ankle, and I crashed flat, face-first into the dirt. The impact knocked the wind out of me, and before I could recover, Bubba was off the horse and on me like a bulldogger. He threw a loop around my wrists, pulling them together tight behind my back. Then he flipped me over.

The big bastard grinned down at me. "Now that's what I call bulldoggin'," he said. "I coulda shot you from a mile off, but I wanted a piece—can't let old Arley have all the fun!" He was trying to force my legs apart with his knee. I squirmed and struggled, but he was much bigger and stronger than me, and he had my hands tied.

He reached down and started fumbling with his belt, and I felt the rope loop around my wrists go a little slack as his grip loosened. "I'll just strangle you after . . . or maybe during . . ." he was saying.

I snapped my head forward, crashing my forehead into his face. The butt stunned him for a second. I snapped my head forward again, and this time I clamped my teeth on his nose.

He yowled, and I felt cartilage crunch between my teeth. I whipped my head from side to side, like a shark yanking a piece of meat off a man's leg, still grinding his nose between my teeth. He flailed his arms, then cuffed me on the side of the head. That finally broke my grip on his nose, and he reeled to his feet. One hand covered his face. Blood streamed out between his fingers. As soon as he was off me I leaped to my feet. It took an instant to shed the rope from

around my wrists and pull the other loop off my ankle.
Then we stood glaring at each other. I gave him a
snarl and a hiss.

"Goddab bidg! You bid off by goddab dode!" He
pulled a big bowie knife out of the sheath at his side
and lunged at me. As he moved I snapped the end of
the rope at him like a whip. It caught him across the
nose, and he fell back, howling.

I whipped the rope end at him again, this time
across the wrist holding the knife. There was a satisfying crack, and the knife fell to the ground. His wrist
was broken.

Bubba bellowed and leaped for me. I sidestepped
easily. For the first time all day I felt I was in control.
It felt good. As he shot past I hit his back leg with an
ankle sweep. He stumbled, and I drove an elbow
strike down onto the base of his skull.

He fell face-first, and I pounced. I planted my left
knee into his back between the shoulder blades, pin-
ning him, with my right leg out wide to brace me. I
looped a coil of the rope around his throat. "So you
were going to strangle me, hmm?" I purred in his ear
as he thrashed and gurgled. "Like this? Is this how
you were going to do it?" He didn't answer. He heaved
himself up onto his hands and knees. He clawed at my
right leg, trying to get a grip. I wrapped both legs
around him, hooking them into a figure four with my
right ankle behind my left knee. I squeezed him with
my legs until it felt like my thigh muscles would pop.
I arched my back and heard his ribs crack. He collapsed. I twisted the rope tighter around his neck.

When I released my grip, he was still twitching.
Maybe he would live. Maybe not. I rolled off him and
lay beside him for a few moments, gasping. My heart
was pounding. I willed it to slow down. I stood.

Deadly Prey

I wanted his clothes. I yanked his T-shirt off. The boots were way too large. Too bad. My feet were a mess. The socks might help. I pulled them off his feet.

I was starting to yank off his jeans when a snort startled me. The heat and the fight must have been getting to me, because I'd forgotten about his horse. Now I realized that it was my ticket out of this mess.

The horse wanted no part of me. It whinnied, it reared. I couldn't get near it. There was a thirty-ought-six Winchester rifle in the scabbard hanging from the horse's saddle. That gun would go a long way to evening the odds against me. I made a grab for it, and got caught by a hoof to my left shoulder for the trouble. It sent me flying. I got back up on my knees in time to see the horse racing off the way it had come.

My shoulder felt numb. My left arm hung. I felt along my collarbone with my right hand. Nothing, nothing, nothing . . . Aaagghh!

It didn't feel like a bad break, but in these circumstances it was bad enough. Damn, I'd gotten greedy! I should have left the damn horse and the damn gun alone!

I turned back to Bubba and continued stripping him. His breathing was shallow and ragged. I found that I could use my left hand if I didn't rotate my shoulder, and that made my work a little easier. I peeled his watch off his wrist, strapped it on my own. It was a good one, a Cartier tank. One-fifteen, it said. Later than I'd thought. I found matches in his pocket, a set of car keys.

A card in his wallet identified him as Robert Elliot Buell, Vice-President for Public Relations, Kincaid Software, Inc. There were credit cards, a few hundred in cash, a picture of his pretty wife and kid. I bet she was real proud of her Bubba. Other cards in the wallet told me he was a member of the El Paso Rotary Club, the Lions' Club, the Chamber of Commerce. A real upstanding citizen. I kept the matches and the cash.

Pretty soon I was dressed in some of Bubba's clothes. His pants were useless, about six inches too long and with a waist at least fourteen inches bigger around than mine. I wore the T-shirt like a minidress, belted with a length cut from the rope. The bowie knife hung in its sheath at my side. Bubba's thick wool socks covered my legs almost up to my knees. His matches and his money were stuffed into the right sock.

The Winchester cap was adjustable, and it kept the sun out of my eyes. I'd used Bubba's belt to strap my left arm across my chest. The less it moved, the less it hurt. I'd cut a twelve-foot length off the rope to use as a whip. I held it coiled in my right hand. I threw the rest of the rope down a gully, along with Bubba's boots, pants, and wallet. I looked down at myself in my new garb. "Well, Selina, girl, you always did have a fine fashion sense."

Bubba let out a groan. I kicked him in the head, and he shut up. Damn, I was thirsty. The sun was high. I remembered reading once that it could get up to a hundred and twenty in the desert. I didn't doubt it for a minute. If I didn't find something to drink soon, I was going to be in real trouble. I set off for the mountains again.

Deadly Prey

4.

I'd found a gully that ran in the general direction I
wanted to go. I guessed that water running from up in
the mountains followed the same course whenever it
rained. Over the years this gully had formed.

It was about fifteen feet deep and about twenty feet
wide. Its best feature was the overhanging shelf that
had been formed by erosion. If I hugged the wall, my
pursuers could look straight down into the gully and
still not see me. Its other virtue was that it was rela-
tively cool. The shelf shaded the bottom of the gully.
The only drawback was that it had been difficult to
get down into it with my injured arm, and it would be
even harder to get out in a hurry if I had to.

I set off at a nice, easy trot. I'd been moving along
at that pace for two hours when I got lucky. The gully
twisted, and around a bend that left the floor completely sheltered from the sun I found a little pool of
brackish water.

I immersed my face in the water. I scooped it up in
my hand and drank deep. It was alkaline, but it was
better than a saucer of fresh milk. I splashed it on my
neck and down my back. I peeled off Bubba's socks
and stuck my burning, shredded feet in the water. It
hurt like hell, but it felt great, too. I closed my eyes,
savoring the moment.

A low growl made my eyes snap open. The big cat
stood tensed on the other side of the pool of water. I'd
intruded on his territory, and he was letting me know
who it belonged to.

It was a leopard, a full-grown male. He was easily
two hundred and fifty pounds of sinew, teeth, and
claws in a spotted coat. He snarled at me, showing

two-inch canines. I sat back on my haunches and forced myself to relax. If there's anything I know, it's cats. He wasn't hungry, he wasn't even particularly angry. He was just annoyed that I had intruded on his space.

"Good kitty," I said gently. "Oh, such a beautiful kitty. Good boy." I trilled a soft leopard growl deep in my throat. I made the chuffing noise that leopards make when they're content and happy.

That got his interest. He cocked his head at me, curious. He knew I wasn't a leopard. At least I didn't look like one or smell like one. But I sounded like one. At last he decided I wasn't a threat. He gave me another growl to let me know who was boss, then dipped his head to lap up some water.

"Man, you *are* a beauty," I whispered to him. "What the hell are you doing out here? Don't you know you're on the wrong continent?" Of course I knew what he was doing here. He was prey for the Kincaid hunting club, just like me.

"What did you do, kitty? Did you figure out how to avoid them? How long have you been out here?" He sat back, regarding me. Then he yawned. He stretched out, sighed, and began to groom himself. So now a human in stolen socks was drinking his water and making cat noises? No big deal. He'd adjust. For however long he'd been eluding the Kincaids and their buddies, he'd made the best of circumstances. He was a survivor. If he could do it, then so could I.

The sound of an approaching helicopter broke my reverie. The leopard was up and running instantly, bounding away down the gully. I pressed my back against the wall, hoping that the overhang would shield me.

The copter swooped in low, passing overhead as it

followed the gully. It roared by. Then I heard the crack
of a high-powered rifle. I took a chance, scrambling
my way up until I could look over the lip.

I was a lot closer to the mountains. Close enough to
take a chance, try to make a break for the woodlands
that started on the nearest of them. I threw a glance
at the copter.

The leopard was racing across the desert floor head-
ing for the woods, and the helicopter was in pursuit.
The rifle cracked again, and the big cat stumbled.
Then he was up and running again.

I jumped up out of the gully and started waving my
good arm in the air. As the leopard swerved the copter
turned to follow. For a moment its nose was pointed
right at me. They had to see me. "Hey, you bastards!"
I yelled. "It's me you want! Here I am!"

Sure enough, the helicopter turned away from the
cat and headed in my direction. The leopard kept going, straight for the timber. So did I. I sprinted for
cover, picking a different line that would take me into
the woods a good half mile from where the leopard entered them.

The rifle cracked, and a bullet kicked up dust a yard
off to my left. I kept running straight. That shot was
just to scare me. I had them figured out. They'd taken
a lot of time and effort to get me here. My guess was
they weren't going to pick me off from a helicopter. It
wouldn't be sporting. As for shooting at the leopard,
that was just something to pass the time. Now that
they'd flushed me, *I* was the prey again.

Then I made it into the woods. I glanced back. The
copter was touching down. Arley Kincaid was at the
controls, with Billy-Ray next to him.

As the copter touched ground Billy-Ray popped out.
"Don't worry, Arley," I heard him shout above the

noise of the engine, "I can handle her! Now get out of here—it's *my* turn!" He had a walkie-talkie in his hand, and he waved it in the air. "I'll call you to come get me when I'm done!" He trotted toward the woods, walkie-talkie in one hand, hunting rifle in the other. The gunfighter rig slapped against his hip.

The copter lifted back up and swooped off toward the east. I bet myself that was where their hunting lodge was. I slipped deeper into the woods. Billy-Ray was coming for me, and I wanted to be ready for him.

My shoulder ached, but otherwise I felt better than I had all afternoon. The water had helped, and now the shady coolness of the woods was a welcome respite from the glare of the sun.

I knew how I wanted to deal with Billy-Ray, but I wanted to be farther in among the trees first. At last I found a nice, open forest clearing. I put my back up against a tree and waited.

My standing out there in the open was so unexpected that Billy-Ray didn't even notice me at first. He entered the clearing with his head down, following my tracks, the rifle cradled in his arms. He looked up and stopped dead, his mouth hanging open.

"What the hell are you doing standing there, girl?" He leveled the rifle at me. "It ain't no fun if you aren't trying to get away!"

I stepped away from the tree. We were facing each other, no more than ten feet apart. He had the barrel of the rifle pointing at my midsection.

He looked me over. "Looks like you've had a hard day," he said. "Maybe you just want me to put you out of your misery."

"I don't think so, Billy-Ray." I let a bit of seductive purr creep into my voice. "I know what you really want." I let the rope in my hand uncoil until most of

it lay on the ground. I'd tied a heavy knot the size of
a fist in the end of the rope. "You want a challenge, a
duel. That's why you wear the gunfighter rig, right?"

He licked his lips and narrowed his eyes. He was
trying to figure me out. I kept talking.

"So *you* get to be the man who killed the
Catwoman. But not with that big rifle. You want to
give me *some* kind of chance, right?"

"What are you getting at?"

"A duel, Billy-Ray. A quick-draw contest."

"You ain't got a gun."

"That's right." I gave the rope a little shake. "I've
got this."

He started to laugh. "You really *are* crazy." He put
the rifle down. We stared into each other's eyes. He
stopped laughing. "All right, then, you talked me into
it," he said, his voice taking on a hard edge. He tied
his holster to his thigh by the rawhide strips that
hung from it. He rolled his shoulders, widened his
stance, flexed his hand over the grip of his Colt. "Anytime you're ready, Catwoman."

"After you, Billy-Ray."

He glanced from my eyes to the coil of rope in my
hand, then back to my eyes.

He went for his gun.

The rope cracked as I snapped it up. The crack of a
whip is actually a miniature sonic boom. I've spent a
long time using and studying whips. Like throwing
a baseball or a punch, the motion doesn't start in the
arm, but in the driving leg. Velocity builds through
the snap of the hip, then accelerates through the
shoulder, the straightening arm, and out through the
length of the whip, until all the force is concentrated
at the tip . . . and whatever the tip strikes. Now seven
feet of rope whipped up at Billy-Ray, with a hard knot

the size of a fist at its end. It was like getting hit by an uppercut at the end of a ten-foot-long arm.

The knot caught Billy-Ray on the point of the chin before his Colt was completely out of its holster. The crack of his neck snapping echoed the crack of the rope. His grip relaxed and the gun dropped back into its holster. Billy-Ray fell back, dead.

I gave him a little nudge with my toe, just to make sure. "I *did* talk you into it, didn't I? You were right, Billy-Ray—you should've cut out my tongue."

5.

I found the little cave just before sunset. The day had gone considerably better after I killed Billy-Ray. He was a small guy, and his clothes fit me fine. Even his hiking boots fit when I wore both his socks and Bubba's. Putting the boots on had hurt like crazy, but my feet got used to them pretty quickly. I kept Bubba's cap. I guess every hunter likes to hang on to a trophy now and then.

I thought about the hunting rifle, but gave up on it. Maybe Rambo could work that thing one-handed, but I couldn't. The Colt was fine, and wearing it strapped to my hip provided a definite sense of security. Normally I don't care much for guns, but I was more than willing to make an exception today. My shoulder still caused me agony whenever I moved it wrong, but I kept my arm immobilized and tried to ignore the pain.

I found a nice little stream in the woods. I waited there after I'd drank my fill, and eventually a jackrabbit came to drink. I killed it the same way I'd killed Billy-Ray. I skinned it with Bubba's knife. I considered

Deadly Prey

cooking it, but smoke from a fire might lead Arley and Lynette to me, and I was too tired for another fight. I ate the rabbit raw. There wasn't much meat on it, and I was still hungry. But it was better than nothing.

The cave was half-hidden behind a clump of bushes. It wasn't a lot bigger than the cage I'd started the day in, but it felt much more homey. It was starting to get dark and the temperature was dropping fast. Better not to be caught outside.

Just before I climbed in for the night, Billy-Ray's walkie-talkie crackled.

Then, "Billy-Ray—where the hell are you?" It was Arley Kincaid.

I couldn't resist. I switched on the speaker. "I'm sorry, Arley, he checked out about two hours ago."

"Checked out . . . ? Selina, you bitch—you killed him!"

"Law of the jungle, sport, kill or be killed. And by the way, you should never call a cat 'bitch.' "

"Where are you?"

"You've got to be kidding. Sounds to me like you can't take the pressure, Kincaid. By the way, how's Bubba?"

"He was still alive when we found him."

"And now?"

"No." His voice sounded shaky.

"Look, Kincaid, I'll make you a deal. Let's call this thing even. You let me walk out of here, I don't come back looking for you and your sister. What do you say?"

I heard squabbling on the other end, and then Lynette came on. "Do you think we're stupid? We know your reputation. Even's never good enough for Catwoman—you always have to win. Well, this time you're gonna lose."

"Have it your way. I'll see you both in the morning."
I clicked the walkie-talkie off. Then I banged it with a
rock until I was sure it would stay off for good.

I squatted in front of my cave. The lair of the
Catwoman. Batman gets the Batcave, I thought. I get
this. Soon it was dark.

I'd forgotten what night is like in the country. The
stars were incredible, spectacular. They filled the sky
with light. Then the moon came out, lighting up the
forest. I lay there in front of my cave for a while,
counting shooting stars and thinking about men. I'd
been betrayed by lovers before, but this was ridiculous.

Maybe I'd take the story to the Oprah show. I could
see it. There I'd be, on stage with several other bro-
kenhearted women, all waiting to tell their tales of
woe. And then Oprah would come to me. "Well,
Oprah, my boyfriend and his buddies drugged me,
took me to a ranch in Texas, stripped me naked, and
set me loose so they could hunt me down and kill me."
Oprah would shake her head. From the audience
would come a couple of shouts of, "tell it, sister," and
"let it out, girl." Then Oprah would bring Arley out to
get his side of the story.

Sorry, Oprah, I thought. Arley's not going to be able
to tell anybody anything after tomorrow. Geez, it was
getting cold. Out here the daytime fried you and the
nighttime froze. Bedtime. I climbed down into the
cave. I pulled Billy-Ray's light jacket around me and
went to sleep.

I was awakened by a dragging sound. I was alert
immediately. I braced back against the wall and held
Billy-Ray's gun out in front of me. Something was in
the cave with me. I could hear it breathing. My left
arm stabbed with pain, but I used it to fumble the

book of matches out of a jacket pocket and light one.
The leopard was in the cave with me. He lay on his
side, panting. He'd dragged what looked like an antelope haunch in with him. That's what woke me.

We stared at each other. He looked as surprised to
see me as I was to see him. We both shivered from the
cold.

I made my friendly-leopard noises. The last thing I
wanted was to have to kill him. He looked at me curiously again. I chuffed and growled. So did he. He got
back up to his feet, painfully, I noticed. He growled
softly and started moving toward me. I hesitated, not
wanting to pull the trigger. Then he was too close for
me to shoot anyway. He ducked his head and rubbed
it against my leg. The match went out.

I lit another one. The leopard lay against me, purring. I touched him gingerly, then more confidently. I
stroked his fur, scratched behind his ears. He loved it.
Catwoman magic, I guess.

I examined him carefully. I'd seen him stumble. I
wanted to see if he'd been shot. At last I found a
bloody furrow gouged along his right hip. The bullet
had clipped him, but it hadn't penetrated. We made
happy leopard noises together and shared his antelope
haunch. He ate most of it. I guess I wasn't really that
hungry after all. We slept huddled together. It was
warmer that way.

6.

I woke at dawn. The cave was filled with the heavy
smell of cat, but the leopard was already gone. I rose
unsteadily. My left arm was numb. I tried to move the

fingers of my left hand. They wouldn't move. I couldn't get the jacket on, so I left it in the cave.

The first step was agony. I was glad I hadn't taken Billy-Ray's hiking boots off last night. I wouldn't have been able to get them back on this morning.

After a few steps my feet began to accept the pain. I made my way back to the stream. At least I had water.

As I leaned over the stream to splash water in my face, I saw a streak of gray out of the corner of my eye. I pivoted toward it, yanking the Colt out of its holster. A whip cracked and the gun went flying from my hand. There was a ragged, bloody gash across my fingers. Lynette stood before me, holding a whip.

She was wearing my costume. The bitch was wearing *my* Catwoman costume!

"Meeooww," she said. "You're a mess! Pathetic! You never deserved this costume! I'm the Catwoman now. You're just another also-ran, and it's going to be a pleasure to kill you!"

I reached for the knife on my belt, and she cracked the whip again. The knife was ripped away from my hip. I looked down at my side. The sheath was torn off, and my blue jeans were slashed. Blood oozed from my side. She was good with that thing, I had to give her that.

"Is this how you want it, Lynette? Just cut me to pieces without giving me a chance to fight back?"

"Fight back? That's a laugh, hon," she said. "You know that Green Beret I told you about yesterday? He was a big, rough, tough handsome thing. Over two hundred pounds, easy. You know how I killed him? With my hands. One against one. Fair fight." She tossed the whip aside. She held up one clawed glove, scratched the air. "Now, if you want to take your cos-

Deadly Prey

tume away from the new Catwoman, you just come on
ahead and try!"

I came at her in a weave pattern, right side forward. Fighting her one-armed wasn't going to be easy.
Especially since she was hanging back, waiting for me
to make a move. Once I committed she'd be all over
me, and I knew from experience what kind of damage
those claws could do. But I'd never been on the receiv-
ing end of them before.

When she was almost in range, I feinted a little
shuffle-skip step, like I was going to shoot a side kick
at her. She was nervous enough to respond, pivoting
to smother the kick. That was enough. I'd gotten *her*
to commit. I changed my movement in midstep, whip-
ping around a spinning roundhouse kick that caught
her in the back of the head, sending her reeling. But
before I could capitalize on it, she rolled through a
ukemi fall and was back on her feet. She was really
good. Maybe if I was fresh and uninjured, I might
have been able to take her. But not today.

She threw a combination at me, starting with a side
kick of her own to bring her into hand range, then
throwing a flurry of raking claws and punches. I
blocked, parried, and countered, but enough of them
got through to rip me up pretty good. She caught me
with a punch to the solar plexus, knocking the wind
out of me. She slashed her left hand across my chest,
leaving a line of bloody scratches. I lurched backward, and she drove a thrust kick into my injured
shoulder. The force of the kick knocked me back several
yards, and I crashed onto my back in a thicket of brambles. I think I blacked out for a second, but when I
came to, she was moving in to finish me off.

That's when I spotted Billy-Ray's Colt, lying in the
thicket not six inches from my right hand. In one

smooth motion I grabbed, cocked, and aimed it. Lynette froze. But she still wasn't scared. Yet.

"Come on, Selina." She hissed my name. "We agreed on a *fair fight*."

She sprang for me, claws extended, and I fired. The first bullet caught her in the chest, knocking her backward. The second nearly ripped her right arm off. The third one tore her throat open.

I got to my feet and staggered over to her. She looked up at me, eyes glazing over, dying. "Those were your words, Lynette," I said, "not mine. Besides . . . when did a cat ever fight fair?"

And a broad-head arrow whacked into my right thigh. I went down screaming with pain and shock, a red haze in front of my eyes. I rolled to my side, grasping for the gun, but it was nowhere within reach.

Arley Kincaid stepped out of the woods.

He stood looking down at me the way I had gazed down at his sister a moment before. He had another arrow nocked in his bow, and it pointed straight at my heart. He gave Lynette a quick glance, then turned his attention back to me.

"You were damn good, darlin', damn good. Everything I hoped for an' more. You got all three of 'em, one way or another." The bastard was smiling. I'd just killed his sister and his two best friends, and now, because *he* was about to kill *me*, he was smiling!

"Doesn't it even bother you that they're dead?" I asked.

" 'Course it does. But terrible hunting accidents happen."

"I thought you loved your sister."

"I'll love her share of the business even more. An' now it's your turn." He began to draw the bow. The pain in my leg was excruciating, but I couldn't let him

see that. I looked up past him, into the branches of
the trees. And I started to laugh.

That got him. He relaxed the bowstring, gave me a
puzzled look. "I'm about to kill you, gal, and you're
laughing at me. Now why is that?" he asked.

"Because I know something you don't know," I answered.

"An' what might that be?"

"I know that *I'm* not the one who's going to die."

A blank look crossed his face. And then he heard
the snarl up in the branches behind him. He half
turned. . . .

I'm sure the impact alone of the leopard hitting him
killed Arley. If not, it was the raking claws that disemboweled him an instant later. Or the fangs that
tore off his face. In any event, he died.

7.

I lost consciousness twice trying to pull the arrow out
of my leg, but eventually I succeeded. I tied a tourni-
quet around my leg and the bleeding stopped. I guess
the arrow missed the major arteries. Using Arley's
bow as a crutch, I hobbled down out of the woods. The
Jeep was waiting at the edge of the desert. I'd found
keys in Arley's pocket and assumed it would be
nearby. Luckily it had an automatic transmission. I
just didn't feel up to working a clutch and shifting today.

It took a little coaxing, but at last the leopard
climbed in and sat next to me. I started the Jeep and
pointed it east.

Less than an hour later I spotted the hunting lodge.

It was a big, adobe ranch house and barn. The helicopter sat out back, and there were several luxury sedans parked beside the house. A dirt road led away to the south.

The cat helped me out of the Jeep. I hobbled into the house, the leopard following cautiously, growling at the human smells inside. I wasn't surprised to find that no one was home.

There was an opened packing crate in the middle of the living room. That's what I'd traveled in from Gotham. My silk dress and my purse lay in the crate. I checked the purse. My wallet was still in there. I was back in business.

I found a bathroom, washed up, and tended to my wounds as best I could. Then I slept.

Later I searched the house. There were hunting trophies everywhere. No stuffed people, however. In Lynette's closet I found a clean pair of jeans, sneakers, a fresh blouse, and a blazer. When I was dressed, I checked myself out in her mirror. Not bad. Considering.

The leopard had been very good, padding around the house, sleeping on the couch. But he was getting understandably restless. He kept telling me it was time to go.

"Just have to make a couple of calls," I told him. I spent the next hour on the phone, making arrangements. When the Kincaids saw the overseas calls on their next phone bill they'd . . . oh, but, silly me, they *wouldn't* be seeing their next bill, would they?

The last call I made was to Otto, my business manager.

"Selina, how wonderful to hear from you! Where have you been these past few days?"

"I took a small vacation. In fact, I'll be out of town for the next few weeks."

"A vacation! How wonderful! You take them so rarely. Where will you be going?"

"Kenya. A friend of mine wants to go home, and I'm going to make sure that he gets settled in okay." I scratched the leopard behind the ear. He licked my hand with his raspy tongue.

"That sounds delightful, Selina. Is there anything you want me to take care of while you're away?"

"As a matter of fact, there is. I want you to sell all my shares of Kincaid Software."

"Really? But they're doing so well."

"I'm afraid that's going to change quite suddenly. I want you to get rid of the stock as soon as we're off the phone."

"Of course. Will there be anything else?"

"Not until I'm back in Gotham. Bye, Otto."

The leopard accepted the leash I improvised. I explained to him that it was only for appearances, and I think he understood. We left the house, being careful to lock the door behind us. For a moment I stood looking at the quartet of luxury cars parked beside the house. "Hmm," I asked the leopard, "which one shall we take?" He growled softly.

"You're absolutely right," I said. "The perfect choice."

We took the Jaguar.

On the Wings of Angel

KRISTINE KATHRYN RUSCH

Fifteen years ago, somewhere in the Midwest

The bus stopped, and Angel got off. She walked across the road, watching the heat rise in waves. No one should have to go to school when the temperature was over eighty-five. Especially the elementary school where the windows barely opened, and no one had heard of air-conditioning. She couldn't wait to get into the house, have a big glass of orange juice, and then go to the creek. The water would be warm against her feet, and she would stay there, in the shade, until her mother called her for dinner.

She walked up the gravel driveway to the sprawling ranch house. Sweat trickled down her back. The house looked quiet. Even the dogs were probably sleeping in the shade. The new trees her dad had planted around the property last spring were still small and spindly. Soon, he hoped, they would grow

Kristine Kathryn Rusch

tall, so no one could see the house from the road. Angel liked seeing the house. It welcomed her when she got off the bus.

The bend in the driveway hid the house from her. Then she turned and felt a small thread of unease. Shadow lay in the driveway—in the sun—sprawled in an awkward position. Usually he ran to her and greeted her, tongue lolling, except on hot days, when he whined at her from the coolness under the porch. Molly, the little poodle, was nowhere in sight.

Both her parents' cars were in the driveway—that at least was normal—but the backdoor stood open, the screen plastered against the wood boards at the side of the building. Odd way for them to cope with the heat. Maybe Mom didn't want to start the air-conditioning in early May.

Angel stopped beside Shadow and crouched. Flies buzzed around his neck and crawled on the matted fur beneath his chin. His eyes were open, but he saw nothing. A thick, bloody stench rose in the air, and Angel let out a small whimper.

Mom wouldn't let anyone touch Shadow. Shadow was her dog—her best friend and guard dog. Only, when she said guard dog, no one ever laughed.

Angel knew that her parents were not like other parents. They never had company and rarely left the house. They would only let her go to school after the bus driver assured them he would pick her up at the driveway and not let her out of his sight until she went inside the school building. She could never have other kids over, and she could never go to their places to play. She knew it was weird, but it had always been like that. Always.

She stood up, wanting to hold Shadow, but wanting

313

On the Wings of Angel

to be away from him at the same time. "Mom?" she
called. "Mom?"

Her voice had more panic in it than she felt. No one
responded.

Angel walked the rest of the way down the driveway, watching the house flicker in the heat waves. Everything had a sharp, unreal edge—the cars, with
their layer of dust; the shed, its door ajar; her swing
set with the chains rusted and the slide in need of re-
pair. Her father had promised to fix it next week. Her
breath was coming in little gasps.

Molly was huddled in a black bundle at the base of
the stairs. Flies buzzed around her, too. Angel bent
over, saw the same wound that ran along the jaw.
Molly was her dog—a present for her tenth birthday
last June. But Angel couldn't cry. Not now. Because
there were reddish-black footprints going up the white
stairs. Big ones. Bigger than her own, bigger than her
daddy's. She stepped beside the prints, careful not to
mar them. She swallowed once, hands shaking. Her
entire body was covered with sweat.

There was no orange juice waiting inside. She knew
that without going in.

More reddish-black stains on the linoleum. The
kitchen stools were on their side, a glass of milk
spilled and dripping off the orange countertop. Flies
filled the house. Her dad's gun was lying in a mess of
papers on the floor. His work papers, covered with formulas and equations he said she wouldn't understand
for a few years yet. The work papers he had shown to
Harold Rosen the night before. Rosen, who had said,
"My God, man. Do you realize what the arms community would pay for this?" Rosen, whom her daddy had
thrown out of the house.

The black notebook was missing from its usual spot.

The one her daddy said to burn if anything should happen to him.

His hand was sprawled, outstretched, near the gun. She knew it was his because of the blunt fingers, the turquoise ring Mom had given him. His arm was bare, raised above his head. Tufts of hair covered his face, but he was as motionless as the dogs. Behind him, Mom huddled. She stared at Angel, but didn't see her.

They had been there since morning. They never spent the afternoons in the kitchen, but in their offices outside of the house. Something happened just after she left. Something awful . . .

A scream built in her throat, but she didn't let it out. No one would hear. No one would care.

She made herself go to the phone, somehow still untouched in the mess the living room area had become. She picked up the receiver, heard the dial tone, and dialed "O".

The operator's nasal greeting made her pause. Then Angel made herself speak.

"Hi," she said. "I think my mom and dad are dead. . . ."

Gotham City—Now

Selina Kyle leaped across the gutter, her fake tail behind her. She tugged on her mask and patted the jewels against her hip. The heist had gone well. The safe didn't have as many jewels as promised, but those that were there were beyond her expectations.

She stopped. A faint cool breeze caressed her face. Some nights she loved the freedom of the rooftops.

On the Wings of Angel

Gotham City looked almost beautiful through the
haze of lights. Buildings rose like shadows against the
skyline, and below, cars moved like well-lit ants. No
one knew she was up here. She stood alone on the as-
phalt roof, a solitary creature hidden from the city.

Better than what she did before. Anything was better than that.

She hurried across the roof, leaped over the space
between the buildings, careful not to look down. She
scurried, letting the darkness and shadows hide her,
until she was only a few blocks from home. Then she
heard a familiar voice.

"Didn't yer momma ever tell you that little girls
shouldn't be out after dark?"

A muffled response, female, then male laughter and
the sound of a chain hitting the wall. Selina made her
way to the edge of the roof, carefully avoiding the
gravel and dirt that would give voice to her footsteps.
Not even the cat, for which she was named, could
move more quietly.

She leaned over the edge and saw below a slender
woman backed against the dirty alley wall. The
woman was young, in her twenties, with light blond
hair and a wiry frame almost hidden beneath her
frothy dress. No concerts were held in this neighborhood; no theaters or fancy restaurants stood nearby.
She had no reason to be dressed like that, unless she
was coming home from somewhere. Unless she lived
here.

Shadows moved around her—six men, boys actually,
the recognized voices. Selina had seen them on other
nights, terrorizing the homeless, frightening old people. One night she had found one of them breaking
into an elderly man's apartment. She had kicked the
hood, knocking him unconscious against the wall and,

Kristine Kathryn Rusch

she learned later, breaking almost all his ribs. He wasn't with the group tonight. He was in the state penitentiary, where they all should be.

She eased her way onto the rusted fire escape. The jewels hit the railing with a clang and she forced herself into the darkness near the side of the building. One of the boys looked up.

"Hear that?"

"I didn't hear nothing."

"Probably a cat."

Selina smiled and looked down. They were all looking up, a bit nervously, she thought, except for the woman. The woman braced herself against the wall, then planted a high-heeled foot into the center boy's groin.

He let out a scream that echoed through the alley. The others turned, and the woman was on them, all legs and feet and flailing arms. Martial-arts training with a touch of something else. She knocked out one of the boys who was bending over his felled companion, and then elbowed another into a pile of garbage cans. They toppled with a clatter, and the three remaining boys started to run. She grabbed a can lid and sent it sailing like a Frisbee into the back of one boy's head. He fell forward, catching a companion's leg, and that boy fell, too. Only one boy escaped, and as he turned onto the sidewalk the red-and-blue lights of a police car bathed the street.

The woman ripped the frills off her dress until she had ten long pieces of cloth. Then she bound the boys hand and foot, leaving them in the alley for the police.

Selina suppressed the urge to shout her appreciation. Police below. She had to be quiet. The last thing she needed was some cop pulling her aside, especially in this outfit, especially with jewels on her side.

On the Wings of Angel

The woman disappeared down the alley, and with one glance back at the police, Selina followed.

He dropped like a bat out of the sky, landing on the garbage-strewn concrete of the alley. The flashing police lights illuminated his masked face, his dark costume, the cloak that looked like wings in the darkness. From what Gordon could see of his mouth, Batman's face held no expression at all.

"You didn't contact me," Batman said.

"We didn't know until one of the tenants called in a 911, reporting screaming nearby. A patrol circled, saw a boy wearing gang colors running out of the alley. When they arrested him, he pointed them here." Gordon ran a hand through his white hair. He had arrived a few minutes after the squads. The five gang members were still unconscious. He was pleased to have them in custody—he had a number of charges to bring against them, not counting the ones their friend would attest to—but the circumstances confused him. Batman was the only person in the city who would take the law into his own hands. At least until tonight.

Batman leaned over the nearest gang member, touched the cloth binding his wrists and ankles. "Tidy work," he said. "Strong knots. You mind if I have one of these strips of cloth?"

Gordon nodded his head. They had more than enough for forensics to go on.

An ambulance pulled up at the mouth of the alley, and two paramedics came out. One of the policemen pointed them to the boy lying next to the garbage-can lid, arms outstretched. "Breathing shallow, lips and fingernails blue," the officer said as he crouched beside them.

"They badly hurt?" Batman asked.

One boy writhed on the ground, bent in a fetal position. He had been rolling and moaning ever since Gordon had arrived. Gordon had seen the boy's hands cupping his genitals and blood running between his fingers.

"God knows," Gordon said. The scene disturbed him. Five boys known for their anger, toughness, and strength, laid flat in an alley. A sixth so frightened he would talk. The commissioner hadn't seen anything like that since . . . well, since Batman came to Gotham City.

"Maybe they·ran up against a more major crime figure, one who didn't like them messing in his territory," he said.

Batman held up the cloth. It changed color with the revolving lights, but not enough to hide the white eyelet pattern of a ruffle. It reminded Gordon of the petticoats his grandmother used to wear. "I don't think so," Batman said. "I think we have someone here we have never met before. Someone who uses her skirts to catch boys."

The woman traveled swiftly by foot, making her way through Gotham's mean streets as if they held no threat to her at all. Selina followed her, careful to remain hidden on the rooftops above. The woman moved with such confidence that Selina was surprised she hadn't noticed her before. Yet no one new to the city would walk that way. No one new to the city would step into the streets without fear.

Unless that person had nothing to fear.

On the Wings of Angel

The woman stopped outside a seedy motel. She stepped over the wino sprawled in front of the doorway and let herself in. Selina crouched on a balcony, waiting to see if the woman would come out.

The cool breeze sent a chill through her. She really had to get home to her cats, to put the jewels away, to think about her next plan—a job that was scheduled in four days, if the shipment arrived. She didn't have time to waste on a balcony, watching a woman she didn't even know.

A light came on in one of the windows. The woman stood by the battered wooden door, a sagging bed between her and the window. The room was rented furnished. Only two pictures on the dressing table and clothes in the closet hinted that it was occupied.

The woman crossed to the window, braced her hands on the frame, and looked out into the night. She was young, pretty, with wide eyes and high cheekbones. But Selina recognized her expression. Cold, empty, unloved.

She needed a cat. Just one would ease the loneliness.

The woman brought the window frame down with a bang that echoed in the darkness. Then she pulled the shade. Selina stared at the window for a moment. Something about the woman appealed to her. Something in the woman's strength and vulnerability reminded Selina of herself.

Bruce Wayne sat in the Batcave. The cave was silent. The bats were out, and would return at dawn fresh from hunting and ready for sleep. Around him, the computers whirred, although he wasn't running a program. The television monitors displayed a variety of programming and scenes from the Wayne Manor grounds, but Bruce had turned off the sound.

He wanted to think.

The piece of cloth dangled before him, like an interesting proposition.

He had been after that particular street gang for days. They had remained out of sight, as if they knew he was searching for them, as if they knew that one more act would send Batman after them.

They had been terrorizing the poor of the city for weeks, beating them, brutalizing them, killing them. The gang had robbed a few well-to-do citizens, probably to keep the members in drugs, but mostly they turned their vicious attention on the less fortunate.

Gordon had asked for Batman's help, and Batman had been willing to give it. Despite his searches, he had found nothing. No trail.

And now all the members of the gang were hospitalized or in prison. They would be tried and convicted, of that Gordon was certain. And for once, Bruce felt left out of the loop.

The cloth was curious. Ruffles from a woman's dress. High-heel prints in the garbage. One man, nearly castrated by something sharp. A good kick to the groin?

Who would do something like that? Catwoman, certainly, but not unless provoked. And the ruffles weren't her style. She would leave a different kind of calling card, something tougher and feline.

Besides, a jewel heist, the first in months, had occurred miles from the attack. Catwoman never struck twice in the same night. Unless she had been caught on the way home.

Bruce steepled his fingers and rubbed them against his lips. Something about the whole attack didn't feel

On the Wings of Angel

right. It didn't look like self-defense and it surely wasn't done out of anger. No. Someone was trying to send a message.

But to whom?

Ralph Lowenstein walked across the tiled floor of the corridor, his rubber-soled shoes making no sound. He loved the silence of the labs, the cool, antiseptic scent of the air. For a time he could forget that he lived in Gotham, could forget the crime and pollution outside, could forget that if he so much as walked through the wrong door, he could get mugged and killed. He was more nervous than usual, with the jewels coming in. Estelle had begged for her jewels for the Gotham Opera's performance of the *Magic Flute*. She was tired, she said, of living like dethroned royalty. She wanted her friends and colleagues to know she was married to one of the richest men in the country. If she couldn't enjoy it while she was young, she said—and he had had to suppress a snort because since when was forty young?—she would never get a chance to enjoy it.

He warned her. No one had caught Catwoman, and jewels were her favorite target. If she knew that Estelle's emerald set alone was worth a half million, imagine how she would drool over the rest of the collection.

Still, he indulged his wife. The years had made him placid. He had turned a tidy profit with formulas and lab work and had thought Estelle his reward. She turned out to be small-minded and dull. Catwoman, he knew, was smart. And dangerous. It had been a long time since he had had his hands on something dangerous.

He could hardly wait to see how something dangerous—someone dangerous—would feel.

He turned into the lab and stared for a moment at the orderly row of microscopes, beakers, and petri dishes. Only a handful of the researchers worked this late, and usually they spent the last hour or two writing up the day's notes. He would download each file, read it, and combine the information. None of the researchers really knew what they were looking for, and only one had ever in all the years questioned Ralph's methods. His explanations sounded airtight, and he played the part of the crazy rich scientist well enough that his employees expected a bit of eccentricity.

Once he made sure everything was in place, he shut out the light, closed the door, and continued down the hallway. He had two more stops and at least three more hours of work before he could go home.

And by the weekend he would have his reward. Catwoman would take the bait. She had to.

Selina usually slept well after a heist, but the next morning she found herself staring at the ceiling long before dawn. Even the cats were still asleep, huddled in their customary night places: Misty at the foot of the bed, Spike sprawled along the headboard, Thorne at the window. The other cats were scattered throughout the apartment, but Selina couldn't see them.

She kept seeing the woman every time she closed her eyes. Something was off, something bothered her. And whenever something was out of phase, Selina had to put it to right.

She got up, showered, dressed, and fed the sleepy, stunned cats. Then she put on a wide-brimmed hat that gave her an air of sophistication, applied makeup to her face, and grabbed a purse. Her pumps were low-slung, but still respectable. Respectable enough, anyway, that a woman who wore dresses in Gotham's back alleys would think Selina legitimate.

Selina waited only a half hour outside the hotel before the woman appeared. She wore jeans, a blouse, and tennis shoes, and walked with the long stride of a runner. She bought a newspaper from a street vendor, then went inside a nearby deli.

Selina smiled. Breakfast.

She waited a moment just in case the woman came out again, then bought a newspaper and glanced at it. The woman's attack on the thugs had made the front page. Selina's heist had been relegated to the inside pages.

She snapped the newspaper as she folded it in half and stuck it under her arm. Inside pages, indeed. Then she took a deep breath and stepped inside the deli.

The air was hot and smelled of baked bread and frying bacon. Behind the counter, the beefy owner shouted instructions to his staff while punching numbers on the old-fashioned cash register. A waitress, hair piled on her head and skirt too short, chomped on a piece of gum as she leaned across the glass partition hiding the baked goods.

Selina scanned the room and saw the woman in the back corner, legs crossed, feet resting on the chair across from her. A glass of orange juice and a cup of coffee sat on the paper place mat. A few of the other tables were full, but not enough to justify sharing a table.

"Just take a seat, honey," the waitress said, waving a hand.

Selina nodded once, not quite willing to make a decision. She didn't know what she would say to the woman, how they would connect, only that they had to.

"Hon," the waitress said. "You want to order out?"

Selina smiled and shook her head. She made her way through the narrow room to the back corner. The woman didn't look up, but her grip on the newspaper tightened.

"Mind if I join you?"

The woman looked around the paper. "There's plenty of tables."

"Yes," Selina said, pulling back a chair, careful that it wasn't the one the woman's feet rested on. "But I want to talk to you. You're new in town."

The woman blinked and folded the paper. "What are you, the Welcome Wagon?"

The comment made a slight flush run through Selina's cheeks. In that outfit, she felt rather like the Welcome Wagon women she had seen on television. "No," she said. "But I have noticed you. And I came to offer you a job."

"A job?" The woman set her paper down as the waitress brought an order of scrambled eggs and ham. Selina ordered coffee and a roll and waited until the waitress left. She needed time to think. If the woman did take her up on the job, she had to have something for her. "What makes you think I need a job?"

"You're not living in the best of places and you don't belong in Gotham. Seems to me a job is what you're looking for."

"Who are you? What gives you the right to follow me?"

"Oh, bad manners on my part." Selina extended a gloved hand. "Selina Kyle. I run a small business near here and I have seen you the last several days. You look a little too wholesome for the neighborhood, and I remembered a friend—what it was like to be new to the city."

The woman took her hand in a firm grip. "My name is Angel," she said. "And I don't need your job. I'm looking for Batman."

Bruce Wayne hurried across the street, his long coat flapping around him. A taxi swerved around him and honked, and another slammed on its brakes. Bruce lifted a hand, as if the power of his gesture could stop them, and jumped onto the curb.

He hated being late for meetings. And the annual stockholders' meeting at Nenex was one of the important ones, especially since he was on the board. Sometimes, when he was busy with other matters—Batman matters—he sent his attorney as proxy. But for meetings like this, when the future of the company was at stake, he always tried to show.

He dodged across the rain-slicked sidewalk and went through the revolving door of the Nenex building. As he stepped into the wide marble hallway the street noises disappeared. A huge expanse of space led to the long desk at the end, the desk where a single receptionist sat, protecting the rows and rows of elevators. Bruce didn't have to stop; the receptionist knew who he was. He just waved and darted for the elevators leading to the top floor.

As he got on, a squat heavyset man got off. His face tanned by too much sun, his eyes dark and slightly slanted, and his clothing's European cut all distinguished him as not from Gotham City. Bruce had seen him before, somewhere. He let the camera in his mind snap a few shots of the man and got into the elevator.

A chill ran up his spine as the door closed. Something wasn't right here. The man didn't belong, especially on the top floors just before a stockholders' meeting.

Then it came to him as the elevator zoomed past the lower floors. He had seen that man on videotape in Commissioner Gordon's office. They were looking at films of international terrorists in a case that broke several months ago.

The man was an international arms dealer.

But Nenex was a genetics engineering firm. It had nothing to do with weapons at all.

"Batman," Selina said. She pulled off her gloves and picked up the cup of coffee the waitress had left. "Why would you want to meet Batman?"

Angel's lips tightened, and she looked away.

Selina took a sip of the coffee. It was made from fresh-roasted beans, but had the bitterness of old grounds.

"I don't even know you. Why should I tell you anything?"

Selina shrugged. "Because I'm curious, and you're lonely."

Angel gave Selina a measuring glance. "I finally found someone I've been tracking for fifteen years."

"And you need Batman's help to capture this person?"

"I don't need anyone's help." Angel pushed a strand of hair out of her face. "And I don't need nosy people hanging around my breakfast table."

"Fair enough," Selina said. She wrote her phone number on a corner of the place mat and ripped it off. "If you need anything, call me. There's things that Batman can never help you with."

On the Wings of Angel

Angel looked up then, startled, as if the idea that Batman couldn't help her had never crossed her mind.

Selina grabbed her gloves, the roll, and the tab and walked to the counter. "Changed my mind," she said. "I'd like this wrapped up." She paid for her food, took the package, and went outside, hands shaking. Batman. Angel wanted Batman. Why was it that young women always thought of Batman as a sort of savior? He wasn't. He only helped the people he thought deserved it.

Selina handed the packaged roll to a wino leaning against a building, then hurried down the street. The encounter with Angel had taken away her appetite.

That night the bat signal flared over Gotham. The yellow light surrounding the black bat dominated the night sky.

Angel stopped along the street outside her hotel, staring up. Then she began to run in the direction of the signal.

Selina looked out her window, swore, and hastily donned her Catwoman outfit. She slipped out the window, hoping she wasn't too late.

Bruce Wayne disappeared from a small gathering of Nenex stockholders, heart hammering in his chest. Within a matter of minutes he had made one phone call to Commissioner Gordon's office and changed, then drove the Batmobile rapidly down Gotham's streets.

Commissioner Gordon hung up the phone, hands shaking, unable to get rid of a feeling of impending doom. Batman is on his way, Gordon reassured himself, but the reassurance felt hollow.

And the two rival gangs who had prompted the

emergency call continued waging war on each other in
the center of Gotham. Only ten boys were involved,
but the amount of gunfire made the small neighborhood sound like a battle zone. None of them glanced
up, even though the light from the signal, reflecting
off the thick clouds, illuminated their faces and made
the automatic weapons easier to aim.

Selina caught up with Angel a few blocks away from
the shooting. Angel was running in the wrong direction, toward the source of the bat signal instead of the
source of the problem. She ran like an accomplished
runner, the distance not tiring her, even though Selina
could feel the same distance in her arms and legs. If
the woman kept going, she would end up at Gotham
police headquarters.

Selina decided to let her run.

Angel stopped suddenly, grabbed the back of one
leg, and leaned against a brick wall. She rubbed.
Selina got close enough to see through the streetlight,
realized there was no blood, probably a cramp.

Then Angel looked up like someone surfacing from a
long sleep, gazed at the signal, and cocked her head,
listening. Selina swallowed. She wanted the woman
out of the way, out of the danger. She thought about
swooping down, leading Angel to the police station
herself, then smiled at the idea. Catwoman leading an
innocent woman into police headquarters. The woman
would disappear in a matter of seconds and Catwoman would be interrogated for hours.

The woman made her own decisions. Selina had no
right to interfere. She hated it when someone inter-
fered with hers.

Angel did a few stretches, then jogged back in the

On the Wings of Angel

direction from which she had come. Selina followed, a discreet distance behind.

The Batmobile skidded to a halt in the center of the war zone. Bullets pinged off the car, damaging the paint, and zinging in another direction. Batman got out and stood for a moment, allowing his cape to swirl around him. The gunfire stopped. He could see movement around the corners of buildings.

Sirens echoed behind him. The police were coming.

Then the gunshots started again. Batman saw a muzzle flare, released a wire, wrapped up the gun, and pulled it back, clattering at his feet. He kicked it under the Batmobile, then confiscated another gun, and another. The sound of running feet blended with the sirens. Without their guns, the boys were cowards.

Squad cars circled the area like wagon trains in a B-movie. Batman hurried after one of the boys who was headed up the stairs in an abandoned building. He caught the boy by the shirt—and hauled him back outside. The shooting had stopped. Police had gathered the other gang members and were separating them into cars.

Two bodies lay on the pavement, both young boys no more than thirteen. Batman knelt by one, closed the staring eyes, and ran a hand along the boy's still-warm face. Then he went to the other boy and saw his chest rising in shallow breaths.

"We need an ambulance!" he cried. He loosened the boy's clothing, looking for the wound. A young woman knelt beside him, her fingers nimble. She pulled the shirt apart, found the two shots evenly spaced on the boy's belly. She ripped a piece of cloth off her skirt and pressed it to the wounds.

"Hold this," she said.

Batman applied pressure, much as she had, relieved to have someone beside him who was unafraid of blood and knew how to handle an emergency. Most people got in the way during emergencies. She placed her ear by the boy's chest, then tilted his head back and began mouth-to-mouth. She kept the boy breathing until the ambulance arrived, a few minutes later.

As they hauled the boy away Batman and the young woman stood. "Thank you," he said. "I'll see to it that the police department commends your bravery."

She smiled and tilted her head. He realized then that she was younger than he thought—midtwenties at most—and beautiful. "I don't need any commendations," she said. "I actually came to see you."

"Me?"

She nodded. "I want to join you. I want to become just like you."

Selina crouched on the roof, watching Angel talk with Batman. Selina leaned over the concrete edge, her tail curling behind her. She hated the way Angel's hand pressed on Batman's chest as they talked, the way they had worked together on that dying boy, the easy camaraderie. She didn't know if the strength of her emotion came because Angel could talk easily with Batman or because Batman was paying attention to Angel.

Selina suspected it was both reasons, and disliked them at the same time.

She had herself. She had her cats. That was all she needed. She didn't know why she wasted her time following a woman who idolized Batman. No sane

On the Wings of Angel

woman would idolize the man. Selina tried hard not to
think of him at all.

Although that rarely worked.

She got up, dusted herself off, then hurried away
from the crime scene. She had another crime scene to
inspect. She had jewels to lift the following night. And
she needed to make sure everything was in readiness.

Ralph Lowenstein walked in the main door of the spacious luxury apartment, already pulling the tie from
his neck. Board meetings left him exhausted. He was
constantly thinking, constantly measuring each word
he spoke. The appearance of Claude a few minutes before the meeting had shaken him. He had had to agree
to a lower price just to get Claude out of the building
before the board met.

He shrugged off his suit coat and threw it over
the nineteenth-century deacon's bench decorating the
foyer. The maid would put everything away in the
morning.

The lights were on, which meant that Estelle was
still awake. He sighed. The last thing he needed was
to face his wife this evening. But she probably wanted
to tell him about the delivery of the jewels, and he
needed to double-check the security. The security company had been in the apartment before he left that
morning, and they assured him that no one could get
in.

He didn't believe them.

He was sending Estelle on an overnight jaunt to
Paris to buy a dress for the opera. She had asked no
questions, and he was pleased. Sometimes getting her
to follow his plans was much too difficult. And this
one he didn't want to try to explain.

Kristine Kathryn Rusch

Tomorrow night he would be home, sitting in the dark, a snifter of brandy in hand. Tomorrow night he would be alone and he would wait.

He knew Catwoman wouldn't let him down.

Bruce Wayne sat alone in the large kitchen at Wayne Manor, clutching a cup of coffee and staring straight ahead. His body was tired, but his mind was alert. He had tried to sleep and found it impossible. He had poured himself a glass of wine, but that hadn't helped, so he worked out in the gym in the basement. Now dawn was creeping over the horizon, and he was no closer to any answers than he had been when he tried to go to bed.

Four hours of computer hacking had finally given him the answer he had been looking for. A notation in the middle of a file recorded in a Chicago orphanage, attached to a missing persons' report for Cook County.

The original file was classified. Angel's father had been a geneticist who was ahead of his time. He had stolen his research material and disappeared in the Midwest. Not heard from again until his body was discovered two years later, along with his wife's. The research materials were missing.

Angel's parents had been brutally murdered when she was a child. She was the one who had discovered their bodies.

I want to be just like you.

He couldn't get the words out of his head. When he closed his eyes, he saw his mother scream soundlessly and fall to the ground, reaching for him. He heard laughter echoing in the distance and felt himself float out of his body, as if nothing that had happened to him was real—the only way he could protect himself.

On the Wings of Angel

I want to be just like you.

"Child," he whispered. "You already are."

No one responded in the kitchen's half-light. His vengeance was his alone. It didn't make him happy, but it did give him a certain satisfaction. Who was he to deny that satisfaction to someone else? Who was he to choose whether or not one young woman learned how to protect herself and how to keep criminals off the street.

He was no one, in that sense. She had already learned. When he saw her, when he heard her speak, he knew she was the one who had attacked that gang all on her own. He didn't have to hold the bit of skirt before her and get her response.

She had done it as a message to him, to show him that she was worthy. And she was more than worthy. If he had to pick a successor, an heir, someone who would take his message and his brand of vengeance out of Gotham, she was perfect.

And that thought terrified him, more than anything had, since his parents died.

Selina glanced out the window. Nothing. The sun was shining through the thick haze that settled over Gotham on hot days, leaving no shadows. A breeze had started, making her thin curtains flow inward. Ash and Cordy were leaning on the sill, sniffing the air—trying to read messages sent in the wind. The other cats had staked out the other windows, and a few slept on the ancient fire escape. They loved the nice weather as much as she did, and were a bit puzzled why she didn't stop to enjoy it as she usually did.

She had plans, and only a little time to prepare for the evening ahead.

Kristine Kathryn Rusch

Still, a small shiver ran down her spine. The odd feeling had been there all day. As if she were being watched. As if someone, or something, was following her every movement.

But no one could. She knew how to track, and she saw no one. The cats weren't spooked. Even if she had missed something, they wouldn't.

Maybe it was time for a vacation. Maybe it was time to take some of her stash and go to some island in the Caribbean, soak in the sun, and think of nothing for weeks.

But then, who would take care of her cats?

She spread the blueprints on her bed and went over them for the tenth time, pleased that they had been so easy to obtain. Architectural firms didn't realize that their computers were as vulnerable to break-in as anyone else's. Most firms didn't have the elaborate security measures on their systems that police departments, governments, and banks did. The firm that built the Lowenstein building didn't either, and she had each detail of the Lowenstein master plan, right down to the secret passages, hidden rooms, and double-protected safe.

Piece of cake. Lowenstein was taking his wife to Paris for an overnight. They had appointments with all the big couturiers. Lowenstein would spend a small fortune to stuff his wife into a gown that would show off her emeralds, and then they would get back, only to discover that the emeralds were gone. Vanished. Disappeared, as they would say in Latin American countries.

From the living room she heard the unmistakable rumble of a cat growling. She got up, moved as softly as she could, and went to the door. Mousse stood at alert, the fur on her back ruffled in the attack posi-

On the Wings of Angel

tion, staring out the window. With one of her over-sized paws, she batted at the screen, then backed away, hissing.

Selina hurried to the cat's side. Mousse screamed, hissed, and batted at Selina, then ran away in panic. Selina looked out the window. It opened over a seven-story drop. The roof was four floors above. Someone would have to be on a wire on the side of the building for the cat to see. No one was that quick.

No one, except maybe Batman.

Commissioner Gordon was on his fifth cup of coffee by the time Batman walked into his office. Batman's cape swirled around him and his leather boots made no sound on the carpeted floor. Even though his face was hidden by the mask, something in his movements made Gordon realize that Batman was tired.

"I was beginning to think I was going to have to flare the signal tonight," Gordon said. He had had word out on the street since early that morning that he wanted to see Batman. It had never before taken Batman so long to respond.

Batman waved a gloved hand. "I had other business," he said.

Gordon nodded. Someday Batman would trust him enough to tell him what that other business was. Not yet, though. "Had an armored-car driver in here crack of dawn this morning, said she couldn't sleep."

Batman nodded, half turned, and stared out the window. Gordon wondered if Batman ever had trouble going to sleep. "A woman driver?"

"Yeah," Gordon said. "Surprised me that they'd let someone that small and pretty drive a security vehicle. But she did look like she had martial-arts training. She said she had been thinking all night about the last stop she made on her deliveries—the only one she's ever made outside a private institution."

Batman didn't look at Gordon. "Did she have light blond hair, this woman?"

"You know her?" Gordon asked.

"We just met," Batman said. He stepped away from the window. "But I interrupted you."

Gordon leaned back. "She left a case of jewels at Ralph Lowenstein's residence. She said the security system was outdated, and the safe would take a grade-B criminal five minutes to crack. Lowenstein made no secret of the fact that tonight he and his wife would be in Paris on a buying spree, leaving over a million dollars in jewels unprotected."

"Catwoman," Batman said.

"Exactly." Gordon took a final sip of his coffee. It was cold. "Something's not right here. But if we know, she knows. And if she knows, she won't stay away."

Batman clasped his hands behind his back. "It's not like Lowenstein to be so careless. The man runs his business as if it contains the secret to national security."

"I don't like it either," Gordon said. "But I thought you should know. This might be our chance to stop that infernal woman."

Batman smiled. "Cats aren't predictable," he said.

Ralph Lowenstein fixed himself a cold dinner of left-over turkey, cheese, and a buttered hard roll. He had an extra cup of tea to keep himself awake. Then, as night settled over the city, he let the streetlights guide him through the dark apartment. The secret room was even darker than he expected. Something rustled behind him, and he turned, heart beating in his throat. He was supposed to be alone here.

He strained, but could see nothing in the total darkness. He wanted to call out. Maybe she was here already. But that wouldn't fit with her pattern. She appeared and disappeared in a matter of minutes. She wouldn't wait in the darkness.

No one would.

He settled in his chair across from the safe. He had thought about using a penlight to read or listening to Estelle's Walkman, but decided that complete silence and darkness was safer.

He settled back and entertained himself with fantasies about the coming night.

He had seen her once—leaping across rooftops, her lithe body well delineated against the night sky. Under the mask, she had to be beautiful. Her grace, and her intelligence, told him that.

If she wasn't to his tastes, he would turn her in and become a sort of hero. If she was, well, Estelle wouldn't be back until the following afternoon. By then, maybe, he and Catwoman would have struck a deal. The secret of her identity kept as a reward for satisfying his passion. She would have to agree to that.

He held a cool glass in his hand—water, not brandy, as he had planned. Setting up the trap had left him tired. The last thing he wanted to do was spoil it by falling asleep.

The brandy sat on the table, two snifters beside it. She would drink with him. Of that he was certain.

Selina made her way across the rooftops with more than her usual silence. The night was cool and a bit

Kristine Kathryn Rusch

breezy. Dust from ancient chimneys, loose particles from rusted tile swirled like sand in the air. She had to stifle the urge to sneeze.

Maybe she should go back. Something about the night felt off center.

But a million dollars in jewels waited. Easy pickings for a short night's work.

Maybe she didn't trust the ease with which she gained the information. Or maybe she had been off center herself ever since she had seen Angel.

Something scrabbled on the rooftop behind her. She whirled in time to see a bit of black disappear behind a chimney. Black against black. She froze, wondering if she should chase it, then decided against it. If that was Batman, he would make his presence known soon enough.

Batman crouched on the edge of the roof across from Lowenstein's apartment. He had been there since dusk, waiting in complete silence. Occasionally he would move just a little, to keep his muscles limber. He wanted to be ready to fly as soon as he saw Catwoman head for the nearest window.

Shivers of unease ran through him. He kept seeing shadows move inside the house. At first he thought they were reflections from across the way, but now he wasn't so sure.

Someone was inside that apartment, waiting for Catwoman. Batman was half tempted to go in and see what was happening. But he decided to wait. If Catwoman never showed, then he had no reason to enter the apartment. If she did and he was inside, she might see him before he saw her.

No, it was better to wait. Something was going to happen soon. He could sense it.

Selina eased herself down the side of the building. Below, horns honked as the traffic lights changed, and taxis hurried to catch the next fare. Sometimes she felt as if she could hang from a building for hours, silent and invisible. But she had work to do, and the quicker she got it done, the better for her.

She stopped beside the large window that was the closest to the safe. She used a tiny laser to cut through the glass, not caring about the sound as glass shattered on the floor below. No one was home. No one would care. She blew powder in the air and saw it illuminate the light beams of the security system. The lights were wide enough apart that her hand could fit between them. She arched her wrist carefully, unlocked the window on the inside, and swung it open.

Fitting herself between those beams of light would be a trick, but it was one she had performed before. She tied her tail tightly to her body. With a lot of skill and slow movement, she slid in the window and waited for the whooping sound of a tripped alarm. Nothing. Then she looked up and noted motion detectors in the corners of the room. They didn't catch her entry through the window, which meant that they had a limited range. She made her way along the wall out of range of the motion detectors until she reached the secret panel.

Hidden in a bookcase. How clever. Every person who built a secret room hid the entrance in the bookcase. Everything else in this apartment had been done simply and with a minimum of imagination. She expected the same with regard to the secret room. She reached under the third shelf and heard a catch slide back. Then she pushed on the shelf and stepped into a pitch-dark room.

Three stairs led to the carpeted floor below. She went down the third step, then latched the door behind her and turned on her flashlight. No motion detectors in here, no cameras, no security equipment at all. Lowenstein showed too much self-confidence. Most paranoid rich would have trebled the security in a secret room; Lowenstein assumed that no one would find it.

She scanned her narrow beam of light on the far wall and saw a portrait of Lowenstein's wife. The obviousness behind the layout made her nervous. Perhaps it was supposed to. Perhaps it was supposed to make her doubt her own abilities or believe that there was an even greater trap waiting for her.

If so, it didn't work. All she believed in was Lowenstein's stupidity.

She walked over to the portrait, pulled it back, and looked at the small safe. A small combination dial covered the front. She would try Lowenstein's birthday first, then his wife's, then—

Something cold and hard lodged in the small of her back. She stiffened. A gun.

"Welcome, Catwoman," a male voice said. "I've been waiting a long time for this."

Ralph's hand was shaking. He was glad for the darkness, glad she couldn't see him. She was as small and graceful as he had hoped she would be. The room was filled with her scent, woman and roses. He longed to touch her, but he knew he would have to wait.

"Turn around," he said quietly.

On the Wings of Angel

She did, arms down and empty except for the flash-light.

He held the gun to her chest and pulled back the trigger. "Now," he said, "remove the mask."

She stared at him. He was about to repeat the command when he heard a rustle and turned. A small woman stood beside the door, holding a gun on both of them. "Harold Rosen," she said. "I've been waiting years for this. And Catwoman. Batman will be so happy with me."

Ralph's shakes got worse. She knew who he was. That little woman knew who he was.

"Angel," Catwoman said. "You don't know what you're doing."

"Oh, yes, I do," the woman said. "I've been following Mr. Rosen for years. Ever since he murdered my father over a man-made disease that could kill certain types of people undetectably. He's made a fortune off of that disease, selling it to more foreign countries than I care to think about."

She reached up and flicked the alarm switch. Sirens whooped outside the apartment. Ralph took that moment of distraction to move his gun away from Catwoman and fire at the girl. She slammed back against the wall. Catwoman kicked the gun from his hand and tried to club him with the flashlight. He ducked, and she almost fell, knocked off balance by her momentum.

The flashlight fell, leaving the room in complete darkness.

He heard footsteps and then the *snick* of a latch. The hidden door pushed open, and he saw a figure with a tail try to get through. The light filled the room, illuminating his chair, the table with the brandy snifters, and the gun at the base of the stairs.

Kristine Kathryn Rusch

He grabbed the gun and pushed his way out of the door as Catwoman tried to close it.

He gripped her wrist and pulled her close.

Batman started across the roof as Catwoman worked the window of Lowenstein's apartment. As he moved, he saw a figure out of the corner of his eye. Angel. He bit back a curse. He didn't want her there. Now he had two people to worry about.

By the time Catwoman was inside, he was hanging from the side of the building, trying to figure out how he could fit through those tiny spaces between the light beams. He didn't want the police just yet. He wanted to talk to Angel.

Then the sirens started whooping, sending his heart beating in counterpoint. He took a breath to calm himself and swung through the window.

A gun went off, and the old remembered terror surfaced. He didn't want her to die. Not Angel. He moved even faster, flying through the window feetfirst and landing in the semidarkness.

Lowenstein was holding Catwoman and brandishing a gun. Angel was a few feet away, braced against the wall, hand on her shoulder, a scream just dying on her lips. In the odd light, her skin looked pale. She was dressed as a black angel, all wings and free-flowing garments. But she lacked the look of malice that a black angel should have. Instead her eyes were wide on her small face, and her lips trembled.

Lowenstein aimed.

Batman lunged.

The gun went off, bang deafening in the tiny room.

On the Wings of Angel

Selina wrapped her arms around Lowenstein's waist and threw him into the wall. She kicked him once for good measure, knocking his head against the floor hard enough to ensure that he would pass out. Batman had his arms around Angel, and it would take a few minutes before they untangled their black clothes and discovered if Lowenstein had hit anyone with his second shot.

A few minutes was all it would take.

Selina ducked back into the secret room.

After all that had happened, she was convinced that Lowenstein had used his own birth date as a combination.

Angel moaned softly, and Batman pushed the hair out of her eyes. His fingers left a trail of blood on her face.

He glanced back, saw Catwoman kick Lowenstein, then turned his attention to Angel. Blood oozed out of her left arm and onto her bell sleeves. He ripped one, tied it tightly around her shoulder, and helped her up.

"You're going to be okay," he said.

Below, he could hear the echo of sirens. He hoped they were smart enough to send an ambulance, too.

"He killed my parents," Angel said. Her voice was thin, ragged. "I was going to kill him, too."

"The courts will take care of him," Batman said. "If you can testify."

"I can testify," she said. "He wanted my dad's research. The night before my parents died, he said that the arms community would pay a lot of money for the formula."

Batman remembered the arms merchant he had seen leaving Lowenstein's office, and he shuddered. Angel's father had worked on the genetic makeup of viruses. He had learned how to create them, and must have learned how to create something deadly. How many people already owned the formula? How many had he himself helped with his sponsorship of Lowenstein's company? He thought they were doing research for humanitarian purposes. But no one stole material like that, murdered, changed his name, and dealt with arms merchants when they were doing humanitarian research.

"She okay?" Catwoman stood behind him.

"He shot her in the arm, but it doesn't look serious."

Catwoman crouched beside them. "Kid," she said, "this isn't a game for amateurs."

"I know who you are."

"No. You only know who you think I am." Catwoman wiped the blood off of Angel's forehead with one gloved hand. "Gotham doesn't need more people in costume fighting on the street. We need people working so that no one is on the street. Maybe you should turn your considerable talents to helping people solve those lifelong hurts instead of trying to fight crime you don't understand."

Batman watched Catwoman. The police were on the stairs. He could hear them coming up. If he kept her talking . . .

"I understand it," Angel said. "Just like I understand what you have in your bag."

Catwoman grinned. Angel stirred in Batman's arms, as if she were trying to sit up. He didn't let her. "She's right, Angel," he said. "We need you doing a different kind of support group—"

"Batman," Angel said.

He ignored her. He wanted her to hear him out. "Maybe starting your own agency, providing help

On the Wings of Angel

where no help is being provided now. Catwoman could
tell you what's needed. Right, Catwoman?"

He turned. But she was gone. The room was empty
save for Angel's ragged breathing. "Looks like you
still need help, Batman," Angel said. "You let her get
away. I tried to tell you. But you were too focused on
your humanitarian vision."

He eased Angel back down to the carpet and went to
the window. Nothing. Maybe he had let her get away.
Maybe that was his gift to her for giving him an idea
about how to work with Angel.

He would always have another chance to catch her.
And besides, she hadn't had time to get the jewels. . . .

Selina slipped into her own apartment, the jewel bag
clutched tightly in her hand. DeeCee slept in the middle of the room, her head buried underneath her
paws. She didn't wake as Selina came in.

Selina peeled off her costume, pulled the shades,
and turned on the lights. She poured the jewels on the
center of the bed. The emeralds gleamed in the incan-
descent light. How precious. Maybe she would keep
those for herself. Mousse got on the bed and sniffed
the jewels, then looked at Selina for reassurance.
Selina smiled.

"Good one this time, huh, baby?" she said. But
there was a price. She would have to find a new apartment. She suspected Angel had believed her lie, but
she couldn't trust a belief. The girl was intent on sav-
ing the world. She had come after Catwoman once,
and she might again.

Or she might tell Batman where Selina lived.

Selina's smile grew wider. That would be interesting, but she wasn't quite ready for that.

Someday, perhaps, when she was sure the Dark Knight would appreciate a cat's sensuality and grace.

Selina chuckled and Mousse started to purr. For the first time in almost a week she felt like herself. She was free of Angel, she had her cats, and she had just acquired a small fortune in jewels.

What more could a woman ask for?

Copycat

JOHN GREGORY BETANCOURT

MILLIONAIRE PLAYBOY MURDERED
CATWOMAN SUSPECTED

By Vicki Vale
Special to the *Gotham Globe*

Bruce Wayne, wealthy socialite and philanthropist, was found dead this morning in his study at Wayne Manor. According to police, Wayne had been "savagely lashed, then strangled to death with a whip," which was found wrapped tightly around his throat. Sources at the coroner's office report Wayne's body was "covered with catlike scratch marks" around his face and hands. Selina Kyle, popularly known as "Catwoman," is currently being sought by police for questioning in connection with this crime.

The body was discovered at approximately 8:30 A.M. by Wayne's butler, Alfred Pennyworth. Pennyworth also noted several Wayne family heirlooms as missing, including an ancient jade Chinese statue of a cat, valued at nearly two hundred thousand dollars. Kyle is suspected of committing a recent string of high-profile burglaries. This latest crime *(cont'd A3, col. 1)*

Catwoman hissed in fury. She crumpled the newspaper without finishing the article, then flung it across her penthouse's living room. A dozen cats watched the paper roll to a stop, before the nearest, a gray-and-white tabby, sprang with blinding speed. Claws flashed. Seconds later the paper lay in tatters.

"That's right, Cleopatra," Catwoman said. The tabby gave her a triumphant look, then began to lick its paws with methodical grace. "Something *must* be done to protect our good name."

Selina reclined, her svelte body barely covered by a leopard-spotted leotard, on a plush, black leather couch in a private suite decorated with handpicked, and personally stolen, objets d'art. She wasn't surprised by the newspaper story. Inconvenienced, certainly. Angry, beyond a whisker of a doubt. But not surprised.

By the time the afternoon edition of the *Globe* had arrived at her secret high-rise hideout, she'd already heard about Wayne's death a dozen times over on the radio. It was a slow day for news, so a millionaire do-gooder's brutal murder by the notorious Catwoman made every news bulletin.

The only problem was, Selina hadn't committed the crime. She'd been lying low the last few days, ever since she'd botched a burglary at Harry Harkins's mansion. *That* had been a real mess. The old man was supposed to be out of town touring his cat-food factories; how was *she* to have known his heart had been acting up and he'd canceled the trip at the last minute? She'd broken in right on schedule, circumventing laser-beam fields and an elaborate alarm system, only to literally bump into Old Man Harkins in the hallway; his well-oiled wheelchair hadn't made a sound as it glided across the carpet.

Shocked, they'd both stared at each other for a second. Catwoman hissed and flashed her razor-sharp claws. Harkins clutched his chest and started to make helpless gasping noises. When he punched the medic-alert button on his wheelchair's left arm, alarms began to wail. Catwoman fled.

Within minutes, a score of private doctors and a hospital helicopter with a huge red cross blazed upon its side had arrived. Catwoman had lingered on the estate's high stone wall long enough to observe the first rush of frenzied rescue activity. When the police arrived with flashing lights and sirens blaring, she slunk home to lick her figurative wounds and bide her time before striking again.

The next day Selina learned she'd literally scared Old Man Harkins to death. His weak heart just gave out. Before he kicked off, though, he'd managed to whisper Catwoman's name, linking her to his death.

The police had been searching for her ever since. Old Man Harkins had a lot of friends—very influential friends—who wanted her arrested for his murder. As a result, she'd decided to lie low for a few days. She hadn't been out of her penthouse since Old Man Harkins's funeral except to pick up a few gallons of cream from a gourmet grocery.

Now it seemed trouble had come looking for her. Someone—some *copycat*—had stolen her modus operandi. Whip marks? Cat scratches? A stolen cat statue? *Murder?*

How dare this upstart put bloody paw prints all over my reputation, Selina Kyle thought grimly. Catwoman didn't like competition. She didn't like getting blamed for crimes she hadn't committed. And most of all she didn't like missing out on pretty baubles like Wayne's jade cat statue. If she'd known it was at the Wayne mansion, she'd have taken it herself. Now she'd never have the chance.

She closed her eyes to slits and stared pensively out the window across Gotham City. Night was falling. Draped in shadows, the buildings looked unusually sinister, even for a city infamous for the ugliness of its architecture. Towering skyscrapers, blackened by decades of smog, loomed above the trash-strewn streets, nearly blotting out the horizon. Barely glimpsed through the vast urban canyons of steel and stone, the western sky glowed the color of blood . . . the color of vengeance.

Copy the Catwoman? Over my dead body, Selina vowed. I'm not going to sit idly by and let some cheap, two-bit hoodlum cash in on my unique persona!

Rising with a fluid grace, Selina Kyle crossed to her bedroom. Inside, in the closet, on plain wooden hangers, were a dozen identical black leather cat outfits, complete with cowled masks and various steel-clawed sets of gloves.

Catwoman will prowl the streets of Gotham tonight—and boy, she thought, am I pissed. The female *is* the deadliest of the species.

Fanny the Ferret was feeling pretty good. A short, narrow-faced woman with long, greasy black hair and

Copycat

a crooked nose, Fanny worked as a professional go-between in the underworld. She'd go between anybody and anybody for a fee. Fanny wasn't particularly bright or ambitious, but she was useful and managed to eke out a rough living that way on the fringes of Gotham's underworld. Tonight, after a long day of numbers running on Gotham's west side, Fanny had decided to celebrate her good fortune and sudden influx of cash. She planned to party her way across Gotham City, starting at Louie-Louie & Gladfelter's Bar & Grill (best known for its illegal slot machines) and work her way east to Bahama Mama's Beef & Leer All-Night Seminude Go-Go (better known for its bootleg hootch than for its has-been, all-too-sagging topless hoofers). Fanny'd made it as far as Jumpin' Jack's (roulette and all-night poker in the back room) and was headed for Queen Bee's (nothing illegal, but great atmosphere) on Seventh Avenue when her plans were abruptly derailed.

As she took a shortcut through an alley a dark shape suddenly hurled itself from the shadows. It struck her sideways like a freight train, sending her flying into a row of plastic garbage cans. Fanny grabbed at a can to stop her fall, but in her semidrunk state she only managed to pull it over, too.

She ended up flat on her back and covered with garbage. Scrambling unsteadily to her feet, she tried to run. Unfortunately the dark shape—how had it moved so *fast?*— blocked the way. She heard metal *tch*ing on metal, like knives being sharpened, and the sound grew louder as the shape advanced on her.

Oh no, Fanny thought, I'm going to die, some maniac bozo's out to kill me, and I'm going to die—

The shape crossed a stray beam of light from an open window two stories up. The figure resolved itself into Catwoman. Her black costume, covering her from head to toe, glistened like oil on a midnight sea. She was striking steel claw against steel claw, making the *tch*ing sound.

Fanny relaxed a little; this wasn't the first time a major criminal had found a use for her. Hell, she'd once run an errand for the Joker—and lived. She took a deep breath. Her pounding heart gradually calmed.

"Catwoman," she said, a petulant whine in her voice. "You scared me."

"That's not all I'm going to do," Catwoman said. One gloved hand closed on Fanny the Ferret's throat. Steel claws pricked her jugular—not hard enough to break the skin, but hard enough to scare Fanny all over again. Jesus, she thought, what did I do? What's she got against me?

"Tell me about Bruce Wayne," Catwoman said. Her voice was soft, a half purr of a sound.

Fanny made a strangling noise.

Catwoman relaxed her grip a fraction. "Tell me about Wayne," she said again.

Say something, Fanny thought frantically. Play along.

"You offed him p-pretty good, huh?" Fanny giggled hesitantly, stopped when Catwoman tickled her throat with one sharp claw, swallowed, then continued. "Y-you want me to sell his statue for ya? It's real hot, but Jimmy the Duke's l-lookin' to buy big stuff these days . . . y'know . . . I'm in g-good with him, right?"

"I'm looking for the one who 'offed' Wayne, as you so succinctly put it," Catwoman said. "She . . . or *he* . . . made it look like my job. I want names, Fanny. Who's new in town? Who's scoring big? Who's playing games with me, Fanny? *Who?*" The last was almost a shout.

Fanny began to cry, tears like lines of grease trickling down her narrow cheeks. Her eyes darted right, then left, then right again, but she didn't dare move. The claws against her throat were digging in, making it hard to breathe.

"P-please . . ." she whispered.

"Who is it, Fanny?"

"M-maybe . . . maybe . . . the Greek knows?"

The claw grip relaxed. Fanny staggered back like she'd been thrown, one hand coming up to her throat. She touched something damp and sticky there . . . blood, she realized. Catwoman had broken the skin on her neck.

When she looked up, the dark shape was gone. Alone, she began to sob, all the nervous terror spilling out in a sudden flood. No more tonight, she thought. Home . . .

She staggered toward the fleabag hotel where she kept a room. It was only a few blocks away, luckily. The three flights of steps up to her floor were an agony.

At last, though, she was safe inside. She locked the door behind her, sank down on the lumpy old bed, and choked back another sob.

What would Catwoman do when she found out Fanny had lied about the Greek knowing anything? Fanny made up the story on the spot. Maybe the Greek did know. He knew a lot of things. Maybe he'd die before he'd admit it. Maybe—

She heard a noise outside her window and jumped, startled, barely stifling a scream. There wasn't anything there when she looked, though.

She kept a bottle of bourbon stashed under her mattress. Yeah, she thought, pulling it out and taking a deep swallow, then another. She drained most of the bottle in seconds. This is just what I need tonight.

Then an alley cat screeched outside her window.
Fanny screamed in terror, and kept on screaming until her neighbors broke down her door.

Danny "the Greek" Chu thought of himself as the
slickest operator on the upper east side of Gotham
City. He called himself "the Greek" partly as a joke;
after all, he'd muscled out a real Greek—Dmitri "the
Greek" Pappadopoulos—for the singularly profitable
job of mob liaison, and he'd assumed the title as part
of the job. He also called himself "the Greek" because
he figured any cop trying to bust someone named "the
Greek" wouldn't look twice at an Asian-American. So
far he'd been right.

Basically Danny made things—useful things—
happen between the rival gangs who controlled
Gotham City's streets. If you needed a hit on a trou-
blesome public official, you arranged it through the
Greek. If you needed fresh personnel for a new whore-
house, the Greek put you in touch with the right dis-
tributors. If you needed booze or drugs or any of a
thousand illegal substances or services, he was your
man. He knew everybody, kept files—mental files,
since he didn't trust paper ones—on every deal that
went down, and cut himself in for a smooth one percent. It didn't look like a lot until you figured upward
of a hundred million dollars in transactions went
through his hands every year.

Since Batman first made his appearance, drug dealing and prostitution and gambling had moved to a
lower level of activity, but it was all still present. Batman had taken out several top levels of management
in the gangs, but the lower echelons kept things running, and new, more careful bosses kept appearing.

Copycat

Life went on in the big city, and vice went right along with it. Especially when flamboyant freaks like the Penguin or Two-Face kept Batman busy.

Right now the Greek was sitting in his study in his inconspicuous brownstone in Gotham's Chinatown, working on the biggest deal of his life. It was already making him nervous. "Spring the Riddler," they'd told him. "We need him out," they'd told him. "He has the key to fifty million in uncut diamonds, and we want them," they'd told him.

So he'd gotten the floor plans to Arkham Asylum and now had them laid out in front of him on top of an antique walnut desk that had once belonged to a senator. He switched on the desk light and stared down at the intricate security system. Who do I know that can handle this? he wondered. Steeleye Cinch? No . . . he's been arrested again. Maybe Sambo the Snake . . .

Even absorbed in thought as he was, though, the Greek heard the slight squeak as the window behind him opened. He never oiled its hinges for exactly that reason. Although he was on the brownstone's third floor, he didn't believe in taking chances, and he didn't like the idea of guests sneaking up on him.

Casually, as though it was an afterthought, he took a sip from his can of soda, then calmly reached for the desk drawer. There was a 9mm Luger inside for just such emergencies.

Just as his hand closed on the drawer's handle, though, another hand came down on top of his. A hand covered in black leather, its nails shiny steel . . . Catwoman's hand.

"Now, now," a soft voice purred in his ear. "Let's not do anything we're going to regret, shall we?"

The Greek laughed and let go of the drawer. My, how these so-called supervillains loved their dramatic entrances! "Catwoman," he said, "how delightful! What brings you here tonight, if I may ask?" He swung his chair around, already wondering if Catwoman would be interested in breaking out the Riddler.

Catwoman leaned back on the windowsill, hands on her very shapely hips, staring down at him from slitted eyes. Danny couldn't decide whether she was wearing slitted contact lenses or if it was a trick of the light on her cowl.

"Information," she said.

"Everything has its price," he said. "Tell me what you're looking for and I'll let you know if I can help."

"Someone . . ." She hesitated, as if not quite sure of herself. "Someone killed Bruce Wayne," she said.

"I know," the Greek said, puzzled.

"I . . . need to find that someone."

"You didn't do it, then." *Or you want me to believe you didn't do it.*

"Do you know who did?"

Slowly the Greek shook his head. "Very sorry, Selina. Everyone thinks you did it. Several fences are already making inquiries among foreign collectors . . . that cat statue sounds like something pretty special, yes?"

"I wouldn't know. I don't have it."

"Should you turn it up . . . come to me first? I may be interested in it for myself."

She tapped him on the nose with one claw. "Find out who did Wayne, will you? Then let me know. There's ten thousand in it for you."

The Greek didn't budge an inch. *Maybe she didn't take it, after all? Or is this some bizarre game?* It was hard to take a woman dressed in a leather cat costume seriously, even if she did look kind of sexy in it.

Slowly he said, "I'll start making inquiries, Selina. If I need to get in touch with you . . . ?"

"Don't worry about it," she said. "I'll be in touch with you."

Meanwhile, he thought, there's more than one way to deal with a cat. "Say," he said casually, "I need someone for a job. There's a cool million—minus my one percent—in it for you."

She leaned forward. "What sort of job?"

"Breaking and escaping."

"Where?"

"Arkham Asylum."

She hissed.

The Greek pressed on. "A few fellows need the Riddler out. They're paying cash up front."

"The Riddler is a psycho," Catwoman said disdainfully. "Not my kind of gig, sorry." A softer, more seductive look appeared in her eyes. "Find out who did Wayne for me, Greek? I'll be . . . very, *very* grateful."

Danny swallowed. Her voice was like liquid sugar and made the hairs on the back of his neck prickle. He couldn't help noticing how tightly the black costume clung to the curves of her body. And what a body! Suddenly he really wanted to know what form that gratitude might take.

"Hey," he called as she sprang out his window onto a narrow ledge. She looked back and her eyes caught the light, like a cat's. "Next time use the front door, okay?"

She laughed, then she was gone.

The Greek folded up the floor plans and put them aside. Taking a deep breath, he began to make a series of calls. If someone else had offed Bruce Wayne, he'd certainly find out about it. After all, whoever sold the cat statue must have done the job, right?

But deep inside he knew he wouldn't find anything.
Catwoman had pulled the job. Why would anyone
want to frame her? It was bewildering. Besides, if
anyone else had done Wayne, he would've heard *something* by now.

CATWOMAN STRIKES AGAIN

GOTHAM MUSEUM LOOTED

By Vicki Vale
Special to the *Gotham Globe*

A priceless Egyptian sarcophagus was stolen last
night from the Gotham City Museum of Antiquities. Selina Kyle, better known as Catwoman, is
currently being sought by authorities for questioning in connection with this crime. The solid-
gold sarcophagus, approximately two feet long, held
the mummified remains of a cat that historians believe may have belonged to the Egyptian queen Cleopatra.

Selina Kyle is also wanted in connection with the
brutal murder of Gotham millionaire Bruce Wayne,
as well as several other recent thefts. Kyle's alleged
crimes all relate to cats in some fashion. Police
Commissioner James Gordon noted *(cont'd A6,
col. 1)*

Catwoman cursed as she stalked back and forth
across her living room. Dozens of nervous felines kept
their distance as their mistress raged.

Catwoman clawed the empty air in her frustration,
wishing it were this copycat criminal's face. She'd
teach Copycat a lesson, all right.

The moment she'd spotted this latest headline at
the newsstand, she felt like killing someone; it was all
she could do to control herself until she got back to

her penthouse. There, she'd discarded the disguise that, for safety's sake, she had been forced to wear on the streets: a floppy hat, a black veil, granny glasses, a white wig, and a dowdy black dress. Clad only in tiger-striped lingerie, her short black hair contrasting sharply with the unblemished whiteness of her limbs, she forced herself to relax.

She crossed to her leopard-patterned sofa, flopped down, and picked up the newspaper again. The headlines screamed at her. Then she examined the grainy black-and-white photo of the precious sarcophagus.

Now I'm really out for blood, she thought. She'd planned to heist that particular artifact herself, maybe even last night. Instead she had wasted the entire evening trying to track down this, this—this Copycat!

She wanted the sarcophagus. She wanted Wayne's Chinese cat statue. But most of all she wanted Copycat within striking distance of her claws.

A sleek Siamese, braver than his compatriots, padded over and hopped into her lap. She stroked the cat's head absently, thinking, I need to plot my next move very, very carefully.

Questioning random underworld figures had proved fruitless; although she'd successfully put the fear of God—and Catwoman—into the local lowlifes, last night's prowling had not brought her any closer to her prey. Certainly she had frightened Fanny the Ferret, and tempted the Greek, and interrogated half a dozen others hard enough to make them spill anything of value they might have known. Only they hadn't known anything. Whoever Copycat was, his or her trail did not wind through the usual underworld circles. She'd have to pursue another track.

Placing the Siamese gently on the floor, she spread

the newspaper out and forced herself to read the whole story slowly and carefully one more time.

At last, frustrated and discouraged by the lack of clues, she noticed the byline. Another Vicki Vale exclusive, eh? So why, she wondered, does this Vale woman always seem to be the first on the scene? Maybe Gotham City's favorite girl reporter had some sort of inside information on Copycat? Did Vicki Vale know more than she let on?

A cold, cruel smile crossed Catwoman's face. She licked her lips in anticipation. *I think I've found my clue.*

The rooftops of Gotham were only slightly less cramped and claustrophobic than the city streets. Conical water tanks rose like missile silos on every other building. Crumbling brick chimneys spewed soot into the sky. Mismatched buildings of varying sizes and designs crowded together like angry commuters elbowing for room on an overstuffed subway. In Gotham City, even structures of stone and steel seemed pitted against each other in a ceaseless struggle for survival.

Catwoman loved the rooftops. She perched on the very edge of a shiny new condominium, twenty stories above a busy street. In twilight, the entire city appeared shrouded in a gentle blue shadow.

Catwoman smiled and stretched, flexing her claws. A coiled black whip hung from a thin silver chain around her waist. It felt great to be alive, in the night, on top of the world, out on the prowl. Her ebony cat suit was like a second layer of skin, transforming her into something more than human, beautiful and unstoppable.

Copycat

A movement directly below caught her eye. Crouching on the roof, she leaned out to watch a red-haired woman, dressed in a stylish green jacket and skirt, exit the building and stroll north on the sidewalk. Catwoman recognized Vicki Vale from various appearances on the TV news. That's another odd thing, she thought. Didn't Vale used to date Bruce Wayne, before his tragic demise? Interesting . . .

Finding Vale's address had not been difficult; she looked it up in the phone book. Now it looked like her patience was about to be rewarded.

Moving stealthily from roof to roof, fearlessly leaping over dizzying drops, she kept pace with the reporter, waiting for just the right moment to pounce.

Vale continued uptown, into a part of the city largely given over to upscale antique and jewelry shops, the kind of ritzy establishments where they kept the front doors locked all day long and wouldn't even buzz you in unless you were suitably dressed. None of the merchandise bore a price tag; if you needed to know how much something cost, you obviously couldn't afford it.

Kind of late for a shopping spree, Catwoman thought. Most of these stores closed up tight after sundown. She felt a tingle of anticipation. What was Vicki Vale doing here, at this hour?

Catwoman found a perch on the roof of a rare coin and stamp shop. A weathered stone gargoyle, whose pointed ears and dour expression reminded her of Batman, concealed her from the pedestrians below. Not that there were many people left on the street; the neighborhood had already started to clear out, the yuppies and shop owners rushing home before the hookers and winos came out for the night. Heavy steel gratings covered every storefront.

To Catwoman's surprise, Vale stopped in front of a narrow alleyway, glanced in both directions, then turned into the alley and vanished from sight.

Jumping swiftly over a darkened skylight, Catwoman raced to keep up. As she did she spied a bent and battered street sign on a rusty metal post: the murky-looking alley was called Catskill Lane.

Cats kill. Selina hurried faster. This was it. She knew it.

Vale was standing in front of the service entrance to a store . . . BRADLEY & ORDOVER'S FINE JEWELRY the sign said. Catwoman padded forward, leaped, and landed silently on the jewelry store's roof.

Cats always land on their feet, she thought. Can copycats say the same thing? She peered into the alley.

Catskill Lane was little more than a glorified crack between the jewelry shop and the expensive boutique next door. The only light came from the neighboring streets, casting a faint grayish glow across islands of trash floating in greasy puddles. Heaps of decaying cardboard boxes had been piled up outside the fire exits.

Catwoman's cold blue eyes widened as she stared at Vicki Vale. The well-groomed redhead was standing atop a rust-flecked iron Dumpster, peering into Bradley & Ordover's through a small back window protected by a sturdy iron grille. As Catwoman watched, Vale removed a pair of black leather gloves from the pocket of her jacket and pulled them carefully over her manicured hands. Then she retrieved what looked like a small perfume bottle from her purse.

Vale sprayed her "perfume" along the top and bottom of the window grille. Metal hissed and smoked where an obviously corrosive liquid touched it. A few moments later Vale tugged on the bars. The entire framework pulled free, leaving nothing but a thin sheet of glass between the respected journalist and the interior of the store.

Catwoman shook her head in amazement. It was working out better than she'd hoped. Vicki Vale wouldn't have to lead her to Copycat—Vicki Vale *was* Copycat. *She's been committing the crimes herself, then using her articles to point the blame toward me!*

Smiling grimly, Catwoman extended the diamond-tipped metal nails of her own black gloves. Time to play, Copycat dear, she thought.

Springing lightly to her feet, she launched herself into the air above the alley, becoming a sinuous shadow against the night sky. She arced over Catskill Lane until she came within reach of the boutique's back wall. Arms outstretched, her claws caught and then tore downward. She turned to snarl in Vale's direction, sliding down the wall toward the alley floor. Her claws slowed her fall enough for her to land unharmed on her feet.

With a startled yelp, Vale had dropped the window grille. It crashed loudly on the Dumpster's steel lid.

"So," Catwoman taunted, "you thought you could follow in my most-wanted footsteps, did you?" She stalked relentlessly toward Vale, a two-legged panther hungry for the kill. "You wanted to have your nice, newsworthy crimes and report them, too? Well, it takes more than a pair of pretty gloves and a couple of lucky breaks to make a girl a Catwoman. You're playing in the big leagues now, and you've lost, big time."

A terrified look on her face, Vicki scrambled off the Dumpster. She glanced desperately toward the end of the alley, toward the avenue and safety, but Cat-

woman darted in front of her and blocked her way.
Then Catwoman hissed and raised her claws.

Backing away, Vale stepped on a bottle of Thunder-
bird. It rolled out from under her and she struggled to
regain her balance. Eyes wide with fear, she kept
watch on Catwoman.

Selina couldn't resist toying with her victim. Unfas-
tening the whip from her belt, she cracked it in Vale's
direction. The reporter flinched; the whip missed her
face by a hairbreadth.

"Tell me something, Scoop-of-the-Century," Catwoman purred. "How did an amateur like you manage to knock off a grown man like Bruce Wayne? I
thought you were supposed to be dating him. Some
sort of kinky fun-and-games, maybe? Things get a little too rough?" She snarled contemptuously. "It
must've been an accident. You're too much of a wimp
to kill a man on purpose!"

She had Vicki backed up against the Dumpster
now. Catwoman wondered if the reporter would fit inside . . . afterward.

Raising the whip overhead, she arched her back to
put all her strength into a flogging Vale would never
forget. But before she could strike, a deep voice spoke
up from somewhere behind her.

"That's enough, Selina. Put the whip down."

No, Catwoman thought. Not him. Not now. Whirling, she saw an ominous figure standing only a few
yards away, framed by the alley's bare walls. He stood
as still and unyielding as a prison wall, an imposing
figure in black and gray. A heavy cape, dark as midnight, was draped over his shoulders. His mask bore
the features and high spiked ears of a bat. A golden
emblem shone on his chest, bearing the black design
of two outstretched batwings.

Even though she'd confronted him dozens of times before, his sudden appearance drew a short gasp from her.

Batman. The Dark Knight of Gotham City.

"Step away from Ms. Vale," he commanded. His voice was deceptively smooth. "It's been a long chase, Selina, but it's over now. You might as well make it easy on yourself."

God, the ghastly irony of it all, Selina thought. For once she was innocent. Her fist tightened around the base of the whip. After all her battles with Batman, the countless minor victories and defeats, she'd be damned if she'd surrender now—and be caged for crimes she hadn't even had the pleasure of committing.

"You've got the wrong kitty this time, lover," she said with a smirk. "I'm just making a citizen's arrest. You want Miss Front Page here. She's the one who broke into this shop, *and* stole the cat mummy from the museum, *and* killed Bruce Wayne!"

Batman's voice remained as sure and implacable as ever. "And what about the late Harold Harkins? Did she murder him as well?"

"Er, no," Catwoman muttered, briefly caught off guard. That killing was hers, sort of. Oh, blast it all, she raged silently, this is a waste of time. Batman's never going to believe my word over Vale's.

"It's a long story, Batman dear, and surely you don't want to hear it in this dank, depressing alley." Keep talking, she told herself as her agile fingers went to work behind her back, detaching a small glass vial from the base of the whip. Then, holding the vial carefully between two fingers, she tied a noose in the other end of the whip. "Maybe we can continue this conversation over dinner at a nice restaurant. I can order a saucer of milk and you can sip a bottle of blood—or whatever it is you bats drink. Ms. Vale can have poison."

Batman stepped forward, gloved fists clenched at his sides. "No more games, Selina," he said impatiently. He reached out an open palm. The edge of his glove had fins like a shark. "Hand over the whip. *Now.*"

Without warning, Catwoman executed a perfect backflip, landing on her feet several yards away from Batman. "Not now, not ever!" she spat, and flicked the noose over Vicki's head. She yanked hard, tightening its grip around the beautiful journalist's throat. Vicki made a harsh, strangling noise.

Batman glanced quickly from Catwoman to Vicki and back again. Before he could make a move in either direction, Selina hurled the glass vial against the broken pavement, where it shattered. Dense black smoke spewed out, rapidly filling the alley with a thick, impenetrable fog.

I learned this trick from you, Batman, Catwoman thought gleefully. She popped nose filters into place and breathed easily through them.

"Find her if you can!" she challenged the Dark Knight. "Before the copycat chokes to death!"

Digging her claws into the jewelry store's wall, she climbed swiftly to the roof, then raced furiously over the top of Gotham City, past TV antennas, satellite dishes, and rickety pigeon coops full of drab, diseased city birds. She didn't halt her reckless, headlong dash until Catskill Lane was dozens of blocks behind her.

Then, breathing heavily, rivers of sweat cooling between her flesh and the tight black suit, she leaned against the graffiti-covered cylinder of a large, looming water tower and tried to calculate her next move.

Despite her bravado, she knew Batman would rescue that miserable papergirl before the noose had done her any serious harm. In this city, Batman was better than 911—and a lot more dependable.

A low growl formed at the back of Selina's throat. This isn't over, she vowed. I know who you are now, Copycat, and there's nowhere you can go that I can't find you. Next time, though, we'll meet on my terms, under my rules, and no misguided Caped Crusader will be around to save you from your just deserts.

Already a plan was forming in her mind . . .

RICH WIDOW SPENDS FORTUNE ON HER KITTIES!
A *Gotham Gab* Exclusive

Mrs. Annabelle McQueen, 84, who recently inherited over twenty-three million dollars from her deceased stockbroker husband, loves her thirty-two housecats so much that she's spent thousands on her pets—and left them her entire estate in her will! These pampered pussies already enjoy the good life, eating their daily meals of caviar and imported Alaskan salmon out of solid-platinum cat bowls that cost over three hundred thousand dollars apiece.

Mrs. McQueen's two-legged relatives, including her surfer son-in-law, are reportedly spitting mad about the cat-loving widow's lavish treatment of her pets, but so far teams of lawyers have been unable to interfere with the Life-styles of the Rich and Feline. Some cats get all the luck.

And remember, you read it first in the *Gotham Gab*!

Posing in front of a full-length mirror in her bedroom, Selina smoothed out the pleats in a drab, matronly,

John Gregory Betancourt

ankle-length black dress. She adjusted her gray wig, done up in an old-fashioned bun, and made sure that none of her own dark hairs were dangling free. The pale pink lipstick she applied to her lips was duller and less glossy than the bloodred hue she preferred, but, Catwoman thought with a sigh, every great scheme required some sacrifices. All she needed now was the right hat and a black widow's veil to complete her transformation into the eccentric Mrs. McQueen.

This particular alias had served her well over the last few weeks, but never, she hoped, as well as it would today.

A cheap-looking tabloid paper, full of huge headlines and brightly colored photographs of Mrs. McQueen and her pets, rested on Selina's makeup counter. She glanced at it and laughed cruelly. The nice thing about sleazy tabloids like the *Gab*, she gloated, was that it was so easy to plant stories in them. Give them a suitably colorful "human interest" item, and they'd practically print it verbatim, without bothering with any tiresome research or investigation. All in all, it was a mutually beneficial arrangement; the *Gab* got a headline and she got to bait her trap. And how quickly that bait had worked.

As if on cue, a buzzer sounded loudly a few feet away. Selina pounced across the luxurious bedroom and pressed the speak button on the intercom unit mounted on the wall. She paused for just a second, to summon up the hesitant, whispery voice of an elderly woman.

"H-hello?" she said into the intercom, then released the button. Another woman's voice emerged from the speaker. Despite some distortion and static, it had the clear and melodious tones of someone accustomed to public speaking.

"Mrs. McQueen? This is Vicki Vale. We spoke on the phone, remember? I wanted to interview you about your cats?"

"Of course, dear," Catwoman replied in her old-lady voice. "I'll buzz you right in. Did I mention I live on the top floor? There's an elevator, though, so you don't have to take the stairs. I wish I could come down and greet you properly, but twenty-six flights is such a long trip . . . and at my age, well, I'm sure you understand."

"No problem," Vicki said. "I'll be right up. I'm looking forward to meeting you and your pets."

Catwoman smiled and licked her lips. "I'll be waiting," she said, and stepped away from the intercom. I know what you're really after, Copycat, she thought, my famous platinum cat bowls. Well, you may find this old lady a bit harder to handle than a soft, spoiled playboy like Bruce Wayne!

"Come along, boys and girls," she cooed to the many, many cats milling about the bedchamber. "We have company."

She placed an old-fashioned pillbox hat upon her white wig, then draped a gauzy black veil over her face; it was like peering out at the world through an intricate spiderweb. She walked quickly into the palatial living room, a battalion of cats falling in line behind her.

A large picture window gave her a panoramic view of Gotham City in all its grim and brooding grandeur; although it was midafternoon, she drew the heavy velvet drapes tightly shut and turned on a couple of small, stylish lamps.

For a moment she paused and scanned her surroundings. Would Vale recognize any of the purloined art treasures decorating the room? She shrugged her shoulders beneath the baggy, black dress. No matter, she reminded herself. The reporter wasn't likely to leave . . . alive.

Finally there was a knock at the door. It took all the patience Selina could muster to walk over as slowly as an aging widow might be expected to. Patience, she told herself. The mouse is here. Let's play with her awhile.

Keeping the chain in place, she opened the door a crack. It was Vale, all right, in a gray blouse and short black skirt.

The reporter smiled pleasantly at her. "Mrs. McQueen?" she asked gently.

"Excuse me, dear," Selina whispered. "I hate to fuss, but could you show me some identification? I know it must seem silly, but what with all the terrible stories one reads about in the paper . . . you know, that horrible Catwoman person and all . . ."

"Of course. I quite understand." Vicki's smile grew even warmer, if possible.

Utterly shameless, Selina thought, impressed despite herself. She squinted theatrically through the veil at the reporter's driver's license and laminated press card. After only a minute or two she closed the door, carefully undid the chain, and invited Vale into the penthouse suite.

The reporter had an expensive-looking camera slung over her shoulder. She walked slowly around the room, looking at the various objets d'art. A legion of cats—black, white, striped, and spotted—began rubbing themselves against Vicki's legs and clawed playfully at her stockings.

"Don't mind my pussies," Selina said, scooping up a plump gray kitty and cradling him against her chest. Moving ever so slowly, she planted herself cautiously on the leopard-spotted couch. More cats swarmed around her. Purring softly, they settled on her lap, around her shoulders, and at her feet.

"How many do you have?" Vale asked.

"Oh, only thirty-two. It seems like more because they keep moving around." In reality, there were more than fifty in the room ... with more waiting in the wings for her command to strike. "Do take a seat, dear," she entreated, gesturing toward an overstuffed chair opposite the sofa.

Vicki sat, opening her purse and taking out a small pocket tape recorder. "Do you mind?" she asked, placing the recorder on the walnut coffee table between them. A slender Siamese leaped onto the table and sniffed the machine curiously.

Catwoman eyed Vicki's purse furtively. Don't forget about that acid perfume, she warned herself. She whispered into the gray kitten's ear and set it down. It stalked across the table and, seemingly of its own volition, decided to curl up and take a nap on top of the purse.

"By all means, use your recorder," Catwoman answered graciously. "I can't believe they're making those devices so small these days. Why, when I was a child ..." And she launched into a long, rambling reminiscence.

Another cat, a black-and-gray-striped tiger, climbed up the front of Vicki's emerald-colored jacket and nipped at the lapels. The redhead kept smiling, but could not entirely conceal a flinch.

Beneath her veil, as she continued to talk on and on about the wonders of modern technology, Selina permitted herself a tiny grin. Afraid of cats, are you? she thought. I can't say I'm surprised, but maybe you should have thought of that before you decided to play in my sandbox.

Vicki patiently waited for "Mrs. McQueen" to finish her long, boring, and completely fabricated reminiscence, then tried, with what struck Catwoman as annoying obviousness, to steer the conversation toward her topic of choice. "So, I'm sure our readers will be fascinated to hear all about you and your plans for these beautiful, and clearly very affectionate, animals. The article in the *Gotham Gab* was quite entertaining, but as I told you on the phone earlier, I'd like to go into a little more depth, tell the full story of your cats and why they're so important to you."

Selina struggled to suppress a yawn. Why was Vale even bothering with this charade, she wondered, now that she'd talked her past the locked door? Did she think Mrs. McQueen was going to hand her the cat bowls?

Vicki leaned forward and pressed the record button on the tape recorder. The striped tomcat slipped off her jacket and landed gracefully on the table. His slit eyes glared at Vicki, and a low growl emerged from his throat.

Selina stretched out her arm and stroked his head until the growling ceased. Not yet, she thought, but soon.

The reporter ignored the cat. "Well, why do you like cats so much?" she asked.

What a stupid question, Selina thought. "Because," she said, growing tired of this game, "they're not afraid to look out for themselves . . . and because they're predators at heart." She stood up abruptly, her back straight, not stooped like an old woman's. The frail, dithery voice vanished, replaced by a low, sultry purr. "And their claws are sharp. Like mine."

Copycat

Vale gasped, then went pale. "Catwoman!" she blurted as she tried to leap to her feet. Selina shoved her back down into the chair.

"What a delight to see you again, Vicki," she snarled. She snatched off her hat and veil and flung them across the room. In the dim light, Selina's black hair glistened like silk and her cold blue eyes gleamed with malice. "Or shall I call you . . . Copycat?"

"Catwoman . . . Selina," Vicki pleaded bravely. "We can talk this over. Don't do anything we'll both regret." She rose again from the chair, more slowly this time, and started to back up toward the door.

"The interview is over, Ms. Vale," Catwoman announced. "It's payback time." She clapped her hands together sharply. All over the room, every cat froze and perked up its ears. "Go!" she commanded them.

Dozens of suddenly frenzied felines raced at Vicki, hissing and spitting. An angry paw swiped her ankle, leaving three parallel, bloody scratches. A score of cats leaped between Vale and the front door.

Slowly, step-by-step, they forced her back across the living room, into the far corner. Claws flashing, the biggest and boldest—a dun-colored Manx—lunged at Vicki. She screamed and threw her arms over her head.

"Wait!" Catwoman snapped.

The cats drew back slightly, forming a half circle around Vale. Fur rose as if electrified along their backs; several hissed, tails lashing. They had her cornered and knew it.

Catwoman cast a loving gaze over her pets. "Aren't they adorable?" she asked rhetorically. Then she glared at Vale and her voice grew cold and hard. "You have two choices, Copycat: You can let my little furry friends tear you apart. Or you can tell me where the treasures are."

"What treasures?" Vicki asked softly. The cats snarled at the sound of her voice, and she drew her feet back even further.

"The Chinese statue and the golden mummy case, of course!" Catwoman said. Reaching beneath the cushions of her couch, she drew out a pair of claw-tipped leather gloves and slipped them on. "Don't play any games with me. Talk fast or you're kitty chow. Where are they?"

Vicki hesitated, staring at the pack of killer cats just waiting for the order to pounce. Swallowing, she took a deep breath and opened her mouth.

Smart girl, Catwoman thought triumphantly. *Maybe I'll only maim you a little bit after all.*

But instead of a confession, Vale shouted as loud as she could: *"Batman! Now!"*

With a deafening sound of breaking glass, the huge picture window behind Catwoman shattered. She whirled. It was Batman—his huge black cape billowing, his feet outstretched. He must have swung down from above on a bat rope, Catwoman realized. She'd seen him do it before.

He landed lightly in front of her. When he released his bat rope, it snaked up and out of sight.

"Stay back!" Catwoman hissed. "I won't allow you to stop me again!"

He stalked forward with grim intent.

"Batman . . ." she said softly, backing up.

He was only a few feet away from her now.

"Lover . . ." she whispered.

He reached out to grab her arm—just as she executed a graceful kick. It was one of the most perfect bits of gymnastic expertise she'd ever performed, and it caught Batman square in the center of the chest. His body armor might stop a bullet from penetrating, but it couldn't stop the force of a blow.

He staggered backward.

Selina did a forward flip and caught him again on the chest with the flats of her sturdy old-lady shoes. Then, dropping to the floor, she pulled her momentum into a tight spin. Her legs struck Batman's knee—and he toppled like a falling log.

"Kitties! Go!" she cried.

As Catwoman scrambled to her feet cats came running from all directions. She could hear them growling deep in their throats—an angry, hostile rumble like distant thunder. As one, they sprang upon Batman, hissing, scratching, biting.

Selina knew they wouldn't stop Batman more than a second or two—but that was all she needed.

That Vale woman was staring in stunned horror at the mass of writhing cat bodies. Selina ran up to her, seized her arm, and dragged her toward the bedroom. Halfway there Vale recovered her wits enough to struggle. Catwoman cuffed her hard across the face several times, until Vale's eyes went glassy and she slumped toward the floor.

With svelte grace, Catwoman picked Vale up and threw her over one shoulder. Staggering a bit under the extra weight, she still made it to her bedroom in record time.

The bedroom door was two inches thick and had a steel core. She threw the huge safety bolts, then dropped a security bar in place. Batman wouldn't be getting through them in a hurry.

Outside, the sounds of the cat fight ended in a series of pitiful mews and a few yelps of pain. She could imagine Batman throwing the cats off one by one, but she knew he'd never hurt them. He had a soft place in his heart for animals, just as she had a soft place in her heart for him.

She'd return that night to pick up her kitties, that or she'd rescue them from the pound. Springing the Riddler was one thing, springing her cats another. Now, though, her first priority lay in getting to safety with Vicki Vale. She'd extract a most painful, lingering vengeance for all Vale had put her through.

She dropped Vale onto the bed and crossed to the windows. Throwing open the huge glass panels, she stepped out onto a tiny balcony. Everything was as she'd left it—a small black backpack sat next to a coil of what looked like gray garden hose.

She pulled the backpack over her shoulder and ran back in for Vale. Hoisting the Copycat over her shoulder, she returned outside, looped the coil twice around her waist, and climbed to the top of the balcony's wall.

It seemed a dizzyingly long distance to the ground below. At least it would be a soft landing: neatly manicured grass and shrubbery filled in the space between her apartment building and the sidewalk.

She took a deep breath and prepared to jump.

"Selina!" Batman's voice called from her right. "Please—don't do it!"

She glanced across the side of the building. Twenty feet away, framed by jagged pieces of glass still stuck in the frame, Batman stood in the hole he'd made in her living room's picture window. She hissed at him.

Then she leaped out into nothingness.

The fall seemed to take forever, but at last the gray line around her waist went taut . . . and began to stretch. It was one of those huge rubber bands used by bungee jumpers—people who, as a hobby, leaped off cliffs or bridges or other high places, only to bounce up and down repeatedly at the end of a giant rubber band rather than fall all the way to the ground.

She knew the tensile strength of this particular bungee cord, and she'd calculated for Vale's extra weight as well; that's why she made the extra loop around her waist.

When the cord stretched to its limit, they were about five feet off the ground. Catwoman released the line. It snaked around her waist like a whip, then shot back upward.

Dropping Vale, Catwoman hit the ground in a roll. She came up on her feet, poised for action. Twenty-six floors above, she could see a dark shape in her penthouse's picture window: Batman, staring down at them.

Didn't expect that, did you? she thought.

Vale was staggering, a confused look on her face. Catwoman took a second to rummage around in her backpack. Finding a little aerosol spray can, she pulled it out, spritzed twice in Vale's face, and waited for the drug to take effect.

It did so almost immediately. Vale's eyes lost all focus and she began to drool a bit. Taking her arm, Catwoman led her to the sidewalk, then around to the apartment building's parking garage. She didn't use cars much, but she had several of them waiting, in case of emergencies.

She chose a silver Jaguar. The keys were in her backpack.

After shoving Vale into the car's tiny trunk, she climbed into the driver's seat, fitted the key into the ignition, and turned it, pumping the gas.

The engine remained stubbornly silent. Where was the throaty roar of power she loved, the ... *It had to be Batman.* The realization came a second too late.

John Gregory Betancourt

"You're going to need a battery to start that car."
Batman's voice boomed from somewhere outside. "I
took the liberty of removing the batteries from all the
cat-named cars down here before I went up to see
you."

Selina hissed silently through her teeth.

Footsteps sounded on the roof of the car. The Jaguar
rocked up and down. When Catwoman peered up
through the window, she could just make out the edge
of Batman's cape. He was standing on the roof of her
car, waiting to pounce when she left.

Quickly she locked all the doors. Then she rummaged through the backpack, looking for—ah, yes,
there it was: a single tiny yellow pill, which carried
the scent of bitter almonds . . . of cyanide. She'd always vowed she'd never be taken alive. Hopefully
Batman believed her.

She rolled her window down a crack. "Put the battery back in the car," she called to him.

"Selina," Batman called, "it's time you knew the
truth. Bruce Wayne is alive. There never was a jade
cat statue at the Wayne estate. And the cat sarcophagus is safe in the basement of the Gotham Museum."

"What?" she screeched.

"It's all been a setup to trap you. You killed Old
Man Harkins. That's going too far, Selina—you're
coming in this time, and you're not going to escape
justice."

Suddenly it all made sense to her. How Vicki Vale
had managed some of the greatest cat crimes of the
last few years. How Batman had been able to trace
her—he'd been watching Vale, and probably had her
wired for sound. How the newspapers had gotten such
detailed stories on Copycat's activities.

On top of that, Batman now wanted to arrest her
for murder . . . a murder she *really* hadn't committed.

"I never did anything to Harkins!" she said. "I just
bumped into him in the hallway, that's all! It's so *unfair* of you to blame me, Batman . . . you of all people
should understand that!"

"Where is Vicki Vale?" Batman demanded.

He cares about her. Catwoman knew then that she
had him. Then she fought a surge of jealous rage. *He
cares more for her than he cares for me!*

"Vale's safe," she said again. "She's safely out of the
way for the time being." Her voice dropped an octave,
to a softer, sexier tone. "Why don't you come down off
your roost and we'll talk about it, Batman."

The silver Jaguar shook again. Batman leaped to
the ground and stood in front of the car, his hands on
his hips, staring at her.

"Well?" he said in that gravelly, sexy voice of his.

Catwoman unlocked her door and slid out. She
made every motion a work of art . . . every gesture
sheer poetry, every movement sublime. She could feel
Batman's gaze tracing the sleek lines of her body even
beneath Mrs. McQueen's unflattering dress.

"I want you to understand, my love," she said, hips
swaying gently as she approached him. "I didn't kill
Old Man Harkins—I surprised him, and his heart
gave out. That's all. His time had come. I didn't *murder* him. Do you see?"

"Where's Vicki?"

"Oh, don't worry about *her*." She leaned her head
against his shoulder and took his arm in hers. "Let's
have a night on the town, you and I. Then you can let
me go. How does that sound, hmmm?"

He hesitated, then forced himself to move away

John Gregory Betancourt

from her. He hated doing it, she saw, but he did it anyway. Selina felt a growing sense of frustration.

"How can you love *that*?" she cried.

"Selina," he said. "Where did you put her?"

"She's dead," she said, annoyed beyond all reason.

Just then a pounding started from the trunk of the
Jaguar. Batman glanced that way.

Catwoman tried to run. He caught her arm and
hauled her in close. Their faces were inches apart.
Selina looked into Batman's eyes . . . and saw forgive-
ness.

"I'm sorry," he said. "I wish there could have been
another way."

"Me too," she said. Before he could stop her, she
popped that little yellow pill into her mouth and held
it between her teeth.

"Good-bye," she whispered. Then she bit down.

A bitter taste filled her mouth, then she closed her
eyes and let everything go limp. Her breathing
stopped.

Batman lowered Catwoman's still body to the cement.
"Selina," he whispered. He could smell bitter almonds
on her breath . . . cyanide? *No—Selina—*

There were tears in his eyes; for a moment he
couldn't see. Biting his lip, he forced himself to stand.

Vicki was pounding on the inside of the Jaguar's
trunk with a tire iron or her shoe or something.
Numb, Batman walked back to the car, took the car
keys from the ignition, went around to the trunk, and
opened it for her.

Vicki Vale sat up and began taking deep breaths.
Her hair was mussed and red lipstick made a long

smear across her cheek. Even so, Batman had never been quite so happy to see her.

"Well," Vicki said, "are you going to help me out of here, or not?"

Silently he offered her his hand. She took it. He pulled her out, and as she stood unsteadily on the cement she looked around.

"What happened to Catwoman?" she asked. "I heard you two talking."

"She—she's dead. Cyanide. She always said she wouldn't let herself be caught, but I never believed she'd kill herself."

"Where's her body?" Vicki said, looking around.

"It's—"

Batman looked, but it was gone. He blinked. He hadn't taken his eyes off her for more than a moment . . . had he? At first he felt a helpless rage that he'd been tricked, then relief flooded in. She was still alive, and she'd made her escape. Chalk it down to nine lives, he thought.

"You win this time, Selina," he said silently to himself. Then he began to laugh.

CATWOMAN STILL FREE
BRUCE WAYNE DEATH "POLICE HOAX"

By Vicki Vale
Special to the *Gotham Globe*

Millionaire Bruce Wayne's recent murder was revealed as part of an elaborate sting operation to capture notorious criminal Selina Kyle ("Catwoman"), Police Commissioner James Gordon revealed today. Also part of the sting operation were fake news stories about cat-related thefts, including the thefts of an Egyptian cat mummy from the Gotham

John Gregory Betancourt

Museum and a valuable jade statue from the
Wayne mansion.

Batman, who took part in the police operation,
was unable to capture Catwoman, although Catwoman's penthouse hideout was discovered. Dozens
of stolen paintings and other works of art have
been recovered.

Batman, with the cooperation of the Gotham police force, Bruce Wayne, and the *Gotham Globe*,
had hoped to put an end to *(cont'd A16, col. 4)*

An Unauthorized Biography

BRIAN M. THOMSEN

Of course I've seen the headlines, Fast-talk," said the statuesque redhead. "Could that bum have taken a more inconvenient time to kick off? We're still at least twelve months from pub."

"That's not all, Billie. Neal and Niederman have canceled the contract and want their money back," said Fred "Fast-talk" Fedderman into his car phone. He was the top literary agent in Gotham City. "They're invoking clauses 13(c), 19(b), and all of section 20. You guaranteed that the book would be timely, on a living celebrity, and with undeniable commercial appeal. You're six months over your last extension, General Southern is dead, and to top it all off, he sold a completed manuscript of his autobiography on his deathbed, which—you guessed it—N&N is rushing into publication immediately. Supposedly he

names more names and dishes more dirt than anyone
expected, including talking about his affairs with two
first ladies and one prime minister. Sorry, honey.
Their escape clause is valid, and you owe them a cool
million. My previously paid commission is nonrefund-
able, so you owe them that, too. Talk to you later,
babe."

Billie Bailey, the "Blitzkrieg Biographer," hung up
the phone. She was in trouble, and she didn't have a
million dollars to pay them back.

Billie Bailey had earned her nickname by authoring
four #1 bestselling biographies in the twelve short
years since she first came to Gotham City. All were
less than scholarly, high on sleaze, and just what the
public wanted. *Alfonsie*, an exposé of Gotham City's
favorite crooner, was greeted by public refutations
from coast to coast, and a rumored Mafia contract on
its author. The public didn't care and it sold millions.
Minister of Money, on the king of televangelism;
Screen Queen, on the closeted life of Hollywood's favorite leading man; and *Photographer Floozy*, on Vicki
Vale, all followed in rapid succession, each for a larger
advance and for a different publisher. Unfortunately,
despite the apparent success of each book, legal fees,
promo costs, and larger and larger returns of unsold
copies, none of her publishers ever made any money,
and sooner or later the more sensational aspects of
each book were disproven, and labeled the result of an
honest mistake, or a researcher's error.

Bailey's profile was still high, but she was becoming
less and less bankable in the eyes of Gotham's publishing bigwigs. She was sure that *Southern's Comfort*
would have taken care of all of that, plus her back-

log of debts, bribes, and attorney's fees that were beginning to get out of control. Now even *Southern's
Comfort* wasn't bankable, she was running out of publishers, and had to do something fast.

Billie fired Fast-talk when he sided with Neal &
Niederman against her. (What really hurt was when
she found out that he was also the agent of record for
Southern's autobiography.) Her lawyers assured her
that they could delay her creditors, including N&N,
for a few more months, provided that their attorneys'
fees were paid.

She needed a new contract, and for that she needed
a hot new subject fast. Perhaps something would turn
up at tonight's benefit for the Gotham Literacy Fund.

Thank God she was still on N&N's comp list, she
thought.

Several hours later it looked like she would have to
resign herself to just another dull evening of charity
favors. Her cheeks began to hurt from too much smiling, and too much biting her tongue when the subject
of N&N came up.

She was about to slip discreetly out a side door
when her arm was grabbed by a petite, smartly
dressed woman of forty who was notorious for never
missing an opportunity to land a new client for her
agency.

"Oh, Billie," said Maura Most, dragging Billie away,
"there's someone over here that you just have to meet.
I hear he has a thing for statuesque redheads."

Their destination seemed to be a devilishly handsome and bored-looking playboy, who Billie thought

seemed awfully familiar. He was probably featured on some society page or something.

Oh, well, she thought, there are worse ways to pass an already disappointing evening than by meeting a handsome playboy. Time to turn on the charm.

"Billie, I'd like you to meet Bruce. Bruce, Billie," prattled Maura. Without taking a breath, she added, "Be back in a minute, one of my clients is talking to Fred Fedderman, and we can't have that, can we?" and she was off and across the room before anyone could reply.

Billie turned her attention to the playboy named Bruce and said with her most inviting smile, "Pleased to make your acquaintance, Bruce."

The playboy seemed to be slightly taken aback. "Why, you're Billie Bailey, aren't you?"

"That's right," she replied. She had seen his type before. He was probably just celebrity shy.

"And we've never met before?"

"I don't believe so," she answered, puzzled at his question. She was sure she could never have forgotten a hunk like him, and she then added in her most flirtatious manner, "But there's a first time for everything."

"I was sure we met somewhere before," Bruce insisted. "After all, how else could I have deserved mention in the acknowledgments for your book on Vicki Vale?"

"I don't understand," said Billie, feeling more and more uncomfortable by the minute.

"I'm Bruce Wayne," he replied, "and I don't enjoy being listed as a source for a scurrilous piece of fiction masquerading as a biography. You are just lucky, Miss Bailey, that Vicki asked all of her friends to let it die and not give it extra notoriety through our protesta-

An Unauthorized Biography

tions. Now, if you would excuse me, I'm sure there must be someone with integrity here I can make idle conversation with. Good night, Ms. Bailey." He turned and strode off in the direction of Commissioner Gordon, and his daughter, Barbara.

Billie called him a prig under her breath and vowed to try to keep more on top of her alleged contacts. She had never found it easy to match names with faces.

The rest of the evening passed without any major incidents, though Billie was continually ambushed in her efforts to extricate herself from the doldrums of the social set. Her luck began to change on the way home.

After last call, she paid one precautionary visit to the powder room, where she overheard two dowagers discussing a recent break-in and jewel theft.

"It was horrible," Billie overheard from the privacy of her stall, "all of the jewels my second husband gave me were taken. Or was it my third husband?"

"Do the police have any idea who could have done it?" asked the other.

"None," said the first. "Though I know it has to have been that one they call the Catwoman. Honestly she has become the bane of everyone of privilege in Gotham City, and it's just not fair."

As the two dowagers returned to their waiting escorts Billie extricated herself from her place of hiding and thought, *Catwoman, the Unauthorized Biography of a Criminal.*

It had best-seller written all over it . . . and a criminal would have a very difficult time trying to take anyone to court.

Delighted, Billie left the powder room and ran right

Brian M. Thomsen

into a tall, geeky-looking fellow whose expensive tuxedo did little to disguise his lack of couth.

"Excuse me," she offered, trying to extricate herself gracefully. She was about to turn away when she recognized him. "Wait a minute, aren't you Maurice Hoffman, president of Trendwide Books?"

"That's right," he replied.

"I'm Billie Bailey," she said, "and do I have a book for you."

A meeting was set up for the following morning between herself, Hoffman, his second in command, and the head of Trendwide's paperback division. Her lawyer, their lawyers and accountants, and a recording secretary were also present.

The triumvirate who would pass judgment on her new project—and on her future, for that matter—reminded her of the see-no-evil, hear-no-evil, speak-no-evil monkey trio.

Maurice Hoffman, called Maury by his friends and detractors alike, was "see no evil." It was rumored that everything he knew about literature came from reading the dust jackets of the books his father brought home. He succeeded his father as president of Trendwide, and even his detractors, of which there were many, agreed that what he lacked in brains, know-how, and leadership skills, he made up for in sheer enthusiasm and goodwill. His ill-thought-out optimism had led his company to buy numerous projects of apparent great potential, and little proof of actual worth in hand. He could see no evil, and for that reason was the perfect dupe for Billie's charms.

To his left, and at the center of the triumvirate was Eva Evans, Trendwide Books' executive vice-president and publisher. She liked to think of herself as the power behind the throne and a hands-on publisher. In actuality her hands-on efforts consisted of a handshake, and a hand-off to a junior editor to do any actual work. Thus she always picked winners—since any losers were easily dismissed as the result of mishandling by someone else. She never listened to any of the advisers she had present and knew in her heart that whenever it came down to it she was infallible. Billie saw her confer with the lawyers and accountants, but had no fear. Eva was "hear no evil."

And finally to her left was Martin Brothers, the director of Trendwide Books' paperback line. Where Maury just wanted to make his father proud, and Eva just wanted to rule the world, or at least book publishing, Marty just wanted to be liked and to avoid being yelled at. By his own admission he had no opinions save those his superiors wanted him to have. He had gotten where he was by copying the successful formulas of the competition and by doing what he was told. If Maury and Eva said it was a best-seller, far be it from him to disabuse them of that notion. Martin was "speak no evil," and Billie knew she had nothing to fear from him.

Despite everything believed by Maury, Eva, and Marty, Billie Bailey realized that she was scraping the bottom of the barrel of the major Gotham City big-money publishers. She knew that they were all too easily impressed with her best-selling track record and sufficiently "out of the loop" to be aware of her problems.

Billie had one chance and one chance only. She either walked out of the Trendwide Books offices with a contract or she was all washed up.

With the winning smile and gracious tone that had

gained her access to the bedrooms, boardrooms, and barrooms of the stars, she began her spiel.

"Gentlepeople," she began, creating her fictions as she spoke, "I'm glad that you are my first appointment, but unfortunately, as I have four other houses to visit before the close of business today, I'll try to be succinct. I have dismissed Fred Fedderman as my agent and will be handling the negotiations for my next project on my own. It is unencumbered by any preexisting option, and my asking price is three million with one and a half million on signing to cover research expenses. I feel that this is fair given the great commercial potential of my next biography."

"Which is about who?" asked Eva, who firmly believed that time was money.

"Like Vicki Vale, the subject of my next book is a woman right out of the headlines of every Gotham City newspaper. Women fear for their valuables, and wish they were her. Men are embarrassed by her audacity, and fantasize about her. Part woman, part feline, she is a mistress of mystery and passion. Yes, the subject of my next book is Gotham City's own lady of the night, the Catwoman.

"Years of research have given me access to her story. For the first time your readers will see the events that shaped her life, the passions that guide her, the goals that inspire her, the instincts that protect her. *Catwoman: An Unauthorized Biography*, the latest number-one best-seller by Billie Bailey. For three million dollars it can be all yours."

The triumvirate was silent. They were about to take her bait.

Billie played them like a pro with one final lure. "Now, if you will excuse me, I have to get downtown for my next meeting."

An Unauthorized Biography

Maury raised his hand to hail her attention, saying, "Billie, am I correct in assuming that we can keep you from proposing this project to any other publisher by meeting your asking price?"

"That's correct," she answered, knowing she was about to land a big one while trying to convey a sense of impatience about leaving for her next fictitious meeting.

"Could you just give us a minute to confer?" Eva asked graciously.

"Sure, but just a minute. I don't want to keep N&N waiting," she answered, closing the door behind her.

By the time she had counted to sixty, Eva and company had called her back in, and with a hearty handshake and salesman's smile; the deal was done and her price was met.

Contracts were signed the next day, and by the time the check for one and a half million cleared a week later, Billie was solvent, with all of her debts paid . . . and she hadn't even put a pen to paper, or opened a book for research, or conducted a single interview.

For Billie Bailey, life was good once again.

Now all she had to do was write the book, and she had eighteen months to do it in.

She was sure she would turn up something.

Fifteen months passed.

As with previous projects, Billie had made her publisher sign a confidentiality agreement that allowed them to divulge that a three-million-dollar deal had

Brian M. Thomsen

been agreed upon without revealing the book's subject matter. This allowed her to research and probe discreetly, without arousing undue attention or fear of lawsuit.

It also allowed her to sell an exclusive leak, revealing her subject matter and some of her most astonishing revelations, to one of Gotham City's tabloids at a later date. This sale was done through a blind, and helped to build excitement before her book was turned in.

As usual she had managed to negotiate a nice six-figure price tag for the upcoming leak ... unfortunately fifteen months had yet to turn up any new or astonishing revelations on the feminine feline known as the Catwoman, so, as she had done before, Billie linked a bunch of tangential materials together with a few well-worn facts and several out-and-out lies, and violà, an exclusive leak on page one of three of Gotham City's favorite tabloids.

Billie had nothing to fear. Whoever heard of a wanted criminal coming forward to clear her name?

Or so she thought.

Page one, the *Gotham City Post* on April 1, 1992:

GOTHAM CITY POST EXCLUSIVE:

NEW BIOGRAPHY ENTITLED

CATWOMAN: AN UNAUTHORIZED BIOGRAPHY

BY BILLIE BAILEY

A confidential source yesterday revealed to the *Gotham City Post* that the subject of the three-million-dollar biography deal between Trendwide Books and Billie Bailey is to be the notorious jewel thief known as the Catwoman.

Among the book's startling revelations are Catwoman's debutante upbringing, her role as student/love slave to former big-game hunter Thomas Blake, also known as the master criminal Cat-Man, from whom she took her name, her affairs with members of the Gotham society set, her cross-dressing fetishes, and her longtime erotic relationship with the Caped Crusader himself.

Bailey claims to have spent years poring over reports and psychological profiles of the felonious feline. The author of four best-selling exposé biographies, including such blockbusters as *Minister of Money, Screen Queen,* and *Photographer Floozy,* about Vicki Vale, formerly of this paper, declined comment at this time, but did admit that the subject sounded intriguing.

Her publisher, Trendwide Books, also declined comment.

Bailey's last book was to be *Southern's Comfort,* a life of Desert War hero General Southern, whose untimely death put the project on indefinite hold.

Upon the announcement of the three-million-dollar price tag for her new book, this paper ran a full-page ad that said BILLIE BAILEY WON'T YOU PLEASE GO HOME.

The ad was paid for by the subjects of her last four books.

As expected, the Catwoman has been unavailable for comment.

At this time this paper has no idea whether Catwoman's true identity will be revealed in the upcoming biography, so we will all just have to wait and see.

Publication is scheduled for the upcoming summer.

Reactions around Gotham City were mixed.

At Trendwide Books, three executives couldn't stop patting themselves on the backs and counting the projected profits on their surefire best-seller, despite the fact that none of them had yet to see any of the manuscript that was due in three short months.

At Neal & Niederman, Bailey's former editor was fired for letting this soon-to-be-best-seller slip through her hands, despite the fact that Bailey's last book had been canceled by a unanimous vote of all three of her bosses, Neal, Niederman, and Schwartz.

At Wayne Manor, Bruce Wayne was not amused.

"You know, Alfred," he said to his trustworthy confidant, "this time she has gone too far. It's bad enough that she is once again pedaling lies as the truth, but this time she is really playing with fire."

"Perhaps the papers are mistaken," Alfred offered. "After all, she never admits that the Catwoman is her subject. The confidential source might be lying."

"She *is* the confidential source," answered Bruce. "It's an old tabloid trick to stir up some headlines. I just hope she hasn't stuck her nose where it doesn't belong."

"Are you referring to Sister Magdalene, sir?" Alfred asked.

"Exactly," said Bruce. "Perhaps Batman should keep a close eye on Ms. Bailey."

"And teach her a lesson, sir?"

"Perhaps, old friend."

An Unauthorized Biography

At the apartment of a recently dismissed police officer, Jake Madison smiled for the first time since he had been kicked off the force for taking bribes. He thumbed through a folder of photocopies.

"This must be my luck day," he murmured.

And in an apartment on the wrong side of town, Selina Kyle crushed her copy of the *Gotham City Post*.

"Lies!" she hissed. "No one tells lies about Catwoman and gets away with it. No one tells Catwoman's story and gets away with it. Cat-Man was a no-good poser. Maybe she's lying now in order to throw me off the trail. Well, *Catwoman: An Unauthorized Biography* will only be published over my dead body."

Selina donned her leather cat suit in preparation for picking up the scent of Billie Bailey's trail.

Billie had a new problem. Eva at Trendwide had called wanting to see if she could move up the delivery date. A meeting was scheduled for Monday, and she still didn't have enough lies to wrap a book around.

The phone rang again.

Billie hoped it was Eva calling to postpone the meeting for a later date.

It wasn't.

"Is this Billie Bailey?" asked a gruff, slightly inebriated-sounding voice.

"Yes," she answered tentatively. "Who is this?"

"If you want the police file on Catwoman, bring one hundred thousand dollars to the Gotham Public Li-

brary tonight just before closing. I'll be in the business
section reading *Sports Illustrated*. Don't be late."

The line went dead.

One hundred thou was all she had left from the leak
money, but if the police file had anything of note in it,
it might be worth it.

It might even have Catwoman's real name.

It was worth the risk, and if she left now, she'd just
make it to the bank and library in time.

Billie grabbed her coat and ran out the door.

Billie arrived at the Gotham Public Library ten minutes before closing. She took a minute to chat with the
security guard at the front door and the one by the elevator before proceeding to the Business Reading
Room. Both guards seemed to appreciate her deigning
to flirt with them and were well within shouting distance if things turned ugly. The money was in an inside pocket of her raincoat.

The Business Reading Room was empty save for a
wino reading a copy of the *SI* swimsuit issue. Bracing
herself, she approached the table where he was
seated.

"Excuse me," Billie offered, "are you—"

"Yeah, I'm the guy who called you. I recognize you
from the picture on your book jacket. Do you have the
money?" he shot back at her like a machine gun.

"Yes, but first I have to see what you are selling."

"Sure, here," he replied. "It's a copy of the confidential file from police headquarters. We lifted a set of
fingerprints from one of her previous heists, where
she lost one of her gloves during an altercation with
Batman. We cross-referenced it with our files, and

sure enough she had a record. No debutante here, but
an interesting history nonetheless."

Billie could barely hold back her joy. It was all here,
and just in the nick of time for Monday's meeting.

Trying to keep cool, she queried him further: "How
did you get this?"

"It's my retirement fund. A cop gets caught making
a lousy mistake, and *boom*, no more pension. I knew
this file would come in handy someday. Now where's
the money?"

She reached into her coat and handed him the envelope, never taking her hands off the all-important
dossier. "Here."

He didn't even bother to count it. "Thank you
kindly, ma'am, and remember I have your number," he
said as he left the room, pausing for just a moment to
add, "See you on the best-seller lists."

On his way out he passed a guard, who had just
come in to announce that it was closing time.

Billie slipped the file under her coat and hurried out
of the room.

Jake Madison couldn't wait to get home and count the
money, so he took a shortcut through one of Gotham
City's many dark alleys. Exultation at his success won
out over his better judgment, and besides he was in a
hurry.

He never saw the young thug with the iron pipe
who bashed his skull in, nor did he see the two police
officers who had ducked into the alley for a little privacy on their break.

Officers Valerie Hobson and Marsh Rogers appre-
hended the assailant immediately, but it was too late
for Madison, who died before the ambulance arrived.

The envelope of money was eventually turned over to the Gotham City Police Department's widows-and-orphans fund.

No one ever found out how the recently dismissed Officer Madison got his hands on so much cash, and no one asked questions.

The money was being put to a good use, so who cared?

Madison died with no known next of kin.

Billie spent all day Saturday and Sunday going over the file that she had recently acquired. The facts of Catwoman's life were better than any fiction she could ever dream up.

The rap sheet revealed that her real name was Selina Kyle, and that she had previously been booked on numerous prostitution charges. Her next of kin was a nun named Sister Magdalene. A nun, for chrissake!

There were also notes from a few years back between a detective named Flannery and some guy named Grant, who was giving her lessons in self-defense. There was also something about some guy named Wildcat. I wasn't too far off with that Cat-Man schtick, Billie thought. I'll just say it was a researcher's error.

There were also numerous notations linking her to the death of some pimp named Stan, but nothing definite was ever concluded.

The file was a virtual gold mine.

Billie quickly fashioned a tale of a poor girl from the sticks who was tainted by the streets of Gotham City. After experiencing every possible degradation, she finally decided to fight back, and was now exacting vengeance on the society who stood idly by while her and others like her were made to swim in the cesspools of sin that were the streets.

There was also that sister angle she could play up, not to mention the crime of passion involving that guy named Stan.

It was during the early hours of Monday that she finally closed the file that she would take to her meeting at Trendwide Books in a few hours.

She looked up to check the time when she saw the leather-clad feline known as Catwoman standing right in front of her, razor-sharp claws reaching for her neck.

Billie had been so engrossed in her work that she hadn't even heard her jimmying the window lock.

Billie pushed back in her chair just out of reach of the claws of death. Faking bravado, she exclaimed, "Why Catwoman, I'm sorry. I didn't hear you come in."

"Oh, I'm sure you would have welcomed me at the door if you had known I was coming," the feline felon purred.

"But of course! Interviews are important in a balanced biography," Billie said, backpedaling as fast as she could.

"There isn't going to be any biography," Catwoman insisted. "All you've done is string together a bunch of lies. How dare you defame me."

"What the *Post* ran was just a plant to throw everyone off the track ... and to act as an indirect invitation to this meeting," Billie said, thinking fast. "You see, I know the truth, but I still want to present your side. I want to show the world what Gotham City has

Brian M. Thomsen

done to you"—she paused for maximum effect—
"Selina."

Catwoman was enraged. "You know!" she screamed.

"Sure," said the now terrified Billie.

Originally Selina had only planned on scaring her
off. Now she realized there was only one way to protect herself, and her sister.

Billie Bailey had to die.

Catwoman closed in on her, claws outstretched.

Both predator and prey were momentarily distracted
when a shadowy figure crashed through the terrace
doors into the living room where they all now stood.

It was Batman.

Billie seized the moment to extricate herself from
behind her desk and to cower in a nearby corner.

"Catwoman, don't do anything rash. I know you're a
thief, but I don't think you're a cold-blooded murderer," said the Dark Knight, offering the Catwoman
his hand.

"There are innocent people who have to be protected from lying scum like her," Catwoman answered,
grasping the gauntlet he offered in costumed camaraderie.

"I assure you that nothing will happen. You and
your sister's secrets are safe from Ms. Bailey's poison
pen. I promise you."

"See to it, Dark Knight," said the Catwoman, "or
I'll be back, and I assure you I'll have her guts for gar-
ters."

And with that, the Catwoman was out to the terrace and over the rail, disappearing into the Gotham
night.

Batman offered a hand to help Billie to her feet. "I hope that will teach you a lesson," he said. "Next time call it fiction. It's what you write, anyway." He turned his back on her and headed toward the terrace door.

"Thank you, Batman," she answered, "I've learned my lesson."

"I hope so," he said, and with that he too disappeared into the darkness.

Billie, of course, had no intention of dropping the project.

If worse comes to worst, she thought, I can always get a bodyguard.

Day was breaking, and Billie barely had time to shower and change before calling a car service to take her to her breakfast meeting with Eva.

The last thing she did was to scoop up the valuable folder with all of her hard-earned research.

She didn't even notice that it was slightly thinner than it had been before.

Seated in the backseat of the limo, Billie nervously went over the notes one more time.

Opening the folder, she finally realized something was amiss.

Clipped to the top was a note, which said: *Billie, I too am a fairly good researcher. Here're some more notes for your files.*

It was signed *Batman.*

In the place of the police report was a dossier on a certain Willie May Balnick, listing her expulsion from

Brian M. Thomsen

Midway High, her two abortions, her dismissal from
the *Midway Herald* for fabrication of source material,
and even the rap sheet for the two arrests for prostitution that she had managed to talk her way out of
when she had moonlighted at the Good Times Escort
Service.

How could he have known that her real name was
Willie May Balnick?

The implication was clear.

Some secrets are better left hidden.

Billie deposited the file in a nearby trash can just as
Gotham City's environmental engineers made their
morning pickup.

She entered the restaurant where Eva and Maury
were waiting.

Summoning her courage, and donning the winning
smile that had saved her more than once, Billie took
her place at the table, saying, "You know, I have a
feeling that the bottom has dropped out of the
unauthorized-biography market ... but I have this
terrific idea for a novel. It's about a glamorous biographer. I see it as a cross between Judith Krantz and
Jackie Collins."

Ten minutes later she knew she had them hooked.

A Harlot's Tears

ED GORMAN
(for Joe Orlando)

David Fisher: 198–

Nothing special about the day. Not most of it, anyway. Rolls into work at 8:22 A.M. Three client conferences to fill up the morning and a fifteen-minute meeting with the new woman in the law library (nice legs) and then racquetball over the lunch hour (yogurt and raisins following) and then a long grinding afternoon-becoming-night of prep. Big court case starting in two days. The kind of thing that could get him a full partnership if the firm won. (And he plans on winning.) And then the parking garage where his sweet little BMW waits.

And then the nighttime city streets

darkness and neon; bus fumes and marijuana smoke; summer heat and the laughter of whores

junkies and hookers and killers and perverts; man

puking in gutter; homeless woman on corner screaming at somebody who isn't there and

He gives himself the He Shoulds.

He Should go home because he's happily married.

He Should have more respect for himself and his
wife and his two children than to give in to this terrible impulse of his.

He Should never jeopardize his law career by traf-
ficking with hookers.

And yet

And yet years ago, just out of college, he used to
cruise like this and it was real exciting

And for some reason

(maybe all the business pressure lately)

For some reason he wants to do it just one more
time

Just once

Because

he loves the danger. Just something about it. Danger makes the sex exciting, the way it was when he
was back in high school, when everything was still de-
liciously forbidden.

And then

He sees her.

Young. Even a little scared looking. Right there on
the corner. The other hookers, all war paint and
sweaty summer blouses, eyeing her with real compet-
itive hatred.

He sees her

and without thinking

pulls over to the corner

and she leans in

and says

A Harlot's Tears

Brett Ewing: 198–

"Hi."

She can't believe what she's seeing.

A) A brand-new BMW convertible. So fine and shiny and red in the grubby neon night.

B) A very handsome, upscale young man with a fifty-dollar haircut and a very expensive-looking summer-weight suit.

C) A very gentlemanly hand extended to help her into the car.

She's been in the city seven weeks now, and so far all her tricks have been rubes and dipshits, including one guy whose BO was so bad she literally threw up afterward.

Kinda neat, romantic, really
   How she gets in
   And he pulls away from the curb
   And neither of them say a word
   Just listen to Anita Baker on the tape deck
   And cruise along the river
   Fresh cool breeze
   Skyscraper lights like red-and-yellow watercolors on the shimmering dark surface of the river
   And he reaches over and takes her hand as if it's a real date not just a trick
   And they drive and drive and drive
   No words yet exchanged
   Just touches
   And glances
   And
   No matter how bad or down or blown out her life

has gotten, she's always kept the dream. The Cinderella dream, where the handsome young prince comes to rescue her. Is this the handsome young prince?

Maybe, she thinks, maybe this is the prince.

And in a couple of weeks or so—after he puts her up in some very nice apartment over near Carver Park—maybe she won't ever have to work the streets again, because to be frank, she really doesn't like it

It scares her

And every time she looks in the mirror she thinks: Slut. You slut.

And so she'd be very very *very* happy if this turned out like Cinderella and they fell in love and

He finds a little nook along the river, many, many miles out along the river

And still without speaking, he parks the car and shifts seats, her straddling him now

and

And afterward, he says, "What's your name?"

"Brett."

"Brett? Really?" Smiles. "I don't think I've ever known a Brett."

Of course that wasn't her name back in Iowa. Eight weeks ago in the small town of Dysart she'd been Donna Mae Hamilton.

"Brett Ewing," she says.

"Aw come on."

"Really."

He laughs. Nice sweet laugh. "If you say so." Grins. "You know what my name is?"

"Huh-uh."

"Lance Sterling."

Now it's her turn to laugh. "Get real."

"Well, if your name can be Brett Ewing, why can't mine be Lance Sterling?"

She does something she's never done with a john before. Gives him a tender kiss. A genuine kiss.

"Wow," he says.

"I really like you, Lance Sterling."

"And I really like you too, Brett Ewing."

The night ends forty-five minutes later on a Gotham street corner.

With David Fisher about to face a wife he loves very much and never wants to hurt

And Donna Mae Hamilton about to face three more johns before this particular night is over

Men she'd never think of kissing in any genuine way

Men who'd just laugh if she told them of her Cinderella dreams

Catwoman: April 1, 199–, 9:28 p.m.

Night is her friend; she can hide in its dark embrace. Night plays its own music, a symphony of moonlight and shadow.

As she herself is shadow. As she herself is cat.

Watch her now as she swings from Gotham rooftop to Gotham rooftop, trailing a man in the ghetto sidewalk seven stories below.

Just as the man himself is trailing the young hooker—who is just now becoming aware of him—half a block ahead.

Hooker walks faster. "Oh, shit, it's him," she mutters to herself. "Shit."

Faster. Faster.

Ed Gorman

As does the man. Faster. Faster.

And thus it is played out as it is played out on so many urban streets every night of the year.

Rape. Or death. Or both.

The man. Closer, closer now.

Hooker reaches the alley. Looks back over her shoulder. And shudders.

"Hey," he says. "You."

She starts to run.

And that's when he closes on her.

Grabs her shoulder. Hurls her into the alley.

Where red-eyed rats and cats with eyes the color of midnight moons . . . watch as

"You remember me?" he says. "Huh?"

His rage is overwhelming.

Bladeflash in moonlight. Switchblade.

"Bitch. Fucking bitch."

Knife to her throat as she tries to scream but his hand too fast clamps too hard on her soft pretty mouth.

"Bitch."

Up comes her knee. Only trick she knows.

But he skillfully turns away and puts the knife deep into her shoulder. Cutting. Cutting.

This time her scream is loose on the night.

"Bitch."

He is just coming for her again when the rats and cats look up and see

catshape of Catwoman silhouetted against the dirty brick of the alley buildings as she

flies down, aiming her feet directly at the back of the killer

slamming him headfirst into the building.

But just as Catwoman lands the wounded girl falls

forward, forcing Catwoman to catch her and hold her
while the killer

blood streaming from his broken nose

runs. slapping footsteps now. retreating retreating.

"Motherfucker!" he keeps screaming, half-delirious.
"Motherfucker!"

And then he too is one with night, beyond even the
reach of Catwoman now as he stumbles to his car and
flees.

Flees.

Selina Kyle: April 1, 199–, 11:47 p.m.

"You didn't recognize him?"

"Huh-uh."

"But he said, 'You remember me?'"

"Right. That's what he said."

"And then he stabbed you?"

"Yeah. He wanted to cut my throat, but I moved
and he stabbed me in the shoulder."

"How's that shoulder doing?"

"Pretty good. I mean, it's really not much of a
wound, I guess."

"I sure wouldn't like to have it."

Brett Ewing smiles. "You're real nice. I appreciate
that. I mean, I have pretty shitty relationships with
other women. It's nice to be able to just relax and talk
to another woman."

They are in Selina's apartment, Brett lying on the
couch, Selina in the chair opposite. Brett has no idea
Selina and Catwoman were the same person. After
bringing Brett upstairs, Catwoman knocked on the
door. Arizona, the young girl presently staying in

Selina's apartment, appeared and helped Brett inside. Catwoman said good night and left, pretending to leave the building but actually climbing in a back window and reappearing to introduce herself as Arizona's roommate Selina.

Brett, who is smoking a cigarette, stares at the ceiling and says, "I guess you've figured out what I am by now."

"Oh?"

"I'm a hooker."

Selina smiles gently at the sad young woman. She was very much like Brett at one time. "Being a hooker is what you do. Not what you are."

"Thanks for saying that."

"It's true. You can give it up anytime you want to."

"And do what? Wait tables?"

"How about going back to school and getting your high-school diploma?"

Yawning, Arizona comes out of the bathroom. She looks snug and warm in her nubby pink bathrobe. "I'm going to stand on the back porch and have a smoke and then I'm going to bed. Just wanted to say good night."

Just off the living room there is a porch that overlooks the alley seven floors below. It's nice to stand there and look out at the city and feel the cool breezes. There is no screen, so with the porch window open it's like being outdoors.

"Night," Selina says.

"Night," Brett says. "Thanks for helping me get that wound cleaned out."

"I still think we should have called the police," Arizona says.

Brett shakes her head. "I've been busted too many times to willingly sic the police on myself."

A Harlot's Tears

Arizona, who once found herself in Brett's trap, nods sadly and drifts toward the nearest bedroom door.

After Brett stubs her cigarette out, she leans over and stares at Selina. "I know who was after me to-night."

"You recognized him?"

"Not recognized him. But I know who he is. 'Harlot,' the guy who's been in the news the past month."

Selina hadn't wanted to alarm Brett, that's why she didn't bring the subject up herself.

In the past nineteen days, six prostitutes had been savagely slain in Gotham. On the forehead of each, in garish red lipstick, the killer had written HARLOT. Hence the name the media had given him.

"I think you're right," Selina says.

"But that's the weird thing."

"What is?"

"It was personal."

"Personal?"

"Yeah, I mean, not like he was just attacking a hooker at random or anything. It was like he knew who I was . . . and hated me. Personally."

Selina stares at Brett for a long moment and then says, "How tall are you?"

"Five-seven. Why?"

"How much do you weigh?"

"About one twenty."

"A wig would make it easy."

"Easy? I don't know what you're talking about."

Selina smiles. "Maybe I don't either. But after we've had a good night's sleep, we'll go over my plan and see if it makes any sense." She stands up, ready to go in, wash her face, put on fresh pajamas, and collapse into bed. "You sure you wouldn't rather sleep in my bed and let me take the couch?"

"I've imposed enough, Selina. The couch will be just fine."

"If you say so," Selina says, and then heads for the bathroom. "G'night."

Brett Ewing: April 3, 199–

Night. Rainstorm. Gutters flooded. Sewers overflowing with filthy gray water. Headlights exposing slanting silver rain. Fender bender forcing three people, including tired-looking overweight cop, into the downpour. Traffic lights—red, yellow, green—watercolors now in the gloom.

Lone woman carrying umbrella walks the city street. Seemingly in no hurry. Smiles at drenched and scared kitty trying desperately to find shelter.

Stoops over. Picks her up. Puts her in raincoat pocket, mother kangaroo style.

Brett Ewing. Walking. Recovered enough now to ply the street corners. Nice round rolling ass beneath the lime-green designer raincoat. Kitty peeking up at her. "Meow."

Brett laughing. Laughing.

Two blocks away she finally finds some action. Street corner that teenage girls and boys dominate. Chickenhawk Avenue, as it's known. Lighted, open newsstand where the kids parade their wares while the droolers drive by and gawk, getting their sweaty money ready in their sweaty hands. She hopes she never has to be as pathetic about getting sex as her johns are.

A Harlot's Tears

Gets closer now. Sees the kids better. From a distance they all look like pretty good merchandise.

But close up:

Pain. Fear. Despair. Of a kind only a teenager who sells her or his body can know. And numbing it all on dope, which also helps you forget all the spooky stories going around. How one hooker was found in a park with her breasts cleaved off. How a male hooker was castrated a few nights later. And always, always some fourteen- or fifteen- or sixteen-year-old being pronounced HIV-positive.

And then she stops, just as somebody says, "Hey, look, that lime-green raincoat! It's Brett! Hey, Brett!" But they can't be sure, the umbrella blocking most of her face.

She turns away before anybody comes running after her.

Walks back the way she came.

The tiny wet kitty sticking her sweet little kitty face up out of the flap pocket and going "meow" again.

Half a block. Footsteps. Hers.

Then other footsteps.

His. Or so she hopes, anyway.

Figured he'd be somewhere around Chickenhawk Avenue. Waiting for her. Probably been here the past two nights while she was recuperating at Selina's.

Raincoat is suddenly hot inside. Sweat. And faint smell of rubber.

"Meow."

"It's all right, kitty. I'm taking you home with me."

Footsteps. Faster now. Hers.

Footsteps. Faster now. His.

When she reaches the alley, she ducks inside, losing herself in the darkness.

Must act quickly now. Away fall the clothes of Brett Ewing to reveal . . . Catwoman.

She quickly scales the side of a brick building, hiding on the shelf of a third-story indentation.

Now the Harlot comes into the alley. Running. Out of breath. Switchblade knife obvious in his right gloved hand.

He stops. Looks around.

Where did she go?

Nobody could get away that quickly.

Bitch, he thinks. Bitch. Tightening his leather grip on the switchblade.

He stops running. She's gone. Just have to face it.

And she was the one he really wanted, too. The others were just practice for Brett Ewing. (The theatricality of the name sickens him now. Some goddamned hayseed come to the big city to make some money on the little rosebud between her legs. Bitch.)

Looks around some more.

Nowhere in sight.

Shoves the knife back in his pocket and begins slowly turning around and walking out of the alley.

Then suddenly stops and looks straight up into the rain falling on him.

As if he's beseeching God himself for a favor.

Bitch.

Sometimes you must wait. Patience. Catwoman could take him down tonight, but she wants to know more about him so that when the police come after him, they won't have any trouble making it a good bust.

She notes his looks; notes his license number as his BMW pulls away.

She strokes the tiny kitty. "C'mon, we'll go home and get you some warm milk."

David Fisher: April 3, 199–

"You're just so tired lately. And you can't seem to get rid of that sore throat."

He lies in the darkness, listening to his wife, Sara.

He's been home for two hours now. After Brett Ewing somehow eluded him.

He's in the same bed where both of his children were conceived. Where he held his wife so tenderly the night her mother died, and where she held him when his father was killed in that terrible head-on car accident.

It used to be so superficial with Sara, his feelings. In college he'd basically liked her because she looked so frigging good in a bikini. Best of both worlds. A feast for his own eyes. The envy of other young men. And the early married years weren't all that much deeper either. Sara was essentially an ornament for his corporate bosses to admire. And David certainly wasn't averse to scoring a little strange nooky on the side.

But somehow the night she'd borne their first child, seeing her face drained yet lovely as she presented him with his baby, he came to love and admire and respect her in a way he would never have imagined possible. Wife. Lover. Sister. Mother. Friend. She was all things to him.

And then that night, several years later, with Brett
Ewing . . .

"You're awfully quiet, honey. Rough night at the office?"

"Yeah," he says. "Boss on my ass again."

"I swear that man has periods."

"I believe it."

And he wants to tell her. Right now. Get it over
with.

But when he opens his mouth and starts to say

he sees her as a beautiful young college sophomore
and then at their wedding aglow in white and then
that night when she gave birth to Kate

and he can't say it

the words, the horrible words, won't come

"You're soaking wet."

"Nightmare, I guess."

"Better go change those pajamas."

Middle of night. Darkness. Rain pattering window.

In the nightmare he was in Dr. Birnbaum's office
again and Dr. Birnbaum is coming through the door
with a single sheet of white paper in his hand and he
says

and that's when David woke up screaming

as he wakes up three, four nights a week screaming

when Dr. Birnbaum comes through the door with a
single sheet of white paper in his hand and says

In the bathroom, he empties his bladder and then
stares at himself in the mirror.

You owe her the truth. Now. Right fucking now and
no more excuses.

But after getting dry pajamas and crawling back in bed, he hears her soft sweet snore in the shadows.

Not tonight. Tomorrow night. For sure.

He feels relief.

My God, how will he ever be able to tell her the truth?

Selina Kyle: April 4, 199–

Uptown there's a guy Selina always calls for background checks on people she's pursuing. The guy lives in a wheelchair, victim of a drunk driver, but he's trained himself to become a sort of poet in the art of computer hacking.

"Here's his license number," Selina says.

"How you been?"

"Fine."

"If I ever get out of this rig, you gonna gimme the first dance?"

"The first ten dances."

"You're nice, you know that?"

"So are you."

She can hear him typing in the Harlot's license-plate number. "This guy a baddie?"

"A real baddie."

"Probably take me a couple of hours."

"Fine. I appreciate it, Richard."

"Toodles."

An hour later he calls her back. As always, he's been thorough.

He tells her the guy's name, age, address, occupation, salary, club memberships, credit rating, and health status.

"God," she says to the information about David Fisher's health status.

"Yeah," Rich says. "Poor bastard."

Brett Ewing: April 4, 199–

Can't take it. Cooped up the last three days this way. Goes for a walk. Selina not back yet as dusk falls.

Writes her a note; *Took a stroll to park. Back soon. Love ya.*

Just before dusk it rained. City smells fresh now. Chilly. But pleasantly so.

She walks over by the park, all the greening grass and green shrubbery smelling tangy in the darkness. The streetlights just now coming on. Selina'll probably be pissed she took off this way, but she was getting claustrophobia in the apartment.

She screams.

A drunk just weaving out from behind a bush.

Thinking instantly: the Harlot!

"Hey, babe," the scuzzy drunk says.

God, he's coming on to her.

She flips him off. Starts walking faster. Deeper into the park.

She always associates pretty yellow and red and pink balloons with parks. And the taste of slightly charred hot dogs with lots of mustard. This summer she'll come back to this very park and bring Selina and Arizona and the three of them will have a good time.

This time it's not a pathetic harmless drunk.

A Harlot's Tears

This time
his hand clamping over her mouth
   This time
his knife finding her throat
   This time
his lips spitting the words "You fucking pig"
   This time it's really the Harlot

Catwoman: April 4, 199–

Took a stroll to park. Back soon. Love ya.
   Selina reads the note in disbelief. Why would Brett go off by herself with the killer still at large? And after all the lectures Selina gave her about keeping all the doors locked . . .

Ten minutes later a silken dark figure, outlined only by pale moonlight, makes her way across the shadows of the city park, shadows in which lovers of every sex hide in whispers and frantic lust; shadows in which the bitter mugger and the troubled sexual derelict wait for victims.
   Shadows in which a man named David Fisher is slashing young Brett Ewing with his knife—
   Catwoman hears whimpers; she glides between trees, down a rocky embankment to a creek and a copse of willow trees.
   And now a muffled scream.
   "Brett!" she calls.
   Another muffled scream.
   Catwoman glances around.
   Where is Brett?

Another scream. This time of pain.

Where is she?

Catwoman sees the small ornamental bridge that children like to ride their bikes across.

Beneath the bridge is a storm drain.

She moves very quickly now, hurtling herself up over the bridge and down into the quarter inch of water that covers the silty mud.

And sees them.

David Fisher has slashed Brett's cheek and is now about to draw his knife across her throat.

Brett kicks frantically, tries to push him off her, but he's too strong.

He's so caught up in his rage, he doesn't see or hear Catwoman until it's too late, until she kicks him in the small of the back then chops him across the rear of his neck.

As he turns, Catwoman's right leg lashes out and catches him in the groin.

He cries out, sinking to his knees in the slime.

Sobbing, Brett throws herself into Catwoman's arms, saying over and over, "I'm gonna die, Catwoman! I'm gonna die!"

Catwoman: April 5, 199–

David Fisher is drinking the bourbon Catwoman offered him. Brett is toking on a joint. Miles Davis plays low on the tape deck, the dirgelike " 'Round Midnight." A dirge is appropriate now. As for the kitty Catwoman found the other night, she is, as usual, lapping up milk with her tiny pink tongue.

At the door, Arizona says, "I'm just going to get a cup of coffee and have a short walk."

"It's getting late. Be careful," Catwoman says.

Arizona nods, then vanishes. She couldn't help but hear what was said here when the three of them came in an hour ago. She can't hack the tension and despair any longer. She needs to get out of here.

After she leaves, Catwoman says, "David, I could have taken you to the police last night, but I sensed that you and Brett needed to talk first. So that's what I want you to do now—talk to each other."

David is on the couch; Brett has been crying off and on. David just seems to swing from cold rage to depression.

"You should've had yourself checked," he says for the fortieth time that night.

"David, I'm a goddamned hick, all right? I run away to the city and a few weeks later I get AIDS. How was I supposed to know?"

He explodes again. "Why didn't you make your johns wear rubbers?"

His rage echoes in the quiet room.

"That isn't the kind of talking I had in mind for you two," Catwoman says gently.

But then Brett falls to crying once more, sobbing really, and David goes back to his scowling.

"You know what you need to do, David," Catwoman says gently. "You need to tell Brett that you forgive her, that you know it wasn't her fault. And then you need to turn yourself over to the police and tell them about how you killed the prostitutes because you were so angry about testing HIV-positive. And then you need to tell your wife the truth and have her get tested, too."

"Just because we tested positive doesn't mean we'll

actually get it," Brett says, more in hope than with any real belief.

"I'm not sorry I killed them," David says, anger overcoming him again.

"In a few days, when you've calmed down, you'll be sorry, David," Catwoman says.

He just scowls and looks out the window.

And then, with no warning whatever, he leaps from the couch, splashes his drink in Brett's face, and then lunges at her, slapping her several times across the face.

Catwoman is up, grabs him, hurls him so hard backward that he trips across the edge of the couch and hits the floor face-first, almost like a pratfall.

He starts to get up, but Catwoman isn't done with him. She grabs a handful of his hair and then slams his head against the wall.

"If you can get pissed, David, so can I. It isn't easy for me to feel sorry for you when I know you killed those women. But I'm trying to be charitable about it, trying to cut you a little slack. But if you ever lay a hand on a woman again—"

She lets him collapse in a heap on the floor.

She goes over and sits on the arm of the chair. Brett is crying again, face in her hands, and Selina leans over and hugs her, friend and mother at the same time.

Then the crying becomes sobbing and Brett reaches out to be held like a child. Catwoman obliges, stroking Brett's hair and saying again and again, "It's all right, Brett; it's all right."

Neither of the women notice David
standing up
(my whole life is over, can't face my wife and my daughter, or my friends)

A Harlot's Tears

and then quickly crossing the room to
the porch just off the living room, where
(he saw a film about an eagle once and the way an
eagle uses the air currents; maybe he'll use the air
currents)
and he does it without thinking really
just gets to the porch and scurries to the window
ledge and
(he sees himself at first Holy Communion devout
looking as a holy card
and remembers fighting Mick Dolan that time after
Dolan made a remark about David's father
and remembers skating that late December dusk
with Mary Lou Malloy the most beautiful girl in seventh grade; how the last of the sinking sunlight shone
red on the ice
and remembers)
is falling
falling
(remembering now his wife the night she gave birth
to their first daughter; that ethereal shine in her eyes,
the eternal nurturing mother
and remembering what it is like to lie with his little
girl when she's sleeping the sweet scent of her hair
the soft purr of her snoring
and remembering)
is falling
falling
and somewhere somebody is screaming, "David, no!
David!"
is falling
falling
all history and memory about to collide with an old
brick alley in a bad section of Gotham
is falling

and all light and all sound will die with him because even if everything goes on he will not be here to
note and comprehend it
 falling
 is falling

Selina Kyle/Brett Ewing: April 10, 199–

The priest is just now saying the last of the graveside
prayers. Two women in black suits and black veils are
sobbing. One is old, one is young. Next to the young
one stands a very pretty little blond girl looking confused about everything going on here. Why is Daddy
in that long, gleaming box? And why are they putting
the box into the ground? Won't Daddy get cold in the
ground?

Selina and Brett stand on the hill, looking down at
the service, at the long procession of shiny new expensive cars, at the half hundred or so mourners just now
turning away from the spectacle of death as represented by the long narrow hole in the ground. Someday all these people will be the stars of their own
graveside services.

Ask not for whom the bell tolls, Selina thinks, and
then wonders if the anonymous note she sent to David
Fisher's wife instructing her to get a blood test will
reach her tomorrow. She hopes so. Sooner the better.

David chose to take his secrets to the grave. The
positive blood test. His killing of the prostitutes. And
Selina is willing to let those secrets be his in the cold
darkness of the waiting earth.

But she wants David's wife to know about the blood

A Harlot's Tears

test so she won't—in case her test is positive, too—give the disease to anybody else.

"It's sad," Brett says.

"Very sad."

"I'm scared, too, Selina."

"I know," Selina says, putting her arm around the young girl, leading her down the hill to the car. Death should have no dominion on a sunny day like this, when the sunflowers are like schoolchildren playing beneath the cloudless blue sky, and the first monarch butterfly of spring flutters past the eyes.

"You up for renting a canoe?" Selina says.

"Really? That sounds great."

"We can even pack a lunch."

"God, Selina, that's a great idea. Thanks."

They walk on in silence, watching an old woman kneel with great difficulty at a gravestone, where she sets down a potted geranium. The old woman crosses herself and bows her head.

"I keep trying to hate him," Brett says as they reach the car. "But I can't."

"No," Selina says wearily. "Neither can I."

Then they are in the car and driving away.

C&W

JON HAMMER and KAREN McBURNIE

Three info-mercials and an old episode of *Ponderosa*. Or was it *Bonanza*? What exactly is the difference between *Ponderosa* and *Bonanza*? He didn't know, but it was a question he asked himself on the graveyard shift on a moonless Tuesday, trying to stay awake at the front gate of exclusive Gotham Woods Estates. Guarding all that wealth, the cream of the Gotham society, and they couldn't even spring for cable in the kiosk? He just had to get off nights before the terminal boredom killed him. But what was that? It sounded like a cat at the door.

"Well, Hoss," he said to the flickering blue screen, "by the power vested in me as security guard, looks like I'll have to play nursemaid to a kitty now. I'd better. Knowing the crackpots I'm working for, that critter could probably buy and sell me ten times." He adjusted his uniform's cap, wondering if by any chance it had fit the last guy.

Another tentative mew came from just outside the booth. He got down on one knee, and slowly, so he wouldn't startle her, he slid the door open. But there wasn't any cat, just a slim, black leather boot. He jerked his head up and saw a black mask. "Meow," said the mask, and then all he saw was black.

"One squirt of my knockout spray and he went over like a blue serge redwood," Catwoman snickered as she hopped into the cab; her faithful hench-kitten Tura rolled the van through the gate.

"Rocky Dexter's estate is a mile up this road. It should be impossible to miss—his front gate is a replica of the one Elvis built at Graceland."

"Blochenstein must be one serious Hank Williams fanatic if he's willing to shell out a half million for these tapes."

"He's a collector, Tura, by definition he's crazy. And they aren't tapes, they're acetate recordings. Please don't ask me what an acetate looks like, all I want to see is that lovely cash at the end of this caper.

"Whoa! This is the joint. Time to go to work."

Catwoman slipped from the van into the cool stillness of the night. With feline grace she gained the top of the wall and paused, every nerve drinking in the scene. This is what the poet meant by the dead of night, she thought. Only the silhouette of the darkened mansion could be seen by the faint starlight, and in the profound silence the only evidence of life was in the air itself. She felt a little breeze on her face and drew in a lungful of the icy wet. It smelled green. Like the immaculate lawns of Gotham Woods Estates and like the piles of crisp legal tender it took to live here. Crouched on top of the wall, Catwoman felt the anticipation building in every muscle of her body, the suspense of a lioness who first glimpses her prey. Noiselessly she slid down into the shadows of the grounds.

This was going to be as easy as five hundred Gs ever gets, Catwoman purred to herself as she glided stealthily toward the mansion. Then suddenly she froze in her tracks, her satisfied smirk dissolved into a wary scowl. She heard a scrabbling noise from behind. Looking back, she saw the figure of a man struggling to the top of the wall with a strenuous grunt. He heaved himself up, clumsily caught a boot on the way over, and landed with a groan, butt-first on the lawn. Catwoman watched from behind a tree as he brushed the dirt off his rear end and loped on up to the side of the house, passing, in utter oblivion, within a few feet of her hiding place. When he was close enough, she could see he was tall, with light hair almost to his shoulders, and he wore suede western boots and dirty Levi's, a denim jacket, and a bandanna around his neck. Who the hell was this rodeo clown?

He didn't go to the door, but instead walked to the side of the house and began trying windows. Great leaping catfish! He was an amateur burglar gumming up her own beautiful plan! This was beyond bad luck. In another minute the jerk would trip an alarm and every doughnut shop in Gotham City would empty out. The cops don't dally when the call comes from this end of town.

She had to move fast. In an instant, as the slim prowler reached for a window sash, she flew at him with a flying kick that knocked his legs out from under him with startling violence. In the time it took for him to hit the ground with a painful thud she had the line off her utility belt and ready. In a flash he lay expertly hog-tied beneath her, as shocked and immobile as a calf at branding time. Angrily Catwoman ripped the bandanna from his neck and shoved it in his mouth, which by this time had begun to gulp rhythmically like a beached carp.

"Next time you're going to have to be quicker on the draw, cowboy," she hissed in his ear. She dragged him awkwardly to his feet. He was easily six feet, but skinnier than she had thought, and she could manage him with a fireman's carry. Cursing him silently with each step, she lugged him back to the compound wall. With Tura's help they got the lanky, writhing obstacle up and over and into the back of the van.

"Tura, get rid of this hick *right now*." Catwoman was seething with rage. "You take the van, leave me the bike."

Tura could only nod and try not to look hurt that she was so abruptly dismissed from the big score.

"I will not allow this bush leaguer to ruin my lovely caper. I'll meet you back at the lair." And before Tura could think of questioning the prudence of leaving Catwoman half-blind with anger and on her own, she was gone.

"Well, I don't know what I'd do to stop her. You don't reason with Catwoman." Tura sighed to herself as she reached around the supine figure on the van floor and extracted his wallet. He was trying to look as brave as he could, gift-wrapped and helpless. Pocketing the cash, she read his driver's license. "And what do I do with you, Alvin Nash?"

Alvin gave her a wink and tried to grin around his red bandanna.

Catwoman's rages didn't last long when there was work to be done, and by the time she had made her way back to the mansion all her faculties were again concentrated on the job at hand. With characteristic speed and efficiency she disabled the alarm system and entered Rocky Dexter's home. The decor appeared to be late seventies rococo Presley. Blochenstein's information about the house proved very accurate.

She located the vault in the floor of Dexter's office and with the aid of this masked cat burglar's most divine new invention—a wafer-thin computer chip that transmitted the safe's combination number visibly onto a wristwatch screen—was soon holding a square metal box containing the lost Hank Williams acetates.

Tura had hidden Catwoman's bike behind the low stone wall to which was attached a sign warning of exclusive Gotham Woods Estates' strict security. Catwoman kicked the vintage jet-black Harley Sportster to life and sped into the night, purring happily with the pitch of the perfectly tuned fifty-five-cubic-inch motor between her knees, a half-million-dollar prize in her saddlebag.

It was thirty minutes' drive from Dexter's estate to the seedy waterfront district. The sky was just beginning to show a predawn blue glow, but the Gotham Fish Market was already a hive of activity as Catwoman rolled up to the warehouse across the street. To the casual observer this building seemed surely to have been abandoned for decades, yet as the Harley approached, the steel riot gate opened with well-oiled efficiency. She was home.

As she got out of the elevator to enter her living quarters, Catwoman could hear the sound of Tura's acoustic guitar. When did she learn that song? In a festive mood she called out, "Tura, have you been taking lessons?"

"Um, yes, Catwoman. You could say that," Tura answered sheepishly, rising to greet her. She let her dark, wavy hair shade her face. Behind her, Kit, another of her hench-kittens, stifled a laugh. Neither of them held a guitar.

Catwoman stopped. She carefully put the metal box on the table, pushing aside a couple of half-nibbled take-out orders of fish and chips. Her eyes narrowed as she strode into the loft. "Tura, you're not trying to tell me . . ." They were trying to tell her.

There on the leather couch with his dusty cowboy boots resting on *her* coffee table was Alvin Nash. Seeing his captor again, he hurriedly set aside the guitar and, country gentleman that he was, rose to his feet with a little bow of his head.

"Good morning to you, ma'am. I hope you won't be too angry with the ladies for showing me the courtesy they done." His hand reached up to his bare head as if to tip his hat.

Catwoman's eyes flashed at Tura. "What have I told you about bringing home strays?"

"But *really*, you don't have to worry," Tura nervously attempted to reassure. "Alvin has no idea where we are! He was blindfolded the whole trip. We just wanted to hear him sing a couple of his songs before we let him go."

Alvin's mother hadn't raised any fools. He'd better break the ice in a hurry or risk another beating. By the looks of it, he'd need every ounce of charm he could squeeze out. That ain't ice, it's a glacier, he thought.

"If you'll pardon me for saying so, ma'am, but you

sure are one mean roper. Have you done much rodeoin'?" Alvin displayed his most winning grin.

She had to admit the boy had nerve. To avoid the impulse to laugh, Catwoman held Tura's paws to the fire a little longer. "A pair of long legs and a mouthful of compliments is just like catnip to you two, isn't it?" She glared at them convincingly. "I'm disappointed. Don't make me think you're too soft for our business."

She watched with satisfaction as Tura's face fell. Her anger gave way to amusement at her kittens' antics. It wasn't hard to see Alvin's appeal. Who wouldn't want a lanky, singing cowpoke for a toy. Only make sure he isn't any more than a plaything. "You can keep him for a while, but then he goes." Catwoman turned, took a few steps, then sharply shot back, "And be certain he can't find his way back."

The girls breathed relieved sighs, happy that they were off the hook. "Alvin has been singing us the most wonderful songs, Catwoman, he's really talented," Kit gushed. "He plays every week at the Wagon Wheel down on Edsel Avenue."

"Oh, really?" CW stretched herself onto the arm of an intricate and fussy-looking chair, the slippery sheen of her cat suit an enticing contrast to the plush splendor of the chair's brocade.

"So what dirty little deed were you up to at Rocky Dexter's tonight, then? I'd think if you were going to force your talents upon the man, you'd at least try it on a night you could crash one of his big showbiz parties."

Tura started to speak, but Kit beat her to it. "He already *has* a contract with Dexter!" she said with an irritated toss of her canary-yellow mop top.

"Oh? If you're such a success, what were you doing

skulking around your boss's estate at three o'clock in the morning?"

"That's a long story," Alvin Nash cut in as he settled back on the couch. "And if I'm to tell it, I'll need to start at the beginning." He took a long, thoughtful sip of his tallboy.

"I come to Gotham City five years ago, hitchhiked all the way from Kewanee, Illinois, with my guitar on my back and twenty dollars in my jeans. I got a room in that dump across from the bus depot—you know the one they call the Motor Lodge, even though they got no place to park your car? Every night I had to go to sleep with all the lights on and the radio blaring just to discourage the roaches from sharing the bed. For a time I was washing dishes and playing my guitar for tips in whatever dive would let me, just to keep body and soul together.

"Then one day this feller in my ho-tel—Lester's his name but we call him Spike 'cause his hair kinda pops up on top like a railroad spike, y'know? Anyhow, he gets a job filling in for the regular bartender over the Wagon Wheel. So one night, it's Spike's birthday and we're all drinkin' his health in the Wheel after hours. Spike gets me up on stage and Mr. Walters—he's the owner—he liked what I could do with a song, I guess, because the next thing you know, I got me my own showcase once a week at the Wagon Wheel! By and by, some girls from Dexter Music started showing up there to see me every Thursday. They kept bringin' their friends and then one night they ac'shly got Rocky Dexter himself down. Guess that was about a year later. Of course, to hear him tell it, he discovered me. I suppose Janine 'n Betsy got a raw deal, but they said it was nothin' new, happened all the time. They would go out and find acts, then Dexter'd take the credit.

"Well, the minute he 'discovered' me, Mr. Rocky Dexter starts barking at me through his paper clip—that's one of his 'eccentricities,' chewing paper clips. It 'pears you can't be a big man in the music biz without cutting up like you ought to be in Arkham Asylum. Anyway, through his paper clip he mutters that I'm a genius and so forth. He tells me to meet him in his office the next day, he's gonna make me a household name, just like Red Pop. Now, recording for a big outfit like Dexter Music has been my one dream since I was a nipper, but at that moment I was busy thinking what a crackpot ol' Rocky seemed to be, and I swear he knew I was thinking it, because just then his secretary, Valerie, she says something to him and he starts cussing at her like a madman. I couldn't tell you exactly why, but I was sure he had that temper tantrum just to impress *me*!

"Dexter's way of doing business spooked me plenty, but I still felt like I was going to strike it rich. I mean, I was more excited than an alley cat given the deed to Disneyland. Oh! No disrespect intended, ladies! I guess I reckoned someone that nuts wouldn't let nothing stop him if he took a mind to make me a big star.

"I signed the contract, recorded some demo tapes, and I—I mean everybody loved the tapes: the producer, the musicians in the studio, the A and R folks. They were convinced I was the next big thing! But Mr. Dexter was in an ornery mood the day he heard it, they tell me. Had a nutso fit and started screechin' that I was 'too country.' He give me the deep freeze, refuses to see me, won't take my calls. I sure didn't know *what* to do. My whole world caved in.

Jon Hammer and Karen McBurnie

"Then a couple weeks later Spike dragged me into his room—the radio was on and he told me, listen to this song. I didn't see at first what he was driving at because it sounded like that kind of awful country pop that ain't *real* country and it ain't real popular with me, but then I realized it was my own song! Rocky had slicked it up so bad I didn't recognize it. After that my songs kept turning up on the radio butchered like hogs in a Tennessee smokehouse—all sung by Dexter's stable of Vegas-styled hillbillies. The kind of cats think the can of snuff in the back pocket of your three-thousand-dollar hand-embroidered jeans by Ralph Lauren makes you a good ol' boy. I was fit to spit. I couldn't understand why Dexter wouldn't give me a chance to do my music my way. By then I realized he had no interest in developing a new talent, he wanted me for another cog in his hit factory. He needed my songwriting to prop up his established acts, as tired a bunch of has-beens as you'll find clawin' at the backdoor of the Grand Ol' Opry. You can bet I kicked pretty hard when I saw the path Rocky Dexter was pushing me down, but it did no good. Once he makes up his mind about anything—an' it's always a snap decision—ain't no turning back.

"One day I got so fed up I had to give Mr. Dexter a piece of my mind. It's always like hunting snipe, getting in to see him, so I had Janine sneak me in to his office. He stammered a bit, caught unawares as he was, and then tells me that he was making me *some* money and I should be grateful, since my singing career 'flopped.' How he figured I was a wash before I even got a record out I do not know. He pulls my contract out from under his lunch and shows me where it says that ninety-eight percent of my song-publishing income was to go to Dexter Music, for promotion, publicity, and so on—well, I never had a thing to promote! I asked where the two percent was from all the hits other folks were making with my songs, and he laughed. He said that with big corporations payments naturally took a long time, given that it all had to funnel through channels: accounting, residuals, taxes, benefits, etce'tra. I told him I wanted my master tapes and my contract back. He looked me straight in the eye and said, 'What contract, my boy? I own you, kid, and the only way you make any money in this business is on my say-so. Get used to it.'

"By then security had arrived to show me the door."

"What about your lawyer, Nash?" Catwoman interrupted.

"Urhhhh." Alvin buried his face in his hands. "Man, I was greener 'n the Joker's hair back in those days. I didn't have a winter coat back then, I sure didn't have a lawyer. When I was about to sign, Dexter recommended this guy Artie Mopp—"

"Artie 'the Cleanup Man' Mopp?" snorted Catwoman.

Alvin shrugged, embarrassed. "Artie represented an arm load of talent, Mr. Dexter told me. 'Course later I realized I'd been had.

"I got the runaround by Artie Mopp's office, too. Then one night he came in the Wagon Wheel, I went right up to his table, and I told him right out, you're my lawyer, you're supposed to be working for *me*!

"He swallowed a mouthful of chicken-fried steak, and cool as January, shoots back, 'When you bring me as much green as Dexter Music, then I'll be playing ball on your team, kid.'

"I told him, why didn't he never give me a copy of my own contract? So then Mr. Mopp drops his fork on his plate, real loud, like to nearly bust it, then picks up the cloth on his lap and dabs his ugly pink lips, says, 'Dexter gave it to you months ago. It's not my fault if you've mislaid it.' Then he turns his back on me!

"Sittin' next to Mr. Mopp were a big, pumped-up goon and a puny mug—he's all dressed up in black silk and stuff."

"Not the Nightlight?" Catwoman growled.

"Mopp called him Louie."

"That was Louie 'the Nightlight' Minescule, Alvin," said Catwoman. "Dresses like a chorus boy in a cheap road-company *Guys and Dolls*, always in black with a white carnation. Always ready for a funeral. He's a common East Gotham racketeer. Even if Artie Mopp *is* a lawyer, I'm surprised he'd associate with the Nightlight."

"So this Louie has his thug throw me out of the Wagon Wheel! My second home! In front of everyone! Then Spike tells me they threatened the management, tellin' Mr. Walters to ban me from there!

"I mean, I ain't stupid, I got me set up with a free lawyer for the arts, Ms. Siobhan Blask, Esq. She worked darn hard and demanded to see my contract and have it declared illegal. That woman endured months of endless runaround with Dexter and eventually threats to her firm and her family. Finally the case took up her time, so she couldn't make a living, and she told me that she'd hafta bow out. Those guys at Dexter Music have a whole floor with nothing but lawyers. Forget till the cows come home, they could sit on my claim, petitioning and making motions till the whole herd up and died of old age. So I'm still singing for my supper in Gotham City.

"Today I just felt so nasty inside, I took to the crazy notion the only thing left for me to do was steal back my contract. Just the kind of dang-fool idea that comes over a fella who spends too much time brooding in an empty glass down at the honky-tonk. I been reduced to being a petty thief."

"That *is* sad. I detest *petty* thievery," cooed Catwoman, the professional condescending to the amateur. Still lying on the arm of the chair, she stretched out all of her muscles and wriggled her fingers in the air. It wasn't a bad bedtime story. But honestly she empathized little with the poor sap. Alvin's a good egg and Dexter's obviously a slimeball; white hat, black hat, the End, and so what? Though she *could* understand what the girls saw in the lanky cowpoke. *Hmm, just for fun . . .*

"Why don't you visit my room in half an hour?" hissed Catwoman, cool as a snake, to Alvin. *Ha! That'll make the fur fly!* She smirked at the steamed looks Tura and Kit traded, even as she knew she would toss him out on his shell-like ear if he dared. *Meow!*

"Myrna! I need cigavets!"

The puffy, silver-haired man barked into the intercom. His red-and-white suede Roy Rogers costume fit him like a sausage casing. Roy Blochenstein's office covered half the fortieth floor of the Gotham Securities Tower. The rest of the floor held thirty of his U.S. staff, a conference room, a gym, a kitchen, and a dining room. His office was decorated in what one newsweekly waggishly dubbed "Bunkhouse Moderne." The walls were covered with split logs salvaged from a Tennessee-hill-country cabin two centuries old. The furniture and western knickknacks were bought at auction from the estate of William S. Hart, the first movie cowboy star. Cowboy-and-Indians curtains one could expect to see in Beaver Cleaver's bedroom framed the huge plate-glass windows. Daniel Boone hats and Tom Mix capguns filled a large display case covering one wall.

Myrna, a sober-looking woman with a brightly colored pant suit glued to her generous curves, walked into the room with a don't-give-me-any-lip look on her face. "All out, Blochy. Sorry." She turned and headed for the door.

"Out! I have to have a cigavet *now*! Why can't you do anyting? You are supposed to have two cartons on hand at all times!"

"Are you going to give me the money for the cigarettes, Mr. Blochenstein?"

"I have no cash. I owe you the dough. *Get me cigavets!*"

"You owe me three hundred and sixty dollars and counting, Blochy. I don't got any money to lend to you today, anyways."

"Then you borrow it from somebody. Get going!"

That deadbeat. Myrna had been a working gal for fifteen years. She'd seen executive big shots of all stripes, and it never failed: the richer they got, the cheaper they became. Still, Blochy took the prize. She stuck her head in her desk drawer and rummaged for change. As she came up with a handful of fuzzy quarters, a black leather glove reached over her desk and buzzed the door to the inner sanctum.

"He's expecting me, doll." Catwoman smirked as she sailed into Blochenstein's office. Geez, Louise, the nuts that guy associates with.

Catwoman scanned the billionaire's digs, a tasteless blend of down-home bric-a-brac and state-of-the-art electronics equipment. "Here's the hotcakes you ordered, Blochenstein."

The startled businessman struggled to retain his composure. Catwoman pulled the container from her satchel and set it on the desk. Blochenstein quickly lifted it off the wood and wiped the surface clean.

"Thank you, my dear." From a ceramic cookie jar decorated with the image of a bucking bronco, he removed stacks of bills, fanned the bundles, and tapped the pile on his desk first vertically then horizontally to even it out.

Catwoman leisurely riffled each bundle of fifty one-thousand-dollar bills. "Thanks, Blochy, but"—her voice was icy—"there's a grand missing." Her eyes drilled into his head.

"Really? I can't imagine how ... I counted it ... but of course, if you say I'm short, I'll ..." He began fumbling furiously for his wallet. "Here! Here it is!"

"Nickel-and-dime chiseling on a deal this size," said Catwoman sadly as she carefully took from the wall a coiled bullwhip. She could see it was a good twelve feet long when she let it slither out on the floor in front of her feet. A label on the handle told her it was the same whip Karl Malden used on Brando in *One-Eyed Jacks*. "Bad Blochy. Now Catwoman spank."

Sweat poured down the trembling billionaire's face. The elegant masked predator before him coolly raised her braided leather weapon, and with an expert twitch of her wrist the cord seemed to spring with a life of its own from the carpet to Blochenstein's thick neck. His hands grabbed at the whip, the lash wrapped tight around him. A wicked jerk of her arm sent him down on his precious knotty-pine floorboards, where he thrashed about, his face first cherry then an unhealthy blue.

"Nice toy, Blochy. I'll take it with me, if you don't object." She planted a black stiletto heel in his chest and loosened the bullwhip. "Next time you pull anything like that, fat boy, I won't be playing."

Blochenstein lay at her feet puffing like a locomotive. The fear in his face disappeared as he watched her laugh down at him. From his humiliated posture he actually managed a sickly leer. "I'll play any game you like, Catwoman."

Catwoman's grin evaporated. "You can sure take all the fun out of torture." She sighed. "Billionaires."

Stepping over the disabled mogul, she strode to the desk. She grabbed the cookie jar and removed the cash, deliberately dropping the ceramic container, which exploded into shards on the floor.

"Oops." She brought a gloved hand to her pouting lips, a mime of remorse as it shattered. Catwoman made for the elevators as Myrna stood at the door, doubled over in laughter.

Rusty Walters wasn't having *anyone* tell him what he could or couldn't do. He'd taken enough of that guff during his twenty years in the merchant marines. On the last day of his last voyage, his career before the mast had left him with two things: a bank account healthy enough to buy himself a tavern, and a deep loathing for all things nautical. He was so sick of the sea he couldn't look a glass of water in the eye anymore. So what if he'd never been inland more than ten miles in his life, he was going to run a cowboy joint. So he opened the Wagon Wheel, where the old salt's eyes need never be offended by the shiny binnacles and lobster traps and antique diving suits that had plagued him through the years in a hundred water-

front gin mills the world over. There would be no
ships built in bottles or superfluous rigging covering
the ceiling; Rusty lived and breathed honky-tonk now.
And he sure didn't take orders from anybody anymore, not in his own place.

Alvin Nash brought in a good, regular crowd; a good
singer and a hit with the broads. The kid was decora-
tive. Rocky Dexter and his goons could take a flying
leap. Yes, sir, Nash was going to play this Thursday
like any other week. Funny thing was, after Rusty
had worked himself up into a state where he could tell
Dexter's gang to go to the devil, they took the news of
the kid's return with uninterested shrugs. That sure
left Rusty puzzled. But he was wise enough not to be
relieved.

"I'm mighty pleased you all could come to see the
show tonight, ladies," Alvin drawled, holding open the
stage door for Catwoman's two apprentices. Tura gave
him a slow wink as they slunk past into the bar. "It's
a shame Miss Catwoman couldn't come too—ugk!"

Alvin suddenly found himself sitting in the alley behind the Wagon Wheel with the wind knocked out of
him, the direct result of a stiff-armed blow to his chest
that had sent him flying through the door. Two pri-
mates wearing matching suits towered over him as he
cautiously rose to his feet. Not only were they both in
gray suits, they were wearing identically sized gray
suits. Tweedledumb and Tweedledumber. Who was
their tailor, Gorillas 'R' Us? One suit leaned on the
door as Tura and Kit pounded on it from inside. The
other jabbed a beefy finger into Alvin's solar plexus,
sending waves of pain tearing through his rib cage.

"Hey." The suit poked him again. "The boss wants you."

Waiting in a darkened corner for Alvin was Rocky Dexter. The muscle tossed Alvin to him like he was playing beanbag.

"I know it was you pulled that job at the house last night," Rocky sputtered, spitting a paper clip on the blacktop. He was apoplectic with rage. "You little crud, you don't know what you're up against, bumpkin. No one does Rocky Dexter. I own this town. I own this street. Heh—I own *you*. I may terminate you—or *ex*terminate, if I get pushed.

"You want I fix it so you can't walk? How about never being able to use those string-picking, thieving little mitts of yours again? Don't be stupid, boy. I've already screwed your career. I've made a mint of your songs! Screwing you was child's play. I screw people for a *living*. It's a business. But you stealing from me, that's not playing the game, Nash. Think hard about it boy, tell me where the acetates are and I may let you live."

"Honest, Mr. Dexter, I—I don't know what you're talking about. I didn't steal anything from you."

Dexter shook his head sadly. "Cowboy, this is serious as cancer. You just don't get that yet. Okay, boys, do your thing. He'll talk, and I sincerely hope it's before he croaks." He turned away quickly and ducked into the waiting limo, which rocketed out of the alley and onto Edsel Avenue.

The car nearly knocked Kit down as she and Tura ran out the front of the club. They sprinted to the mouth of the alley in time to see one of the goons crushing Alvin in a bear hug. The other thug, humming to himself like a busy craftsman, twisted the

singer's hand up in his face for a good look at his own
finger bent back until it touched his wrist.

"This little piggy's hurting real bad, ain't it, soldier?
In ten seconds it'll be busted, but don't worry. I got
nine more to play with. Where's the stuff at?" Sweat
and tears flooded Alvin's eyes, so he could barely see
his tormentor's face. He was shaking so violently the
other hood had to hold the singer's face still with one
massive paw to keep the mangled hand in front of his
eyes.

Running to Alvin's aid, Kit sent a distress signal to
her boss via the microminiature radio attachment of
the pink-rhinestone-encrusted cat collar that encircled
her wrist.

Tura attacked, followed closely by her partner.
When they were nearly upon them, the goon holding
Alvin charged. He made a grab for Tura, getting a
handful of her hair. With the split-second timing of a
well-rehearsed acrobatic team, Kit slammed her Doc
Marten boot down on his instep, forcing him to release
Tura, who instantly aimed a roundhouse kick that
split the thug's face open. He screamed and fell to his
knees, pawing at his face. The other villain finished
breaking Alvin's finger, then put the singer out of
commission with a swift cross to his jaw. Alvin
promptly crumpled. He began to get the feeling he
might die then and there, beaten for something he
hadn't even done. The one with the good nose ran
headlong at Tura, but Kit, who had bounded to the top
of a Dumpster, took a flying jump at him, landing both
boots in his kidneys. By this time the other goon had
found his legs and gotten a hold on Tura. Between
trading blows with King Kong she was able to yell out,
"Get out of here, Alvin. *Now!*"

Jon Hammer and Karen McBurnie

He shook off the pain enough to stumble to the door of the club, yelling, "I'll call the cops!"

"No!" screamed the torpedoes *and* the cat gals in unison at the mention of Gotham's finest.

Tura and Kit knew working on the thugs separately was their only hope. The guy with the broken nose was on his feet now, but he was slightly dazed. The girls each grabbed an arm and smashed his head into the steel fire door of the club and he went down like the *Titanic*. Kit ran over the fallen thug and into the Wagon Wheel.

Tura tried to follow but the other man mountain snatched her arm, jerking her back into the alley. She heard the door slam behind her as she took a punch to the gut and fell in a heap.

"Now it's payback time for Miss Busybody." He giggled maniacally. The murderous creature pulled out a gleaming straight razor, ready to autograph her pretty face.

But as he lowered the blade to Tura's pale flesh, he was distracted by a high-pitched *whir-click, whir-click*. It was Catwoman throwing back handsprings down the alley, picking up speed and momentum with every flip. The gorilla turned to see a fifty-mph kick coming straight at his head. He went flying ten feet, all the way to the rear of the alley, the razor embedded in his own thigh. His scream was the stuff of nightmares.

"Thanks, boss," panted Tura, "that was a—"

"Yeah, a close shave!"

Amid floor-standing vases of fragrant flowers and silver trays of complicated Italian pastries, Catwoman's gang and Alvin recuperated in the safety of the hideout. Her spectacular ultramodern sound system was tuned to WGC, broadcasting vintage bebop jazz. But sweets and music weren't doing the job tonight; Catwoman was still in a rage. She ground her teeth. She wrung her hands and paced the floor, still seething over the beating her protégés had taken.

Kit, sipping coffee from a nineteenth-century porcelain cup, tried to lighten the mood by suggesting they roll Dexter in cornflake crumbs and fry him in oil. That got Catwoman howling with laughter, though Tura's laugh was halting and suppressed by the pain of two cracked ribs. She was sporting a nasty black eye. Alvin was looking mighty black and blue, too, plus half his right arm was in a cast and sling. The cast was decorated with cartoon cats bearing greetings from Kit and Tura. Kit was missing a patch of hair. They looked like what the proverbial cat dragged home.

"I know!" said Tura, intent on lifting their spirits, "We find an empty pool, right? And we kidnap Dexter, throw him in it, don't feed him for like a week, then we get real big hooks and bait 'em with cheeseburgers and . . ." Kit and Catwoman were passing champagne through their noses at this point. Alvin stared at these wild women, nearly incapacitated by laughter, and wondered if it was all talk.

"Darrrrling! Don't worry!" Catwoman tried to reassure him when she read his worried expression. "We'd never do something so ridiculously—*unprofitable!*"

Alvin joined in the think tank. "If you all are serious about getting revenge, you think about this; only one thing in the world Rocky cares a rat's behind about and that's Dexter Music. Why don't we start our own label and put Rocky Dexter out of business?"

"Because that would involve *working nine-to-five,*

dearest." Tura laughed as she licked cannoli cream from her fingers. "You couldn't see us all laboring like *that*, could you?"

Alvin shook his head in agreement.

The cunning grin that always signaled one of her more brilliant brainstorms lit up Catwoman's face. "You've given me a purrfect idea for a caper, *mon petit chou*," she said, strolling over to Alvin to reward him with a little caress. "We want to ruin Rocky Dexter, and as Alvin suggests, the only place to really hurt him is in the wallet.

"You, my dear," she continued, stroking Tura lightly behind the ear, "must begin practicing your singing. Alvin will tutor you and write some music for you. Kid, I'm gonna make you a star! Ah, there is nothing so sweet as revenge, my kittens, and we're going to have a ball every step of the way."

Alvin was at no loss for inspiration. He dashed off some songs faster than he ever had in his life. Coaching the beautiful Tura from morning to night proved to be no chore either. When he wasn't working with Tura, Alvin met with Catwoman to tutor her on the ins, the outs, and the who's whos of the Gotham music game.

Finally Catwoman and Alvin developed their strategy in detail. Kit and Tura were briefed on the step-by-step plan. Studio time was reserved, and Tura cut her single with the help of Alvin and his band. To safeguard their anonymity Tura and Kit wore wigs and cat's-eye masks. Alvin and the other musicians tied bandannas over their faces, train-robber style.

They found a tiny independent company called Spare-Time to press and distribute the new single by

Tura's new alter ego, Tabby Jo Jeter. As soon as the record was pressed, a video was made.

Working in her new identity as Tabby's manager, Simba Voleuse, Catwoman had already planted outrageous rumors in the gossip columns guaranteed to keep her the talk of the town: a Kuwaiti prince tried to pay cash and livestock for a date with her. Her record played backward gives her recipe for corn bread. She was a famous child star who married at fifteen. . . .

Ms. Voleuse traded hundred-dollar bills for the *Gotham Intelligencer* and *Globe* to run photos of Tabby Jo Jeter in her signature costume: a deep red jumpsuit with jewels and rhinestones, around her hips a big Elvis-style utility belt with a glittering cat's-head buckle. Tabby Jo T-shirts and buttons were distributed free to concert-goers. Publicists were given island vacations in return for arranging their clients' cameo appearances in Tabby Jo's debut video.

One afternoon Kit and Tura were surprised by a sleazy-looking stranger who had somehow gained entrance to the hideout. The guy's hair was trained into a classic salesman comb-over. He was dressed in loud mismatched plaids and sporting a gold chain around his neck. Kit and Tura looked at each other, then rushed to pin him to the wall, knocking the breath out of him. "Whoa, Tura! Kit! It's me! Alvin!" The girls did a double take and dissolved in a giggling heap.

"What happened to you, cowboy? Were you kidnapped by a band of used-car salesmen?" hooted Kit.

"These are my promotin' duds! I've been visiting the radio stations, pushing the Tabby Jo song. Dig this." He slapped Kit on the back and boomed in an FM deejay voice, "Hey, how ya doin', pal? You the program director here?" He put out his hand for Kit to shake. She gave him her hand, which he commenced to pump vig-

Jon Hammer and Karen McBurnie

orously, and after he finally let her go, she found a folded bill pressed into her palm.

"I bring you the new release from Spare-Time Records, by superstar Tabby Jo Jeter. Sure hope you can give her a listen." The girls examined the portrait of Ben Franklin.

"It's real, if that's what's worrying you. And that's nothing but getting-in-the-door money. We're going to be spending thousands at every radio station in the country to get this thing played. It's without a doubt the biggest payoff ever. Your boss sure likes to spend her dough!" said Alvin, still unconsciously wearing his happy-huckster grin.

"But, Alvin," said Kit, "your songs are so sweet even Tura can't wreck 'em! We don't have to bribe 'em to play the record." The glamorous Tura stuck out her tongue at her sister-in-crime.

"Aw shoot, if it only worked that way." Alvin frowned. "The world ain't so honest as all that. These guys at the stations are bought. If you don't pay, they don't play! Geez, listen to the radio and you'll know that without a doubt. I honestly think they don't give a hoot about music no more. They're not in their jobs for *love*, they're in it for *dough*!"

As soon as "I Got a Two-Timing Hell-Raiser in a Civil Ceremony" hit the airwaves, the country was in love with Tabby Jo. Alvin's catchy tune and tight arrangement had romanced pop fans and solid country listeners alike. That and the most blatant payola radio has seen since the fifties. The song was a bona fide crossover hit, charting on the country, pop, and even, absurdly for a country tune, the urban contemporary charts!

Naturally it didn't hurt the cause any when Simba Voleuse messengered *Musicday*, the top industry tipsheet, a little gift to show appreciation for the swell job they did. This little token of esteem was not cash this time, it was a squeaky cat toy filled with a fine white powder. Tabby Jo Jeter's debut single went to number one that week.

A modern, streamlined, shockingly vulgar, cream-colored limousine sped around one of the Gotham expressway's high curving overpasses. Cradled in the rich leather cocoon of the backseat, Rocky Dexter set the copy of *Billboard* down next to him. Tabby Jo Jeter on the front page *again*. This chick comes out of literally nowhere and now you can't pick up the paper or turn on the radio without she's on it. He felt a small g-force tugging at his sensitive stomach as they took another turn. He slapped the chauffeur's glass angrily. *Oi.* Where were the frigging Tums? His ulcer hadn't flared up this bad in years. When his stomach turned sour, it meant one thing: Rocky was yearning. He wanted, he lusted, he pined for, and his gut hurt like the devil. He *needed* to sign Tabby Jo Jeter!

"Artie," Rocky screamed into the cellular speaker phone, "tell me the word on this broad Tabby. And Spare-Time Records? Who the hell ever heard of Spare-Time Records? They're *nobody* and they're *killing* me!"

The distant voice of Artie Mopp rasped through the speaker. "Who knows? The last record Spare-Time put out was a home instruction, you know, like 'Stop Smoking While You Sleep' kind of thing. All of a sudden they have this Tabby kid and the crumbs are paying the deejays twice what you are, Dexy. Word is they've upped your notes all over town. And for them program directors who are arctic explorers? Spare-Time ain't tossin' 'em a gram, they're shellin' out like a half an ounce of the happy powder."

"Idiots!" screamed Dexter. "Do you know what I'll have to come across with to top their chart buys? Five figures! How can we spend that kind of loot every day? How do *they* spend it?"

The car whizzed by a towering Tabby Jo Jeter billboard. Tabby's teeth sparkled and Dexter's stomach writhed.

"I got to have that Tabby Jo character. I got to get her away from these nuts at this Spare-Time Records just to save my own hide! Who can compete with the money they're spending?" Rocky shrieked.

"Think you can?" Artie asked. "She's already hitting like a ton of bricks. You'll have to pony up plenty wampum to steal."

"Nobody romances talent like Rocky Dexter! I'll get the studio to pull some more of that jerk hillbilly yahoo's songs and cut one with Tabby Jo!"

"Sure, Rock, but there's a lot a bread behind this chick, maybe her manager's loaded."

"Yeah? Then I'll bet the skirt'll kill for *more* dough. Just who is this Simba Volulla anyway? A lucky rookie, that's who. A green manager with a nobody label and one fluke hit. Kid might never crack the charts again. Could be all washed up, forgotten. She knows if she links herself with Dexter, she's a player. She's in with us big spuds."

"Don't forget, Rock, she's already playing the game," stammered Artie Mopp. "You can bet she's no pushover."

"Hmm. Artie, my boy, in that case, double the reason to get Tabby Jo Jeter on Dexter Records."

The biz had never seen as manic or as public a display of spending as Rocky Dexter laid on in the courting of Tabby Jo Jeter and Simba Voleuse. Monday, there was the videostrobe in the middle of downtown's entertainment district, glaring for all to see: a thirty-foot Rocky Dexter offering a rose, with the headline I LOVE YOU AND GOTHAM CITY LOVES YOU, TABBY JO! over and over for seventeen long hours. Tuesday's lunch at the Gotham Yacht Club brought the paparazzi out in full force, and they got a lensful. Dexter gave Tabby and Simba matching Mercedes convertibles. Catwoman traded hers in for cash on the way home. Wednesday, Dexter hosted a reception in Tabby's honor at the Czarina Room of the city's most over-the-top hotel and presented a diamond watch to Tabby and a ruby bracelet to her manager. By Friday the cash was in the envelopes. He'd purchased Tabby Jo's contract from Spare-Time Records. Tabby Jo signed her telephone-book-thick Dexter Music contract that same day. So confidential were the particulars of the deal—the hefty advance monies, shares of Dexter Music stock, and perks—that the company's file clerks were only permitted to store sealed copies of the document. One important clause in the agreement was that Alvin Nash would be released from his own contract.

Tabby Jo's single was to be immediately rereleased on Dexter Music's label. And Tabby was scheduled to go into the studio that night—with Alvin Nash and his band—to rush-record an album. *Musicday* snapped a picture of Rocky Dexter positively beaming. Yeah, he could buy anything, anyone, anytime.

Jon Hammer and Karen McBurnie

The automatic eye of the wrought-iron gates opened smoothly to admit the sleek, midnight-blue automobile, then slowly closed behind. Darned if they don't always make me feel secluded, thought Bruce Wayne.

He was feeling rather lonely lately, anyway. And particularly after tonight's charity event, one more room full of hopeful ingenues who could stimulate his eyes but do little for his mind and soul. Finding stirring, intelligent people to converse with was always a difficult task. Thank goodness Commissioner Gordon was due for dinner tomorrow evening, Bruce thought as he pulled the car around the front of the house and stepped out onto the cobblestone drive. He walked up to the great arched doors of Wayne Manor and let himself in.

Alfred, polishing the silver coffee service to an immaculate shine, did not notice the heir's return. As he worked he busily performed a sort of bizarre shuffle to some lively music coming through the earphones of his Walkman. Bruce allowed an amused smile to brighten his dark features when he said, "Evening, Alfred."

"Oh! Good evening, Master Bruce! I regret to say I failed to hear your entrance."

"Yes, Alfred, apparently lost in a musical reverie. What were you listening to? Vivaldi? Or Tchaikovsky perhaps?"

"I blush to admit, sir, that it was a selection of a somewhat more plebeian kind, though, I hasten to add, no less moving for its humble origin," said the butler. "A new hillbilly chanteuse. Miss Tabby Jo Jeter is her name, I believe, sir."

"Alfred, you surprise me! Frankly I've never had any patience for that brand of twangy caterwauling. I confess country music has always left me cold."

Bruce Wayne's ever-faithful manservant discreetly lowered his eyes and uttered with deference, "Perhaps, if you'll forgive me, sir, that is because you have never lost your woman nor taken to strong drink."

"Alfred, I believe there are depths to your soul that I shall never plumb!"

Entering his darkened study, Bruce Wayne glumly tugged on the black silk bow at his neck. What a colossal waste of his talent these charity dinners sometimes seemed. But that was selfishness. He knew the Wayne Foundation was as important a force for good as his alter ego, the Batman. Bored, that was his problem. He flicked on the television and bounced the remote on the taut, red leather couch, then wrestled his massive shoulders out of his dinner jacket. A tabloid entertainment news show materialized on the blue screen before him. He picked up the remote to zap it over to CNN, but paused when he saw it was a story about Tabby Jo Jeter, Alfred's new sensation. Amazingly erudite old bird that Alfred; Bruce Wayne chuckled to himself. Just imagine, Horatian odes *and* hillbilly love songs both buzzing about that wonderful brain! Let's see what all the fuss he was making is about.

"Dexter Music mogul Rocky Dexter has signed Ms. Jeter to a contract which sources say is *the* most generous deal in history. In addition to the splash she's made with her hit single, Tabby Jo is making waves in the music business establishment with her mysterious masked manager, Simba Voleuse. No one seems to know why Voleuse chooses to present such a bizarre public persona, but all agree her business savvy is unequaled. Industry insiders and fans alike will be watching Tabby Jo's fairy-tale success unfold, Mary."

"I know *I* will, John!"

Jon Hammer and Karen McBurnie

Simba Voleuse. Something about that name made the short, coarse black hairs on the back of his neck bristle. He clicked off the set and stared unseeing at the blank screen. The Batman knew his sensitive instincts were not to be ignored. His French was rusty to say the least, but he was almost certain *voleuse* meant "female thief."

"Alfred! Step in here a moment, please. How's your Swahili, old fellow?"

"Not as comprehensive as it might be, I'm sure, Master Bruce," the faithful retainer intoned as he swept into the study.

"But you would say that 'simba' is a kind of a cat, correct?"

"A rather large cat, sir. It's not my language expertise speaking, sir, but rather my knowledge of old adventure films. I believe the people use it to describe the lion."

"I thought so. Simba Voleuse. Alfred, fantastic as it sounds, I suspect your favorite singing sensation may be managed by none other than Catwoman!"

"Yes, I see sir!" The canny old gent's eyes, like those of his master, shone with excitement. "I agree that this bears looking into."

"At once, my friend. Not a moment to spare when 'the game's afoot' as Holmes says."

If it was Catwoman, what could be her angle? Actually appearing to *work* was not her style at all. Entering a legitimate business venture was too out of character. That worried him.

A week later, deep beneath Wayne Manor, the Batman sat before the bat computer, hunched like some medieval scribe. He pored over the mass of information ready at his fingertips through the world's largest anticrime data base. A polite "ahem," audible over the low hum of the powerful mainframe, interrupted his labors and the Batman turned from the terminal to find the trusty Alfred wheeling a tea cart off the elevator.

"Pardon the intrusion, sir, but as the hour is late, I took the liberty of preparing refreshment."

"You're a mind reader, Alfred," said the cowled crusader, taking a cup of steaming cocoa and a smoked mozzarella-and-tomato sandwich from the tray. "Fuel for the engines of justice, eh?"

"If I might ask, sir, how is your investigation of Catwoman's latest endeavor proceeding?"

"Interesting developments, Alfred. I've certainly uncovered a vast network of corruption in the record business. But even in an industry where tax fraud and conflicts of interest seem to be the norm, it's hard to fathom why Dexter Music hasn't been investigated before.

"To give you an idea of how much power this Rocky Dexter commands, in the past ten years over one hundred civil suits have been brought against him. None of them ever reached a judgment. Each was dropped. Now, maybe his lawyer is an expert at settling out of court, but looking at the company he's known to keep, I sincerely doubt any of the cases have been settled, period. I think intimidation is a more likely explanation."

"So it seems this captain of industry is a common hooligan, sir?" asked Alfred.

"All signs point to yes, my friend."

"But—" Alfred began.

"But why is he permitted to operate so blatantly on the fringes of legality?"

Jon Hammer and Karen McBurnie

"Why, yes, sir."

Batman leans back on his chair. "Several factors contribute, I believe. First, in as flamboyant a business as his, Dexter's devilish ways are for some reason an emblem of his power. Because he acts like a gangster, he is treated with the highest degree of respect by his peers. Secondly, he's a very wealthy man. Finally, Dexter contributes generously to many political campaigns, which naturally wins him much influence. Photo opportunities with celebrities provide invaluable publicity for politicians. I've brought this to the commissioner's attention and his investigation is sure to bring those involved to justice."

"But what, sir, of Catwoman? What is her interest in this man's schemes?"

"That is what still puzzles me night and day, Alfred. Night and day."

"I'll leave the tray here, sir, should you desire additional nourishment. If there is nothing else you require, I shall retire now. Good evening, Master Bruce." Alfred glided from the room.

The Batman continued pondering. There would be no sleep until he found some answers. What would Catwoman want with such a sleazy but still fundamentally legitimate business? Well, if Gotham City's music industry was as profitable and as crooked as his findings indicated, perhaps she merely wanted a piece of the pie. Or perhaps she was hoping to beat Dexter at his own game, and so, to rid himself of competition, he approached her and made it worth her while to join forces. Perhaps the two crooks had planned more diabolical activities and the record company was merely a front for their association.

Or could she have been planning to *take over* the multimillion-dollar corporation that was Dexter Mu-

sic? God knew, she was clever enough to obtain most
anything she wanted.

There was another possibility. Bruce had no hard
evidence that Catwoman was involved in this business at all. But that's the most pathetic brand of wish-
ful thinking I've ever been guilty of, thought the
Batman. No one but she could call herself Simba
Voleuse. And yet he couldn't help but think maybe
this one time she wasn't planning the crime of the
century. Perhaps Catwoman *had* finally abandoned
the life of crime! Now that she found herself a huge
success in a colorful business, perhaps her appetite for
fun and power and wealth was satisfied. It was too
good to be true, though. As for me, Batman thought, I
know I'm only human, the mind susceptible to the
thoughts of my own pleasure. As much trouble as
she's brought on herself, I can't deny I've enjoyed her
company. . . .

My *God* it must be late, and I must be weary! How
could I even *think* . . . In the end she's nothing but a
thief! She uses her charms as just another weapon in
her criminal mischief. What a colossal fool I am to forget that, even for an instant.

"Sid! All right already, Sid. If you'll just stop busting
my chops for ten seconds!" Rocky Dexter howled
hoarsely into the car phone. Phew! No rest for the
wicked, Rock. In my own car people got to give me an-
gina. "Look, Sid, in case you forgot, *I'm* the president
of Dexter Music, *you* are a bean counter! What, I don't
know the company's cash poor right now? Am I a
dope? I sign the artists, I decide how much we spend
on promotion, you jut cut the checks, pal. Understand

me? Am I getting through to you? You're a pencil pusher, you can't know from talent."

"I'm sorry if you think I'm pushing, Rocky." Sid's voice sounded thin and metallic. "But it's my duty to tell you Dexter Music is tapped out. This Tabby Jo Jeter signing has drained us. At this point we have two assets: the catalog and the artists' contracts, and now I hear we may have to sell off some rights just to pay the bills."

"Yeah? Well, you didn't hear that from me. That back catalog is worth millions. Why, the Hank Williams stuff alone could bring in enough to cover the overhead for a year." Sure, if I knew where in Hades the acetates were. "I'm waiting for the optimum moment to release the package, that's all. Anyway, this Tabby Jo is worth every nickel. When her album hits the street, we'll be riding higher than my great-uncle Osgood's trousers."

"I hope you're right, Rocky. If this record isn't the biggest hit in our history, we are sunk."

"Okay, Sid, you keep the bill collectors away a couple more weeks, I guarantee we have the smash of the decade. In the meantime I have an idea that may save some money. So long!"

Rocky hung up and reached for a Cuban corona out of the limo humidor. He squinted at the streets of Gotham rushing by the window as he nipped off the end. Trimming a little fat around the office wasn't a bad idea. He picked up the receiver of the cellular.

"Hello, Hollander? I have an idea to cut down our overhead. Listen; when Sid Schulman goes out for lunch, I want you to put a wall over his office door. . . . Yeah, build a whole wall! You deaf, or what? Leave his stuff where it is, I want it to look like there never *was* an office there, get me? When he comes back, you let him look for the door awhile, then security tosses his can out of the building. Forever ... I don't want to hear your bellyaching! Just do it."

The clock on the top of the Gotham Securities Tower read 4:17 A.M. as the Batmobile flashed by a lone garbage truck as it made its leisurely rounds. Bruce Wayne had just spent much of the wee hours outlining the results of his investigation of Dexter Music to Commissioner Gordon and his guests, two high-ranking officials of the FCC. The payola, the extortion, the tax evasion had all been laid before them in unimpeachable black and white. Now subpoenas were being issued. A grand jury would convene within a week to determine if there were grounds to indict Rocky Dexter. The feds were confident Dexter Music would be shut down in a matter of weeks, but there was something missing. There was still nothing to tie Catwoman to Rocky Dexter, save the large stock deal her protégée, Tabby Jo Jeter, received on signing with Dexter Music. The Batman couldn't shake the suspicion that he was letting Catwoman slip through his fingers. The Batmobile streaked soundlessly through empty midnight streets. He knew this case wasn't yet closed.

That afternoon, in the posh offices of the Katz, Mauser Brokerage House, mere blocks away from Gordon's office at Police Plaza, a svelte young woman in a crushed-velvet bodysuit was concluding an important transaction with Jeremy Katz.

"That's right, I want you to sell every last share. Simple as that."

Jon Hammer and Karen McBurnie

"I apologize, Miss Jeter, if I seem a bit mystified." Jeremy glanced up at the portrait of his grandfather glaring at him from over Tabby Jo's shoulder. Old Man Katz looked none too happy, but what could Jeremy do? "As you say, it's your money, but all our projections show great potential for Dexter Music. It just doesn't seem prudent or, forgive me, even logical to divest at this stage of the game, especially since you own over a third of the shares offered by the corporation to date."

"Look, Jeremy, the bottom line is I wouldn't bet a dime on the future of Dexter Music. Gambling, that's all the market is, right? So we understand each other, I came to you because you have a reputation for discretion."

Tabby Jo gave him a wink. Oh, God, so that's it, thought Jeremy. She heard that I handle the Penguin's portfolio!

"I need efficiency in this matter. This is the number of a Swiss account. I want all the shares sold and the cash deposited by the end of the day," she said, rising.

"Yes, but . . ."

"No 'but.' Yes will do."

She flew from the room, leaving Jeremy alone to gaze at Old Man Katz. His dead grandfather's oily stare seemed more disapproving than ever.

The wind ripped through the Batman's cape as he peered through the violet night to the glowing sodium grid of the streets fifty floors below. At these sterile heights, the city spread out at his feet, surrounded by the cool, silent spires of midtown Gotham, he could almost forget the evil that prowled the streets. The impassive architecture spoke nothing of the corruption he had spent his life fighting.

On another floor of this skyscraper Tabby Jo Jeter was making her television debut on a live late-night comedy/variety program. Batman had watched in secrecy as Tabby Jo and her guitar player arrived by limousine. Her manager, "Ms. Voleuse," had followed the car on a slick, early-model motorcycle. The Batman knew time was running out. It was the eve of both the release of Tabby Jo's album and the convening of the grand jury. If he was ever going to find out what Catwoman's angle on all this was, it had to be tonight.

When she and Alvin Nash left after the show, Tabby Jo Jeter found that hiding behind her movie-star shades didn't do anything but attract more attention. She found a dozen autograph hounds waiting at the stage entrance.

For the first time in her short career Tabby Jo was not accompanied by her manager. The fictitious Ms. Voleuse was nowhere to be seen, but Catwoman in full costume had preceded the two musicians out of the studio.

"You and Alvin better stay and satisfy your public," teased the feline mistress of crime. "I have to go drive the last rusty nail into Rocky's coffin."

While Tabby Jo signed autographs Catwoman mounted her Harley Sportster. Kicking over the motor, she called out, "Enjoy it while you can, Tura. This was your last appearance."

"I didn't forget," Tabby/Tura replied huffily.

A wide-eyed woman wearing something between a housedress and a muumuu in a pattern of fluorescent

pink daisies the size of sunflowers, broke from the
pack and ran over to Catwoman.

"Catlady! Catlady! Can I have your autograph
there? You're my all-time favorite criminal."

"Very flattering, I'm sure," said Catwoman graciously. She signed the dog-eared book on the page after Eartha Kitt. As she sped off, a pair of dark eyes
quietly marked her every move from a loading dock
across the street.

He had to take every precaution not to alert his
quarry. The Batman knew just how slippery she could
be. Luckily Simba/Catwoman had been careless
enough to park her motorcycle where he could easily
find it. He had tagged it with a homing device that
could be tracked by the Batmobile's computers from a
distance of five miles away. He settled into the
sculpted interior and watched the dot of green light on
the screen. It was moving west on State Avenue. She
was headed over the river.

He followed her for nearly an hour, hanging back a
mile or two, through the vast industrial wastelands
that lay across the water from the great metropolis.
Past the mammoth storage tanks and oil refineries
and fetid canals, mile after mile of crumbling
nineteenth-century factory buildings bordered by
lonely stretches of toxic marshland, she rode on
through each circle of this industrial inferno until she
came to a large warehouse adjoining a CD pressing
plant.

By the time Batman crept stealthily up to her
Harley, Catwoman had already cut her way through
the wire fence and broken the lock on the door. Stepping out of the floodlit yard and into the shadow of the
warehouse, the Dark Knight pulled his cape around
his body. He would wait in ambush for her exit.

The minutes ticked by, the buzz of the sodium lamps the only sound. Then a flurry of sharp footsteps and Catwoman burst through the door at a run. Suddenly the Batman pounced. From the near invisibility of his hiding place he came at her with the speed of a cobra. Startled, Catwoman aimed a kick at the crime fighter's head but failed to connect. Pivoting on her toe like a dancer, she spun at him again, this time dealing a blow with her knee that caught him in the stomach. He grabbed for her leg as she threw a third kick, this one to the chest. Though off balance, he was able to pull her off her feet. Catwoman landed on her back, but with a quick roll she was up again. This time the Caped Crusader launched himself at her before she could unleash another volley of blows. His superior size and strength easily overwhelmed her at close range. Catwoman found herself struggling in vain, crushed in the viselike grip of his iron arms.

"Simba Voleuse, I presume?" the Batman scolded into her ear. "I knew it was you the first time I heard that ridiculous alias."

"Like I care," she spat, squirming to regain the upper hand. She jerked an arm free and quickly sent a karate chop to his temple. In a flash he grabbed her wrist and with a painful squeeze forced it behind her back.

"Your foray into the music business is over, Catwoman. Rocky Dexter is going to be arrested in a matter of days and I doubt that his company will survive the payola investigation the government is beginning this week." The Batman's voice was low and even, despite the exertions of the battle.

As he spoke Catwoman's frantic writhing stopped abruptly and she looked up at him in amused sur-

prise. Then she laughed, a cold vengeful laugh. His
stomach sank a little at this strange reaction.

"Ruined Rocky Dexter, did you? Thanks, Bat-dope.
But in the future, if I need your help, I'll ask for it."
Catwoman smirked. Still held in his powerful grasp,
she twisted her arm until she could just see her wristwatch. The mocking tone left her voice. She looked at
him earnestly. "In the meantime, big boy, I strongly
suggest we move away from this warehouse in a
hurry. Unless you have nine lives."

Before he could consider where this trick might
lead, Catwoman, applying every last ounce of her
strength, spun the Batman around until his broad
back faced the warehouse. In that instant an almost
supersonic thud shook the ground. The doors of the
building exploded outward in a wall of flame, the force
of the blast knocking the cowled crime fighter flat on
top of Catwoman. Shaken for a moment by the blast,
the Batman took a savage right cross to the jaw from
Catwoman, who made a dash for her bike.

The Batman stumbled to his feet and listened to the
roar of the Sportster fade into the night. The street
was littered with melting CDs and jewelbox cases.
None of this made any sense to him. He would have
thought Catwoman had more pride in her own abilities than to stoop to sabotaging her competitors' product. Absently he flipped a burning jewelbox over with
his toe and watched, amazed, as the name Tabby Jo
Jeter turned to ash. Why? Was Catwoman a Svengali
destroying her own Trilby?

"Kit, darkling, bring us two bottles of champagne
from the cooler. The ones from the Cannes heist last
year."

Candles warmed the huge parlor room, and perhaps, Catwoman hoped, their soothing glow would
calm. Tura, still in heavy television makeup, readied
the ice and silver bucket, never for a moment taking
her eyes off the display of *Introducing Tabby Jo* CDs
that decorated the mantel. "Wow," she said to herself.

Catwoman turned on the news. A fashion show was
on the screen. ". . . don't think we'll be seeing these
ensembles on the streets of Gotham this season or
anytime soon. Eliza Press, Seventh Avenue."

"Thanks, Eliza. Now here's a late-breaking story
sure to have deep repercussions in the business world
and the music industry all the way down to the con-
sumer in the record shop: in a press conference today,
businessman Roy Blochenstein announced his take-
over of the collapsed Dexter Music."

The squirrel face of Blochenstein appeared on the
television screen. "It's a tremendous opportunity!" he
sputtered.

The news reader continued, "The troubled Dexter
Music corporation had fallen on hard times of late.
First, rumors that huge cash and stock offers made in
the wooing of overnight sensation Tabby Jo Jeter,
compounded by declining profits for the second year in
a row, crippled the company financially. Sources say
Dexter was hoping to recoup their fortune with the re-
leases of Jeter's album and a rare lost Hank Williams
session. Now we learn Rocky Dexter has been named
as the key figure in the largest payola scandal in over
a decade."

"Ha! We really hit him where it hurts! Rocky won't
have two dimes to rub together after the government
is through with him. And now that twerp Blochenstein is buying his company out from under him,
how about that?" Tura laughed as she turned to

Catwoman. The smile perished when she saw the ice in Catwoman's eyes.

"Yes, how about that," the mistress of crime said grimly. "We did a good job ruining Rocky for our own purposes, we did an even better job of driving down the price of his company so Blochenstein could buy it for a song. That dumpy little freak is no Hank Williams fan, he was after Dexter Music from the start. And like a sap I helped him do it for free." Catwoman flung the crystal goblet she was holding across the room, where it shattered into a million shimmering bits. Tura and Kit froze in fearful anticipation of the next violent expression of rage. "*Blochenstein*. He'll pay for thinking he can use Catwoman!" she bellowed.

Alvin Nash, out of bravery or stupidity, ventured a comment. "He'll pay, that's for sure. If not in this world, then in the next."

Catwoman shot him a withering glance.

"Well, what I mean is this," stammered the flustered cowpoke. "That ol' boy bought himself more than a record label. He bought perdition!"

"Thank you, Rod Serling," Tura snorted.

"No! Now, I'm serious. After what I seen of the music business, and I know Rocky Dexter ain't unique, I believe there must be a special circle of hell reserved just for record executives."

Alvin managed to get this out in his folksiest drawl wearing his winningest grin, and that was enough to break the spell. A purr began to emanate from Catwoman, which changed to a chuckle. Tura and Kit traded looks that told how relieved they were the mood had lifted. For now Alvin Nash has extinguished the Catwoman's fiery temper. His remark had helped level the delicate scales of Catwoman's strange justice. She no longer felt she had been bettered. For now.

About the Authors

JOHN GREGORY BETANCOURT has been writing science fiction and fantasy for twelve years. His novels include *Johnny Zed*, *Rememory*, and *The Blind Archer*. He currently lives in New Jersey with his wife, Kim, amidst their ever-expanding collection of books, computers, and cats.

MORT CASTLE has published more than 225 stories in a variety of magazines and anthologies: *Twilight Zone; Mike Shayne's Mystery Magazine; Cavalier; Pulphouse; Masques* (volumes I-IV); *Still Dead*, and others. His 1990 horror novel, *Cursed Be the Child*, was called a "classic of its kind" in a five-star review in *Rave Reviews*. Active in comics since 1989, Castle has written for and/or edited *Horror: The Illustrated Book of Fears; Leatherface;* and *J. N. Williamson's Masques*.

GARY COHN has been a free-lance writer for over a dozen years. He trained in the craft at the Clarion Science Fiction Writers Workshop under the tutelage of Damon Knight, Kate Wilhelm, and several other prominent SF authors. He has written numerous comic books, both on his own and with his writing partner, Dan Mishkin. Together they created the *Blue Devil* and *Amethyst* series for DC Comics in the mid-1980s. Gary has also sold stories, articles, essays, and young-adult novels. Recently he has completed coursework toward a doctorate in American history, and looks forward to pursuing his dual careers as writer and teacher.

GREG COX is an assistant editor at Tor Books in New York City. He is the author of two books, *The Transylvanian Library* and *The Pirate Paradox* (with Nick Baron).

KAY DEMIJOHN, born in the highlands of Scotland in 1954 to Croatian and Hungarian refugees, has traveled across Europe and Asia working as a translator and interpreter. She is fluent in 14 languages and holds advanced degrees from 4 different universities on three continents. Her interests have lately turned to writing, and *"The Cat's-Eye Crown"* is her first published work.

The Bloomsbury Review recently called **ED GORMAN** "the poet of dark suspense." The British magazine *Million* said he is "one of the world's great storytellers." Gorman has written in a variety of genres but is probably best known for his suspense novels *The Autumn Dead*, *A Cry of Shadows*, and *The Night Remembers*. He lives in the midwest with his wife, the novelist Carol Gorman, his stepson, Ben, and Tasha, Crystal, and Tess, the family cats.

KAREN McBURNIE enjoys listening to vinyl and sometimes wears it. **JON HAMMER** mixes plaids. They are presently collaborating on a screenplay called "Monkey Chaps."

PAUL KUPPERBERG is a veteran writer in the comic-book field with over 500 stories to his credit, both in the U.S. and Great Britain, including work on *Superman*, *Batman*, and *The Vigilante*. In addition, he has written both the syndicated *Superman* and *Tom & Jerry* newspaper strips and is the author of the novels *Murdermoon* and *Crime Campaign*. He is currently an editor for DC Comics' Development Group and lives in Connecticut with his wife, Robin, and their cat, Cassie, both of whom contributed to the story in this volume.

As Kenneth Robeson, **WILL MURRAY** continues the long-running *Doc Savage* adventure series for Bantam books and ghostwrites the *Destroyer* novels for New American Library. He has written for *Starlog*, *Comics Scene*, *Fangoria*, *The Armchair Detective*, *Mystery Scene*, *DC Comics*, *Marvel Comics*, *Lovecraft studies*, *Twentieth Century Crime* and *Mystery Writers*, *The Dictionary of Literary Biography*, and National Public Radio. He is also the creator of Squirrel Girl.

A former comic-book editor for DC Comics, Warren Publishing, and Atlas Comics, **JEFF ROVIN** became a free-lance writer in 1975. Since then, he has written over 80 books, including the 5-million-copy best-selling *How to Win at Nintendo Games* series, *The Encyclopedia of Superheroes*, the novelization of the cult film *Re-Animator*, and original novels such as the thriller *Starik* and the horror tale *The Madjan*. He is a regular contributor to *Ladies' Home Journal* and *Mad* magazines and writes a monthly film column for *Science Fiction Chronicle*. He lives in rural Connecticut with his wife and two Batman-loving sons.

KRISTINE KATHRYN RUSCH has written a number of critically acclaimed short stories and novels. She edits *The Magazine of Fantasy and Science Fiction* from her home in Eugene, Oregon.

BRIAN M. THOMSEN is a former nominee for two of science fiction's most coveted awards, the Hugo and the Tucker. He has contributed to numerous anthologies, and currently resides in Brooklyn, New York.

ROBERT WEINBERG divides his writing time equally between fiction and non-fiction. In the horror genre, he has written four novels, the most recent of which is *The Dead Man's Kiss* from Pocket Books. He has had short stories in numerous anthologies including *Chilled to the Bone*, *The Ultimate Werewolf*, and the upcoming *Tales of the Riverworld*. A two-time winner of the World Fantasy Award for his non-fiction, his latest work is the *Louis L'Amour Companion* published by Andrews & McMeel.